I0662592

THE SILENT WITNESS

by

David Y. B. Kaufmann

Tasikov Press
ISBN-13: 978-0615495538
ISBN-10: 0615495532

This is a work of fiction. Names, characters, places and incidents either are the product of the author's imagination or used fictitiously. Any resemblance to actual persons, living or dead, events or locales is entirely coincidental.

Cover design and photography by
Rivkah Kehaty

To my Father

who taught me how to read

PRELUDE

Winter, 1990, New Orleans

Chapter 1

Shammai Danielson rushed through the front door. "Just a second," he shouted to no one in particular. He stopped for a second to enjoy the mix of pre-Shabbos smells, then dashed into the bedroom; he threw his briefcase onto his bed, tossed his jacket and tie onto the briefcase and took a deep breath. Hopefully Hannah was just busy. "Sorry I'm late," he called out.

He entered the living room, empty except for the aroma of chicken soup. "It took longer with Josh than I thought."

"Get the boys out of the bath and set up the candles," Hannah answered from the kitchen. "Did you get the message about Mr. Levinsky's printer?"

She's in a good mood, he thought. "I fixed it. I'll tell you about it in a minute."

The bathroom stood half a dozen steps down the hall. He tried the door. Locked. He banged on it.

"Aaron, Moshe, hurry up in there."

"We have to wash our hair," Aaron called back.

"Make it quick."

That translated into the boys starting to pour the shampoo by the time he'd gotten the candles set-up.

Less than an hour to Shabbos and what was left to do? The house looked cleaned, the rug vacuumed, and the table set, though the *challahs* weren't out yet. The food must be almost done, judging by Hannah's voice.

He suddenly realized a tuna sandwich at eleven AM couldn't compete with the breaded chicken and whatever else it was Hannah just took from the oven. Maybe he could grab something as he got the candles.

He entered the kitchen just as she shut the oven. "Not done yet," she smiled. Two large pots - *cholent* and soup - made bubbling sounds on the stove.

"How much longer?"

"Relax," Hannah said, "everything's under control." She started washing the dishes.

"I have to take a shower."

"So do I. But Elie and Dinah Chaya are done. I put aside some fish and salad for you," she said, answering his question before he could ask.

He opened the refrigerator, searched a moment, then found the plate. She'd even put a fork on it. Josh's documentation compared poorly to the gefilte fish and cole slaw before him. He took out the horseradish.

"So why are you so late?" she asked, almost as an afterthought.

He raised his eyebrows. Things must really be under control.

"Where's Elie?" he asked, spreading the horseradish thin.

"In his room. I just need to bake the cake. You can set up the stove-cover right before you leave."

He nodded, made a *brocha* and took a bite of the gefilte fish. The horseradish was hotter than he thought. He quickly got a glass of water.

"Whew," he said. "You really want to hear?"

She nodded.

"Well, Josh kept me later than I planned."

"A problem?" she asked rinsing off some silverware.

"No. A conversation. Or argument."

"About?"

"Guess.'"

"Not again!" Hannah said, scrubbing a plate.

"Do you want me to do that?"

She shook her head. "This is it. Go on."

"I don't know why everyone thinks I have such influence over Mr. Enstein. If anything, he's the one with --"

"What happened with Josh?" Hannah interrupted, adding some soap to the pan.

"Kashdan's trying to ship Mr. Enstein off to an old age home, so Josh thinks he should move in with us."

"Really?" she laughed.

"No," he said, taking a forkful of salad. "But they're worried about his living alone, even though we send Sheila there twice a week to clean and that nurse comes every Friday."

"Tell me the rest later," Hannah said, drying her hands. "You'll have to get out the candlestick and tray. The candles, too."

He put down the plate and got the box of candles from on top of the refrigerator. He put it on the counter, careful to keep it away from the film of water. He didn't want to chase fifty candles all over the house. "Even if I could convince him, Elie would be crushed." He leaned on the box of candles, without putting his weight on it.

"Are the boys out of the tub yet?" Her tone changed the subject even more emphatically.

"I doubt it." He took another bite, then went to the pantry. He took out the polished silver tray and six-branched candelabra. "Where's Dinah Chaya's candlestick?"

"She probably packed it. She's staying at Sarah's, remember?"

"Oh, yeah. Will she have time to drop off the *challahs* at Mr. Enstein's, or do I have to drive her?"

"Depends on how much longer it takes her to do her hair. She was supposed to leave five minutes ago."

Balancing the tray and candelabra in one hand, he used the other to take another bite of fish, careful to knock off excess horseradish and spear some lettuce as well.

4

"No mail for you. I got my women's newsletter, though. I'm going to sit down and flip through it. Call me in five minutes if I'm not back. I've got to turn off the soup and *cholent*."

"I can do that," Shammai offered. "What about the chicken?"

"It's got another fifteen minutes, at least. When you take it out, put the cake in. It'll stay until right before candle-lighting. The kugel just needs to be heated, so I'll put it in with the chicken when I take the cake out."

Shammai followed her out of the kitchen, putting the tray on the table. He centered the candelabra on the tray.

Before going back and getting the candles and matches, he went to the bathroom door and knocked loudly several times.

"We're out," Aaron said.

"Finish up. Your mother and I need to use it."

"Daddy, will you put the *challahs* for Mr. Enstein in a bag for me?" Dinah Chaya called from behind her door. Her room was at the other end of the hall from his.

"Sure. Where is it?"

"On top of the refrigerator."

"The ones you baked?"

"Uh-huh. And a couple small ones Mommy made."

"Okay."

He went back into the kitchen and got the matches from the pantry. He counted out six candles and put the box back on top of the refrigerator. Seeing the *challahs* there, he made a mental note to bag them as soon as he was done.

"Elie!" he called.

No response.

"Elie!"

"Yeah?" His son's voice came muffled through the kitchen wall, his room being right behind it.

"I could use some help."

"In a minute."

Right, he thought. That means as I'm walking out the door. Now if it had been Mr. Enstein calling . . . It was his own fault. He'd encouraged the friendship. Well, at least Elie read Torah every week. And only six months after his Bar Mitzvah.

At the table, he began fixing the candles in their holders, melting the bottoms when necessary.

Aaron and Moshe came marching by, Aaron with his pants, undershirt and tzitzis on, Moshe holding his clothes and wrapped in a towel. Both boys were barefoot.

"Bathroom's free," he said to Hannah.

"In a minute. Will you turn off the *cholent* and soup?"

"Sure. Want me to put the cake in the oven, too?"

"Not yet. The chicken's not done."

Now, what was he supposed to do next? Oh, right, the *challahs*.

He went back into the kitchen and brought all the *challahs* out to the table, along with the plastic bags.

"How many for Mr. Enstein?" he shouted.

"Dinah Chaya made three," Hannah answered from the couch. "And there's some rolls. Take four or five."

He separated them, leaving the rest on the table. As he bagged them, he asked, "Any guests?"

"Just Lazar. But tell Elie he can invite one of his friends if he wants."

"Maybe a college student or two will show up at *shul*. They do sometimes if not much is happening on campus."

"Well, invite them if no one beats you to it," Hannah said, getting up. "Keep an eye on the chicken. No more than another ten minutes."

"Anything else?"

She shook her head.

6

"I'm going to finish my snack, then. I didn't eat much for lunch."

She lowered her magazine and gave him a patronizing look.

"By the way, did you say you fixed Mr. Levinky's printer?"

"I got your message. The problem was easy. But --" He hesitated.

"What?" Hannah asked immediately.

"Well, you know how he and Mr. Enstein feel about each other?"

She sighed. "Do I have to hear all the gossip about Mr. Enstein right before Shabbos?" She sighed again. "What did he say?"

"A lot of things. He said he liked the *shul*, his wife liked the ladies. He said it's a good, honest place."

She laughed. "And small enough not to be a bother. What else?"

Shammai paused a long time.

"He said Mr. Enstein was the soul of the *shul*."

"I'd agree with that," she said. "So what's the problem?"

"Why did he say it to me?"

"Because you were there? I'm taking my shower. Don't forget what you have to do. And try to get the boys dressed."

He went back to the kitchen, wondering if he could sneak another piece of fish. He had enough horseradish on the plate for two.

As he stood, eating more slowly, Dinah Chaya came in, holding a small suitcase in one hand and brushing her hair with the other.

"Don't do that around the food," he scolded. Holding the handle of the brush in her teeth, she unzipped the suitcase, then dropped it in.

He looked at her as she rezipped the suitcase. In less than a year, she'd be spending every Shabbos at someone else's house. He fought off his resentment at her leaving for this one.

"Do you have your candlestick?" he asked.

She nodded. "Can you get me a grocery bag to carry the *challahs*?"

He went to the pantry, rummaged for a minute, and found one for her.

"Do you need a ride?" he asked as she packaged the wrapped challos.

"Do you have time?"

"Not really, but I'll drive you if you want. I don't want you to be late for Shabbos."

"I've got more than half an hour and it's only a fifteen minute walk."

Into the awkward pause that followed her observation, he said, "Mr. Enstein looks forward to them."

"I guess that means he's too excited to say thank you."

"Don't start."

"Sorry. I've got to go now. Good Shabbos, Daddy."

"Good Shabbos, Dinah Chaya."

She hefted the grocery bag in her free hand, then left.

Just like that.

He suddenly remembered he was supposed to turn off the *cholent* and soup. He jumped to the stove and turned off the burners. He might as well set up the counter-cover now, too.

That done, he felt something else should be done. Reviewing everything in his mind, though, he couldn't think of anything. Pretty good. Still over half an hour left before Shabbos.

He went through the boys' room to Elie's.

"You all ready to go?"

"Uh-huh." Elie looked up from his book. "Are you driving?"

"Probably."

"I'm going to walk over in fifteen minutes."

"Why?"

"In case Mr. Enstein wants to walk. He gets nervous when you drive up at the last minute."

"Is he going to check your Torah reading?"

Elie looked up.

Stop pressuring him, Shammai thought.

"Do me a favor," he said, more gently. "Before you leave, take the chicken out of the oven and put the cake in, if it's not already done."

"I thought mom was doing that."

"She asked me to, but I'll probably be in the shower."

"OK."

With a few minutes to spare, he decided to look at that new Rambam translation while waiting to get into the shower. His "library" wasn't very big, only one bookcase with four shelves, but it had the essentials. Nothing like Mr. Enstein's. But then, he'd never be a scholar. At least Elie had the right start. He'd gotten that much right, even if Mr. Enstein seemed to become more of a curmudgeon, deliberately, every day. Putting up with Mr. Enstein's complaints and criticisms seemed a pretty cheap price for his son's education.

Well, in thirty years, maybe someone would look at his collection, as he looked at Mr. Enstein's, and wonder if he knew what was inside all the books. Between now and then, maybe he'd even have time to actually read a few.

He pulled the book off the shelf. The main thing was to try. What did the rabbis say? A chapter in the morning and a chapter in the evening. Or even a verse. The main thing was to learn something.

"Shower's free," Hannah called.

He smiled to himself and put it back. Tonight, after dinner, he thought, knowing he'd be lucky not to fall asleep at the table. Never enough time, he thought. Too much work, too much family, too much of everything. And when he could sit down and try to learn, he didn't get very far.

Not true, he told himself. All it took was a little more discipline.

He went into the bedroom to get his clothes. Hannah passed him on her way out.

"Did you put the cake in?"

"Chicken wasn't done. I set up the blech." He never could say the Yiddish word for the counter-cover without a smile.

"Take Aaron or Moshe with you to *shul*. Or both."

He nodded. "Elie's leaving before me."

He showered quickly, suddenly feeling the lateness of the hour.

He went into the bedroom to brush his hair and get his shoes and jacket.

As he was tying his shoes, the phone rang.

"I'll get it," he shouted, annoyed at whoever was calling while he was in a rush. But Hannah would be busy in the kitchen.

"Hello?"

"Daddy, come quick. I think Mr. Enstein's had a heart attack."

For a moment, he couldn't respond.

Then Dinah Chaya's terrified sob roused him from his trance.

"Did you call 911?" he asked, his mind suddenly clear and sharp.

"Yes. They said a TEMS will get here quickest."

Good thing they lived so close to the university, he thought. Its emergency ambulance service was around the corner and wouldn't have to fight traffic.

"OK," he said, trying to calm his daughter with his voice. "Where's Mr. Enstein?"

"He's on the floor, holding his chest."

"Is he breathing?"

"I - I think so."

"As long as he is, just leave him. Loosen his tie if it's on. If he starts to struggle, push on his chest. I'm coming now."

"Please hurry, Daddy."

He dropped the phone, grabbed his keys and wallet and ran to the door.

He caught a glimpse of Hannah watching him from the kitchen, worried.

"Mr. Enstein's had a heart attack. Dinah Chaya's there. She's still on the phone, I think."

That would have to be sufficient explanation. He ran out the door.

He started the car, pulled out of the driveway with a squeal and raced up Burthe street. At Lowerline, he honked his horn instead of stopping, ignoring the gesture and responding honk from the driver he'd cut off.

Two cars waited ahead of him at Broadway. With the late afternoon traffic, it could take five minutes to get across. He tried to see down the street, but his vision was blocked by the corner house. While he debated whether to honk again, the first car turned right.

One car ahead of him, but it had its left turn signal on. That meant it would have to cross both lanes of traffic. He hoped the driver, a college student, would have sense enough to pull across to the neutral ground at the first break.

Now he could see the oncoming traffic. The signal couldn't stay green much longer.

He had no idea how heart attacks worked, he realized. How much time did Mr. Enstein have? He hoped the college students who manned the emergency service were well trained. They should be there by now.

Poor Dinah Chaya. She didn't deserve to see something so traumatic. He should have gotten home sooner. Always trying to squeeze in a last minute of work that didn't matter. Then he could have driven her to deliver the *challahs* and he would have been there.

Or maybe not. Maybe no one would have been with Mr. Enstein.

The light turned red. The last car had half a block behind it and the one turning from Freret. Plenty of time.

The college student didn't move. The free space would close, as three other cars also turned.

He pressed his hand to the horn. The college student made a gesture in the mirror and stopped inching out.

Shammai pulled around him, onto the curb. He shot between two of the just-turned cars into the median, causing one to swerve. His mind, already at Mr. Enstein's house, shut out the other drivers' anger.

He looked the other way, inching out, playing chicken with the drivers. The first didn't stop, but the second let him through. He waved and pushed the accelerator for half the block, slowing just enough to make the turn.

Another block. This time the light was with him and he zoomed right, just ahead of some cars coming his way.

Was there a pre-Mardi Gras parade tonight, the floats up the street stalling traffic? He could never remember the nights or routes.

If not, it shouldn't take more than a couple minutes, he thought. Palmer was the next street after the light.

No oncoming traffic. Probably a parade. He took a chance and sped down the wrong lane, horn honking.

At the corner, he cut off another car to make his left turn and again accelerated. A glance at the speedometer showed fifty. The half-block to Mr. Enstein's house flew by and he slammed on the brakes.

He jumped out of the car. Where was the ambulance? Hearing its siren, he looked down the street and saw it speeding away, already the other side of Willow. Good.

The front door was open.

"Dinah Chaya!" he called as he raced in.

She sat in the rocking chair, shivering, crying softly, a book in her hand.

"How is he?"

"I thought he was going to die."

He took a deep breath. That meant the ambulance got there in time.

"How are you? Thank G-d you were here."

With her free hand, she wiped her eyes. "OK, now. I guess."

He took a step forward and almost tripped on her bag.

She looked at it. "I don't think I want to spend Shabbos at Sarah's."

"Of course not," he said gently, picking up her bag. "I've still got time to drive you home."

She nodded. With an effort she stood up, still clutching the book, he noticed.

He checked to make sure the door was locked and took the key from the inside handle. He used it to turn the bolt from the outside. He assumed Mr. Enstein had been taken to the university hospital. He'd find out after Shabbos and take care of whatever needed to be done.

A thousand details and consequences thrust against each other, demanding consideration and action. Time enough to sort out what Mr. Enstein's heart attack meant and what had to be done for him after Shabbos, Shammai thought. Right now, he had to concentrate on his daughter and getting to *shul* before Shabbos.

He looked at her. She walked slowly, visibly composing

herself. She knew it was almost Shabbos, he told himself. By the time they reached the car, she'd stopped trembling, her red, swollen eyes the only evidence of her tears.

She sat, staring down and covering the book with both her hands.

As he started the engine, he asked, "What happened?"

"I rang the bell and Mr. Enstein didn't answer. I didn't think anything about that, other than to be annoyed because I'd have to really hurry. You know how he was, I mean, is, he likes to keep people waiting. I rang again and he still didn't answer, so I tried the door."

She paused to take a breath. "It was open so I went inside. He wasn't in the living room, so I called out his name. I heard something from the back. I called out again, saying I'd come to bring him *challahs* and should I just leave them on the table with the books - there were two or three besides this one - or wait for him. I hoped he'd say just leave it, but he said wait. I didn't tell him I was in a hurry.

"Anyway, he came out a few minutes later, all dressed for Shabbos. He started talking about how nice Mommy was, but I should come earlier and I wouldn't have to rush and he knew how young people didn't have patience for old people, except Elie. He said something else nice about Elie and I said he really liked Mr. Enstein. That seemed to annoy him, or maybe he just pretended. But he said Elie used him like everyone else, including you. I guess he was upset because Elie hadn't gotten there to walk him to *shul* yet, or something. Maybe he was anxious to see Elie, or you, but I got angry and said, if that's the case, why don't you make your own *challahs* and I'm going to be late for Shabbos thanks to him."

Shammai looked at his watch and then the traffic. Should still be enough time. "What happened next?" he prompted.

She took a deep breath. "Nothing really. He just said, why

don't I leave the *challahs* on the table and I put them down, starting to move the books to make room. That got him upset. He said not to touch them, especially this one, I was my father's daughter - he said that like it was something he was afraid of, or almost terrible. He had a funny sound to his voice. And then it happened."

He waited a moment before speaking, making sure she had control of herself. "You must have been very scared."

"I didn't know what was going on at first. I thought he was just making fun of me or being nasty. He gasped for breath, grabbed his chest and fell. I almost just left, but then I realized he was in trouble. I bent over and called his name. He whispered, 'heart,' really struggling to get out the word.

"I don't know how, but I managed to call 911, then you. I kept staring at him, wondering what I should do, and he kept looking at me, his face going from real agony to anger to almost begging. Finally, he called my name and I went over to him.

"He struggled to get up and I said he should lie down and be quiet, but he wouldn't. He took this book -" she raised it slightly, "then fell on the floor. He held it out and said, 'To your father, it's for --" She stopped with a convulsive sob.

"For what?" Shammai asked.

"That was it. He became unconscious. The ambulance came up almost right after that and I watched them press his chest and do a few other things, put him on a stretcher and say he was still alive and might make it. I don't remember anything else until you got there, not sitting down, nothing."

Shammai held himself back from saying or doing anything other than concentrating on the traffic, fighting a sudden rush of fear and excitement. Had Mr. Enstein known beforehand? What did it mean?

He pulled up before the house to let Dinah Chaya off.

"Tell your mother. Take some aspirin and lie down. I've got

to rush back to *shul*. We'll talk more when I get home."

She smiled at him, picking up her bag. "I'll be all right."

She put the book down on the seat.

He watched her walk into the house, feeling helpless, knowing there was nothing more he could do for her right now, or for Mr. Enstein. He was running out of time.

As he drove off he glanced at the book. It was so old it had to be worth a fortune. He suddenly felt giddy. He opened it. On the inside front cover were names and dates, going back at least two hundred years.

It was a siddur.

Interlude 1 - 1845

"His beard. What I remember seeing first was his beard: white, full, long but rounded at the end. Some beards, especially the longer ones, straggle. Or they grow in all directions. But his curved, perfectly, not a hair out of place. You have to understand, beards were common, practically universal, among the poor Jewish peasants in Russia. I myself had one at the time. I had no choice, of course; who would give a shave to the village idiot? That would just have been one more thing to make me different, and those simple villagers, well, they weren't cruel.

"Anyway, in a world of beards, his was remarkable. But then, everything about him was remarkable. The eyes, for instance. Deep-set, ocean-blue, they always looked through the things of this world." Father shivered, as if again encountering those far-sighted, penetrating eyes, and sighed. "Thank G-d, they did, or I would never have recovered and you wouldn't be here."

The affection in his own eyes embarrassed me - so I gave the reins a snap, focusing on some additional speed from the horses, instead.

I'd heard father's story before, of course, many times. But for me, his eldest son, it was like a prayer familiar and well-said, the repetition of which, if one concentrates, actually creates a newer, more meaningful experience. I treasured father's story, as he told it, as much as I treasured his siddur, which had saved his life and been for me, as for him, a Bar Mitzvah gift.

"Uriel, we won't reach Strasbourg tonight, no matter how hard you drive the horses," father remarked. "Believe me, I'm as anxious to get there as you - not to see the factory. It hasn't produced any textiles for months and won't again until we get it reorganized - if it's salvageable at all."

"We didn't have to be the ones to go," I said, voicing the question - or complaint - I'd harbored since we left yesterday. "Our little business venture includes three other Strasbourgers and a Strasbourger in-law, all equally qualified to inspect the factory. "

"True," father said, fingering his moustache, "but the family name didn't rescue them from the oblivion of amnesia. I owe the city a thank-you. Don't worry, your Rosa and little Giselle will be safe until you get back."

A flock of birds passed noisily overhead. I glanced up, noticing the broken pattern of their formation - a sure sign they had just begun to fly, not yet organized. That made me aware of the increased wind which had, imperceptibly, been growing stronger. I glanced over my shoulder, noticing another broken formation organizing as it flew toward us - that af grey storm clouds. I faced b akward, to the clear spring day, now fleeing before us. No reason to panic, but could the horses be urged to greater speed? Father could finish his story just as well inside an inn beside a fire as on the open road in a driving storm.

I saw he had also noticed the coming storm.

"So which is it that saved you," I said to distract us, "the siddur, the Rabbi's brocha or your name?"

"All three," he answered seriously. "Ah, Uriel, I hope you never know the smell of war. It stinks - from the grease on the cannons to the parade of animals to the mass of unwashed men. But the worst stench is the terror as the shells explode, as the tree you just passed blows up, as your companion - who just last night told you his deepest secret - stops, spurts blood, then collapses into it."

He covered his eyes with his hands. The memory was always painful, even after more than thirty years. In a sense, I had lived father's pain, without the memory, all my life. As he regained his composure, I gently urged the horses on in an impossible race against the fast darkening sky.

He looked up and smiled at me. "I never knew which shell, or whose, did it. But if I hadn't stopped and pulled the siddur, my grandfather's bar mitzvah present, yours now -" he added with an affectionate touch on my leg - "if I hadn't taken it out to offer a silent prayer before the battle began - I always did, during the whole march through Europe, from Paris to the edge of Moscow - if I hadn't stopped and fallen behind, I would have been like the score of men around me. As it was," he sighed again, "I lost three years."

He closed his eyes and didn't speak for a moment. "Three years," he whispered as the first drops, more a mist, began to fall. "And who knows how many days or weeks I wandered from farm to farm, stealing a bit of bread or a blanket against a Russian winter night. Well, I took more from Russia than Napoleon. Napoleon," he spat, "he was no friend of the Jews, I promise you." He shook his head. "He had his exile, and I had mine. For those three years after the constable looked in my knapsack, saw the siddur, realized I was a Jew and turned me over to the village council, I was an amnesiac, nothing more than the village idiot whose only possession was a valuable siddur."

"And then the great rabbi came," I said. I knew by heart this story from the heart. Even as we spoke, I looked desperately for some shelter, if no inn could be found.

"Yes. I never found out who he was, though I have a good guess, or why he was passing through. But they brought me to him and made me show him the siddur. He was the only one I let touch it during that time. He looked at it for a long, a very long time, then looked through me - yes, through me - briefly. He gave me a brocha for a complete recovery. I remember his words. 'Yaakov Strasbourger, because you have guarded and honored this siddur, may its prayer for healing and health, physically and spiritually, be fulfilled for you.' From the moment he mentioned my name, my mind began to open, the clouds of amnesia to part."

I smiled. Father always attributed his recovery to the great Rabbi's blessing. Who knows? There are stories of tzaddikim, those righteous men. I'd never met one, though. Still, who knows? "That he recognized our family name as a French town, made inquiries and had you returned home didn't hurt, either." I added.

"True," father said, "but if I hadn't inscribed my name in the siddur, how could the rabbi have known? It's starting to rain. There should be an inn just over that bridge, around the sharp bend. I wish you'd written your name in it at your bar mitzvah, like I had. Or at any time since. Maybe you'll do so when we get home? Hurry, it will be a deluge soon."

The horses needed to be controlled, for the onset of the storm had begun to panic them. I need not worry about their speed now.

But, even if the siddur was officially mine, so long as my father was alive, I would not write my name in it.

ASSESSMENT

Chapter 2

Shammai walked into *shul*, dazed yet acutely aware of the *tallis* bag held loosely in his hand. Kashdan, Josh, Mishael, Lazar, the boys - everyone was there. But - the thought shocked him again - Mr. Enstein wasn't with him.

He walked toward the bookcase, to put his *tallis* bag in its niche as he did every week. Only now, he had to concentrate on the previously unconscious routine. Somehow, Mr. Enstein's *siddur* had made its way inside the plastic cover. Suddenly, but not for the first time, it momentarily seemed to weigh more than he could carry. The unpredictable adrenalin-induced distortion passed quickly, but left him, again, temporarily disoriented.

Should he have gone to the hospital? It was Shabbos, and what could he do? Besides, he didn't even know which one.

He sensed, rather than saw, the greetings and stares of the others, but they brought to mind what he had suppressed in his rush to arrive before Shabbos, what had unconsciously plagued his thoughts from the moment Dinah Chaya called.

Where was Elie?

He dreaded the moment of telling his son. How could he explain Mr. Enstein's heart attack? How could he tell his son he had failed?

Lazar came up to him, a big smile on his face.

"Cutting it close. What was it, a symphony or some new commentary?" referring to Shammai's favorite radio station.

"What?" His mind was far away from Lazar's humor.

Now Josh approached. Why couldn't they leave him alone, for a moment at least, to clear his mind? Didn't they know already? Didn't they see the *siddur*?

Josh stopped short. "What's that?" he asked, pointing to

Shammai's *tallis* bag.

Shammai's gaze followed the gesture. "A book. A *siddur*. Mr. Enstein gave it to me."

Josh whistled, as Mishael and Kashdan came up.

"Some gift. It looks like it's a hundred years old. So that's the reward for a weekly escort, *challahs* and listening to the old man kvetch. I guess you were right when you said patience has its rewards."

"That's not what I meant," Shammai said sharply. Why now, of all times, did that offhand comment come back to haunt him? It had been a witticism, provoked by "joshing," and words he'd regretted.

Kashdan said. "Where is Enstein, anyway?"

"He's not here," Shammai said, as yet unable to explain why. "He won't make it tonight."

"Too bad," Kashdan said. "I hope he's feeling alright. We better start *mincha*, then. It's late."

Shammai put his *tallis* bag away and mechanically took a *siddur* - not Mr. Enstein's - as Kashdan began *Ashrei*.

Elie, talking excitedly with Benjie Sagalman and Malachi, turned, catching his father's eye. Shammai saw his son's face change, the satisfied smile of everything-in-its-place, the delight of recognition, fade to worry.

Awkwardly, Elie approached, his questioning, apprehensive look draining the small measure of composure Shammai had found in Kashdan's chanting.

Absently, he noted that Lazar was still beside him. Lazar knew - or at least guessed something was wrong.

"Hi," Elie said, awkwardly, timidly, ignoring the service. "Where's Mr. Enstein? I got there before Dinah Chaya, so he said I shouldn't wait. He needed his *challahs*. I knew you'd give him a ride."

23

"He's not coming," Shammai said, angry at his voice for shaking.

"Why?"

In the question, Shammai heard the hope, the fear, the accusation and the cry for comfort of a little boy. Strange. How had he thought his son was almost an adult?

"Mr. Enstein had a heart attack."

He said the words calmly, quietly, looking straight at his son, prepared, he thought, for any reaction.

"Oh, my --" Elie screamed.

Kashdan stopped, just before *kaddish*, and turned. The whole *shul* turned.

"He's all right," Shammai said quickly, his voice lacking conviction, he realized. "An ambulance got there in time. He's at a hospital. Dinah Chaya was there."

Elie recoiled at his sister's name, and Shammai knew that had been a mistake, a part of the event he should have recounted later.

"*Mincha*," Shammai said. When Elie just stared, he said, "Mr. Enstein would want us to *daven mincha*. We can say some *Tehillim* for his health."

Elie nodded. He understood that.

Somehow they got through the afternoon service, including the repetition, without a word. Shammai wasn't sure whether or not to be thankful for its shortness.

At its conclusion, everyone quickly gathered around him. He sat down, staggered by their closeness, affected most by Elie's silence and averted gaze.

"I don't know any details," he said, feeling surrounded. "Dinah Chaya called, desperate, and I raced to Mr. Enstein's house. I'm surprised I didn't have an accident. By the time I got there, the ambulance was leaving. According to Dinah Chaya, he was still alive. I don't even know what hospital they took him to." He said the last sentence almost as a plea.

"Probably the university hospital," Kashdan said, visibly shaken. Shammai hadn't expected Kashdan, who seemed more Mr. Enstein's sparring partner than *shul* co-founder, to be so upset. Thinking about it, he shouldn't have been surprised.

Josh shook his head. "We were afraid of something like this. But if they got to him in time, he'll be OK. Once they get him past the emergency, they've got medicines. Of course, he'll be in intensive care for a while."

"If he had a heart attack and was already in the ambulance before you got there, how'd he manage to give you that book?" Lazar asked.

"He gave it to Dinah Chaya and told her to give it to me. I'm - I don't quite know what I feel."

"We'll have to do something for him, of course," Kashdan said.

"We don't know where he is," Lazar pointed out, "and I doubt he'll be in any condition to receive visitors for a while."

"We should do something," Kashdan insisted.

"We should say some psalms," Mishael said. "Anyone know exactly how old he is?"

"Eighty-one," Elie muttered.

Everyone turned. Shammai realized that the last thing his son needed now was an audience. How could he divert their attention? "Bob, what happens with a heart attack? I mean, what does it take to survive one?" The question switched the focus to Dr. Sagalman.

"Basically, the regular rhythm goes chaotic." Sagalman smoothed the hair over his left ear. "There's all kinds of treatments, both immediately and for recovery. It all depends on how severe and the condition of the patient. A man Mr. Enstein's age -- it's hard to tell. But if he made it to the hospital, Lazar's right, his chances are better."

"You know," Josh said, "it's kind of strange. Why would he give you just one book? I'd think he'd either give you everything, or be in too much pain to think about it."

Shammai shrugged. "I don't know. It was right next to him and maybe that's all he could think of through the pain. A legacy, just in case."

"What are you going to do with it?" Kashdan asked cautiously.

"Keep it, of course. At least, until he recovers." He watched Elie, who had deliberately turned away.

"I'll make some calls after Shabbos," Bob Sagalman said. "Find out where he is, how he's doing."

"What if he dies on Shabbos?" Benjie Sagalman asked.

"He can't," Elie said.

Thankfully, no one responded.

"I'm sure Dinah Chaya told the ambulance drivers who he was, whom to contact," Mishael said practically. Shammai saw Elie wince.

"Would they have time to listen?" Lazar asked.

"They're trained to get information while working," Mishael said. No one questioned how he was so confident. "He won't die on Shabbos."

"Any one know his next of kin?" Kashdan asked. "Just in case."

Nobody spoke.

"We've got almost thirty-five minutes until *maariv*," Josh said into the silence.

"We should learn something," Lazar said.

"Psalms first," Mishael said, going to get them.

He passed the books around and everyone said a few chapters, beginning with eighty-two.

Through it all, Elie stood apart, participating, but not part of the group.

Shammai looked at the congregation, the *shul*. So few of them. Barely a minyan. And everything seemed smaller, less stable now.

Shammai suddenly realized how much they needed a rabbi. Oh, they'd talked about it for years, but their size and the salary stopped them from looking. They could have used a leader now.

If they'd searched, would they have found someone? They could have hired any number of people with the right papers; but finding someone who could listen without judging, who could find solutions without compromising Torah, who could keep the favor of the moneyed members without giving in to them, who could inspire them to be more observant and still bring in new members - well, where could they find such a rabbi?

"*Maariv*," Kashdan said at last.

Mishael led Kabbalat Shabbat, the accented beauty of his voice cutting through the emptiness.

Afterwards, everyone said Shabbat Shalom quickly, anxious to leave. Elie and Shammai met at the door.

Outside, Josh remarked, "You better take care of that *siddur*. It looks valuable."

"The *shul*'s safe," Shammai said.

With a downcast face, Elie led the way. Lazar walked beside Shammai, Bob and Benjie Sagalman right behind.

"It's funny," Bob Sagalman said, "I never thought it would happen this way."

"What do you mean?" Lazar asked.

Sagalman shrugged. "Geriatrics isn't my field, but someone like Mr. Enstein - I figured it would happen gradually. A broken leg, maybe, something that would give him time to get things in order."

"How do you know they aren't?" Shammai asked.

"He has a will," Lazar said. "I know, because he wouldn't let me see it."

"No," Sagalman said. "I meant he'd have a chance to make a few last comments, try to set up the *shul* to continue the way he wanted. Too stubborn to go quietly and too much in control to go suddenly."

"Maybe that's why it was this way," Shammai said. All the time, he watched his son. Even in the dark, from behind, he could see the tension in Elie's bowed head and stiffened shoulders, sense the anger in the silence and clenched fists.

"He's not dead, yet," Shammai said. "Maybe we shouldn't be speculating like this."

"You're right," Lazar said quickly. "I'm sure he's fine."

"Didn't Dinah Chaya say the ambulance people told her he had a good chance to survive?" Benjie Sagalman asked over his shoulder.

"Good thing she was there," his father added.

Shammai noticed Elie withdraw even more at the mention of his sister.

"Can we ask Dr. Cramer to find out?" Benjie asked.

"A colleague who lives on the next block," Sagalman explained. "He'd make the calls for me, if I asked."

"I don't know the *halacha*," Shammai said. We need a rabbi, he thought again. "I'm not sure we can ask a non-Jew to do that on Shabbat." He wondered what he would say to Elie if they were alone. Would any words of his help?

"Well, if I happen to meet him, I'll mention what happened and let him decide."

Lazar shook his head.

Shammai looked at him.

"He should have let me see his will," Lazar whispered, so Elie wouldn't hear. "That *siddur* he gave you - I don't know. What

28

about the rest of his books? Or his other property?"

Shammai shrugged. "If he has a will, I'm sure he's taken care of things."

"Mr. Enstein never let go of anything he controlled," Lazar said.

"How do you control books?" Shammai asked. "I always thought they controlled you. Isn't that how we live? At least, we're supposed to. The Torah "controls" us. The *Shulchan Aruch* "controls" us. Otherwise we have chaos."

"I know, we're most free when we follow the rules," Lazar said. "I guess Mr. Enstein was like one of his books, then."

"I'm sure he'd take that as a compliment."

The conversation died as they approached Mr. Enstein's house. Once in front of it, they stopped.

"You locked it?" Sagalman asked.

Shammai nodded.

"We'll have to go in after Shabbat," Lazar said.

"I've got the key," Shammai said. "But I think we should get his permission first. If it's possible."

They watched the darkened door, in silence.

"We're such a small group, but I wonder if we really know each other," Sagalman finally said.

"Can we leave the philosophy to the experts, like funeral directors?" Lazar said with uncharacteristic irritation. "We can't do anything practical right now, for all we know Mr. Enstein will be back next week, annoying everyone as always, and we'll just have wasted our morbidity. What's really changed?"

Elie had taken a step towards the house, separating himself from the others.

They watched him, but he seemed reluctant to go further with their eyes on him.

"Well, perhaps you're right," Sagalman said. "It is Shabbat, after all."

Still no one moved.

Shammai felt compelled to break the awkwardness. Should he call his son back or join him?

"My family's waiting," Sagalman said, sparing Shammai the decision. "I'll let you know tomorrow if I find out anything. I don't think I will. Come on, Benjie."

Benjie reached out a hand towards his friend, but withdrew it. He followed his father, several times looking back.

Elie waited. But with only Lazar next to him now, Shammai felt no need to rush his son. Let Elie deal with this in his own way, he thought.

"What's he going to do?" Lazar whispered as Elie slowly took another step.

Shammai shrugged.

"It's almost like he's testing you, wanting you to say something, to stop him or encourage him," Lazar observed.

Shammai had had a similar thought, but dismissed it. He waved Lazar to silence. They watched as Elie simply stood in front of the door.

"Maybe he doesn't know himself," Shammai said, thinking aloud. That wasn't right. Elie was trying to find a connection, some gesture to express not only his sorrow, but his determination to keep alive what he'd learned.

Elie reached up and touched the *mezuzzah*. He brought his hand down, kissing his fingers, then turned and came back.

Of course, Shammai thought. What's written on the *mezuzzah*? These words - the words of Torah - you shall inscribe them on your doorposts. And these words - the words of Torah - you shall teach them to your children.

Without another word, they continued the walk home.

They passed the university library, it's lights still on, but with only a few students outside.

Lazar slowed down and Shammai matched him, letting Elie get ahead of them.

"You know," Lazar said, "I was just thinking. If Mr. Enstein survives, he's going to have to explain to Elie why he didn't think of him. If he doesn't, you'll have to explain why he left you a gift instead."

Shammai nodded. "I was just thinking the same thing, wishing Mr. Enstein had had the presence of mind to leave something for Elie. Maybe there's something in his will."

"I hope so," Lazar said, then paused. "Have you thought why he left you that particular book?"

Shammai shrugged. "It's what he was studying at the time."

Lazar shook his head. "He could have named anything in the house with the same effort. There's something about that *siddur*."

"What should I do, have it appraised?" Shammai joked.

"Not a bad idea."

"I think I should wait. If - when - Mr. Enstein recovers, he won't appreciate that."

"He doesn't have to know."

"But I will."

Lazar shrugged. "As long as you're sure of what you're dealing with."

Elie waited for them at the corner, watching them, aware they were discussing Mr. Enstein, obviously not wanting them to do so.

When they got to the house, Shammai knocked lightly.

It practically flew open. Dinah Chaya stood there, waiting, her face questioning, worried. Hannah's expression mirrored their daughter's.

"Where are the boys?" Shammai asked.

"In their room," Hannah answered. "I didn't know when you'd be back."

Elie passed in front of him.

"Elie," Dinah Chaya said, but he ignored her, heading back to his room.

Lazar shut the door quietly. "We don't know anything more. Sagalman may try to get a neighbor to find out which hospital they took him to, but I don't think he will. It's Shabbat."

Shammai heard Elie open the refrigerator.

"I did everything I could," Dinah Chaya said, her voice pleading, her eyes on her father.

"I know," he said gently.

Elie came out and put the wine on the table, along with the *kiddush* cups.

"I'll get Moshe and Aaron," Hannah said.

Shammai and Lazar began to sing Sholom Aleichem. Shammai watched Elie sing quietly to himself.

How much longer could Elie hold it in? And how would his reaction - explosion or implosion - affect the rest of the family?

Moshe and Aaron came into the living room, followed by Hannah. They all took their places around the table.

Shammai made *kiddush*, poured the wine into the little cups and passed them to Hannah, Moshe, Aaron and Lazar. Then he handed the wine to Elie.

Elie stared at him, an empty stare.

Then he poured the wine, lifted his *kiddush* cup, closed his eyes and made *kiddush*.

Lazar broke the silence that followed.

"OK, let's eat," Lazar said, clapping his hands.

Hannah led the procession into the kitchen. Elie continued to sit. Shammai stood by his chair, waiting for the others to wash, as he always went last.

For a moment, only he, Elie and Dinah Chaya were in the room.

She turned to Elie. "It's not my fault," she said.

He lifted his head, eyes angry.

"You could have waited for him," she continued. "You could have been there, too."

At first, Shammai thought his son hadn't heard.

"We'd have been halfway to *shul*," Elie said in a low voice. "I wouldn't have gotten to a phone in time."

Dinah Chaya breathed a sigh of relief. "I thought you'd be mad at me. He was my teacher once, too."

"I don't want to talk about it," Elie said. He shut his eyes against the tears. Then he blurted, "He told me to leave. He knew. He said I should go on without him, that maybe he'd get a ride. But he knew."

"Elie," Shammai said quietly.

"Don't you see, he knew - and he kicked me out!" Elie pushed his chair back. Going into the kitchen to wash, he added, "Right now, I don't want to talk to her."

Shammai looked at his daughter. She was in tears. "What did I do, Daddy?"

"You saved his life."

"Then why is Elie mad at me?"

"That's why."

She wiped her eyes. "I wish he'd seen Mr. Enstein lying there, fighting to breathe, his face all twisted. I just wish he'd been there."

"So does he. Be patient with him," Shammai said. "Right now he's angry with everyone, especially himself. It's a normal reaction, to feel guilty, to turn that into anger, and direct that against someone close, someone who did more than he did.

"There's always the what if," he said, realizing he was speaking to himself as much as to her. "What if I had been there? Would I have done differently? Better? Worse? Would I have been able to say what I want to say now? And in Elie's case, why did Mr. Enstein tell him to leave?"

Dinah Chaya wiped her eyes. "Well, he's not the only one who's upset and I'm not going to suffer because he can't handle it," she said. "And anyway, Mr. Enstein's not dead." But she didn't go into the kitchen until Elie came out.

Shammai went in with her. They washed, said the *brocha*.

Shammai sat down, made motzei and started the meal. Someone would have to find something to talk about, something to bring them all back into the mood of Shabbat. Usually, he could count on Lazar for something controversial or amusing. But tonight, Lazar seemed to be taking his cue from the family.

"Is Mr. Enstein going to die?" Aaron asked.

"Some people want him to," Elie said bitterly.

"Elie!" Hannah said.

Shammai motioned to her. "I don't think so," Shammai said. "But we should talk about something else tonight. What did you learn in the *parsha*?"

"Aaron's two sons died," Moshe said. "They offered a strange fire in the Sanctuary."

Shammai shot a glance at Lazar, who gently shook his head.

The fish came to Elie, but he didn't take any. Shammai reached over and took the plate.

"We learned about kosher animals," Aaron said.

"Good," Shammai said, relieved. "What are the signs of a kosher animal?"

"Pass the horseradish," Dinah Chaya said.

It was right in front of Elie, but he didn't move.

"Split hooves and chews its cud," Aaron said proudly.

"Please pass the horseradish," Dinah Chaya repeated.

"What about fish?" Shammai asked.

"Fins and scales," Moshe and Aaron said together.

"Please pass the horseradish," Dinah Chaya said again, exasperated, her voice rising.

Shammai realized Elie hadn't responded to the request. He reached over.

Suddenly, Elie shoved his chair back and ran from the room.

A door slammed.

Everyone looked at where Elie had sat.

"I suppose you're going to blame that on me, too," Dinah Chaya said.

"No one's blaming you," Hannah said.

"All I did was ask for the horseradish."

"I know."

"I'm not going to let him make me feel guilty because he didn't wait and Mr. Enstein didn't want him to," Dinah Chaya said, standing. "Does he think Mr. Enstein was stupid? If he'd known, he would have told Elie to call the ambulance. I wish he would have."

"Sit down," Hannah said firmly. "No one said you should feel guilty. But you also shouldn't imitate his behavior."

"I'm upset, too," she said.

"We're all upset," Hannah continued. "But you're not going to spoil Shabbat dinner because of Elie's distress."

"He gets to run away."

"Exactly. He's running away. Why do you want to leave?"

Dinah Chaya stared at her mother, then lowered her head. She took the horseradish and put too much on her plate.

"I'll go talk to him," Shammai said tentatively, waiting for his wife's approval.

"Make it brief," she said. "You have to set the example."

He nodded as he stood.

Lazar touched his sleeve. "It's the *siddur*."

It took Shammai a moment to understand. He didn't think Lazar was right, but he'd see. He put his napkin by his plate and went to his son.

He found Elie sitting at his desk, shadowed by the light from its lamp. The Tikkun lay unopened in front of him.

Elie didn't look up when he came in. "If you're not going to eat any more, you need to say *birkat haMazon*," Shammai said.

Elie's lips tightened.

"It's not right," Shammai said gently. "Not on Shabbat."

"He could have said goodbye."

"Who says he needed to? Or realized he might have to?"

"He didn't even think about me."

"How do you know? Did he have time?"

"He didn't say anything. I'll bet he was mad at me for not waiting. I should have waited."

Shammai decided it would be best not to touch his son, despite the impulse to do so. "Even when he told you to leave?"

"It doesn't make sense. He knew. Why kick me out? Why not call an ambulance right then?"

"Maybe he didn't know. Maybe you said something that upset him. Anyway, I don't think he had time to order his thoughts that well."

"He had time enough to give you something."

Maybe Lazar was right. Shammai put his hands behind his back. "Are you worried about Mr. Enstein? Or are you upset he didn't say anything about you? That's rather selfish."

Elie looked up, blinking rapidly. "You don't understand."

"Maybe not," Shammai shrugged. "But I don't intend to keep the *siddur*."

"You better." Elie looked down again.

"You're right. I don't understand. Explain it to me."

Elie clenched his fists. "That's all he had to pass on."

"Maybe. He has a house full of books, you know. And a will."

"So why only that one? He knew."

"I don't think he did," Shammai said. "Anyway, why not hope for the best?"

Receiving no answer, Shammai reached over and opened the tikkun. "Why don't you do something for Mr. Enstein? Something he'd want you to do?"

Elie slammed it shut.

"When you're ready, don't forget to come back and say birkat."

Shammai turned.

He hesitated outside the door. As he started to go, he heard pages being ruffled, followed by a low, tentative chant.

He sighed and shook his head.

It was the *siddur*.

Chapter 3

Between *Hamavdil* and *ben kodesh* the phone rang. Shammai's effort to ignore the ringing while finishing *Havdalah* only increased his - and the family's - tension. As he sat down to drink the wine, Dinah Chaya handed him the candle, as ready to run as Elie.

He doused the flame, saying, "I'll get it."

He reached the phone by the end of fourth ring.

"Hello?"

"Shammai, Bob Sagalman. Mr. Enstein's at the University hospital. He's in stable condition at ICU, but they're not allowing any visitors."

"What about you?"

"Yeah, probably, but not without his cardiologist's OK. I won't be able to get down there until tomorrow morning, anyway. They promised to page me if there's any change in his condition."

"I appreciate it," Shammai said automatically.

"Well, it's not just a favor for you, after all." After a pause, Sagalman added, "I'll have more for you tomorrow."

"Any word about next of kin?" Shammai asked.

"None they would give over the phone. We'll just have to wait until the morning."

Shammai looked at his family's expectant faces. "Patience is in short supply here, but OK. When?"

"If I can get through with my rounds before minyan, I'll stop by beforehand. Otherwise, I'll go down right after. Maybe you can come along."

"Thanks."

He hung up.

"Well?" Hannah asked.

"He's at the University hospital, stable, in ICU, no visitors, and no more information until Dr. Sagalman can get down there in person."

"But what if something happens?" Dinah Chaya asked.

Shammai instinctively glanced at Elie "I'm sure they've either located his next of kin or whoever has power of attorney. They're just not giving that information over the phone."

Elie started to leave the room.

"Can't we find out?" Dinah Chaya asked, a hint of desperation in her voice.

The door to the boys' room slammed shut.

Shammai counted to ten, then answered her question. "I'll call Lazar in a few minutes. Maybe he's got some legal connections."

He went back to the dining room to make the after *brocha* and clean up after *havdalah*. Dinah Chaya followed him as Hannah pushed Moshe and Aaron to go clean their room.

"You'll have to wait a few minutes to use the phone," Shammai said as he picked up the plate and wine.

"I wasn't even thinking of that," she said, taking the candle and spices. Her voice had her best I-need-my-father's-sympathy tone. "Elie hasn't said a word to me all Shabbos."

"He hasn't said much beyond the perfunctory to anyone," Shammai said, putting the plate in the sink. "But I don't think he's still angry."

"How can you say that?"

"Because no one can stay that angry this long." He picked up the phone.

"I'll straighten the table," she said, going back to the living room.

Lazar answered before the first ring finished.

"No word, Shammai," Lazar said, without any greeting. "They won't tell me if they've located his next of kin, but assure me, rather huffily, they have authorization to provide medical treatment."

Shammai wasn't surprised that Lazar knew it was him or what he'd ask. He wasn't even surprised that Lazar had an answer. "Any suggestions?"

"None. Kashdan's trying to locate any relatives. On Monday, I can make a few phone calls."

"Sagalman's going down there tomorrow."

"It's funny. We're the only ones who care, and we can't do anything."

"I'm not sure about either of those statements."

"I am. And it worries me."

Shammai sighed. "You've got to stop being so cryptic."

"I prefer to think of it as aphoristic."

"Whatever it is, it doesn't change things. We're still just going to have to wait."

"Shammai." Lazar hesitated. "I'll mention it just once more. Get that *siddur* appraised as soon as possible."

"Why?"

"Because if I have to go to court, I may need something to show that Mr. Enstein intended to entrust his property to the *shul* - or someone from it."

"It seems kind of premature to be worrying about his property, especially since we don't have any real right to it," Shammai said.

"Do you know anyone with a better right?" Lazar challenged. "Besides, there's more at stake than an invaluable personal library."

Shammai waited for Lazar to explain, then gave up. "I don't get it."

"If that *siddur's* worth something, his gifting it to you may show he was giving you power of attorney."

40

"That's weak, and I'm no lawyer."

Lazar's turn to pause. "I know. But it's the best we've got."

"Do we need it? If he recovers, he can take care of himself. If he doesn't, it won't matter."

"What happens if Kashdan can't locate any relatives, or they want to do something we know Mr. Enstein wouldn't approve? What happens if he doesn't recover, but remains, well ..."

Shammai understood. "But the hospital told you they have authorization."

"Do you want some doctor who doesn't know him making those decisions?"

"I'm not sure I want to."

"Who else?"

Shammai nodded. "Well, nothing more I can do tonight. Call me."

They hung up.

Please, he thought, no surprises.

Hannah came out of the boys' bedroom. "All quiet," she said. "Elie?"

"His door's shut, but not all the way. I saw him lying on his bed, staring at the ceiling, a book beside him."

"Should I talk to him?"

She thought a moment, then shook her head. "Not unless you can tell him something. Let him sort through his feelings."

"He's been doing that all Shabbos," Shammai said, with some exasperation.

"I didn't know he had a time limit."

"Score one for you." He smiled at her. "I'm going to try to read."

She smiled back. "Good luck."

He went to the bookcase and took down the volume of Maimonides he'd been working on.

*

When Shammai arrived in *shul* at eight o'clock Sunday morning, he looked for Bob Sagalman.

"He's not here," Lazar said, adjusting his *tefillin*.

"Late rounds, I guess." Shammai started to put on his *tallis*. Elie put his *tefillin* down a couple chairs away and rolled up his sleeve.

By the time Shammai finished putting on his *tefillin*, they had a minyan, even without Bob Sagalman. While everyone stood around, chatting, waiting, Elie, without invitation, went to the front and started leading the service.

"Have you talked to him?" Lazar whispered.

Shammai shook his head. "I don't know what to say. Any time it looks like I'm going to, he avoids me. He'll be all right. He just needs some time. And we just need some news."

"I hope you're right," Lazar said, shrugging, then picking up his *siddur*.

All during the morning service, Shammai kept looking at his son. But Elie prayed as if nothing had happened. Or everything.

Afterwards, he waited for Elie to join him before taking off his *tallis* and *tefillin*. Silently, Elie unwrapped the straps from his arm.

"You did a good job," Shammai said.

Elie didn't respond, but simply took the *tefillin* off his head. Shammai continued to remove his *tefillin*.

As Shammai folded his *tallis*, he caught Elie watching him.

"I'm going for a walk," Elie announced.

"Want some company?"

Elie looked at him, mouth tight, eyes watering. "Not right now."

Shammai watched his son ignore Benjie and Malachi and walk out.

Had that moment of eye contact been a silent breakthrough? Shammai had been waiting for his son to reach out, to ask for help, to seek understanding, to solicit compassion - to simply talk with him. Sometimes, he suddenly realized, a silence or a withdrawal was a communication, an outpouring more potent than words.

Mishael and Kashdan came up to him.

"I've got to open the store," Mishael said. "Can you lock up?"

Shammai nodded.

"I've made some phone calls," Kashdan said. "All I can do is wait. But if you ask me, he doesn't have any relatives."

"Nobody asked you," Josh called from the other side of the room. "Come on, if you want a ride."

Kashdan shrugged his shoulders. "Sorry."

Shammai watched them go.

"I'm going to the office," Lazar said. "Call me if you hear anything."

Shammai nodded again.

He found himself alone in the shul. Something had changed, almost been lost. The quips and jests, which often served as their lubricant or bond, had been subdued. It seemed as if the very nature of the *shul* lay in the hospital with Mr. Enstein.

Would he have the same feeling if someone else - Kashdan, say, or Josh - was gone? Maybe. Certainly each of them brought a characteristic to, helped define the nature of the shul. And each one had a place, almost like a limb of a body. Remove an organ, an arm, even a toe and the body's not complete.

They didn't have a head, no one who led them, gave them a sense of direction. Of course, many synagogues with rabbis also didn't have a head. Mr. Enstein, well, he wasn't exactly the heart.

Maybe the liver or spleen. Shammai smiled to himself.

And what am I?

He shook his head and started to turn off the lights. Already, there seemed to be a shift of focus, an adjustment, an unspoken consensus a void no one wanted to fill, that couldn't be filled, would have to be.

The loss of one life is the loss of a world.

He's not dead yet, he thought, as he started to lock the door.

The phone rang. He raced to the back of the building to catch it before the answering machine.

"Hello?"

"Oh, good, I caught you." It was Bob Sagalman. "Sorry I couldn't make minyan, but a patient developed a complication and then I got caught up trying to find out about Mr. Enstein."

"Well?"

"No change and no visitors. He hasn't regained consciousness. Their authorization comes from a hand-written document in the custody of the nursing service."

"I'll call Lazar."

"Good idea. I've got a call in to the administrator. I think I can convince him to have me added as a consultant."

"And?"

"And we wait. His condition hasn't changed, which means he's no worse and there's hope. Still, in my opinion..." he hesitated. "In my opinion, if he doesn't respond in the next twenty-four hours, it's all in Lazar's hands."

What's in Lazar's hands, he thought? Burial arrangements? We've got no claim on Mr. Enstein's property.

"Hello?"

"Sorry, Bob. Thanks. The news is really comforting."

"That's the way it is. And this affects the whole shul, you know," Sagalman said, annoyed.

"I know." Shammai felt drained. "We're all doing what we can." And I'm not doing much but listening.

He hung up.

The hardest part, he thought as he locked the door, was not being able to visit. The medical and legal technicalities he could leave to Sagalman and Lazar. They didn't involve him and there was nothing he could do about them. But the anxiety of his family, the stress in the shul, his son's hopefully premature grief - for these he had become responsible. And he hadn't yet come to terms with his own reaction.

Automatically, he started the car and began to drive home, thoughts jumbling, pushing each other in and out of his mind in a chaotic urgency, none in the forefront long enough to define itself.

Without planning it, he found he'd turned onto Mr. Enstein's street. Having done so, he rationalized it: he had the key to Mr. Enstein's house and it should be checked.

He stopped the car, got out and stopped. Elie stood in front of the door, back to him.

He debated with himself, then slammed the car door, so the noise would draw Elie's attention.

Elie turned and watched his father approach.

Shammai didn't say anything until he stood next to his son. Together, they stared at the door for a minute.

"I've got the key," Shammai said quietly. "I'm going to make sure everything's all right." He unlocked the door and opened it, but didn't enter. Let Elie decide.

Elie reached a hand up to the *mezuzzah* and then walked in. Shammai followed.

The living room looked undisturbed. Reverently, Elie went toward the bookcase.

"I'll check the rest of the house," Shammai said.

Elie gave a quick nod - of acceptance or approval, he

couldn't tell.

The house had not been disturbed. Shammai made sure the windows and back door were secure and returned to the living room.

Elie, oblivious, stared at the books. Shammai cradled the moment.

He took a deep breath. Almost a day and half had passed. It was time to talk.

"Everything's in order," he said quietly, taking a step forward.

"Not the books," Elie responded.

"What do you mean?"

"It feels to me," Elie said slowly and quietly, "like the books have lost their souls. Can you feel it, Dad?"

Shammai hesitated, not sure what would keep his son talking. At last he simply shook his head. "No."

"Oh, they look the same, they sit on the shelves like before, with the same dust and everything - but they can't live any more. Not without him."

"They - or at least one - can live with someone else." He reached to put an arm around his son's shoulders and suddenly found himself hugging Elie, who had broken into sobs and buried his head in Shammai's chest.

When he got a chance, Shammai put his free hand under his glasses, wiping his own eyes. "He taught you skills, how to learn, how to choose the right books. How to make your own inheritance."

Elie broke away. "That's not it. Don't you see? That's not it."

"What's not it?" Shammai asked.

Elie paced in front of the bookcase. After a few turns, he impulsively sat down. "What do you remember? What's your best memory?" he asked.

Shammai thought a long time, then broke into a smile. "I don't know that it's my 'best memory,' but it's the first that came to mind. One Shabbos afternoon - you were three or four - I went to visit him before *mincha*. A neighbor - he lived two houses down, across the street, but he's moved - had a dog, a big brown thing like a shepherd or doberman. It got loose just as I passed and came tearing across the yard. I ran across the street, but it followed, not attacking, just snarling and backing me up.

"Mr. Enstein must have heard the commotion, because he came onto the porch. He took a look at me, in my hat and Shabbos clothes, sweating and shaking, a look at his neighbor, half-running with a leash and mumbling, and a look at the dog, growling, baring its teeth, ready to spring. Then he looked at me again, shouted, 'Where's Elie?' and went back inside." Shammai laughed. "At the sound of his voice, the dog turned tail and ran whimpering right back to the house like it had been beaten. It never bothered me again. What about you?"

Elie held his head in his hands, then stood up. "I never told you this. It's kind of hard even now." He stuck his hands in his pockets. "My first memory of Mr. Enstein is on Simchas Torah. I don't know how old I was, but it was before Aaron was born. I remember being on your shoulders a lot. Then I remember you putting me down and I cried because I didn't want you to. Then an old man gave you a Sefer Torah to hold and he picked me up to kiss it and he held one hand and you held the other, with your free one, and we danced." He had moved away from the books, toward the door. "Can we go?"

Shammai nodded, heading for the front door.

As they stood on the threshold, Shammai asked, "Are you more upset that Mr. Enstein might die, or that he didn't remember you?"

His back was to Elie. He didn't look back.

"I don't know," Elie said. "Are they my only choices?"

Shammai tried to smile and ended with a shrug. He locked

the door and they went down the steps together, not looking at each other.

"Do you want me to take a walk with you?"

Elie shook his head.

"Do you want a ride home?"

"I just want to be alone."

"OK. But promise me, when you're ready, you'll talk to me."

"If you'll talk to me."

Shammai stood by the car door. "Fair enough."

For a while, he just watched his son go down the street.

He got into the car and sat, hands on the steering wheel. What should he do now?

He looked at his *tallis* beside him and had a sudden impulse. He started the car and drove back to the shul, his mind focused on one thing.

He unlocked the door and went to the phone.

He waited impatiently for someone to answer.

"Hello?"

"Hannah? I'm at the shul."

"Why? Where's Elie?"

"We stopped at Mr. Enstein's house to make sure everything was all right." He paused. "We talked a little. Nothing important. But we talked a little."

"I guess that's a start." He could sense her relief. "Is he with you now?"

"No, he went for a walk. I think he'll be OK. Bob Sagalman called after minyan and said that Mr. Enstein's condition hasn't changed."

"Is that good or bad?"

"Sagalman isn't hopeful, but who knows. Anyway, I need to go downtown for a little while, if that's all right."

"The boys are quiet and Dinah Chaya's with friends. I don't

mind. But what are you going to do?"

"I'm not sure."

"It's about the *siddur*, isn't it?"

She knew him so well. "Yes. I'll tell you everything when I get home."

He hung up and went to the ark. He opened the bottom section, beneath the Torah scrolls, and took out the *siddur*. He'd left it there, not feeling right about keeping it with him.

But it belonged to him now.

He ran his fingers over the aged leather cover, noting the bruises, indentations, and smooth spots. Carefully, he opened it, gently turning the leaves from the middle, so as not to further damage the ragged edges.

On each page, a commentary, in Rashi script, surrounded the central text of a prayer. He noticed some writing in the edges in a small, precise handwriting. He recognized only a few letters, partially because of the peculiarity of the script, partially because of its size. But who would make notes in so valuable a book?

He opened to the flyleaf, scanning, at his leisure now, the list of some half-dozen names and dates of previous owners inscribed on the inside cover.

If books truly had souls, truly said something about those who owned them, what did this one say about all these vanished names, Mr. Enstein, himself?

He shook his head and closed the book. No sense delaying any longer. It shouldn't matter, this trip downtown. But would he really feel better knowing?

As he left the shul, cradling the *siddur*, he answered his own question. Somehow, it might help bring him and Elie closer.

He drove to the French Quarter, his hand occasionally straying to touch the *siddur*, a gesture of reassurance that annoyed him when he became aware of it.

He deliberately left the radio off, preferring to let his mind wander or remain empty as it chose. Any distraction would focus his thoughts where he didn't want them.

Traffic was usually light on a Sunday after football season - except for the two before Mardi Gras, of which this was one. But it was early enough that he could get into the Quarter without too much of a problem. He found an open-for-business parking garage only a couple blocks away from his destination.

The Quarter catered to tourists and strangers, and in some ways he felt like one now. Clutching the *siddur* tightly, he made his way to Royal street and the Oak Tree bookshop. He found comfort in the dim lights, dust and slight smell of mildew that greeted him. Books were lined up everywhere, on the floor, on shelves, chairs, in boxes, in no apparent order.

Mr. Heuerstein, whom he knew from previous, though infrequent visits, was nowhere in sight, but he heard voices. He went into an aisle and waited. He had time, and what he wanted required privacy.

A middle-aged couple, tourists by their dress, preceded Mr. Heuerstein, who went behind the desk.

The man held out three books and Mr. Heuerstein took them, opened them and called out prices. The woman held out two more. He gave them a total. The man pulled a twenty out of his pocket. Shammai noted with amusement Mr. Heuerstein's surprise at not having to bargain.

"Thank you, and enjoy your stay in New Orleans," he said.

Shammai turned to look at the books on the shelf before him as the couple passed, not wanting to appear to have been listening.

As soon as they left, Shammai stepped forth. Mr. Heuerstein's glasses still hung from a chain around his neck and his tight smile seemed too small for his gangly height.

"So, are you buying, browsing or chatting?" Mr. Heuerstein

asked, remembering him.

"None of the above," Shammai said, showing him the *siddur*. "You appraise the value of books?"

He looked at the book in Shammai's hand, squinted, and raised his glasses to his face. "Yes, for a fee. Of course, I can't always give a price instantly."

"I understand." Shammai held onto the book. "Still, I don't want to let this out of my possession."

"Of course," Mr. Heuerstein said, extending a hand. "Something that old and rare, I don't blame you."

"How much?"

The man looked up at him. "Oh." He smiled. "My fee is fifty dollars minimum, assuming a certain age and value. Recent books I only do as part of a collection."

Shammai hesitated. That was a lot of money.

"It's negotiable," the man assured him. "I don't charge more than five percent of its worth. One percent if you make me the dealer of record, for such time as you might wish to sell."

"I won't be selling," Shammai said, "but that sounds OK."

He handed him the book. "It's in Hebrew," Shammai added. "Will that make it harder?"

The man stared at the book without opening it, his mouth agape.

"What's the matter?" Shammai asked.

"Where did you get this?" the man asked harshly.

"Why?"

"Because I procured it for Mr. Enstein. I remember it well, because it was an expensive proposition. Half my profit was taken by lawyers who shouldn't have been necessary."

"Really?" Shammai asked.

"I'd never forget this book. It was in storage in a small village in Czechoslovakia, in what passed for a bank. Some local notable had the key to get it out, but could only do so in Mr. Enstein's presence. The number of affidavits and notarizations of Mr. Enstein's signature was ridiculous. I even called the place with Mr. Enstein here. It took us years to get it out. And he gave this to you?" Mr. Heuerstein asked, incredulous.

"To my daughter for me, actually." Shammai felt uncomfortable explaining how he'd gotten possession of the book. "He had a heart attack and she was there. He gave it to her to give to me."

"I see," Mr. Heuerstein said, nodding. "And you want to know how much it's worth so you can sell it?" He had a look of disgust on his face.

"Not at all. I told you it's not for sale, even before you told me how he got it over here. I know it's quite valuable, and I just want to know how valuable." The man continued to stare at him, so he added. "So I can best keep it safe for him when he recovers."

The man handed the book back to him. "I don't quite believe you, but there's nothing I can do about it. It's worth at least fifty thousand dollars."

Shammai almost dropped the book. "Fifty thousand?"

"Minimum. That was fifteen years ago. I imagine it's worth a lot more now."

Shammai looked at the *siddur* as if for the first time. "All these years," he said in a whisper, "for this book. No wonder he wanted me to - " he looked up, feeling Mr. Heuerstein watching him - "wanted me to be so careful."

"Maybe you should just put it back," Mr. Heuerstein suggested.

"But that's not what he wanted. And he's in the hospital now." Shammai shook his head. "If anything should happen to this..."

How many other volumes in Mr. Enstein's library were worth

a small fortune? What was the whole collection worth? He'd better call the police and tell them to keep an eye on the house. And he himself would stop by more often.

"Thanks," he said, breaking away from his thoughts and pulling out his checkbook.

Mr. Heuerstein held up his hands and shook his head. "No charge. I didn't need to do any research. All I ask is that you take care of that book and guard it. Mr. Enstein was a good customer. And I treasure anyone who values books as he did."

"He still does," Shammai said, somewhat annoyed. "And I assure you, if nothing else, I've learned to value books with souls as much as him."

Outside, to calm himself, Shammai opened the *siddur*. The inside front cover, with its list of names and dates, caught his attention again.

Interlude 2 - 1885

"*Well, that's the proposal.*" *Mr. Notta took an embroidered handkerchief from his coat pocket, politely coughed into it - once - and folded it back into his pocket. He gave us a tight little smile which curled the ends of his petite, stylized moustache. Apparently, he thought his little ceremony should have given us enough time to have made a decision. When we didn't respond, he pursed his lips and looked from Mattis to me twice. "Well, that is the proposal," he repeated, with emphasis.*

I looked at Mattis. There should have been something more. But of course, there could be no more, not for Tova Naomi.

I appreciated what Mr. Notta was trying to do, but I so wanted him to leave. I needed to cry, to draw strength from Mattis, before I could answer.

"*So, that is the proposal," Mattis said, nervously rubbing his hands on his legs. "Yes, that is definitely the proposal." He began twisting his head to and fro, as if the idea demanded a physical pro-and-con. "Well, as you say, it is a proposal. It's certainly a proposal we haven't heard before."*

"*No, I thought you hadn't," Mr. Notta said, smiling. "That's why I rearranged my schedule, making the arrangements for your daughter Tova Naomi a high priority."*

Mr. Notta had completely misread Mattis. Poor Mattis! He gave me one desperate, plea-for-help look then, rubbing his hands on his knees again, started to stand. Halfway, he sat down again.

"*Naturally, Kalman Hoch is expecting a prompt response. He deserves no less," Mr. Notta added.*

"*Oh, that's certain, no one would question that," Mattis said, now standing, preparing to lead Mr. Notta to the door. "Kalman Hoch is a fine boy. I've seen him in the synagogue and on some* business." *Mattis looked at me, then away, not expecting to see the pain in my eyes . "A fine boy," Mattis continued, at a loss. "Quite clever, they say, and I can say that at least he's not the opposite, not by any means, from the times I've talked with him - only for a minute, of course."*

"And a heart of gold," Mr. Notta added. "Don't forget he has a heart of gold."

"Yes, so you say," Mattis said, looking uncomfortable. "And so, in fact, I've heard. Of course, he is still a little short."

Mattis said this understatement diffidently, worried about its effect on Mr. Notta. It had none.

"True, true. Kalman Hoch is far from perfect, everyone knows that. Why, Kalman Hoch admits it himself. But if Kalman Hoch did not have his own physical - deficiencies, shall we say? - would I be able to bring from him a proposal for your Tova Naomi? After all, cheerful and pleasant as Tova Naomi is - highly desirable in a wife, I assure you, a girl can never be too cheerful or pleasant in my business - cheerful and pleasant as she is, it is not quite compensation for, pardon me, being unable to walk." He glanced at me and added, "Pardon."

I looked straight at him. "Just because Tova Naomi is a cripple - you see I can say the word - and must be practically carried everywhere, do not think we will grab desperately the first match offered."

"It might be more accurate, begging your pardon," Mr. Notta said, "to say the 'only' match offered."

"But he's so fat," Mattis protested, rejoining the conversation before I could demand Mr. Notta leave.

"Fat, muscle, he will be able to carry Tova Naomi everywhere. That he has declared his willingness to do so testifies he has, indeed, a heart of gold."

"You're sure there's no other way?" Mattis asked, glancing

at me. But I was thinking only of my daughter. Had I started a trend of tragedy at a young and tender age for the girls in the family? Before I was three, I was orphaned - physically by my drowned father and emotionally by my distraught mother. And Tova Naomi has been a cripple since the same age.

"Kalman Hoch was quite firm about that," Mr. Notta said.

Mattis looked to me again and took my silence as approval, not distraction. "If only it wasn't so much," he said. "We don't have those kinds of funds, or access to them."

"A shame," Mr. Notta said, rising. "On this point, I can safely say on behalf of my client, that without the capital to invest in his business venture, any marriage, let alone one with the restrictions that Tova Naomi would necessitate, would be unthinkable."

"Can you give us some time?" Mattis practically pleaded.

"Certainly," Mr. Notta aid. "I will call on you this time tomorrow for your answer." So saying, he rose and left us alone.

Mattis began to pace. "It's such a large sum, Giselle. If we had it, in an instant I would accept Kalman Hoch's proposal. What should we care about money if our daughter can be married, something we dared not think about before?"

"Kalman Hoch is no businessman," I said. I wiped my eyes quickly, so Mattis wouldn't see they were wet.

"Well, has he had a chance? Many who barely make ends meet in one line of work become quite wealthy in another. But what's the use? We haven't the money or any access to such a sum."

I wiped my eyes again. This time Mattis saw; but he said nothing. "We could borrow it," I suggested. "You have a connection with Monsieur Charbonier, don't you?"

"Not a real connection," Mattis said, sitting down and rubbing the back of his neck. "A client of mine occasionally does some work for him. Still, I could get an introduction. It's worth

56

trying, for Tova Naomi's sake." For a minute, he didn't say anything, but just sat rubbing the back of his neck. Then he jumped up. "What am I thinking? How can I approach Monsieur Charbonier for a loan of such an amount? Even if he would be interested, he would want something as a pledge, as collateral. What do we have of any value?"

The tears flowed freely now. "My father's siddur," I said.

"No!" Mattis practically shouted. "Absolutely not! I accepted that siddur from Rosa as a pledge, to honor the memory of your father and grandfather, and to pass it on within the family. Your mother gave it to me only because I was marrying you."

"For our daughter's future - for a grandson to whom you can pass it on, my father would approve. Besides -" and the tears stopped - "I was barely a year old when my father died."

"Yes," Mattis said, waving his hand, "that sudden storm, the collapse of the bridge that killed both your father and grandfather. That's exactly my point: it was the ambition for more that put them there."

"No," I said, surprised at my own vehemence. "It was their love for their children, concern about their future, that drove them." I stood. "I say they would approve, for we pass on the siddur itself for the same reasons."

We stared at each other, until finally Mattis looked away. "Very well. I will get an appointment with Monsieur Charbonier and ask him for the loan. I will offer him the siddur as collateral, and suggest a ten-year period for repayment. I'm sure he'll accept. The ten years should give our new son-in-law, Kalman Hoch, time to make his business successful enough to repay it himself, if need be. But the wedding expenses come from our own pocket."

I nodded, crying for joy. "Maybe they will name their first son Uriel," I said. "I will tell Giselle now."

ARRANGEMENTS

Chapter 4

Shammai picked up his coffee cup and winced. Too hot. It always seemed too hot or too cold. He put it down and decided he was hungry. Should he have cereal or a bagel and cheese for breakfast?

He went to the kitchen and opened the refrigerator. It looked empty. It always did on Tuesday; it would seem to overflow on Friday, though.

He didn't see any cheese, so he took out the milk, got a bowl and spoon, then searched for the cereal which seemed to have the least sugar.

As he sat down again, he reviewed his day's schedule: some paper work at the office, a report for the insurance company, a proposal to the engineering company that responded (at last) to his letter of inquiry. A slow day.

He poured the milk over the cereal.

Hannah came into the room.

"The children get off to school all right?"

He nodded. "Mishael drove this morning."

"Your coffee's getting cold," she said, passing into the kitchen.

He continued eating his cereal.

He heard her put water into the kettle and turn on the stove. "Did Bob Sagalman call?" she asked.

"Not yet. If he doesn't call before I leave, I'm going to page him from the office."

Bowl and spoon in hand, she came and sat next to him. "What are you going to do?"

"What can I do?" he shrugged. "It's still Mr. Enstein's *siddur*.

I just hope he pulls through."

"Will that solve it?" she asked. "But I meant about Elie."

He took a sip of coffee and made a face.

"I told you it was getting cold," she said, standing as the kettle whistled. "I put in extra water."

"Thanks." He watched her go into the kitchen, then turned around and finished the cereal.

She came back, a cup steaming with coffee in one hand, the kettle in the other. He waited for her to fill his cup, put the kettle back in the kitchen, and return.

She blew on her coffee once and started drinking.

"I don't see how you can drink it that hot."

She smiled. "So what are you going to do?"

He leaned back in his chair. "Do you think I should tell him?"

"What do you think?"

"I think if he learns that Mr. Enstein gave me a *siddur* worth over fifty thousand dollars, he'd be devasted."

"He's got to learn sometime."

"Why? If Mr. Enstein recovers, I give it back and that's the end of it."

"Unless Mr. Enstein tells him. And if Mr. Enstein doesn't recover - don't look like that, you told me what Sagalman said yesterday - he's going to want to know why Mr. Enstein's gift is in a safe deposit box instead of here."

"Yes, but if Mr. Enstein left Elie something in his will - "

"Assuming he has one," she interrupted.

"Then I can tell him without all the - repercussions."

She put her cup down. "It's almost as if Mr. Enstein planned all this," she frowned. "Why do you think he did it?"

He shrugged again. "Who knows? Maybe he just had this one nearby when he had the heart attack, and wanted to make what might be a last gesture of thanks."

"Some thanks."

He raised his eyebrows ruefully. "Yeah."

"You know," she said thoughtfully, "that probably means he hadn't included you in his will."

"So?"

"Nothing." She poured out some cereal. "It might also mean he hadn't disposed of his books in it."

"You're assuming he could think straight at the time."

"If he could think straight enough to give it to Dinah Chaya with instructions, he could think straight enough to know what he was doing. He could have said anything. 'Tell your father my books are his.' 'Tell Elie the top row belongs to him.' He could even have said something to you earlier."

"No, because then he'd never know if our kindness was genuine, or for an inheritance."

"Now don't you play his game," Hannah said. "It was all very well for him to pretend there's an ulterior motive - other than our children's education - and for you to go along with his 'cake and eggs' accounting, if that sort of hands-off posturing is part of the masculine mystique. But protecting Mr. Enstein's property is a different matter than protecting his ego. Or yours."

"But protecting it from what? Or who?" He got up, taking his bowl and spoon to the sink.

"Your coffee'll get cold again."

"I like it that way," he said irritably.

"No, you don't. You just never drink it when it's the right temperature for you."

He pushed his chair in. "Hannah, what were we doing fourteen years ago?"

"Why?" she asked suspiciously.

"Just answer the question."

"We'd just moved to town. Dinah Chaya was a little more than a year old. You were working downtown on an engineering project for the Defense department. I was three months pregnant and had a temporary, part-time job as an accountant."

"What else?" he prompted.

"We didn't live here. Josh Green found us an apartment on the other side of the university. That's how we got involved with the *shul* and Mr. Enstein."

"What were your impressions of him then?"

"You expect me to remember?" She picked up her coffee. "Now mine's as cold as yours," she said. She furrowed her brow. "Probably the same as now. An old man who'd been through a lot, without anyone, perceptive, cranky, possessive, who played petty little power games for reassurance. And he went out of his way to make sure we were taken care of."

"You thought all that?"

"Probably not. I didn't know him. I would have made him *challahs*, anyway. He took an interest in us."

"So did everyone else in the shul," he said, his mind drifting back.

"True, but Mr. Enstein's interest came from the same place as his gruffness - the heart."

"I'd say the spleen. Or the liver," Shammai said.

"What?"

"Never mind."

"Why do you ask?" she said.

He walked away from the table. "Because fourteen years ago, Mr. Enstein started to get this *siddur* from its hiding place in Europe."

"Hiding place? You didn't tell me any of this."

"I didn't know it until Sunday, and with running the kids around when I got back, I forgot. Not really a hiding place, it was in a bank vault in a small village. But it might as well have been hidden. I'm just trying to figure out if there's a connection."

"Well, don't waste your day on it."

"I won't," he promised, picking up his briefcase. He stopped and looked at the bookcase on his way out.

"What are you thinking?"

"How few we have. How it would look here." He'd left it in the shul. He turned and smiled at her. "I'll call you later."

"Let's hope there's some good news."

He nodded.

\#

Shammai came back from lunch at the Creole Kosher Deli and checked his messages. The third, from Bob Sagalman, he returned immediately.

He got the receptionist.

"Is Bob Sagalman in?"

"Who's calling?"

"Shammai Danielson. I'm a friend. He called while I was at lunch. It's pretty urgent."

A pause. "He's with a patient right now. I'll have him call you."

"Please. As soon as possible. I'm at my office. He has my number."

He looked at his to-do list, including the other phone calls to return, but was too nervous to do anything but speculate why Sagalman had called. He paced the room a couple times and finally sat down at his terminal.

The phone rang.

"Hello?"

"Shammai. Bob Sagalman. I've got good news and bad

news."

Shammai leaned back in his chair and watched the screen-saver kick in, making trails of geometric designs. "Let's have it."

"He's out of the coma. He should be able to have visitors."

"When?"

"By the time you get there. I'll meet you."

"Don't you have patients?"

"I'll manage."

Shammai leaned forward and hit a button to change the design. "Do you have to?"

A pause. "Don't you want me there?"

Shammai's turn to pause. "I just want to understand the situation."

"No, I don't have to be there." Sagalman sighed. "I'd like to be and I think it'd be better if I was."

"Because of the *shul* or because you're a physician?"

"Both. It'll make it easier for you."

"Okay." He leaned forward. "What's the bad news?"

"He's not going to make it."

"Is that official?"

"As official as anything can be in medicine. He's too old for any surgical procedure. His body couldn't stand the shock. And his heart won't keep going much longer, even with the machines."

Shammai picked up a pen and doodled. "When?"

"No telling. He should last long enough for a visit. He may even last a week. But I don't think he'll leave the hospital."

Shammai looked at his watch. "Encouraging. Give me a time."

"I can break free in half an hour."

Shammai nodded. "I'll meet you in forty-five minutes." He started to hang-up, then had a thought. "Can I bring Elie?"

The question surprised Sagalman. "Sure. I don't know how

many visitors he'll be allowed, or for how long, but why not?"

"Okay." He hung up.

He looked at his doodles a minute, then called Hannah.

She answered before the second ring.

"Bob Sagalman just called. Mr. Enstein's out of the coma. I'm going to visit him."

"Maybe you should take Elie out of school," she suggested.

"I was planning on it. There's something else."

"What?"

"Official prognosis is he's not going to make it."

She drew in her breath. "I'm sorry. What are you going to tell Elie?"

Shammai doodled again. "I don't know. Maybe I won't tell him anything."

"Is that fair?"

"Well, maybe I'll wait until after he sees him. It'll be hard enough as it is."

He waited for her response.

"Use your judgment." She paused. "What about the *siddur*?"

"What about it?"

"What are you going to do?"

"I don't know," he said irritably.

"Maybe you should call Lazar."

"Good idea," he said, still annoyed.

"Anything I can do?"

"No. It's too early to make funeral arrangements, I guess. Sagalman doesn't know how long."

"Shammai, call Lazar."

"I will." He had to smile. She knew him so well. He would have put off the call.

"And let me know what I can do. What happens."

"I will."

He hung up and stared at the phone. He checked his watch. He had time to call Lazar before picking up Elie.

Lazar answered the phone himself.

"Where's your secretary?"

"Out to lunch. My partners are meeting with a client. I'll plead the Fifth to any other questions, unless you tell me why."

Shammai smiled. "Bob Sagalman just called. Mr. Enstein's out of the coma. I'm going to visit him. With Elie."

"Great."

"Not so great. He also said Mr. Enstein's not going to make it."

Silence.

"Hello."

"Sorry," Lazar said. "I started thinking of the complications. Professional hazard. Of course, our esteemed doctor doesn't know when."

"No," Shammai said drily.

"So," Lazar said, his tone becoming artificially facetious, "aside from making sure I receive the latest bulletins, no doubt out of concern for my feelings, knowing I hate to be left out, to what do I owe the pleasure of this call?"

Lazar's mockery, used to mask emotions he feared to express, this time annoyed Shammai. It just wasn't appropriate. "Does Mr. Enstein have a will?"

"As a matter of fact, he does. I found out this morning I have the dubious privilege of being executor, which I strongly suspect will place me in an interesting conflict-of-interest. I just love his little secrets."

"He's got more than we suspect, I'm sure. You've seen the will?"

"I most definitely have not. It's in a safe deposit box, to be opened only by an officer of the bank upon receipt of written

66

notification of Mr. Enstein's death. At which time I will receive further instructions."

"That doesn't make sense, but how did you find out?" Shammai looked at his watch and stood up. He'd probably have to cut this short.

"I was notified by said officer," Lazar explained, continuing his mimic of courtroom style, "who was notified by the nursing service, which was informed of Mr. Enstein's condition by the hospital, which in turn learned of its legal obligation upon application to his insurance company."

"How did the hospital know which one to contact?"

"Because Medicare had it listed," Lazar said, dropping the banter and letting his own irritation show. "I wasted almost two hours, worth three hundred dollars, futilely chasing this down, only to have it all laid before me with a five minute phone call. Even a lawyer can have a surfeit of deviousness."

Shammai chuckled. "I'm sure Mr. Enstein had his reasons." About to hang up, he remembered Lazar's remark. "What do you mean by a conflict-of-interest?"

"Unless you or yours are named sole heir, which makes things too simple and too honest an expression of gratitude for Mr. Enstein, I refer to the *siddur*."

The difficulties were suddenly becoming real to Shammai. "You're assuming I'll want to keep it, and want you for my lawyer. I'll call you later."

With that, he hung up, pleased that he'd been able to leave Lazar on the receiving end of a jibe for a change.

Chapter 5

He got in his car and headed for the school, a ten minute drive. It'd take about half an hour to get downtown and park, so he should get to the hospital about the same time as Sagalman.

Absently, he turned on the radio. The sound of a not particularly notable piano sonata filled the car. He placed it in the Romantic period. He made a face at the melody, but became too busy merging into traffic to turn it off.

Getting Elie out of school wouldn't be a problem. Figuring out what to tell him would. He scratched his head and adjusted his glasses. Hannah was right, of course, it wouldn't be fair not to tell Elie. On the other hand, it might not be fair to Mr. Enstein to say anything. Sagalman could be wrong. Even if he wasn't, making Elie more depressed hardly helped him fulfill the mitzvah of visiting the sick.

He pulled off the interstate and his stomach tightened. Elie might guess the truth, in which case he wouldn't lie. Could Elie handle it? He reassured himself somewhat, with the thought that G-d doesn't give us a burden we can't handle.

For the next few minutes, he concentrated on getting around the traffic as quickly as possible. As he futilely willed a red light to change, the pianist came to an annoying fortissimo and he flicked it off.

He pulled into the parking lot, glancing at East Jeff hospital across the street. Instead of drugstores, maybe they should put a hospital on every corner. He got out of the car and was in the school office without having resolved what to say.

The secretary looked up when he came in.

"I'd like to take Elie out of school early. There's someone in the hospital he needs to see."

She looked at him dubiously, with why-can't-you-wait-until-after-school written all over her face. "What about your other children?"

"No, just Elie."

"Wait here, please."

She got up and went down the hall.

He looked around the office, noting with disgust and dismay the obsolete computer the school used. He'd have to see about getting a newer one donated, he reminded himself again.

The secretary soon came back with Elie, whose expression showed a mixture of fear, submission and defiance.

"Mr. Enstein's out of the coma," Shammai said, surprised at the matter-of-factness of his voice. "Dr. Sagalman suggested we visit as soon as possible."

"We?" Elie said.

"Well, I thought you might like to come."

Elie stared at him, clearly trying to learn something more.

"OK," was all he said, as neutrally as Shammai.

They got into the car without saying anything else. Shammai waited until he was on the interstate before trying the radio again. This time, some cacophonic modern concerto was playing. He switched it off. So much for that excuse.

As he slowed into the downtown traffic, Elie finally spoke. "What did Dr. Sagalman say, exactly?"

"I don't remember his exact words," Shammai said, immediately realizing Elie's last word was simply generational jargon, "but he said Mr. Enstein was out of the coma, could receive visitors, and we - I - should come as soon as possible."

"Because he might go back into a coma?"

"Something like that," he said drily. Elie would understand - no need to say more. "I didn't go into the medical details. I called your mother and then came for you."

Elie fiddled with his seat belt, an annoying habit. "Is he all right?" His voice rose slightly.

"A man that age is never all right after a heart attack."

"You know what I mean."

Shammai sighed, waiting until the exit before answering. The crawl of cars gave him time to consider his words. "No."

He couldn't find any others.

Elie seemed to accept the assessment, as though he'd anticipated it. Waiting for the light to let him onto Tulane avenue, he stole a glance at his son. Elie gazed into the distance, his face a blank.

The light changed.

"Can we listen to some music?" Elie suddenly asked.

"We're almost there," Shammai said. The garage was two blocks ahead.

"It doesn't matter."

Shammai nodded and Elie turned on the radio. Beethoven's Moonlight Sonata.

The concrete and steel of the garage didn't mute or distort it. Selfishly, he hoped he wouldn't find a parking place until it was finished, but now, of course, he found one quickly.

He pulled in and started to turn off the car.

"Wait," Elie whispered.

A minute later, in the middle of the movement, Elie said, "OK," and got out of the car. Shammai followed, puzzlement chasing away any yearning for the music.

Elie must have seen his bewilderment. "Mr. Enstein once told me that music is the pen of the soul," he explained. "I didn't think children's tapes fit right now, and that's all we had."

He nodded.

They walked the steep incline to the elevator without a car

passing, went down two stories to the crossover and stopped at the information desk. Getting directions to Mr. Enstein's room, they went to the hospital elevators, walking past nurses and patients and around wheelchairs.

Two other people, an old man and a middle-aged woman, were in the elevator. Neither got off at their floor.

They stepped from the background hum of the elevator into a hall almost devoid of sound. Their footsteps, echoing off the antiseptic walls, seemed amplified.

They turned a corner and the weight of the silence seemed to lift. They almost passed the visitor's lounge without looking, but a sudden movement caught Shammai's attention.

"Mr. Levinsky!" he said in a stage whisper.

Simultaneously, the short, heavy-set man - grayed, his face age-marked though with fewer wrinkles than one would expect - dropped a magazine, got up and approached. He looked out of place without a phone in his hand, Shammai thought.

"What are you doing here?" Shammai asked, surprised. Though Levinsky paid dues - as he did at two other shuls - and occasionally came for the holidays, he wasn't a regular. The antagonism between him and Mr. Enstein accounted for that, in part.

"Coming to challenge an old friend," He said in his thick accent. Funny how he had more of one than Mr. Enstein. Shammai hadn't thought about that before.

Mr. Levinsky glanced down the hall at the nurses' station. "They won't let me see him. I've been here almost an hour, waiting. Now that I need a doctor, I can't buy one." He looked back at Shammai. "Sagalman's there waiting for you."

"I didn't think -" Shammai started to say, then stopped himself.

Levinsky snorted. "That why you like the computers so much, because they don't think either, like you said? But he's like me, stubborn. But he never had suppliers and customers. And I was never his kind of Jew."

"I'm sorry," Shammai said, acutely aware of Elie beside him.

"It doesn't matter. Whether I'm old or not, I'll soon have to stop thinking of myself as young. For a while, things went along. I wrote checks that made sure he had a *shul* and he said prayers that made G-d forgive even me. And we both thought the other missed something. But now. . ." he shrugged.

"I could --" Shammai started to offer.

"No," Levinsky, said, holding up a hand, then turning it outward. "But if I come to the *shul* - well, honors I don't need any more. *Gabbai?* But Enstein, he knows old Levinsky hasn't forgotten his Torah." He looked at Elie. "I thought your son might like to know that."

He pushed past them, obviously intending to leave. He stopped and turned around. "I'll come again tomorrow. Don't tell him I was here."

They watched him disappear around the corner.

At the nurses' station, they found Bob Sagalman waiting, looking over a chart. He looked up and smiled as they approached, putting down the chart with a nervous flip of his hand.

Shammai glanced at Elie, but Elie's attention was diverted by the activity.

"Welcome to ICU," Sagalman said, shaking their hands, and using the other to sweep around the ward.

Located at the end of the hall, the nurses' station formed a rectangular barricade, open in the middle of each side, to the five, curtained rooms in a semi-circle behind it. Three nurses occupied it, one sitting opposite Dr. Sagalman and putting the chart away, another at a computer terminal, and the third standing, back to them, manipulating vials of medicine.

The quiet was denser than even the normal hospital silence,

broken only by the beeps of monitors and the background hum of life-preserving machines.

Shammai felt Elie beside him, anxious, nervous, but refusing to be overwhelmed or frightened.

"A different type of sanctuary," Sagalman said, putting on his bedside manner for them.

"Which room?" Shammai asked.

"Five," a nurse replied automatically.

"When can we see him?" Elie asked Sagalman.

"I'm waiting for authorization from Dr. Reading," the nurse answered.

"Staff cardiologist," Sagalman explained. "Very good."

"Is he Mr. Enstein's doctor?" Shammai asked.

"He's the one who saved his life," the nurse said. "But Dr. Fields is in charge of ICU."

"I've already gotten his written OK," Sagalman said, reassuringly. "Dr. Reading said he'd call before six."

Shammai looked at the clock on the wall. "You mean we might have to wait a couple of hours?"

"I don't mind," Elie said.

"No," Sagalman said. "I paged him when I got here. If he doesn't call in the next fifteen minutes, I'll page him again."

"He's quite busy," the nurse said. "Sometimes he gets an emergency surgery. You can sit down over there." She pointed to a row of three connected chairs. "There's also a visitor's lounge down the hall."

"We passed it," Shammai said.

"I'll wait here," Elie said firmly.

The nurse shrugged and swiveled her chair around.

"I haven't seen him yet," Sagalman said to Shammai, "though I could invoke physician's privilege."

"Why not?"

Sagalman shrugged. "I wanted to wait for you. Also, I don't know how many visitors or for how long Reading will authorize. I don't want to step on any toes." He smiled. "I'm giving you right of first refusal."

The phone rang and the nurse picked it up. She nodded her head and wrote, twice stopping to respond with a yes. Then she held out the phone.

"Dr. Reading wants to speak with you, Dr. Sagalman."

Sagalman took the phone, listened, said thank you and handed it back.

"One at a time, five minutes only. If a nurse comes in, leave immediately. It means something's wrong." He stopped to look at them. Shammai and Elie both nodded. "He's hoping to get here within the half-hour and is most reluctant. I owe him. But then," he added with a rueful smile, "he hasn't collected on any of his debts yet. Go ahead."

He stepped aside for Shammai.

Shammai took a step and stopped. What had Sagalman said? The right of first refusal. "Elie, you go first."

Without a word or a glance up, as if expecting this of his father, Elie walked around them. Shammai suddenly wondered, though, if Elie thought his words a gesture, a noble sacrifice, or into just another command.

Elie walked to the curtain, hesitated, and slipped inside.

Shammai turned to Sagalman. "Is he even conscious?"

"Yes," the nurse said, "though don't expect him to be too alert. They sleep most of the time here."

Sagalman settled himself comfortably in one of the end seats. Shammai took the other.

"It's not good, is it?" Shammai said.

Sagalman shook his head. "Could be tonight. Tomorrow. No more than a week."

"How do you know? Physicians are only given skill to heal, remember."

"I remember." Sagalman smiled and looked away. "But we don't rely on miracles, either. His heart's gone. I don't know how else to put, except with terminology that doesn't explain why."

Shammai thought about the words. "I'd think that would be the last part of Mr. Enstein to go." Sagalman looked at him. "He's so stubborn."

"Things are going to be different," Sagalman said.

"Things are always going to be different."

Sagalman hesitated. "They'll be most different for you."

Shammai looked at the curtain.

"I don't mean for Elie," Sagalman said. "He'll grieve, but Mr. Enstein's not his grandfather. I mean for you. Whatever he left the shul, you've got a personal legacy from Mr. Enstein."

Shammai turned to him, meeting his eyes. "You know, in the fourteen years I've known him, I haven't heard anyone call him anything except Mr. Enstein. Except when he's called to the Torah."

Sagalman's eyebrows went up.

"Dr. Sagalman, it's been three minutes," the nurse said.

"Dr. Reading said five," he responded without turning. "What do you think they're talking about?"

"Can he talk?" Shammai asked. "The nurse said he might not even be awake."

Sagalman just cocked his head. Shammai chuckled.

"Yeah, for me he'll be asleep."

The curtain parted slightly, and Elie emerged.

Shammai rose. Elie grinned then wiped his eyes.

Before Shammai could take a step, the nurse was at the curtain, ordering Elie aside.

"What's the matter?" Shammai asked.

Dr. Sagalman was ahead of him.

"The monitor indicates stress," she said curtly. "Please wait here."

Sagalman went to the nurses's station, checking the monitor and conferring with another nurse.

In a moment, the nurse came out.

"He's sleeping," she said. "Everything's stabilized."

Shammai exhaled. "Can I go in?"

"I'm sorry, not without Dr. Reading's approval. I can't risk another disturbance. If you want to wait for Dr. Reading..."

Shammai looked at Sagalman.

"I'll page him again," Sagalman offered, going to the station. He passed through the nearest opening and picked up the phone.

"Page Dr. Reading, please," he said. "I'll wait." He motioned twice, open-hand downward.

A moment later, he put the speaker to his mouth. "Sorry to bother you again. One of the visitors just went in. ... No, two, his son came with him. ... The son. ... After he left, there seemed to be a momentary problem, but he's asleep now. Can he go in for a look? ... It might be - okay, I understand. ... No, I agree. I'll explain it to him." He hung up the phone and came over to Shammai.

He shook his head. "In his state, Dr. Reading doesn't think it's a good idea. If Elie's visit exhausted him that much, he's clearly not up to it. Even your presence might, well -"

Shammai nodded, surprised to find he felt, in the midst of his disappointment, a little relieved. Had he feared a confrontation, a last harangue, or just a retraction of the gift? A quick examination of his conscience rejected all three. A reluctance to let go, then, most likely.

"Should I stay around or come later?" he asked.

"No telling. I've got to get back to my office soon, myself."

Without Sagalman to procure Dr. Reading's permission, it seemed pointless. "Call me and let me know as soon as I can see him."

"Sure. Or if anything happens."

Shammai headed down the hall, looking for Elie, who had wandered off when the nurse came out.

He found Elie in the lounge, flipping through magazines, ignoring the overhead TV. Elie stood up when his father entered.

"Will you get to see him?" Elie asked.

"Not right now," Shammai responded, lightly. "Hopefully I'll see him later tonight or tomorrow." He put a hand on Elie's shoulder. "Let's go. Your brothers and sister will be home from school by the time we get back."

They walked to the elevator, rode it down and crossed into the parking lot without a word. There didn't seem anything to say.

About a mile from home, stopped at a red light, Elie suddenly said. "Let's talk, Dad."

"OK About what?"

"You're the father. You tell me."

Shammai looked at his son. The joyous earnestness, genuine, masked something deeper, more disturbing. But all he cared about right now was that his son wanted to talk to him. But what should he say?

One question kept repeating itself in his mind.

"Do you want to be like him?" Shammai asked quietly.

"I don't think so." A pause. "Sometimes I felt, I don't know, like I was one of his books. That's how he treated me. It was a good thing, because it meant he respected me. I don't think there's enough respect for the books. Or for the ones who teach them."

"Or for the ones who learn them?" Shammai asked.

"Maybe. The thing is, I think he appreciated what was inside me."

"But you don't want to be like him?"

"No. I was his student, not his clone."

Elie hopped out of the car. "By the way," he said as the car alarm beeped, "I liked that piano piece we listened to in the garage."

That was it? Shammai thought.

Chapter 6

Going to a funeral erev Shabbos was not exactly the ideal way to prepare. He'd gone to the hospital Tuesday and Wednesday, waited for half-an-hour, then left both days without being allowed to see the still comatose Mr. Enstein. On Thursday, he'd rearranged his schedule, gone early and had a brief encounter with Dr. Reading. That afternoon, Mr. Enstein had passed away.

Hannah sat on the couch, ready to go, her face taciturn, anticipating the experience of unpleasant feelings to come.

"Dinah Chaya and Elie are in their rooms, getting ready. They'll be out in a minute," she said.

He nodded, unsure what to do.

"Is everything taken care of?" she asked to fill the void.

He adjusted his glasses. "I think so. Mishael and Bob Sagalman are on the *Chevra Kadisha*, so they took care of things from that end. Josh Green offered to help if needed. Lazar handled the legal stuff."

She raised her eyebrows at him.

"I know, I guess I should have helped, but I'm not a member of the *Chevra Kadisha* and I felt funny coming just this once. Maybe I'll join."

"No you won't."

He smiled at her. "You're right. Anyway, I made all the arrangements with the funeral home. Aryeh's going with the casket, they've got xeroxed *tehillim* to hand out and -- well, everything seems ready."

"Who's paying for all this?"

"Oh," he said with a wave of the hand, "Mr. Enstein had insurance. Lazar's executor, you know, so he's taking care of that."

She shook her head. "It seems strange there's not more for

you to do. Who's conducting the funeral?"

"I asked Rabbi Blumenthal and he agreed. We thought maybe someone from the *shul* should say something, too, but that's not definite."

"Who's we?"

"Jonathan Kashdan, Bob Sagalman and myself. I guess if any of us feel like it, we will."

He went to the bookcase and looked at the *siddur*, sitting in the middle of the top shelf. It seemed out of place. But it was his now, and he couldn't very well abandon Mr. Enstein's legacy. It belonged in his house.

"Are you upset?" Hannah asked.

"About what?"

"About not seeing him before he died."

Shammai thought about the question. When the call came from Sagalman's office that Mr. Enstein had gone into cardiac arrest, he'd told Hannah to make other arrangements for the children and raced to the hospital. Sagalman and Lazar were there waiting for him. By the looks on their faces, he knew he was too late.

His thought at the time had been that at least Elie had gotten to talk to the old man.

Since then, he'd been too busy to think about his own feelings.

He turned around. "I guess I should be disappointed. But, given his condition, I'm not sure what I would have said anyway." He sat down in the rocking chair. "You know, I don't even remember my last conversation with him. I guess it's better that way. I can always imagine it was something particularly significant. Or - more likely - just the usual trivialities that formed the relationship." He shrugged. "At least Elie got to see him. That's important."

They sat for a minute, not saying anything. Impulsively, he bolted out of his chair. "Where's the paper?"

"On the table," Hannah said. "It's open."

The obituary page lay before him. He found the entry for Mr. Enstein, halfway down the first column. It took all of five lines. Eighty-one years old. Joined the community twenty years ago. Retired. Holocaust survivor. No profession listed. No known relatives. Funeral today at eleven AM. Memorial donations to the shul.

He folded the paper with a sigh. It wasn't much for a man who'd lived as long and done as much as Mr. Enstein. But anything else seemed superfluous now. The facts of Mr. Enstein's life weren't particularly noteworthy and how could they sum up all the little things that would make him missed? Shammai wasn't sure he could ever put them into words.

He remembered how Elie had reacted to the news. Shammai had driven to the school, numb except for an uneasiness how to handle Elie's blame. He'd decided to avoid the problem by telling Dinah Chaya at the same time.

The secretary had brought them both to the office. Although he felt sure they knew when they'd been called from class, or at least by his expression, they still surprised him by their silence.

He spoke the words. Dinah Chaya just cried.

At first, he didn't think Elie had heard. But then Elie had looked at him, searching for words, saying, "Baruch Dayan Emet," when he'd remembered.

After that, Elie had turned to the wall. Shammai had just waited, feeling helpless and more uncomfortable than if either had reacted more strongly.

"I just came from the hospital," Shammai had said, forestalling questions about details and the funeral.

Elie had faced him, dry-eyed. "I guess we better go back to class."

And that had stopped Shammai's questions about their

response. For once, Dinah Chaya followed her brother.

"Shammai." Hannah's call broke his reverie. He looked up. She motioned him to come over.

"What did you and Elie talk about last night?" she asked in a hushed voice, glancing at the back of the house in case Elie came out.

"On our walk? Not much. I know we were gone a while, but the conversation was sporadic. I tried to say a few good things about Mr. Enstein, but he didn't want to hear that. I guess he felt I was condescending to him. He did say --"

He stopped as a door shut. Dinah Chaya came out. He exchanged a look with Hannah that said he'd finish later.

"I hope I don't cry too much," Dinah Chaya said.

"You'll cry as much as necessary," Hannah said, standing. "And you won't be alone."

"I'll get Elie," Shammai said, but just then his son came through the kitchen.

"Let's go," Elie said impatiently.

They all started for the door. Hannah had been right to insist Aaron and Moshe go to school. Mr. Enstein wasn't their grandfather, and they were too young for a funeral.

He stopped by the bookcase and hesitated. Should he bring it? He wasn't even sure if he was going to say *kaddish* - that was really the rabbi's job - and there'd be another *siddur* there. Still, gratitude seemed to demand he at least use the gift at Mr. Enstein's funeral. It was a *siddur*, not a museum piece.

He pulled the book off the shelf and said, "Let's go," repeating Elie's words.

He locked the door, the ancient prayer book tucked tightly under his arm.

The silence of the drive weighed heavily and several times he was tempted to break it with something other than Dinah Chaya's occasional sobs and Elie's short-tempered response.

A crowd had already gathered by the cemetery gates when they arrived.

"More than I thought," Hannah said.

Shammai half-expected Elie to say "not enough," or words to that effect, but he just got out of the car, as subdued as his sister.

As they walked toward the crowd, Shammai felt oddly proud of his children. Their appearance and manner reflected well on their parents, he thought.

Shammai glanced skyward. Dark clouds rolled by swiftly. The air smelled of rain, but seemed content to merely threaten. He wondered if the dirt for the grave, covered by a tarpaulin, was moist. He remembered one funeral on a hot summer day where it had been unexpectedly muddy, making the burial laborious and more trying for the mourners. He shook his head. Hopefully, there wouldn't be any such difficulties today.

Some people already stood inside the covered alcove. The rest stood outside, talking quietly.

"Surprised?" Hannah whispered.

"At what?"

She nodded her head. "The number of people."

Shammai surveyed the crowd, picking out individuals. He recognized most of them. A large number were elderly, but quite a few younger - and not from the *shul* - had also come.

"Not really. Mr. Enstein had a lot of respect around town."

At the gate, Hannah and Dinah Chaya went inside, joining a knot of women to one side of the alcove. Shammai saw Rabbi Blumenthal talking to them, but waited outside. He was one of the pall bearers.

Where was Jonathan Kashdan? As a kohen, he couldn't enter the cemetery, but he should be here. He craned his neck, searching, and saw him by the iron-wrought face, standing alone and looking in.

He made his way to Kashdan's side.

"Shammai," Kashdan acknowledged, without looking up.

Shammai looked at the grave in front of them.

"My mother," Kashdan said quietly. Then he added, "They'll be here any minute. I called on my car phone just before you came."

"Are you all right?"

Kashdan nodded. "There are times -" he sighed. "Mr. Enstein and I didn't get along very well, did we?"

"No, not really," Shammai said ruefully.

"I didn't dislike him. I just wanted the *shul* to grow and Mr. Enstein wanted to keep it small enough to dominate." He sighed. "And, I wanted the power."

"Not much of that in our little place. With your money, you could have joined one of the larger synagogues and been president." Shammai shuffled his feet, kicking at some loose gravel. The conversation, and his participation in it, surprised him.

"Too easy. I built that department store from nothing. I wanted to do the same with a shul." With his hands in his pocket, huddling in his coat against the damp chill, Kashdan didn't look so formidable.

"I guess you can, now. None of us will stop you."

Kashdan gave a short laugh. "I know. Do you think mother would approve?"

Shammai raised his eyebrows and Kashdan turned around.

"You've got his *siddur*, I see."

"Should I donate it to the shul?" Shammai asked, not really serious.

"No, of course not. Then I'd never beat him. Besides, you should take advantage of his momentary weakness."

The crowd stirred and they turned to see the hearse drive up.

"I don't think it was that at all," Shammai said, leaving

Kashdan.

The crowd parted as the hearse parked next to the entrance. Rabbi Blumenthal came out and shook hands with Shammai and Josh Green, who had just come running up.

Elie stood by the curb, waiting for the doors to open.

The driver and funeral director got out, opened the door and pulled out the cart. As they set it up, Rabbi Blumenthal asked, "Who are the pall bearers."

"I'm one," Josh said. "Shammai, Mishael, Lazar, Bob Sagalman."

"We need a sixth."

"Malachi," Shammai reminded Josh. The boy, though not yet fifteen, was, like his father, quite strong.

The casket was pulled out and set on the cart.

"Three on each side, please," Rabbi Blumenthal instructed.

Josh, Malachi and Bob Sagalman went on one side. Mishael and Lazar took the ends of the other. Shammai stepped forward and suddenly realized he had the *siddur* under his arm.

"Maybe you'd better give that to someone else for the moment," Rabbi Blumenthal suggested.

Shammai looked around and saw his son, isolated, in front of the casket.

"Elie." Elie looked up from the casket to his father. "Would you like to take my place?"

Elie's eyes shifted from the *siddur* to his father, his expression blank.

"Or hold the *siddur*?" Shammai added.

Without a word, Elie stepped into Shammai's place.

Suddenly not knowing where to be, Shammai, looked around, deciding to stand next to and slightly behind Rabbi Blumenthal, following the casket. This is where the mourners stand, he thought, feeling someone should be there. And who better than him?

Rabbi Blumenthal led them inside, slowly, and motioned for them to stop under the alcove. The crowd assembled around the walls, those forced outside occasionally glancing skyward. The clouds continued their march.

"There are many customs for observing the anniversary of a *tzaddik's* death," Rabbi Blumenthal began. "For instance, on Lag B'Omer, when Rabbi Shimon bar Yochai passed away, in Israel they light bonfires and some give their three-year old sons their first haircut, introducing them to the world of mitzvot. A *tzaddik's yahrtzeit* marks the completion of his life's work. On that day, it is said, we see the full effect of his spiritual efforts and it is a propitious time to recall his accomplishments and invoke his aid from Above."

Rabbi Blumenthal paused to survey the crowd. "When preparing a few words to say, I was struck by the appropriateness of the comparison. Mr. Enstein devoted his time while in our community to the work of a *tzaddik*. He studied, he taught, he involved himself in the problems of groups and individuals. No organization ever held a testimonial dinner for him. He didn't sit on any boards or committees. But he was known throughout the city, in all the synagogues, at the JCC, wherever we Jews gathered, we always looked to see if Mr. Enstein was there.

"He had no relatives, at least none I'm aware of. He didn't talk of his past, of the difficulties - and horrors - that he experienced prior to moving here. He didn't talk much. He didn't have to. His presence was testimony enough, proof that a life lived through Torah justified itself."

There was a rumble overhead. Shammai looked up, but the roof blocked his view. Outside, umbrellas rustled.

Rabbi Blumenthal continued. "Mr. Enstein had a reputation for bluntness, for a sharp tongue, for the impatience we too often assume accompanies old age, but may just be the byproduct of our own indifference to our elders. Still, it seemed like he was everywhere in the community. And the respect he had he rightfully earned. One incident puts Mr. Enstein in perspective, for me. That incident reminded me of a story associated with Rabbi Levi Yitzchok of Berditchev, a story about the generous miser."

Shammai saw Levinsky walk up, quietly, almost surreptitiously so as not to drawn attention to his lateness.

"Perhaps you've heard the story," Rabbi Blumenthal continued, "of the rich man who, when he passed away, was castigated by the townsfolk until Rabbi Levi Yitzchok revealed how this man who never gave to charity openly, secretly supported the needy and indeed, gave --," he paused, apparently confused.

Shammai took the opportunity to glance at his family. His wife and daughter shared the expectant look of the crowd, but Elie - he seemed to be finishing his own eulogy.

"Well, for instance," Rabbi Blumenthal continued, "once a merchant left his family to seek his fortune, telling his wife to collect a salary for the journey from this rich man. When the wife, not knowing her husband had made up the story so she would acquiesce in his departure, came for the salary, the rich man's secretary, who had never seen her, began to chase her out. The rich man, hearing the commotion, came out and promptly instructed his secretary to pay her weekly. When the merchant returned, his fortune made, the rich man refused repayment for his mitzvah."

Rabbi Blumenthal paused again, but this time as preparation for his conclusion. "A generous miser. So I thought of Mr. Enstein. And the incident I witnessed? Simple enough. It happened about four years ago. I'd only been in town six months and was still getting to know my congregation, so I hadn't had much of a chance to familiarize myself with others in the city, though I'd heard about Mr. Enstein. Cantankerous Mr. Enstein, was how he'd been described to me. My first impression seemed to confirm all that I'd heard."

Levinsky inched closer, until he was next to Shammai.

"Once, a prominent member of the community - a member of our *shul* - had yahrzeit. Because of the time of year and other circumstances, we'd had difficulty getting a minyan for a few days. This person was not the type, despite his wealth and importance, to draw attention to himself, and it was questionable if there'd be a minyan all three times.

"But at *maariv, shacharis* the next morning and *mincha* we unexpectedly had nine visitors, at least one from each shul, different men each time, each with a different reason for being there. This individual was able to say *kaddish*. I found out later that they had all been sent by Mr. Enstein, that he had known this individual had to say *kaddish* and we were a few short that week.

"And why didn't Mr. Enstein himself come? Because he and this individual were not on speaking terms." Rabbi Blumenthal drew a deep breath. "A generous miser."

"That was me," Levinsky whispered to Shammai. His voice seemed mixed with anger and sadness. "That was me."

"Now," Rabbi Blumenthal concluded, "Mr. Enstein has no resaon to be a miser, to hide his generosity. And neither do we. May we all, then, be only generous, with each other, and with his memory." Rabbi Blumenthal looked around the crowd. "Mr. Enstein had no relatives, but if anyone would like to say something, I invite them to do so."

"He didn't get him right," Levinsky whispered. "Someone should get him right."

Shammai glanced at Levinsky, expecting him to step forward. Levinsky looked up and shook his head.

Rabbi Blumenthal motioned to the pall bearers and they picked up the casket. The procession to the grave began, Rabbi Blumenthal reciting Psalm ninety-one and stopping the traditional seven times. Shammai clutched the *siddur* tighter as they approached the grave. He kept thinking about Levinsky's words.

At the grave, the non-Jewish cemetery workers removed the tarpaulin and the pallbearers lowered the casket. Shammai's attention shifted from the casket to Elie. He shouldn't have asked his son to take his place.

He glanced back and saw Dinah Chaya wiping her eyes, occasionally with a sob. Everyone else, as far as he could see, remained dry-eyed.

The pallbearers stepped back. Shammai looked around, saw Jonathan Kashdan leaning against the fence. If Kashdan weren't a kohen, he would have said something. He always had something to say about Mr. Enstein.

Rabbi Blumenthal opened his book. Impulsively, Shammai stepped forward. He had been given the *siddur*. It was his responsibility, if it was anyone's.

"Can I still say something?" he asked.

Rabbi Blumenthal looked at him, then nodded.

Suddenly, all eyes shifted to Shammai and he fought for the words which had seemed so appropriate a moment ago.

"I knew Mr. Enstein for fourteen years," he began, then stopped, lost. Hannah caught his eye and gave him a quick smile and nod. It was enough. "I knew Mr. Enstein for fourteen years," he started again. "It was my privilege - though sometimes I thought I was doing him the favor - to walk him to *shul* in his later years, to have my wife prepare *challah* for him. He was the most difficult man I ever met. I often wondered why I bothered."

He glanced at Dinah Chaya and Elie, then continued. "I bothered because I learned from every encounter, every obstacle he placed in my path to openly liking him. Mr. Enstein was a teacher. He was also a lover of books. And what he taught was the life and truth that was in the sacred texts he cherished.

"He taught my children. His refusal to openly express

gratitude - I know now, maybe I always knew, he felt it taught us the truth that the kindness we do is a favor to ourselves. G-d has many agents. If we don't take the opportunity to be one, G-d will find another. But we will have lost.

"His name was Mordechai, and I'm reminded of the story of Purim. There, G-dliness was hidden, and Mr. Enstein hid himself, but that revealed, as no other way could, the true source of his kindness and the true assistance received.

"Rabbi Blumenthal said he had no known relatives. But Mr. Enstein was a grandfather to my children."

He stepped back, feeling he should have said something else, that he still hadn't gotten Mr. Enstein right. Maybe nobody could.

Rabbi Blumenthal recited the Tzidduk HaDin, the justification of the Divine decree. When he finished, he said, "We are taught that we can do no greater kindness to another than to give one a proper Jewish burial. I ask the pallbearers to be the first to bury Mr. Enstein."

One by one, Josh, Mishael, Lazar and Bob Sagalman took the shovel, thrust it into the pile of dirt, lifted and emptied it backhanded into the grave. The earth thudded against the casket.

Bob Sagalman handed the shovel to Elie. Once, twice, three times Elie filled the shovel and emptied it over Mr. Enstein's casket. He held it out for his father.

Reluctantly, Shammai handed the *siddur* to his son. He added his shovelful, passed the shovel on and turned. Elie hadn't moved. He let Elie stand there, holding the *siddur*.

When everyone had passed by, the grave was half-full. The cemetery workers started to pick up the shovels, but Mishael stopped them. He, Lazar and Josh Green continued to fill in the grave. After a while, Bob Sagalman, then, briefly, Elie and Levinsky relieved them. Soon the casket was completely covered.

"It is time now to recite the mourner's *kaddish*," Rabbi

Blumenthal said. He looked at Shammai, who stepped forward.

Elie handed him the *siddur* and Shammai opened it, slowly reading the mourner's *kaddish*. He recited it mechanically, surprised at his own numbness. He searched for a feeling of regret or grief, but found within himself only a sadness at the finality of the silence the words proclaimed.

He knew then that, while he would recite *kaddish* for Mr. Enstein on his *yahrtzeit*, he would not be a mourner reciting it for a year.

When he finished, everyone filed out of the cemetery, slowly, some stopping to toss a handful of grass over their shoulders, wash their hands at the gate, or deposit something in the *tzedakah* box by the entrance.

While washing his hands, Shammai glanced back. The cemetery workers nonchalantly evened off the mound.

The crowd broke into groups as it dispersed. Over by his car, Mishael talked to his son Malachi and Benji Sagalman. Elie soon joined them. Josh Green and Lazar, with Jonathan Kashdan approaching, waited for Shammai. Clutching the *siddur*, he walked into their gaze.

Levinsky walked by him quickly. Catching Shammai's eye, he shook his head.

"There's the matter of *kaddish*," Jonathan Kashdan said, reaching them the same moment as Shammai.

"Can we rotate it among the members?" Josh asked.

"Let's ask Rabbi Blumenthal before he runs off," Lazar said.

"No need." They all looked at Shammai, expecting him to take the responsibility. "I'm calling a yeshiva this afternoon. If you want to help pay for someone to say it, I'll accept any donations."

"You're not going to do it?" Kashdan asked, pointedly looking at the *siddur*.

Shammai shook his head. "I'm not related, I'm not a rabbi,

and I don't think any of us can do it for a year without resenting Mr. Enstein. That's not a proper tribute."

"Tribute or legacy," Lazar said, "he's left something to be considered."

"What do you mean?" Shammai asked.

"I'm executor of a will I haven't seen. And I don't think any of us intends to pretend he didn't exist. Even if he's disposed of his property in such a way that it doesn't affect the shul, or some of us in it, which I doubt, it'll be a while before we do anything without looking over our shoulders." He looked at each of them as he talked, but most intensely at Shammai and Jonathan Kashdan.

"Where's Bob Sagalman?" Kashdan asked.

"Probably running back to his office," Josh said. "By the way, Shammai what was the point of having Elie take your place?"

"Come on, Josh, we know why," Kashdan said.

"I doubt it," Shammai replied. "But Elie had more right than any of us."

"I hope he thinks so," Lazar said, looking off. "But it's an inheritance or a lesson from Mr. Enstein. We trust young people less the older we grow."

"You sure you didn't take philosophy lessons from him on the side?" Josh said.

"No, but those of you with familial obligations have people waiting. And I have a legal obligation at least as onerous," Lazar said.

"Well, the *shul* will survive," Kashdan said, "and we have time to see what Mr. Enstein left. us. If anything."

Shammai said goodbye to them and left. Halfway to his car, Lazar caught up to him.

"I think your daughter was the only one to cry," Lazar said casually. "I wonder what that means."

"Maybe that we also grow less sensitive the older we grow."

"Or maybe more sensitive," Lazar responded. "But I'm not convinced he didn't leave some problems behind. Don't be so sure that book is yours."

Shammai shrugged. "If not, I haven't lost anything."

"Maybe." Lazar stopped, putting a hand on Shammai's arm. "Listen, I don't know if I'm going to have the courage to tell you this later. Being a bachelor has the advantage of letting me pretend to some objectivity. Elie's going to have a lot to sort out. Don't let him do it alone."

"I don't intend to," Shammai said, annoyed. He pulled his arm away.

"That's not what I mean. You think there's a void in Elie's life now, and you're going to spend a lot of time trying to be what Mr. Enstein was. It won't work and Elie saw through Mr. Enstein, anyway."

"If there was anything to see through, then he was the only one."

"Well, just don't let it come between you."

"Expert advice?" Shammai asked. "Or have you just forgotten what it's like to be a teenager?"

"I haven't forgotten what it's like to have children."

Shammai stopped, startled. Lazar never referred to his failed marriage to a non-Jew, or the child he no longer saw.

"Come for Shabbos," was all Shammai could say as they reached his family.

Dinah Chaya was still wiping away tears.

"Are you all right?" Shammai asked.

She nodded. "It's just that I saw him die. I wish I had some other last memory. I'd rather almost anything other than to see him so helpless. It scares me and, like, makes me angry at him."

"But you were able to do him a kindness no one else could," Hannah said. "Be grateful to him for that." Thank you, Hannah, he thought. She could always find solutions when he couldn't. He knew that his gratitude would be insufficient for her strength, his confidence in her inadequate to suppress his amazement at her understanding. But he wasn't surprised, because it had always been like that between them.

Elie joined them. "Thanks."

Thank you, Shammai thought, for taking my request as a "gift," as intended.

They got into the car.

"I feel like we should do something else," Dinah Chaya said.

"There's no one sitting *shiva*," Elie said, mostly to himself.

"Don't worry," Hannah added, "Your father and the other men will make sure something's done."

He followed the line of cars back onto the highway.

"I wonder what it's like to be old," Elie said to himself.

Maybe Mr. Enstein wondered what it was like to be young, Shammai thought. I do.

They didn't say anything on the drive home. Shammai left the radio off, sensing the silence drawing his family closer. For a moment, perhaps his children realized how precious they were to their parents, just as he, and he knew Hannah, felt especially protective of them right now. Confronting mortality did that, but Shammai considered there was more to it. They had buried an outsider, a guest, in a way even an intruder, into their family. And yet, Mr. Enstein had been more than that. So much more.

He pulled up in front of the house, and as he stopped the car, for the first time felt he'd lost something that afternoon, something more precious than Mr. Enstein.

They walked to the house, together, closer than usual.

"I liked what you said, Daddy," Dinah Chaya said.

"Thanks."

"It was better and shorter than Rabbi Blumenthal's eulogy,"

Hannah added.

"I'm not a rabbi."

"Yeah, I think you got Mr. Enstein right," Elie said, surprising him.. "Only," he paused.

"Only what?"

"Only, you know, he wasn't our grandfather."

Chapter 7

Shammai drank his coffee and read the paper, feeling more relieved than he had in a week. *Shiva* would have ended this morning, had there been any relatives. He could have arranged minyanim, but, having sent the check to the yeshiva the day of the funeral, he'd accepted that the practice of hiring someone to say *kaddish* would have to suffice. He could not have committed himself to saying *kaddish* three times a day for a year. He'd had a thousand arguments with himself, with periodic surges of guilt followed by hours of justification, self-explanation, reconciliation and acquiescence. It had been a hard week.

Hannah slept unusually late this morning. Even though he got the children ready on days he didn't drive carpool, she almost always got up, if only to spend a few minutes with Dinah Chaya and then join him for coffee.

In fact, he thought, putting down his coffee, she'd been rather withdrawn the last few days, ever since Shabbat. She said she felt all right, but he suspected she'd come down with something. She didn't show her usual excitement about her job or interest in his work.

He'd always appreciated that, though she never touched computers, she wanted to know about his projects. Talking to her about them rarely clarified any problems, but did give him a sense of progress. The last two days of private breakfasts impressed on him how much he missed the perspective she helped him achieve.

Well, if she wasn't feeling better by this afternoon, he'd suggest she call the doctor. Maybe he'd ask Bob Sagalman to join him for lunch at the deli and ask him if something was going around.

Thinking of Sagalman brought his thoughts to the shul. Shabbos had been subdued, which was to be expected. Mishael had taken Mr. Enstein's place as *gabbai*, without discussion or protest. It seemed strange not to have Mr. Enstein, with his tart comments, interruptions and practiced grumpiness. Maybe they all realized how much that contributed to the camaraderie of the shul.

He got up and stretched. Time to get to work. Lazar hadn't mentioned anything about the will on Shabbat, so he assumed everything was taken care of. Still, it would be nice to hear something, have his ownership confirmed.

He strolled over to the bookcase. He had cleared the top shelf - it had taken some rearranging Sunday afternoon - and put up two soft-sided bookstops to hold the *siddur* firmly in place in the center. He'd have to get a special case, he decided, maybe from one of the antique dealers.

What was on his schedule? He had a meeting with that engineering firm (the one that had finally responded to his fourth letter of inquiry last week), that membership list really needed to be loaded into the new database, and, with a little extra work, he could finish the billing program for the old age home. He should also have time to return Levinsky's call, reminding himself that Levinsky had called twice, personally, while he was out.

In the car, he flicked on the radio. Something post-Stravinsky, which he didn't like, but he didn't want to make the twenty-minute drive in silence. So he endured it, hoping it would end soon. Unfortunately, it continued until he got off the interstate, and then the announcer, with the usual ineffectiveness of a classical deejay, made small talk. He turned it off before he got to the office, not wanting to get annoyed if he liked the next piece and couldn't listen to it.

Inside, he switched on the computer, started the coffee, got his papers from his briefcase, and went through the rest of his routine for starting the day. He liked his work; he had plenty of time to himself, but met a lot of people as well.

He called up the mail program and saw that the half-dozen

electronic mail messages could wait. He started his answering machine; only one message, and he'd already returned that call late yesterday. He decided to prepare a preliminary report for the engineering firm. It could be a big contract, and they could provide some good referrals.

He'd been at it for half an hour when the phone rang.

"Hello."

"How'd you like to be impressed? I haven't had anyone in here all week sophisticated enough to admire my carpeting or wall of certificates and diplomas," Lazar said.

"Only if you'll be impressed by the management information system I'm designing."

"Since I don't even understand that, I'm impressed already. When can you come over?"

Shammai switched the phone to speaker and went to the coffee machine. "What's up?"

"Are you alone? Recording a conversation with your lawyer isn't allowed. It's supposed to be the other way."

"Come on, Lazar, I'm busy."

"I've got the will, it's been recorded at the court and it's official."

He put down the pot, his cup only half full. "I thought you had it already."

"Yes and no. It was handwritten and I had to have it transcribed at the bank, with me double-checking. It took all the time I could spare Monday and Tuesday. I do have to do some dishonest work to get paid."

"So? Is it mine?"

A pause. "Come read it for yourself and tell me."

Shammai went over to his desk. "That sounds like bad news."

"A lawyer doesn't get paid if he brings bad news. But in this case, I'm not getting paid, not by you or Mr. Enstein. Anyway, you need to read it. It's not urgent."

"But I'm anxious. I'll be right over."

Lazar's office was in mid-city, close to the courts downtown.

When Shammai walked in, the secretary smiled up pleasantly. Lazar had two partners. One of them walked out and nodded at Shammai.

"I'll buzz him," the secretary said.

Shammai had just sat down and picked up a magazine, when the secretary told him he could go in.

The building was a converted four bedroom house, with the offices arranged along a narrow hall, one room serving as a conference/library. Lazar's was the last one on the left, the smallest, but with the best view of the busy street. Shammai walked in without knocking and shook off the chill from the open window.

Lazar, on the phone, waved him into one of the standard plush burgundy chairs. Shammai sat, waiting.

"OK," Lazar said, "but I still want a disposition. ... Yes, we've got a deal, but I'll need something to show my client. ... Of course it's more than money, Tom. It always is. ... Right, stay out of court yourself."

He hung up the receiver as if he'd been holding something fetid.

"Now that's a true shyster," he said grudgingly. "Actually, my client couldn't care less about anything but getting some money, but I have to keep Tom honest. Or dishonest. Anyway, his client's been kicking and screaming about his liability and I want some justice. Besides my fee."

"Where's the will?" Shammai asked.

"What, no hello? No, how's that Supreme Court case coming?" Lazar said as he opened a desk drawer.

"You don't have a Supreme Court case," Shammai said drily.

"But you're not supposed to know that." Lazar put a large brown folder on his desk, opened it, pulled out a sheet of paper, and pushed it across the desk toward Shammai. "Want some coffee?"

"No," Shammai said. "My nerves are dancing on themselves as is."

"Well, take your time. I've got some research to do and my next client's not due for half an hour. You should be done by then. If not, I'll kick you out to the conference room. I'll be in and out, but don't pay attention to me. Not that I have to tell you that."

Shammai reached over and picked up the papers. Typed single-spaced with a wide margin, the text of the will crowded the header and the signatures at the bottom.

"Isn't this kind of long for a will?"

Lazar was already at the door. "Depends. It's not a novel, but then most novels about wills don't have a happy ending."

"A lawyer who reads? No wonder they want to disbar you."

"Don't get any ideas about blackmail. That's a lawyer's job. Enjoy."

He shut the door and Shammai settled back. The first thing he noticed was the date. Fourteen years ago.

"For one such as I to write a will assumes that I have something of value to leave to my heirs. But I have no wife or children or grandchildren, and have as much interest in other relatives as they have in me. Over the course of a lifetime such as mine, it would be odd if I had been unable to acquire something of worth, but for those things in my possession I can claim to be no more than a caretaker.

"I can claim no special distinction in my life, other than to have survived the tests G-d presented me with my faith intact. No one will write my history and I do not know how those who chose to let me influence them will remember me.

"I have accumulated no monies, save enough to bury me and care for ordinary medical expenses. The executor of this testament will see, however, that I have a large and perhaps valuable collection of books. I learned firsthand the truth that 'when a new holy text is obtained, it enhances all the holy texts which one had previously.' Seforim are associated with the wisdom of holiness. I claim neither, only a close association with both, an association which I preserved through the terrors. My life has been spent in amplification of small points.

"I read once that books must be 'more than a library,' that 'they must be redeemed from their state of captivity' in which I, too, have held them, though not for selfish reasons, for I know somewhat of captivity. May whoever inherits me do better. May he remember that books have souls."

When he finished reading, Shammai sat for a few minutes, trying to figure out what Mr. Enstein meant. He'd heard about ethical wills, but this seemed more like a puzzle.

Lazar came in, quietly, for some papers, but seeing Shammai had finished, sat down.

"Well?"

Shammai smiled weakly. "Enigmatic, of course. What does it mean?"

"You're asking if you get to keep the *siddur*?"

Shammai nodded.

Lazar stretched out a hand for the will. "Well, on occasion I've had more specific documents to work with." He shrugged his shoulder and tossed the will on his desk. "I'd say it's yours. In fact, if you want, I can make a case that all of them belong to you."

"I don't know how you can do that," Shammai said.

"Oh, that's easy enough," Lazar said with a wave of his hand. "The will's vague and no one else has a claim. Why not? I could argue that the gift of one was the gift of all."

Shammai thought for a minute. "You think any one will dispute it?" he asked, not really wanting the responsibility of all the books.

"Not the document. And who's going to have a better claim on them?" Lazar leaned forward. "The *siddur*, at least, is yours. Congratulations. Or condolences."

Shammai laughed and shook his head. He felt embarrassed, yet happy.

"I guess that vindicates a lot, doesn't it?" Lazar asked.

"That's not it," Shammai said, still smiling. "Contrary to popular belief, I did not expect to be mentioned in Mr. Enstein's will. And I was right."

Lazar smiled back. "Oh, I believe you. I don't think Kashdan or even Josh will, but that doesn't matter. But he did, in effect, mention you in his will."

Shammai leaned forward to glance at the document. "Why do you think he didn't make any changes in fourteen years?"

Lazar shrugged. "Why should he? Especially considering how vague that was."

Shammai frowned, his joy fading. "When you told me the *siddur* was mine, I felt ecstatic. Not because I got 'paid' for the mitzvah - I always felt that there was a, well, spiritual reason for having to put up with his - obstinateness, I guess I'd call it.

"No, I was happy because I thought it proved my instincts right - that Mr. Enstein was worth the trouble."

"The fact that the book is close to priceless didn't affect you, though."

"Only in the sense that I will now have to give it worthy companions."

Lazar leaned back and swiveled in his chair. "Come on, Shammai, don't start playing games with me now. You could have bought books any time you wanted. But you'd rather have a few books you can read than a lot you can't. A big personal library is an embarrassing reminder of how much time we waste."

Shammai shrugged. "Maybe. But I don't think Mr. Enstein would have given me the centerpiece of his life without thinking about it."

"He was hardly in a condition to do much thinking."

"Exactly. So why not write a codicil? Why take the chance he might die in his sleep and have his wishes remain unknown?"

Lazar looked at his watch. "I've got an appointment in five minutes. How about a drink?"

Shammai shook his head, then changed his mind. "A miniscule one."

"In the conference room," Lazar said, standing. "So don't you want it?"

"Of course I want it, though how I'm going to find a way to keep it at home without having my own heart attack from worry, I don't know. It's just that it wasn't like Mr. Enstein to do something like that. If he had enough control to say something and give it to Dinah Chaya, he could have said anything - or nothing."

"Maybe the fact that she was there inspired him." Lazar opened the door for them and Shammai stepped out first.

"Maybe. Anyway, I'll never know."

Lazar led him into the conference room and poured the drinks, his into a large cup. "I'll register it this afternoon." He recited the blessing, took a large swallow and grimaced. "Whoa. My stomach feels like it deserves an ulcer." He patted his midsection. "But what are you going to do?"

"That's easy. I'm going back to the office and call my wife. Then I'm going to spend the rest of the day between daydreaming and making phone calls to find a way to keep it safe. I can't see putting it in a safe deposit box. That's the same as sticking it in a museum somewhere. Mr. Enstein knew its value and kept it in the open. He wanted it used. He wanted it to belong to a family." Shammai swirled the liquor around in the cup.

"What?" Lazar said.

"I'm thinking of something Elie said, about books with souls. There's a connection from soul to soul. Jewish books have Jewish souls and we can't abandon them. Isn't that what learning Torah's all about?"

"Finish your drink," Lazar said, "you're getting philosophical and I've got clients. Both are bad signs."

Shammai made the blessing and drank. His cheeks flushed immediately. "I see why your courtside manner is so casual."

"Casually effective," Lazar corrected. He looked at his watch again. "I'm getting some money from this case, if I can convince the client to follow my advice. But, well, congratulations again," Lazar said, sticking out his hand. Shammai took it.

"I'm on my way out. Thanks."

"I certainly hope so. If you need an attorney, let me know and I'll try to find you a good one."

"Why would I need an attorney?"

"So he can make lots of money representing you and I can feel jealous."

"Right. Anyway, thanks for your help."

"You're welcome. I think." Lazar walked Shammai halfway down the hall. "I know you'll keep me informed if it brings you a sudden increase in good fortune." He stopped. "And do me a favor, tell the secretary you're leaving and I'm ready."

Shammai nodded. He suddenly turned. "What happens if I don't want the rest of the books?"

Lazar's eyebrows shot up. "I guess we'd have to search for

other heirs." Lazar smiled, then he thought a moment. "Seriously, I don't know. We'll get the rest donated someplace, I guess. Maybe to a university." Lazar shrugged. "Or you could buy a new house."

Shammai adjusted his glasses. "And I've got something worth fifty thousand to use for the down payment, right?"

"That might work," Lazar laughed. "Anyway, there's time to think about it - and his other property isn't your concern. Now go celebrate, and prepare yourself for some insightful comments from Kashdan and Josh."

Shammai smiled. "Right."

He got in his car and sat for a few minutes, deciding what to do. Should he go back to the office or home? He had a full day of work in front of him and he could just call Hannah. But he wanted to tell her in person. Wait, he thought, today was Wednesday. She worked half a day. He better call first.

He went back inside and asked to use the phone. No answer at home. She'd been sick; she should be home. Maybe she'd gone to the doctor or felt better and had gone into work. Back to the office, then; he'd try again in the afternoon.

Now that he was certain it was his, how it would affect his family? At least Lazar could get the rest of Mr. Enstein's books - and his other things - turned over to a trust or something. Of course, he'd have to do something special for the *siddur*. Buy a new bookcase, with a special glass shelf. A shame he couldn't bring a few of the books home; surely some belonged with the *siddur*. He'd have to live with the comments for a while, but if he ignored Kashdan, he'd stop. Josh would respond to a polite request.

At the office, he called the business where Hannah did bookkeeping on Wednesdays, feeling a little guilty he hadn't thought about calling there earlier, when he was in Lazar's office.

She was there, and the secretary got her on the phone.

"How are you feeling?" he asked.

"Fine. My stomach's a little queasy, but I'm eating Tums." Her tone asked why he called.

"I just got back from Lazar's. I saw the will."

"And?"

She should have been enthusiastic, even if she was sick. "It's mine. I'll come home early and tell you about it. I think we can make sure Mr. Enstein has a fitting legacy, one that'll even satisfy Elie."

"As long as it satisfies you. Ooh."

"What?"

"My stomach."

"I guess you're not up to going to the Deli for dinner, then?"

"I wouldn't think of spoiling the celebration. I can not eat there as well as home, and this way I won't have to worry about cooking or cleaning up."

"OK. When will you be home?"

"About three."

"I'll be there."

He hung up, feeling very satisfied.

\#

He didn't get back until after four. Hannah was lying on the couch.

"Don't tell me I look as bad as I feel," she said.

"On the contrary, pale becomes you."

"Ouch. Don't make me laugh."

"That bad?"

She shook her head. "Not really. I called the doctor. He said there's a forty-eight hour bug going around. As long as I limit myself to chicken soup and tums and avoid roller coasters, I'm fine."

He laughed. "You must be very frustrated, not knowing if your stomach knots are from the office or the virus."

"Ouch. Is this how your computers feel when they get a virus?"

He threw up his hands. "Enough. I like it better when you're well."

"You just don't appreciate my humor." She closed her eyes and pressed her stomach. "Another wave passed. It's like being seasick. So, what did the will say? What did Lazar tell you?"

He sat down in the rocking chair. "Basically, the will didn't say much, so it's mine. Like a dying bequest. Lazar said he could make a case that I should get all the books, but I don't think I want to fight the state and go to court and all that. But," he shrugged, "who knows?"

She looked around the room. "But where would we put all those books?"

"Well, maybe they could stay in Mr. Enstein's house." At her puzzled look, he continued. "You know, turn the place into an Enstein memorial library."

"That's a nice idea, but unless you're planning on retiring and becoming curator, I think you better just let Lazar work out what goes where and be satisfied you got anything."

He sat silently rocking. He reached out to turn on the stereo, but remembered the university station had a national news program on, so he left it off.

"That *siddur's* worth a lot of money. Is it safe to keep it here?" she asked quietly.

"At least as safe as in Mr. Enstein's house. I can't sell it."

"I don't expect you to. I just hope everything goes as smoothly as you plan."

"Lazar doesn't see any problems."

"Lazar's not perfect."

A car honked.

"The children are home," he said.

She sat up and immediately put a hand to her head.

"Lie down," he said, standing. "I'll take care of them."

"It's all right. I want to sit up."

The door opened and the children burst in, talking.

"Quiet," Shammai commanded. "Your mother's sick."

They didn't stop talking, but lowered their voices. Aaron and Moshe rushed over to Hannah, interrupting each other.

"Go put your things away," Shammai said. "We're going to the Deli for dinner."

"I'll stay home with Mom," Dinah Chaya said.

"I'm coming, too."

"But you're sick."

"Missing a night out with my family will make me sicker. Let's get ready. You all have homework."

Elie paused by the bookcase, staring.

Shammai went over and put a hand on his shoulder. "It looks kind of lonely."

"It should." He gave his father a quick smile and went to his room.

Shammai looked at Hannah. She shrugged.

A few minutes later, they had all gathered by the door.

"I know why we're going," Dinah Chaya said.

"Then don't say anything," Hannah said.

They got into the car. On the way, Shammai asked about their day at school. At first, he got only short answers, but when Aaron mentioned what Yaakov had done, they all started talking about the teachers and other children.

Shammai let them talk.

At the Deli, they took over a table, saying hello to the people they knew. Nahum came over to take their orders.

"Hamburgers and french fries," Shammai said. "And a bowl of chicken soup."

"Right."

Josh Green walked in with his family. They waved to each other. After Josh had seated his family, he came over.

"So, a *mazel tov* is in order, I guess," Josh said. Shammai pretended not to understand. "I called Lazar and he told me."

"Told you what?" Elie asked.

Josh suddenly looked embarrassed. "*shul* business. Enjoy your dinner," he said, hastily walking away.

Elie and Dinah Chaya looked at Shammai.

"I was going to wait until dinner was here, but," he shrugged. "I saw Mr. Enstein's will. The *siddur's* mine. His library, in the absence of heirs, will probably get donated to a university library. Of course, there'll be a memorial plaque inside each volume."

"I knew it," Dinah Chaya said. "All the girls were talking about it this week."

"Are we going to have to catalog them first? I'm not a librarian," Elie said.

Shammai was surprised. "Mr. Enstein taught you a lot from those books, and I'm sure he'd want you to continue to learn from them as long as you can."

"I can't, without a teacher."

"I don't think I can go back in there, into that house," Dinah Chaya said, playing with a napkin.

Nahum brought their food.

"Everyone wash," Shammai said sullenly. He'd expected a better response.

Elie waited until his siblings had gone to the sink. "Dad," he said quietly, "have you ever thought what that *siddur* means?"

"I know what it meant to Mr. Enstein."

"Is that what it will mean to us?"

Something in his voice warned Shammai the ground was thin. "Elie, what's the matter?"

"Nothing. I just wonder how fortunate we are. It didn't make Mr. Enstein very happy to have to get it and then take care of it, I don't think."

He went to wash.

Shammai turned to Hannah.

"What are you thinking?" she asked.

"If books have souls, are they ever ours?"

"You might say the same thing about children." She stood up, looking pale. "The smell of the food is making me nauseous. I shouldn't have come."

She practically ran to the bathroom.

And that, Shammai thought, may be Mr. Enstein's legacy.

Chapter 8

"Hannah? Anyone here?" Shammai called through the doorway. They couldn't all be sleeping this late, even on a Sunday morning. He shrugged, took a deep breath and hefted the long narrow box, almost losing his footing as he tried to balance it.

It's bulkier rather than heavy, he told himself as he dragged it inside. He held up the front end, afraid of scratching the floor, and tried to pull the rest in after him. The bottom of the box caught on some bump in the door's weatherstripping. He took another deep breath, yanked, and suddenly lost his balance and grip as the box flew free.

He whirled his arms and dance-hopped on one leg; his other foot and the box found the floor at the same time. As he brought his various internal alarms to rest, his family appeared, curious and concerned.

He looked at his wife, daughter and two youngest sons with a mixture of embarrassment, exhaustion and annoyance.

"Are you all right?" Hannah asked.

"Of course I'm all right," he answered, now only annoyed.

"What is it?" Dinah Chaya asked.

"What does it look like?"

She stared at it.

"It doesn't bite," he said by way of encouragement.

"A portable sukkah?" she asked hopefully, looking to her mother for support.

"It's not even Pesach!" Shammai said. "Be serious. Aaron? Moshe? Where's Elie?"

"He's at Mr. Enstein's," Hannah said quietly.

Shammai looked at the box on the floor. He knew I was coming home with this, he thought. I even asked him to come with me. He said he was too tired.

"What's he doing there?" Shammai said sharply. "And how'd he get in?"

"Getting an early start on the week's Torah reading, I think," Dinah Chaya said. As Hannah turned to stare at her too, her gaze shifted from one parent to the other like a trapped animal.. "And we do have a key, right? I mean it's not like he's trespassing or something."

"It may very well be he is trespassing."

"He should have told me he was going," Hannah said quietly.

"He told me," Dinah Chaya said instantly. "You should be happy he's talking to me again."

"What I'd like to know," Shammai said, "is why he can't study at home."

"Why don't you ask him?" Dinah Chaya shouted and ran to her room.

"A most pleasant start," Shammai muttered, kicking the box just hard enough to hurt himself. If the fall hadn't broken something, his kick probably did.

Aaron and Moshe ran up to him and started climbing over the box.

"What is it?"

"Can we keep the box?"

"Can I open it?"

"No, let me."

"It's heavy."

"Is it for our room?"

Shammai's hands shot out, each grabbing a shoulder. Eyes shut, he said, "It is a bookcase for the living room, which you cannot open. If you remain quietly in your rooms the rest of the morning, you may play with the box outside." He released them. "Now, go," he added, opening his eyes.

"Can we watch you put it together?" Aaron asked, subdued.

"I'll help," Moshe offered. "I can hold the tools for you."

He took a deep breath. "I'll think about it. Right now, go back to your room."

He waited until their footsteps faded, then sat down and started tearing at the box. It felt like opening a present.

"Do you want me to leave, too?"

He turned around, startled to hear Hannah's voice. "What? No, of course not. I just asked the boys to leave because they'd gotten out of hand."

Hannah folded her arms. He stopped in mid-motion, a strip of cardboard in his hand, ready for an argument about the children.

But she sighed, shook her head and gave him a half-smile. Apparently she'd decided the empty room was argument enough.

"Where are you going to put it?" she asked.

"In the middle."

"There's no room."

"Yes, there is. I measured it this morning."

"You got up early for a Sunday."

"I wanted to pick it up before the unveiling. I knew we'd be tied up all afternoon and I didn't want to wait another week."

He expected her to ask why, but she just looked around, rearranging the furniture in her mind to accomodate the newest addition. "Can we afford it?" she asked.

As an answer, he pulled at the cardboard, which yielded with a satisfying rip. He worked it until he'd peeled it off the the box lengthwise, remembering too late he'd promised the boys they could play with it. Well, it was too narrow for a tent, anyway.

"What do you think?" he asked, looking up at Hannah. "It's solid wood."

"I'll let you know when I see it up."

"I like the shade. But it's darker than the others," Dinah

Chaya said.

Shammai turned, startled by her unexpected return.

"Is it hard to put together?" she asked.

He shrugged. "We'll see."

"Isn't it kind of big for just one book?"

"That depends on the book, doesn't it?" He ripped another section of cardboard. "But there may be others to join it."

He finished working the cardboard apart, exposing the pieces of the bookcase.

"It looks complicated," Dinah Chaya said.

"It looks heavy," Hannah said. "Maybe you should wait until Elie gets home."

"Won't have time," Shammai said, detaching a little bag of screws taped to the top board. Inside were the instructions.

He started reading them. It seemed easy enough. Three sides, four shelves, the double-glass door for the top shelf and the optional sliding doors for the bottom, twenty-eight screws and an allen wrench.

Obviously the first thing to do was count all the pieces. He leaned forward and felt a slight pressure on each shoulder. Aaron and Moshe had snuck back in and were trying to see what he was doing. He grunted to himself and held the bag out to Aaron.

"But don't open it," he cautioned.

Aaron held it like a treasure and wouldn't let Moshe near it. That almost caused a fight until Hannah assured Moshe he'd have something important to do in a minute, too, with a wouldn't-he glance at Shammai.

"Well, he can count the pieces as I take them out of the box," Shammai offered.

That seemed to satisfy Moshe. So, as Shammai took out each piece and laid it on the floor, Moshe counted.

"Eleven," Moshe announced triumphantly.

"All there," Shammai said. "And surprisingly the glass didn't break." He put the two glass doors aside, still bubble-wrapped. "Now we have to count the screws."

He held out his hand for the bag. Aaron, realizing what was going to happen, started to cry and wouldn't let go.

"Oh, for -- now do you see why I sent them to their room?" he asked Hannah, frustrated, not knowing what to do.

Hannah leaned over and said, "Daddy and Moshe have to count them, but when they're done counting, everything goes back in the bag for you to hold until Daddy needs it to build the bookcase. OK?"

Aaron nodded reluctantly, then, with eyes shut, held out the bag to Shammai.

"Why don't you watch us count?" Shammai said, taking the bag.

Aaron looked at Moshe, who shrugged, and then settled down on the floor next to Shammai.

Carefully, Shammai emptied the bag on the floor, making a circle around the screws and allen wrench with his free hand.

"Now, put them back in the bag as you count," he told Moshe, holding onto the allen wrench.

The process was painstaking and slow, with Moshe losing count twice and skipping from fourteen to sixteen. But Moshe finished before Shammai's patience began its own countdown.

He separated the three sides, making sure he had the back one flat on the floor. Using the allen wrench, he screwed the left side in place.

"Dinah Chaya, can you hold this straight?"

She unfolded her arms and did as asked. He screwed the right side into the back, thinking it would be easier if Elie was there.

"Hannah, can you hold this side up?"

He got the top on and told them they could let go.

"I want to hold the bag now," Moshe said.

"Why don't you help me with the pieces instead?" Shammai said.

Moshe nodded agreement and helped Shammai carry over the three shelves and bottom piece.

"Almost done," he said as he put the sliding doors on the bottom row.

"Good," Hannah said, "because we have to get ready soon."

"How are you going to pick it up?" Dinah Chaya asked.

"I'll help," Aaron offered.

"Me, too," said Moshe.

"I think I'll wait for Elie," Shammai said, as he carefully took out the glass doors.

When he'd finished, he stood up to admire the bookcase, though it still lay on the floor.

"Are you going to put anything else inside the top row?" Hannah asked, pointing at the glass doors.

"I don't think so."

"I'm hungry," Moshe said.

Hannah looked at her watch. "It's eleven-thirty and the boys haven't eaten."

"Neither have I," Shammai and Dinah Chaya said simultaneously.

"We have to get ready in half an hour," Hannah said. "I'll get breakfast ready. Or lunch. Or both."

"I'll get Elie," Shammai said, picking up the phone.

"No need." Elie stood in the doorway. "What's that for?" he asked, pointing to the bookcase.

Shammai's first impulse was to reprimand his son, but not wanting a fight and needing his son's help, he changed his mind.

"Help me pick it up," Shammai said.

Elie got on one side and the two of them lifted it.

"Don't start moving things around now. It's getting late," Hannah called from the kitchen.

"We don't have enough books for this," Elie said, running his hand over it and frowning.

"Well, it's really just for one book. At least to start with. It should look nice inside the glass, don't you think?"

"It's a shame you can't just leave it at Mr. Enstein's house."

"Why would I do that?" Seeing his son's face, realizing he had misread the statement, Shammai instantly regretted the sharpness of his automatic response.

Elie shrugged, a gesture clearly meant to hide his distress. "You told me it would be nice if the books could stay together and be like a library."

"I didn't mean --" Now it was Shammai's turn to shrug. "Anyway, I said that because Lazar mentioned the collection might have to be broken up if more than one library put in a bid or something. Speaking of which - "

Shammai's discussion of Elie's unauthorized visit was interrupted by Hannah calling them both to eat.

Moshe, Aaron and Dinah Chaya were already sitting around the table, the boys having some cereal with their milk and sugar, Dinah Chaya eating crackers and cheese.

The Sunday paper sprawled around the cereal boxes, milk carton, sugar bowl, cracker box and cheese container, a maze of information surrounding the outposts of modern nutrition. Shammai gathered pieces from reluctant hands and moved the misshapen bundle off the table. In the kitchen, the coffee water boiled.

Hannah came in with two cups of coffee as Dinah Chaya, stuffing a last cheese-laden cracker in her mouth, stood.

"Sit down and finish," Shammai chided.

Dinah Chaya bounced up and down on her toes, her head bobbing and hands waving along in rhythm as she tried to chew faster and explain why she had to get ready now.

"Let her go," Hannah said, "I haven't started cleaning her room for Pesach yet anyway."

Shammai sat down with his coffee and reached for a bowl. "I'm not really hungry," he said, to no one in particular. A box of cereal appeared next to him, moved by an "invisible" hand. "Thanks."

Moshe dropped his spoon and started drinking the rest of his milk. Aaron, on the other hand, began slurping from his spoon. Shammai shut his eyes and poured the cereal.

"It'll spill," Elie said.

Shammai put down the box, opened his eyes and added a little more. As he poured the milk, Dinah Chaya swallowed hard and started to rush out.

"Make an after *brocha*," Shammai said, receiving a dirty look from his daughter and wife.

"Well," he shrugged to Hannah.

"Aaron, Moshe," she said, "go get changed. Now. And," she added, stopping their race after three steps, "take your bowls and spoons with you."

Their exit was slower this time.

"I want to get ready, too," Hannah said. "Will you clean up?"

Shammai, his hand on the Metro section, nodded.

He figured if he read one column, then cleaned up the table, he'd have time enough to get ready without being rushed or having to push the children. He ate in measured spoonfuls.

"Do you think everyone should go?"

Elie's voice surprised him. He forced himself to stop in mid-sentence, put the paper down and look at his son.

"What?"

"Do you think everyone should go?"

"What do you mean?"

118

Elie's expression changed; he looked like he regretted having asked. He shrugged and rustled the sports section in front of him. "You might be late if you have to drop Moshe and Aaron off."

"It's on the way." He looked at the clock.

"Maybe I should stay home with them," Elie said.

The declaration momentarily stunned Shammai. "You're not making any --" He stopped. The bookcase. Well, he wasn't going to let Elie brood about and criticize that for another week. "Your brothers are going. You're going. Each to his appointed place." Shammai spoke firmly, his voice low.

Elie shrugged again and got up. "I'll make sure they're ready."

"Wait. I want to ask you something."

Elie stood indifferently, while Shammai sped through an internal debate.

"Why is it everything I do to honor Mr. Enstein makes you angry?" he said at last.

Elie's lips tightened. After a long pause, he said, "Because I'm not sure."

"Of what?"

Elie remained silent, looking forlorn.

"That it's to honor him?"

"That it does honor him, or that he deserves it."

"Now, look," Shammai said. "I realize I'll never live up to Mr. Enstein's expectations, nor will I ever be able to teach you like he did. And it may be that one day when you do live up to his expectations - and you probably will - you'll be able to tell me how he should have been honored. But until then, I've got to take care of the *siddur* as I see fit and do the best that I can."

To calm himself, Shammai started to gather the cereal box, milk and bowls in his hand.

"I didn't ask for him to be my teacher," Elie said, fists

clenched, voice vehement and cracking. "I didn't ask to become his favorite, to be the only one spared his sarcasm, who could do no wrong. I knew I could never do enough to please him, but that was okay, because I knew you wanted me to learn. His books and me -" Elie looked around for something to do with his hands, but couldn't find anything; he seemed suddenly unable to find his passion, as well. "You still don't get it, Dad," he said quietly. "It's not the *siddur* at all."

Shammai gathered the spoons and coffee cup deliberately, hovering over the table until Elie had escaped.

#

The conversation on the way to the cemetery was subdued, and practically non-existent once Aaron and Moshe had been dropped off. As he drove, Shammai kept one hand on the *siddur*. He and Elie had made a silent peace. Again.

"You need a minyan, don't you?" Dinah Chaya asked.

"We'll have one," Shammai said resolutely, as if his words determined it.

This, he knew, was farewell. How often would someone visit the grave? Shammai wanted his family with him when he said goodbye to Mr. Enstein.

Maybe trying to keep something together wasn't such a good idea. Lazar should find a way to donate the books to a university or a yeshiva, already. He could sell the *siddur*, perhaps using what he got to help the synagogue hire a rabbi. Hannah would support him in any decision and Dinah Chaya wouldn't care.

And Elie - would Shammai ever do anything right in his eyes again?

Two more right turns brought them almost to the entrance of the cemetery. The street came to a dead end fifty yards from the entrance; opposite the cemetery was a cheap apartment complex.

"It's really in a corner, hidden away," Dinah Chaya said, as they stood around the car for a moment. "It's so claustrophobic."

"I've been told that this used to be open field around here," Shammai said.

"I see Lazar, Mr. Green, Mishael and Mordechai," Elie said.

"That's six with us." Shammai looked at his watch. "We've got a few minutes yet." He pointed at the stone-canopied shelter a few feet inside the entrance. "Why don't you and Dinah Chaya go sit down," he said to Hannah.

Hannah nodded and went ahead with Dinah Chaya. Shammai and Elie followed more slowly.

Lazar detached himself from the others and hurried past Hannah. He gave Elie a strange look, then said to Shammai, "I hope you can afford me."

"What?" Shammai stared. "I thought you said that, with a little creativity, the state would accept the claim as a routine case of intent."

"Oh, the state will. Even though it would make money, the hassles and expense of going to court - and they'd lose, anyway."

"Then what are you talking about?"

"Our minyan."

"What about Dr. Sagalman and Benjie?" Elie asked. "Or Mr. Kashdan?"

"Sagalman had an emergency," Lazar said, answering Elie but speaking to Shammai. "If Benjie can get a ride, he'll be here." He shrugged. "As for Kashdan, well, he is a Kohen."

Shammai clutched the *siddur* closer. "That's only six, then."

"Eight," Lazar corrected.

"Who?"

"Come on, we could get charged for conspiracy, standing around like this," Lazar said, too obviously avoiding the question.

As they walked towards the cemetery, Shammai kept wondering why.

"I don't think Mr. Enstein would have liked all this," Lazar said softly. "But then, maybe he planned it."

"Not having a minyan to say *kaddish* at his unveiling?" Shammai asked.

"No, having *this* minyan."

More mystery.

Shammai's confusion cleared up as an immaculate Lincoln Continental pulled up and parked in front of the entrance. Levinsky got out, throwing a smallish cigar in the gutter. Benjie Sagalman came around from the other side.

"Eight," Shammai said. "Maybe Mr. Levinsky has a car phone."

They were close enough to wave. Those under the shelter came forward to greet the newcomers. Lazar, Shammai and Elie walked a little faster.

"Such a family reunion," Lazar muttered, as they all formed a circle and exchanged greetings.

Shammai didn't understand Lazar's cynicism; he for one was glad Levinsky and Benjie showed up, and said so.

"Next time I visit him," Levinsky said, looking around at the graves, "it'll be to join him. And he knows it."

"I tried to get a ride with Josh or Lazar," Benjie explained, "but they'd already left. I stopped by the *shul* and met Mr. Levinsky."

"We've got eight here," Josh said. "I guess we should get them. Lazar?"

Lazar nodded. "Is that an assignment?"

Before Lazar could move, however, two car doors shut. Shammai followed Lazar's gaze. Two men approached, clean-shaven, and from the similarity of their features, pose and walk, clearly related. By the way they struggled with the black silk yarmulkas, it was also clear they weren't very observant.

Shammai knew Lazar well enough to recognize these men were somehow a threat, which put him on his guard.

"Who are they?" he whispered to Lazar.

Lazar took Shammai's elbow and propelled him through the circle. "Let me introduce you," he said, stopping inside the gate to wait for them. "Earl and Simon Osterik, this is Shammai Danielson," he said as the two entered the cemetery.

Cautiously, Shammai took their extended hands, each in its turn. "Glad to meet you." Shammai felt them staring at his other hand, at the *siddur*.

Before anyone could speak, Lazar said "Let's start," loud enough to be heard by all. So saying, he walked briskly, drawing Shammai reluctantly, but almost magnetically, after him.

The small party moved solemnly toward the grave, Shammai and Elie passing Lazar and joining their family, at the moment accompanied by Levinsky.

Josh Green passed out xeroxed pages of the psalms as they went.

They formed almost a full circle around the grave. Elie stood as close as possible, placing himself on Shammai's left, between the *siddur* and everyone else. The protectiveness of the gesture surprised him.

"We'll now recite the Tehilim, the psalms," Josh announced, his voice displaced, like a phantom in the wind. He read slowly, verse by verse, almost unheard, waiting for the murmured response to stop before starting the next.

As Shammai recited the words, he listened to his son. Elie pronounced each word with deliberation; after a few verses, Shammai realized Elie was trying to match him, to join their voices.

He heard Hannah's and Dinah Chaya's voices, as well,

fighting the wind's effort to carry them away.

Suddenly, momentarily, he felt they were a chorus, speaking in song-like harmony, not to memorialize the deceased or elevate a soul, but to unify the family. A singular warmth radiated from that central unity, barring and silencing the wind howling around.

When the psalms were finished, everyone looked expectantly at Josh. He shifted nervously, seemingly unprepared for his role.

"I'm not, uh, that is --" he took a deep breath. "A rabbi usually gives a *hesped*, a euology, now, but--" he shrugged. "If anyone would like to say a few words?"

Shammai anticipated the usual diffidence such a request brings, expecting someone might eventually volunteer or be volunteered. But, surprisingly, Levinsky immediately took a step forward and raised his voice.

"I just want to say one thing. He gave his life over to what he left behind. Everyone should understand that."

"Um, thanks," Josh said, as startled and perplexed as everyone else.

Clearly Levinsky had a specific meaning in mind. Shammai thought he knew what it was.

Josh looked at him. He almost started forward, but stopped and shook his head. He had no more to say.

Josh removed the cloth covering the gravestone. Instinctively, everyone leaned forward to see. It was simple, with only Mr. Enstein's name and the dates of his birth - this a guess - and death.

Mishael started singing the *kel malai rachamim*, the words fluttering around him, the genuineness almost palpable.

"And now it's time to say *kaddish*. Shammai?"

Shammai nodded and opened the *siddur*. He felt eyes on him, but forced himself to see and feel only the words before him. He spoke loudly, clearly, slowly, waiting until the last echo of each "amen" had faded before beginning again.

Finished, he closed the *siddur* and searched for the eyes: Elie - respectful; Hannah - apprehensive; Dinah Chaya - tearful; Levinsky - approving; Lazar - withdrawn.

And then he found two more pair, the strangers, Earl and Simon Osterik-- and he recoiled.

"Thank you for coming," Josh said. "Some have the custom of placing a small rock on the gravestone as a sign that there has been a visitor." So saying, he bent down, searched, and put a pebble on the top.

A line formed. While waiting, Shammai felt himself stared at again.

He let Elie go before him. Silently, the line traveled around the grave and toward the cemetery's entrance.

As they passed through the stone-canopied shelter, everyone put something into the wooden charity box standing there.

The tension evaporated at the cemetery gate.

Shammai turned to Hannah. "I have to ask Lazar something before he leaves," Shammai said quickly, seeing Lazar unlocking his car.

Shammai half-ran, arriving just as Lazar got in.

"Who were they?" he said, too breathless to make it a demand.

"Mr. Enstein's nephews. Great-nephews, really, though I wouldn't call them that."

Shammai stood stunned and speechless.

"You'll hear from them. A lot." Lazar started the engine. "And that's before the trial. If we get one." He closed the door and backed out down the street.

As a reflex, Shammai reassured himself by opening the *siddur*, checking again the names and dates on the inside front cover.

Interlude 3 - 1899

Had I not already seen Vilna, Warsaw and Berlin, I no doubt would have gaped out the carriage, thus proclaiming my amazement and vulnerability, as we clattered through the streets of Paris. As it was, over the three months of my journey, in exchanging the clothes of the peasant, which I had comfortably worn all twenty-two years of my life, for the attire of a gentleman, which had finally stopped scratching my neck, I had also acquired the appearance of sophistication that goes with them. Of course, Paris being my final destination, and being about as far from my native Dubrovno as I wanted to go, I allowed myself to glance - casually - at the visual attractions.

It seemed to me, on first impression, that, aside from fashions in clothing and building design, which surely had no substance or permanence, no significant differences between the great cities - or between them and a smaller village - could be found. I held onto this impression so as not to be overwhelmed by the sheer numbers and mass of what confronted me: if Paris was only more people, more animals, and thus more business and more garbage, I could manage quite well simply by remembering that no matter how much the city limits contained, the amount of people, business or whatever I could personally come in contact with would not, in all probability, ever exceed that to which I had grown accustomed in Dubrovno.

Still, I wondered why the rebbe of my yeshiva not only permitted me to go, but rather insisted I accept this inheritance. I rubbed the packet of letters between thumb and forefinger - a slim lot - just as the carriage wheel hit what elsewhere would have been thought a rather large chasm, but from my experience in the metropolises of Warsaw and Berlin, could be called no more than a small hole. Had it been a real Parisian pothole, the carriage roof would have needed as much repair as my new hat did from the contact. Although I had seen the driver secure my valise rather tightly, and had heard nothing strike the cobbled street (though it might have disappeared into the small hole for all that), I still risked a nervous glance out the back, for the moment not caring if a native deduced my naivete thereby.

Reassured by - or maybe just resigned to - the slower, steadier jolting, I turned my attention to the letters between my late uncle - whose estate I had come to inherit - and my mother, who had passed away some five years ago. They had not seen each other for over forty years and the sum total of correspondence amounted to about two letters a decade on either side. They testified that the uncle I never knew retained a remnant of family loyalty: beyond naming me as heir, which was not obligatory, his letters gave sufficient hints to assure me that I would find, upon examining his accounts, the source of our survival since my father's death in a pogrom shortly after my birth.

I pulled out the top letter, from the estate executor, and read it again. It still seemed unlikely my uncle would simply give me such a large inheritance, without some preconditions or requirement. But, aside from furnishing proof I was me (easy enough even for a poverty-stricken youth), I need only appear within six months to claim the entirety of the estate.

Even as I finished rearranging the precious packet, the carriage turned down a smaller, quieter street, deliberately slowing down. Observing - casually - the construction and aspect of the houses, I concluded we must be nearing my uncle's home.

Within a short distance, the carriage stopped, confirming my suspicion. The driver was down with the door open before I could adjust my battered and bruised hat. As soon as I had stepped to the ground - and while I was momentarily pre-occupied with making the *hat as presentable as possible under the circumstances - the driver leapt up, tore through the ropes and landed cat-like at my side, prepared to double as a porter.*

"The house of Monsieur Charbonier," the driver said.

I still didn't know why my uncle had changed his name from Tzivies, but it didn't matter.

I allowed the driver to carry my valise and paid him handsomely for both duties. I must admit to an anxious moment, for on his gratuity alone (assuming his fare honestly assessed) I could have eaten for a year. Yet from the executor's advance, I still had enough for ten such trips. I realized I would have to be careful with my new-found wealth: better to handle the funds of the rich from the perspective of the poor than to gain the perspective of the rich and be left with the funds of the poor. (I winced, imagining my rabbi's reaction to such a witticism.)

The door opened and I showed the lawyer's letter to the butler. He examined it carefully, then returned it, saying they had been expecting me. He picked up my valise and led me down the hall into my uncle's study. Waiting for me was the executor and another man.

"I am Jacques Lyotard, your late uncle's lawyer, executor of his estate, and, I may say, a close personal friend." He extended his hand and we shook. "This is Francois Foucalt, a lawyer from a different firm, who will serve as witness."

"Chaim Ephraim Tzivies," I said, fumbling in my coat for my Russian passport. I showed it to the two lawyers, who examined it, nodded their heads in unison, and then returned it.

"All seems in order," Jacques Lyotard said, giving my packet of letters a significant look. "There is but one last test. Monsieur Charbonier had a rather unusual sense of humor. His safe, which you see there on the wall, has a new combination, one which he set shortly before his passing. In his last communication with me, he

gave me instructions for opening it, but not the combination."

I looked at him with curiosity, especially as he pointed at my letters.

"The combination is a code based on the name of his sister, for whom he had an unusual affection and sense of obligation. Something from their youth, no doubt." He shrugged. "It's a simple enough code. Each letter corresponds to a number, in sequence. We know her name in French and Russian, but it does not seem to work."

"It must be in Hebrew, then," I said, smiling. "Her name was Leah Goldah, so the combination must be 30 - 1- 5 - 3 - 6 - 30 - 4 - 5."

Too surprised to speak, the two lawyers exchanged glances, then bowed me toward the safe. With trembling fingers, realizing this was a final test of my identity, I turned the lock. At the last number, the tumblers clicked into place. The handled turned easily enough and I opened the safe.

There, before me, was my inheritance: piles of papers - securities and bonds, records of transactions, bank records - on one side; on the other, a large sum of ready cash, beyond a lifetime's earnings.

And in the middle, on a velvet cloth, the most beautiful siddur I had ever seen. Where had this aged, priceless family heirloom come from?

PRE-TRIAL

Chapter 9

"It's Lazar's fault, of course." Shammai shut the door gently but firmly behind him. Stalking into the room, he still felt like slamming it.

Hannah looked up from the Sunday paper. She checked her watch and her amusement turned sour. "Your excursions are getting longer and you're getting more worked up. Since the unveiling you've had - is that three walks to calm yourself down and five friends accused, or the other way around?"

He stopped pacing for a second to face her, then again began tracking his frustration back and forth across the floor. "Nevertheless, it's Lazar's fault. He should have done the legal work sooner, filed the motions or something."

"Let's see," Hannah said, looking at the ceiling and counting on her fingers. "It's Lazar's fault for not filing a motion, and Mr. Enstein's fault for not writing his will or speaking before witnesses, and Kashdan's fault for answering the *shul* phone when the nephews called, and your fault for caring - about anything." She smiled at him, unpleasantly, and wiggled the uncounted finger. "You've got one more left. Who's it going to be? Me? Only don't take an hour to figure it out, because it's dark and late and I've had a rough afternoon, too."

He smiled ruefully and shook his head. "It sounds silly, but it's serious, Hannah. They're here to take away the *siddur*. And I don't know if I can stop them."

She pushed the paper aside. "Maybe you shouldn't."

"What? Is this another joke?"

"No." She looked at him intensely, standing to confront him. "Our family's been in turmoil ever since Mr. Enstein got sick - even before. Elie's always about to explode at Dinah Chaya, you can't talk to him, she's in tears half the time, and the other half she's about to explode at everyone - and it's not just because they're teenagers. You buy an expensive bookcase we don't need and start talking about making a library with books we don't own and who knows what else. Mr. Enstein gave you one book, that's all. Even if the nephews didn't show up, why should we get the rest? Where would we put them? They belong in a real library, not your dreams."

"I know." His whole mouth taut, he strained the words between his teeth and lips. "But for all these years, I've watched his collection grow. It doesn't seem right for part of it--"

"Then give back the *siddur*," Hannah burst out. She turned away instantly. Shocked, he searched for a response. Before he found one, she faced around, glaring at him. "I wasn't going to say anything, but --" She drew a breath. "It's worth a lot of money. What if it gets stolen?"

"He kept it."

"It was his."

He stared back at her. She looked away first.

He walked over to the bookcase and touched the glass door. He spoke with his back to her. "He gave it to me. His death wish. What am I supposed to do?" he whispered.

She came next to him. "Do you feel he owed it to you?" she asked softly.

He shook his head. "No. I feel I owe it to him. And you. And Dinah Chaya - what other compensation does she have for what she saw?"

"And Elie?"

He nodded. "And Elie."

He sat down and took off his glasses. "I don't care how much it's worth. Who knows what Mr. Enstein went through to get that *siddur*, to safeguard it, to retrieve it? Then, as he was dying, he gave it to me. It has to be preserved, used and passed on. Elie will get it, of course. Maybe a wedding present, I don't know.

"That doesn't matter. The point is, I - we - have a responsibility. It'd be like putting a *sefer Torah* in a museum vault. Dead, irrelevant things go there. A living Torah, a living relationship makes demands on us. We have to sacrifice. We have do things we don't always understand, things that don't make sense. A logical mitzvah, a convenient mitzvah - that's easy. This *siddur's* part of Torah. Mr. Enstein was a teacher of Torah. He gave it to me, but it's for the children."

The silence grew. He looked up, saw her studying the mess she'd made with the newspaper. "So," she said, "what are our options?"

He started straightening the papers. Having her support removed so much of the tension. "I don't know. I've tried to get in touch with Lazar since dinner, but he's not home - at least he won't answer the door or the phone. There or at the office."

"Well, at least I know where you went on your various rambles. And I should compliment you on acting so well in front of the children all afternoon."

He put the papers on the table. "I was at my office half the time."

"I know. Doing what?"

He shrugged. "A little work, a lot of pacing, even more thinking. By the way, it's rather quiet for so early."

"Dinah Chaya's at a friend's house, as usual, Elie went to a basketball game with Benjie Sagalman and Aaron and Moshe are asleep."

"So there's nobody to worry but you and me."

"Something like that. I'll fix some coffee and you tell me what you've figured out."

He sat down. "I don't know how these two nephews found

out about Mr. Enstein passing away. I made some phone calls, but nobody knew."

"What do you mean?" Hannah called from the kitchen.

"I thought maybe someone from the *shul* had contacted them." He bit his lip. "You know, like Bob Sagalman or Kashdan."

"Why them?"

He shrugged. "They're the officers. And Josh. But he wouldn't think of looking for a next-of-kin. If Mr. Enstein had left a note or record or something in the shul, then --" He lifted his glasses and rubbed his eyes. "It's strange. They just appeared from nowhere."

"Maybe they're imposters."

"I thought of that, but Lazar didn't think so. I'm sure they contacted him, as executor of Mr. Enstein's will. When we got to the unveiling, he obviously knew something he didn't want to tell me. They were it. But how did they find out?"

She brought in the coffee and sat down. "Maybe they've got a subscription to the Times-Picayune and read the obituaries every day."

"Seriously."

"Maybe they did it by computer."

"Now that's an idea," he said, thinking about networks, drumming the table as he thought.

"So these two nephews of Mr. Enstein's appear from nowhere and --" she said to get his attention back.

"And nothing. They're going to sue me."

She said a *brocha* and took a sip of coffee. "Funny how we didn't know about them all these years. You'd think Mr. Enstein would have said something. They must not have gotten along."

He reached for his coffee.

"Yours is too hot for you." She took a drink, then held the cup between her hands for the warmth. "So shouldn't all the books belong to them?"

"Well, Louisiana law -- ouch." He put the cup down and shook his fingers. She gave him an I-told-you-so look. "--says that unless otherwise provided for, property goes to the next of kin. I'm pretty sure of that. So no library."

"And they should even get the *siddur*."

"I don't think so. It was a gift at the time of death, which is like a change of will, I think. But that's why I've got to talk to Lazar, to find out what the options really are. Mr. Enstein's will is no help. But at least it doesn't hurt."

"Do you want some cake?"

"Not right now." He stood up, but just leaned on the chair. "Maybe these two guys - Earl and Simon Oster-whatever - don't have a claim after all these years without contact. But there are other questions: Is the *siddur* part of the estate or was it a gift before death? Does Mr. Enstein's involvement with the *shul* count for anything, since he didn't name any inheritors?"

"And does your having looked after him have any effect?" she said. "A lot of questions."

"And no answers, except that I'm sure we're in for a fight. Uh, I'll have that piece of cake now." Guiltily, he added, "Well, I changed my mind."

She got up and went back to the kitchen. As she opened the refrigerator, she said, "Maybe they'd agree to a *beis din*."

"They don't look too observant to me."

"Still," she said, putting the pan on the counter. "Or maybe some form of arbitration, so we don't have to pay expensive lawyer's fees."

"I doubt it. I'll ask Lazar, though. I can't see him doing this gratis. I don't know that I'd want him to."

"Oh, if he gets some good publicity out of it, like going to the supreme court, he'd probably pay you." She put the cake and a couple of plates on the table.

Shammai laughed and took a piece.

"So," she said, after he'd made a *brocha*, taken a bite and nodded his approval. "What do we do now?"

"Wait until tomorrow and talk to Lazar, I guess."

"How do we pay for it?"

He shrugged.

"What about Bob Sagalman or Josh Green? Can they help with any of this? Or anyone from the shul?"

"I don't know." He finished his piece of cake. "I just don't know."

She stood up to clear the table and he stood to help. "How do you think we should handle all this with the children?" he asked.

"By telling them the truth," she said.

He followed her into the kitchen.

Putting the dishes into the dishpan, she said, flatly, "An uncle of mine was involved in a lawsuit. It dragged on for years and practically destroyed him."

"I remember. You told me the story before we got married. The last appeal was rejected during our *sheva brochas*."

She bit her lip. "I don't want that to happen to us."

"It won't. I promise you, before it gets anywhere near that, I'll - I'll I don't know what. But I've got to see this through. I won't let it destroy us,. though."

She studied him a moment. "There's something else, isn't there?"

He hung his head. "Yeah." Leaning on the counter, his hands gesturing, he turned around, unable to explain himself and look at her at the same time. "I can't help but wonder, with all the jokes and rumors and raised eyebrows, have I really been expecting something from Mr. Enstein? Or was I -- were we -- watching out for him, helping him, because that's the way it's supposed to be?

"I'd like to think that for just one thing, in some way, I was doing what the Torah said, the way it says, without any other motive or thought. I'm not a *tzaddik* - as you well know - but --" he paused and looked at her over his shoulders. "I guess I want to prove to myself I'm not a complete rosha, completely wicked, either."

She started to speak, but he stopped her with a gesture and continued. "I don't mean literally evil or wicked. I mean spiritually, in my mind's eye. If I can do after Mr. Enstein's death exactly what I did or would have done while he was alive, then I can hope."

He straightened up. "That it might require some sacrifice..." he shrugged.

She looked at him in silence, giving his words some respect. "I understand."

"Now," he said lightly, "I have a question for you."

"What?"

"How are we going to handle our teenagers?"

The phone rang. "Dinah Chaya," she said. She dried her hands and went to answer it. "I think they'll let us know."

#

As he waited, Shammai catalogued the signs of Monday morning in Lazar's office: the receptionist yawning and bleary-eyed; the two para-legals rather loudly and intermittently reviewing their weekend activities while trying to sort through the confusion left behind Friday afternoon; the phone ringing every thirty seconds; the unstudied entrances of Lazar's partners - one artificially jovial, another bewildered and disheveled, the third trailing a client like some oversized bass from a fishing rodeo.

Shammai looked at his watch. Lazar had said he'd be in by eight-thirty, but to give him fifteen minutes just in case. It was now ten after nine and he began to wonder if the receptionist had actually buzzed Lazar. He had a *tehillim* in the car, maybe he should get it. The two dozen or so magazines lying on the coffee table didn't interest him twenty minutes ago, and he was sure that old newsmagazines, slick, picturesque home and garden digests, an odd law journal or two, and three months of a sailing publication with an individual's name rather than the firm's still wouldn't interest him.

Of course Lazar had expected his call. In fact, Lazar sounded as if he'd been about to call himself, though six-thirty a.m. was two and a half hours before Lazar usually got up. But then, the unusual seemed to become routine of late. So, even though Shammai had called as late as one a.m. without an answer, neither Lazar's alertness nor evasiveness about where he'd been all Sunday evening and late into the night surprised him.

He stretched. First he'd ask the secretary to buzz Lazar again. Then he'd get the *tehillim*.

As he approached the desk, she glanced up. Her harried, what-now look he'd seen on many different secretaries under many different circumstances, but he hadn't expected to see Lazar's direct it towards him.

Every other time, though, he'd been a visitor (except for a couple of minor things that required no more than a phone call or signature), one who had no legitimate demands on her. Their exchanges therefore had only been social. Now, she saw him as a client and he had, through Lazar, a claim on her time. She saw, or rather knew from experience, that, like any client, he would expect activity and commotion, whether warranted or not. The waiting, thinking and researching necessary to a case, because unseen, offered little proof to the anxious client that this law firm and its attorneys would help.

He laughed at himself for wanting proof of competence beyond his friendship with Lazar. How quickly perspectives change, he thought, how awareness arouses desire, which corrupts attitudes and distorts self-perception. The *yetzer haro* at work.

She picked up the phone, just as it buzzed.

"You can go right back," she said, not catching the irony of the "coincidence."

The sense of change increased as he walked down the hall; the nonchalance of friendship turned, with each step, into the nervousness of dependence. Even the smell of the coffee -- and he suddenly really wanted a cup -- reminded him that amenities were only a courtesy to outsiders.

At Lazar's half-open door, he knocked. "Come in," Lazar said, then waved him indifferently to a seat. Lazar finished making a few notes and Shammai found himself getting annoyed. That, too, was new. Previously, he'd waited paitently for Lazar's attention; previously, though, he'd only come to visit.

Finally, Lazar looked up and flashed, for a moment, a familiar smile.

"I didn't expect this," Lazar said, waving a hand and shaking his head over the papers and books on his desk. "One of these can serve as a placemat." He pushed a button on his phone and leaned over it. "Two coffees, please. One black, and add extra sugar to mine." He looked up at Shammai. "Actually, I'd like to use them all as rags," shuffling the papers over the desktop.

"I've been here since eight-thirty."

"I've been here since seven-thirty," Lazar said, now making a pretense of tidying his desk. "And I was in the law library until almost two. Until when did you call? I should get an answering machine."

"You knew this was coming?" Shammai asked, keeping his voice neutral.

"I am neither a prophet nor the son of a prophet." Lazar leaned back, his hands behind his head. "But when two previously unknown relatives show up from nowhere, unannounced and with

not much civility, it's a tell-tale sign. I did not expect to see this --"
he lifted a manila folder with papers on it -- "waiting for me."

"What is it?"

"It is a letter from their attorney, which is being registered
with the court even as we speak, demanding that I, as executor,
release all of Mr. Enstein's property into their possession, as sole
heirs, as of noon today. Attached is a copy of the suit they will file
tomorrow if I don't comply."

"Maybe I should go back and just take all the books right
away," Shammai said. "Possession being so important to the law."

"Oh, right." Lazar threw his hands up and almost tipped his
chair over backwards. Righting himself, he looked at Shammai.
"Theft and-or fraud. Can we stay out of the criminal code, please?
We'll have enough to do as it is."

The door opened and the secretary brought in the coffee.
Shammai and Lazar thanked her and waited until she left. Lazar
whispered the *brocha* and took a deep, satisfying drink. Shammai
held the burning cup between his hands.

"Anyway, I can just see Hannah's reaction as you haul all
those books into your living room, bedroom and kitchen," Lazar
said, picking up the conversation. "Not to mention Elie's and Dinah
Chaya's."

"Why, what objection would Dinah Chaya have?" Shammai
asked, then laughed at the absurdity of the question in the
circumstances.

Lazar put his coffee down, reached behind him and opened
the shades. "Anyway, it wouldn't help. Your claim on everything but
the *siddur* is very weak. You'd have to prove that by giving you the
one, he gave you them all. And there's no evidence for that."

"Then there shouldn't be a problem," Shammai said, looking
for a place to put down the cup. Lazar indicated anywhere. Shammai
looked for the spot on the desk with the fewest papers. "Just give

them the key to his house when they come."

"I don't plan to be here then," Lazar said.

"Why?"

"Because you, my friend, are going to be sued and I want to reserve my righteous indignation for the court. Besides, I intend to make that claim - that by giving you one he gave you all - until the judge throws it out in preliminaries, which he will. I will do this to confuse the enemy and buy some time."

"Well," Shammai said, smiling. "Hannah made a similar point about the rest of the books. It was just a daydream, anyway." He stood and stretched. "You really think they're going to cause trouble?"

"How much is the *siddur* worth?" Lazar asked. "How much are the rest worth? If you wanted to sell all the books, would you do it without the *siddur*?"

"If you put it that way, ..." Shammai said. Lazar didn't have to elaborate. The *siddur* was worth fifty thousand and had to be the centerpiece of the collection. How many books that valuable could Mr. Enstein have?

"I wish I wore glasses," Lazar said at last. "That way I could pull them off dramatically at a moment of tension. Like now." He gulped the rest of his coffee. "Oh, well, I'll save the gestures and flourishes for the judge."

"Lazar."

"OK. The will doesn't help. It doesn't hurt that much, either, considering the circumstances."

"So, what do I do?"

"Depends."

Shammai looked at him sharply.

"On whether or not you're going to hire me," Lazar explained.

"Of course."

"Then I accept, on condition you listen to my advice."

"I'm not a lawyer."

"No, but sometimes you're stubborn enough to be one."

"What do you mean?"

Lazar paused. "Are you willing to compromise?"

"How?" Shammai asked, puzzled.

"Exchange the *siddur* for some of the other books."

Shammai thought about it, then shook his head.

"Give it back to his natural heirs for a 'thank-you' fee."

He shook his head again.

"Give it back outright," Lazar continued, leaning forward.

"No."

"Sell it to someone else."

Shammai didn't bother to respond.

"Sell it to them. Fair market value."

"No, and you're fired!" Shammai said.

Lazar smiled. "Well, at least I know your bottom line. OK, I'll take the case."

Shammai folded his arms. "You really think they're going to sue? On what grounds?"

"Did Mr. Enstein make a dying bequest - a disposition mortis causa in my jargon - or --" he stood and took a couple steps, "was it obtained under duress?"

"I wasn't even there," Shammai protested.

"Ah, but all that time you spent with poor old, confused Mr. Enstein." Lazar shook his head and clicked his tongue for a moment. "It's called undue influence. Ironic, considering your relationship." Lazar took a deep breath. "And then, let's say we prove the gift is legitimate, is the donation to you excessive? Earl and Simon, as the legal heirs --" He leaned against the wall. "They didn't travel from who knows where just to look. It won't be pretty." He leaned back and waited.

"I just don't understood how they found out," Shammai said, mainly to himself.

"They probably called during Pesach, being dutiful nephews, found out the number had been disconnected and went from there. I'd bet that, according to when Mr. Enstein died, we could have had possession for six months." He sighed. "It would have helped, their being absent for so long. But we can't do anything about it now."

"So, what do we do?" Shammai asked.

"Wait. Write letters in response. Depends on what they do," Lazar said. "I can't decide on a plan until I know their strategy, what angle they're going to attack with."

"But you can start preparing, looking at possibilities, can't you?"

"I already have. Two a.m. remember?" Lazar stood and stretched. "Which brings me to the next point. And for that, we'll need the conference room." He picked up the coffee cups in one hand. "Come on."

The walk down the hall, though short, seemed to Shammai unnecessarily formal, and hence unexpectedly tense.

The conference room was furnished with the large, solid wood, overbearing table and high-backed, plush rolling chairs almost required of law firms. The room also had a sink, refrigerator and small microwave. Lazar nonchalantly slid the cups onto the counter and sat down next to a pile of papers.

"Where should I sit?" Shammai asked.

"How much exercise do you want? We've got to pass some papers back and forth."

Shammai took the second seat from Lazar. "Speaking of passing, does this table substitute for a practice field when it rains?"

Lazar smiled. "We've got to keep our distance from each other around here, especially in conference. The first one's easy," he said, passing a set of papers to Shammai. "It's our agreement to represent you and your authorization for us to perform the legal mumbo-jumbo to win the case. Standard stuff."

Shammai gave a glance at it, shrugged, signed both copies and returned one. "What else?"

"Here's a copy of the will, and the motion I file today to have you declared sole heir of all movable property and the *shul* of immovables - the house. You'll see by the date I wrote this two weeks ago."

"Why?" Shammai said, scanning the papers, which made little sense.

"A whim. I also have motions requesting the *shul* be named sole heir of all property, sole heir of all books, the house to be sold and the proceeds to establish a clerical fund for the shul. Etcetera." Lazar riffled through a thick file as he spoke.

"You did all this in the last two weeks? Didn't you have anything better to do?" Shammai asked.

"I like the mental exercise," Lazar said, giving him a do-you-have-to-ask look. He tossed him a manila folder. "Your copies. You'll see, by the way, I didn't make too strong a push for any investments or cash. Thought I had to give the state something. Now it''ll be Earl and Simon, instead."

Shammai looked at the long sheets dubiously. "Do I really need all this?"

"No, but I think you'll want your own file, so I'm starting you off right. If you're going to ask questions, you've got to have the source. Just remember that ninety percent of this is smoke and mirrors. I don't believe it, their attorney won't believe it, but the judge will hopefully believe it's serious enough to be ruled against, which gives us time. Do us both a favor and make sure you don't believe any motion, petition, etc., unless it's from us and the judge rules in our favor. Even then, don't believe more than half."

"What if the judge rules in their favor?"

"Hope I can find a counter-motion."

Shammai raised his hands in a gesture of helplessness. "Is all this necessary? Maybe we could talk to them, explain things. After all, they will get the rest of the books, right?"

"With the *siddur*, the books may be worth two hundred thousand dollars, maybe more. We'll have to get them assessed. Without it - is it a complete collection? It'll be worth less than the minus fifty thousand, that's for sure. Anyway, I didn't see any *tzaddik* label around their necks."

Shammai shook his head. "I feel like I'm getting in up to mine - and beyond." He folded his hands. "I helped, my family helped, Mr. Enstein because we were available, we felt sorry for him, for a lot of reasons, none of which included getting his property."

"I know that and you know that. It's my job to convince the court of it," Lazar said quietly.

Shammai continued, as though Lazar hadn't interrupted. "But Mr. Enstein fought hard for those books. Maybe saving them was his own private war. He didn't redeem the books from captivity just to have them institutionalized or something. I can't save them all, I guess, but I can save one, at least." He noticed the table reflecting his face, hand and the papers he held. "Doesn't the Talmud tell us that saving a life is saving a world? Well, if books also have souls, like Mr. Enstein said, I'm going to save a world."

Lazar leaned forward "Just remember those words if you're on the stand. By the way, I think Mr. Enstein felt the heart attack coming, that he had some warning before Dinah Chaya got there. That's why he 'happened' to have the *siddur* - he wanted to give it to you before he died, to remove any doubt. It just turned out she showed up for you."

This startled Shammai."How do you know?"

"I don't, but that's my instinct, and if I can get the judge to entertain that as reasonable - and I'll need a doctor as expert witness for that - it'll help get him to consider intentionality our way. If Mr. Enstein had the presence of mind to specifically select it right before or even better during a heart attack, well, that's some heavy-duty undue influencing."

"So that's the defense?" Shammai asked.

Lazar nodded. "That's the defense." He picked up the papers, shook and knocked them straight, and said, as he was putting them away, "That's it. Now get something productive done, because this could drag out for a while. Find a project to occupy you for a couple months or years. Lawsuits are notoriously long-winded."

"I don't want this hanging over my family. I want it finished as quickly as possible," Shammai said. He let his thoughts wander a moment, then suddenly stood and stuck out his hand. "Thanks."

Lazar took it.

"One more thing," Shammai said, rubbing the back of his neck. "You haven't said anything about getting paid."

"That's because there's nothing to say." Lazar looked uncharacteristically uncomfortable.

"You're not doing this for nothing," Shammai said emphatically.

"You're right, I'm not. But that doesn't mean you have to be the one to pay me." He hesitated, looking around the four walls of the conference room, as though there might be some window somewhere.

"Lazar, I have to pay you something."

There was a long pause. "No, *somebody* has to, even though I will work on contingency," Lazar said. He walked to the door. Before he left, he added, "And I can take my fee in something besides cash."

Chapter 10

Shammai looked at the clock on his office wall. Two P. M. The mail must have come by now. Monday was always the worst. A whole weekend to speculate and wonder and listen to all his expert friends at *shul* and around town. At least the reporters hadn't called since the initial story, nearly two months ago.

Now that had been torment, to say the least. A good thing Lazar said to expect them and tell them all to go away. Though disappointed, they'd been reasonable enough about respecting his request to be left alone. Of course, there really hadn't been anything to say. It had caused such turmoil in the house, though. He'd thought about being on the news since then, wondering what he would have said if given the chance, what he would say if they asked after the court decided. He saw how easily he could have trapped himself into the illusory chaos of significance, with its self-defining importance; he understood the temptation of the lean and hungry quote.

The story had its appeal: a poignant legacy, a faithful friend, conniving relatives, law versus justice. Such stories could destroy families, though - and not just in novels.

He walked the length of the office, picked up the phone, put it down and walked the length of the office again.

This is ridiculous, he told himself. A weird way to count the Omer - and beyond: to call home almost the same time every day just to find out if they'd received a copy of the latest motion or counter-motion being filed, even though Lazar had already told him all about it. He turned the air-conditioning down. The beginning of June already felt like mid-summer.

Lazar had kept his word about fighting paper with paper. His own personal melodrama, with only Hannah watching. He knew it wearied her, but she understood - most of the time. His calling wouldn't start a fight - not that they hadn't had a few. She wouldn't let him quit, though.

So what made him hesitate today?

Of course - the children. This was their first Monday home for the summer. No more school. Adjustments and aggravation in the house. And phoning would add to it.

He called home. Hannah picked up on the fourth ring, just before the answering machine clicked on.

"Hi. Hold on a second, the mailman's just getting to the door."

She put the receiver down, and he heard her footsteps fade, then approach again. She sounded cheerful enough, almost relieved that he'd called. It had become that routine for them.

"OK. Let me just get rid of the junk."

"What kind of junk?"

"Coupons for treif food. Some form letter from a roofing and siding company."

"We - "

"- don't have the money to do anything to the roof," she finished. "Do you really want a catalog of the junk mail?"

"No." He paused. "By the way, how did you know it was me?"

He could sense her smile. "A lucky guess."

From her tone, he thought, better not ask about the kids. "Maybe I should have Lazar send it all here to the office."

"Don't you dare," she warned. "Then you'd hide half of what's going on."

"Maybe I should."

"Not if you want my support. It's bad enough you're obsessed, you're not going to - Aaron! Stop that!"

The phone dropped with a thud. She picked it up

immediately. "Sorry."

He leaned forward in his chair. "I tell you everything Lazar tells me."

"So far."

He could hear the rustle of envelopes through the phone. "Well?"

"A couple of bills, an appeal and - " She stopped.

"And what?"

"A letter from their attorney."

"What?" He jumped up. "How do you know?"

"I can read a return address and by now I think I know the name," she said drily. "Shall I open it?"

"Yes. No. I'm coming home. Wait until I get there." Everything else had been routed through Lazar's office first.

"Don't you have work to do?" she asked, her voice tensing slightly.

"Some. But I won't be able to concentrate on it now. I'll come back tonight if I have to."

"Maybe you should just call Lazar. I'm sure they sent him a copy."

Shammai thought about the suggestion. He knew she didn't like him coming home in the middle of the day, even if he had business in the Central Business District and just stopped in for lunch.

He checked his calendar. He had to modify a system for a doctor's office off Napoleon Avenue later in the week. He could probably move it up.

"Let me call you right back," he said. "But don't open it."

"You'd think it was a birthday present or something," Hannah said, annoyed. "All right. But make it quick, I've got some things to do."

Shammai called the doctor's office and asked the receptionist if he could come by later today instead. She put him on hold. One minute. Two minutes. They must think I'm a patient, he thought. Just as he was about to hang up and try again, the receptionist came back, said hello and dropped the phone.

"Four o'clock?" she asked, offering no explanation for the delay.

"Fine," he said.

Now, to call Lazar.

He dialed the first three numbers, then stopped. No. So far, Lazar had controlled everything about the case, explaining what this motion meant and why that affidavit had to be signed and telling him which letters should be ignored and citing this precedent and that district court to show the purpose behind filing, questioning, subpoenaing.

Of course, as the lawyer, that was Lazar's job. But this wasn't Lazar's life - it was his. It was his - Shammai's - family that had been affected, and it was his - Shammai's - life that had been thrown into turmoil. The *siddur*, with its unknown history, was his responsibility.

It would be an insignificant, almost silly step, Shammai told himself as he turned off the lights and locked the door. After all, weren't they required by law to furnish Lazar a copy of documents in the case? That would apply even more to the client on the other side, one would think.

But impressions were important, first ones most of all, and he wanted to form his of this letter free from Lazar's analysis and instructions. That would come later.

He called Hannah and she graciously, though skeptically, accepted his explanation of a downtown appointment.

He found himself in a surprisingly good mood on the way home - the concerto on the radio no doubt helping - despite the way this lawsuit was absorbing his life, marginalizing all his relationships. So far, almost everyone from the *shul* had been depositioned. It was threatening to fracture. He shrugged to himself, sure it would lurch on, seeing it only as further proof that there must always be a leader.

The concerto ended someplace along Carrollton Avenue, which meant either listening to the announcer's attempt at banter or the streetcars' stop and go screeching along the neutral ground. He chose the latter, turned off the radio, and left it off until he got home.

He found Hannah sitting on the couch reading, waiting for him. "It's on the table," she said without getting up.

As he picked up the letter, she stood. "Lazar called."

"Oh?" He paused. Not that he hadn't expected it.

"He wanted to know if the letter came."

"What did you tell him?"

"I just asked him if it was supposed to come here. He said yes, it should arrive today and call him as soon as possible. You must have just left your office."

"He knew it was coming, and coming today. That means he knew about it beforehand," Shammai said, tearing the envelope.

She took tentative steps forward as he started to scan the letter.

"I don't believe this," he said, dropping it onto the table.

"What?"

"I don't believe it."

Now she rushed across the rest of the room. He picked it up again, still dazed.

"Listen to this," he said, trying to hold it so she could read it with him. He skipped the greeting. "'In regard to the claims of my clients against you concerning the disposition of the property of the late Mr. Enstein, particularly his valuable collection of old and rare books, and even more specifically, the prayerbook currently in your possession - quite illegally - my clients are willing to make you an offer of settlement, as follows.'

"Here it comes," Shammai said, curling one hand across the top of a chair. Hannah did the same thing, and leaned forward. "'In exchange for a written revocation of all rights, interest or claim in any and all of the property of their deceased relative, including return of any currently within your domain, my clients have authorized me to offer you ten thousand dollars, payable immediately upon receipt of your revocation.' Etcetera and so forth," Shammai said, dropping the letter on the table, and heading for the kitchen.

"What are you going to do?" Hannah asked.

"Get a cup of coffee."

"I meant about the letter." Her smile at his comment took away some of his tension. "Are you going to accept it?"

The question in her voice surprised him. "I wasn't planning on it," he said.

"It's a lot of money," she said, dubious.

"And there's more behind it," he said with assurance, as if the fact that more could be offered was reason enough to reject any offer.

Her reply didn't come immediately. "What do you think Lazar's going to say?"

"I don't know. But I'm sure he's already got his answer. I'll give Lazar this much credit. All his petitions and filings and motions kept Mr. Enstein's books right where they were, in his house. I'm sure it drove them crazy, not being able to get their hands on anything." He poured the coffee, wondering why since he'd leave before drinking it. "That's why this letter, I'm sure. Anyway, I'll call him later."

"But what do you think of the letter?" she suddenly insisted.

"I don't know. I'm not a lawyer."

"You know what I mean," she said, coming into the kitchen.

"Why do I think they sent it? How's it going to affect us?" She nodded and he shrugged. "Why did they send it? To avoid a fight, they think they're going to lose, or - I don't know." He shrugged again. "How's it going to affect the family? It's bad enough trying to guess what they're going to try next and how it'll affect me. I should speculate on the children now, too?"

She turned away and shook her head. "It's become our family obsession - or heirloom. The anxiety's inheritance enough from Mr. Enstein," she said, more to herself than to him. She looked up. "Go ahead and call Lazar." Her voice had a surprising edge of bitterness.

"Hannah?"

She averted her face. "Never mind." After a moment, she added, without looking up, "Sorry."

He expected her to walk away, but she stood, waiting.

"Are you angry with Lazar?" He asked, confused. "He's done all right with the case so far."

"No, I'm not angry with Lazar," she said, turning back. "I'm angry with you."

"Me?" He put his free hand to his chest. "Me?"

"Yes, you. Your only concern now is that *siddur*. What about the rest of Mr. Enstein's books? Do you owe them anything?"

"That's what's bothering you? Should we amend the lawsuit?"

"No, that's not what's bothering me." She threw up her hands and made a full circle in exasperation. At its end, she looked at him, lips ready to speak, but unable to do so. Exhausted by her inner battle, she suddenly sat down, saying weakly, "This whole business is not a family obsession, it's yours. And I'm getting tired of it."

Shammai sat down, too. "Are you saying I should drop the whole thing?" He tried to make it a neutral question, but was sure some anger had crept into his voice. This was not what he'd come to expect from her.

"Now that's going to make a great impression on the children," she said sarcastically. "I can see how we'll explain that: 'Oh, it's OK. Yes, we made sure Mr. Enstein was all right when he was alive, but now that he's dead, we don't have to care. Yes, your father was going to make sure things were done right, that the will was followed, that we'd preserve the legacy of the *siddur*, but he doesn't want to now.' Shammai, who were those people whose names are inscribed? I've looked at the different handwritings inside the front cover and wondered. Did they struggle, did they suffer, were they happy?"

Shammai shook his head. "I don't understand. You want to continue, but you say I'm obsessed? Should I take the settlement or not?"

"I don't know!" Hannah said, throwing up her hands. "I don't know what the options are, how you feel about them, anything. You'll ask Lazar, we'll talk about it and you'll decide. As always. But that's not the point."

"Then what is the point?"

"The point is," Hannah said, leaning forward, "that you've been ignoring the children through all this."

"I --" Shammai started to protest. Was it true? "What have I done differently?" he challenged. "I've been home for supper just the same, helped with homework when needed just the same. How have I ignored them?"

Hannah sighed. "I mean you've been ignoring their feelings. How do you think they feel, knowing their father is worried, tense, involved in some kind of battle, that he's trying to do something Mr. Enstein wanted, show him some respect - and you won't talk about it with them. Half the time you don't tell me what's going on."

"That's not true. I've always turned to you right away. Besides, what am I supposed to tell Moshe and Aaron. How are they going to understand?"

"They don't have to know the details, but you should let them know in a general way. More important, you should listen. How do *they* feel about it?"

He looked at her dubiously. "And Elie? Dinah Chaya? I'm supposed to turn this business into a psychology session?"

"No, you're supposed to communicate with your children. Dinah Chaya was there, remember? She saw him almost die, she got the *siddur* for you. Don't you think she's got some strong feelings about all this?"

He wished he didn't have a too-hot cup of coffee in his hand. "I hadn't thought about it that way," he conceded, still feeling resistant. "I guess, if I thought about it, I just figured that they knew what it was about, knew it was important, and supported me." He looked at her. "Like you."

"Of course, but that misses the point."

He saw her hesitate, debate whether she'd gone too far or not far enough.

"And then there's Elie," she whispered.

Too far. "There's always Elie," he exploded. "Maybe that's the problem. Maybe they should think about me, ask me how I'm feeling." He got up, feeling claustrophobic. "Listen, I still have work to do. I'll be home for dinner." He decided not to add an offer to continue this conversation.

He looked around for a place to put the cup, couldn't find one, stomped to the kitchen and poured it out, then stomped to the door.

He paused. "I still need your help deciding what to do about this settlement offer."

He waited for her response.

"Any time. You know that."

Chapter 11

He'd spent a lot of time driving today, Shammai thought, looking at his watch. Almost 6:30 and he was only half way home. Good thing he'd called Hannah and told her he'd be late, please wait for him for dinner.

After his mid-afternoon stop at home, he'd gone to his excuse-appointment. Everything seemed to take twice as long as it should. A fifteen minute drive turned into a forty-five minute disaster, due in part to the interstate bypass construction, but due mostly to poor driving through traffic snarls. He'd had too much on his mind to get upset until near the end, when, three blocks from his destination, he was rerouted because someone tried to beat a yellow light and someone else tried to anticipate a green one and they met at the red.

He'd arrived late, annoyed and sticky - even a new car's air-conditioning would be hard-pressed to deal with June's late afternoon heat for that long, and he had neither a new car nor its air-conditioning. His client had been understanding, but anxious. After a cold drink, he'd checked the problem, made some preliminary observations and reasoned, to himself, that normally he'd need about an hour on-site or two hours in his office to fix the problem. In his current mood, however, between the letter, his conversation with Hannah, and the delay, the hour on-site could easily become two or three. He took a print-out and a floppy-disk copy of the program to work on it when less distracted.

Now he was going home to a wife who accused him of child neglect, children more irritable than usual because dinner was late, a nuisance from work that should have been finished but would now annoy him all evening - and the question of the settlement offer still undecided.

If it wasn't for the aggravation, the day would have been wasted.

He tried to shut out all thoughts on the way home and managed to have all thoughts fighting for his attention.

He knew it would not be an easy night as soon as he got out of the car and heard the noise from the house.

He opened the door to Dinah Chaya's screaming, Moshe crying, Aaron pleading - and the phone ringing.

"It's for you," Elie said, on his way out.

"Where -"

"I'll be back in five minutes."

Shammai stared at the closed door.

"Shammai!" Hannah called from the kitchen.

"You promised!" Dinah Chaya screamed. "I can't believe this! Why don't I just walk to camp right now?" She ran into her room.

At least it was getting quieter, Shammai thought, as he headed for the phone.

"I didn't do it," Aaron said to him as he entered the kitchen.

"I'm sure you didn't. Now do what your mother told you. Go!" The last cut off any further protests. Moshe had subsided into sobs.

He picked up the phone. "Hello?"

"Hi," Lazar said, a slight, almost indetectable tension in his voice.

"I read it."

"And?"

"And?" Shammai returned, but with more vehemence. "And what? You said at the beginning to expect it. Now that it's here, you tell me. That's what you're supposed to be getting paid for."

"Now you promised no blackmail," Lazar said in a mock-offended tone.

"The *siddur's* worth five times the offer," Shammai said. "At least."

"True."

"Josh always tells me about the real estate market, how the buyer shouldn't insult the seller by making too low an offer."

"So you think it's too low?" Lazar prompted.

Shammai looked around at Hannah and, to her anxiously raised eyebrows, just shrugged. "Sounds like you're advising I negotiate."

"That depends on their motive for making an offer at all, doesn't it?"

"Guessing motives is your field, not mine," Shammai said. "Or a psychiatrist's."

"Touché. OK. Either they want to avoid a fight, or they think they're going to lose, or they think they're going to win."

"My words, almost precisely. So?"

"So I don't know which it is. It may even be posturing, you know, to tell the judge they tried to reach a compromise."

Shammai chewed on his lower lip. "Should I take it or not?"

"I get in trouble answering that type of question."

Shammai reached his exasperation point. "So get into trouble. What are friends for?"

"Am I your lawyer or your friend?" Lazar hesitated before continuing. "Normally, I'd give a client advice. Lots of it. Unsolicited and uncharged. And if he didn't want that, I'd insist on analyzing his options, laying out the choices." He stopped, and this time the pause was so long Shammai thought Lazar was through. "But not with you, Shammai, and not with this case."

"Why?"

"Because when it's over, I still want a place to go Friday nights. And whatever I say, even if you decide to agree, you'll resent it. At some point, you'll wonder, "what if?" which will lead to, "if

158

not for..." And I don't want to be at the end of that sentence."

"You don't know me very well, then," Shammai said, almost hanging up on him.

"Maybe not, but I know parties to a lawsuit very well. It's personal. Talk it over with Hannah, then let me know."

"At least help make sure I've got my options clear."

"Three: take the offer, negotiate for more, or refuse to settle."

"If I don't want to settle now, can I change my mind?"

"Sure, but so can they. One of the risks."

Shammai nodded, holding up a hand to Hannah's anxious expressions. "Do you know why they offered to settle now?"

"I have some ideas, but we'll discuss them after you decide, if you're still interested."

"OK. I'll call you."

"Let me know tomorrow," Lazar said, and hung up.

"Well?" Hannah asked.

Before he could answer, the door opened and Elie came back in.

"I wanted some quiet," he said defiantly. "What did Lazar want?" Shammai looked at Hannah. "We got a letter from the other side. They've offered to settle."

Elie's jaw tightened. Other than that, Shammai saw no reaction. "How much?" Elie asked.

"I don't think --" Hannah began.

"Ten thousand," Shammai interrupted.

"It's worth at least five times that much," Elie said.

"I know."

Elie was looking at a point behind Shammai, at something in the past or future. "I'll set the table," he said suddenly.

Hannah motioned him aside. "Why'd you do that? Why did you tell him?"

He watched Elie come back, cradling the dishes in his arms.

Ignoring his parents, Elie carefully put down the plates.

"You said I'd been ignoring the children. You're right. This isn't just my fight. It affects all of us. So, let everyone be a part of it. What's for dinner?"

"Spaghetti."

"Meat or milk?"

"Look at the tablecloth. I've got some things in the kitchen to finish."

Milk. He wanted to ask her what Dinah Chaya had been screaming about, but thought better of it. Elie came back with the silverware, humming a *nigun*.

He might as well see what he could do to help.

"Put out the salad and water and get the boys to wash their hands," Hannah said as soon as he entered, before he could say anything.

He did as instructed, doing his best to keep his thoughts on hold.

Elie was carrying the grated cheese and salad dressings, and Hannah the spaghetti, as he went to the boys' room in the opposite direction.

"Dinah Chaya! Dinner!" Elie called.

"Don't shout," Hannah said.

Shammai knocked on the boys' door, then opened it. "Dinner," he said, poking his head in.

"I didn't do it," Aaron said.

"We'll discuss it later. Wash your hands and come to the table."

"I'm hungry," Moshe said.

"Good, then you'll eat a lot."

"I want spaghetti and meat balls."

"We're having spaghetti and cheese. Milchig's tonight."

"I'm not hungry."

Shammai counted to ten. "Go wash your hands and sit down. This is all you're getting tonight."

He followed the boys to the table.

Hannah was busy dishing out the spaghetti; Elie, pouring sauce on his plate, ignored his sister's request for it. Shammai closed his eyes and waited. He might as well let them squabble while the food was being served and passed. They wouldn't stop until they'd eaten something, anyway.

After making sure Aaron and Moshe had said their *brochas*, he settled down to eat. He suddenly realized how hungry he was himself.

"So," Elie said abruptly, "what does Lazar say?"

"About what?" Dinah Chaya asked.

"Your father got a letter today," Hannah explained. "They made a settlement offer."

"Great," she said, pushing her chair back. "That means the phone'll be tied up again all night AND I won't get to the mall in time. Maybe I'll just stay home this summer."

"Camp doesn't start for another month," Shammai said, surprised.

"Daddy, you just don't understand."

He started to argue, but stopped himself. "Maybe you're right. Maybe I don't. But I'm not going to be on the phone all night. As for going shopping, I'll be glad to take you."

That caught her off-guard - and embarrassed her. "There may not be time, anyway," she said quietly. "I mean, like, I've got to help Mom and talk to Sarah and - you know."

"Well, the offer's there. Pass the salad, Elie. The car's free for your mother to take you, as well."

"So," Elie said, picking up where he'd left off, "what did Lazar say?"

Shammai took a drink. "He said he'd leave it up to me, but

that I had three options."

"Can I be excused?" Dinah Chaya said.

"Why?" Shammai asked, surprised again. Surprising him seemed her task for the night. "You're not finished yet, are you?"

"No, but --"

"Go ahead," Hannah said.

"But I want her input, too," Shammai said.

"Sometimes it's still too much for her," Hannah explained in an elaborate whisper.

Shammai looked dubiously at his daughter, standing in the doorway, and shrugged. Some indiscretion caught his eye.

"Moshe, stop that," Shammai said. "Sit up and eat nicely."

"Don't blame that on me," Aaron said.

"I won't, but you have to eat some salad. Where was I? Oh, yes. The three options are to accept the settlement, to negotiate or to reject it."

"I wish you'd just accept it and get it over with," Dinah Chaya said from the doorway, her voice wistful. "But I know you won't. You'll probably just reject it. But I'm not coming back from camp for this."

Shammai raised his eyebrows and looked at Elie.

"I think you should talk to them," Elie said quietly.

Elie's turn to surprise him. "Why?"

"To see how much they think it's worth, for one thing. That might help at the trial."

"How?" Since the unveiling, Elie had been strangely silent about Mr. Enstein, even trying to avoid conversations when he was the topic. But he always wanted to know all the details - the technicalities, strategy and evidence - about the lawsuit. He'd even called Lazar a couple times. So he knew Elie had been thinking about it.

"If they'll admit that the value was well-known and obvious, then Mr. Enstein couldn't have made a mistake in giving it to you. Even in the midst of a heart attack, he would have had to know what he's doing."

"We've established its value already, without talking to them," Shammai said.

Dinah Chaya sat down again, drawn back. Aaron and Moshe were making their way through the spaghetti, teasing each other in the process.

"But if he knew what it was worth and knew what he was doing, anyway, you couldn't have had undue influence over him," Elie said vehemently.

"That's a thought," Shammai said. "But couldn't Lazar get that information at trial?"

"If he's good enough. But if you talk to them, you might also find out something about their strategy."

"Can we talk about something else?" Dinah Chaya pleaded.

"In a minute," Shammai said. "OK. Elie says I should negotiate, but not accept any offer. Dinah Chaya wants me to accept it."

"I didn't say that. Go ahead and reject it."

"OK." He'd grown tired of her game, especially since he didn't know her rules. "Aaron, what do you say?"

Aaron, who'd been aiming a carrot at Moshe, was so startled to be included in the conversation, he dropped his fork and the carrot dropped into his spaghetti.

"I didn't do it."

"I know, but what should I do?"

Aaron looked around suspiciously, as if he was being trapped. Elie laughed. "Whatever Elie said," he announced triumphantly.

"OK, Moshe?"

"Whatever Dinah Chaya said," he said, sure he'd gotten the

right answer.

"Hannah?"

"I guess it wouldn't hurt to talk to them," she responded reluctantly, "assuming Lazar thinks it's a good idea."

"But don't settle," Elie emphasized. "I know you're going to win."

Shammai smiled. "Thanks for the vote of confidence. OK, I'll call Lazar in the morning."

He started to finish his supper and noticed Dinah Chaya blinking hard and wiping her nose.

"You know," he said gently, "with all this lawsuit nonsense, and school, and summer, it's been a long time since we've done anything as a family. I remember we used to take outings all the time. Let's do something this Sunday. Aaron, where would you like to go?"

Aaron thought a moment. "The Jump-Off. I like the trampolines."

"That's a possibility." He caught Hannah smiling at him. "Moshe?"

"Bowling!"

The look on Elie's face told Shammai he better skip him. He spoke to Hannah. "I remember when they were first fixing up the zoo. We went there a few times. That was one of the first places we went when we got here. Remember how Dinah Chaya used to make elephant noises during the elephant show? Why don't we go to the zoo?"

He glanced at his daughter as he asked this. She graced him with a brief but grateful smile.

"A great idea," Hannah said. "Dinah Chaya, it's your turn to clear the table."

"I think I'll have a cup of coffee," Shammai said.

They finished eating and everyone but Dinah Chaya and

Shammai went to their rooms.

"Want some help?" he asked as he watched her.

"No, thanks."

He held the cup as she came back and forth from the kitchen. When she got to his plate, he put his hand up to stop her. "Sit down a minute," he said.

She sat.

"I just want to tell you something that's been on my mind."

"If it's about the phone bill. . ."

"It's not about the phone bill, or Elie, or Mr. Enstein or the lawsuit or anything. It's about you."

"Me?"

Ha! His turn to surprise her. He took a big swallow of the coffee. For once, it wasn't too hot for him. "I just want to say that in a few weeks you'll be off to camp and out of the house. But this year it's different, because when you come home, you'll pack your suitcases and leave for school. You may feel like you're already gone, or like I think so. But that's not so. Even when you're not here, I - well," another sip of coffee. "We don't talk much these days, not like when you were six or seven."

"I remember," she said, swallowing hard. "We'd take walks alone, hand in hand, and discuss why the sunflower grew as tall as me, and the bees seemed to like the purple flower better than the pink one."

"And why the magnolia had a big white flower," he continued for her, "And why the street names were inlaid into the sidewalk, and why you liked your hair in a ponytail, and why Chavie was your best friend."

He looked at his little girl, so busy with her plans for camp and shopping with her mother and discussing trivial, yet critical, items with her friends. How they relied on her to help with her brothers and relieve them from some household chores - he would miss that. He'd even miss her challenges, the way she flaunted her adolescence and dared him to confront her and create a shouting match or crying scene.

Elie wasn't his only child with whom he shared a silence. With Elie, it was a burden, a struggle they shared, that each had to fight, next to each other, but apart. Dinah Chaya was different. The silence wasn't shared, it was an unspoken agreement, a barrier between them, the one thing they couldn't discuss - that she, and she alone, had witnessed Mr. Enstein's heart attack and received his inheritance for him; that Mr. Enstein had spoken to her, not to him.

Someday, he hoped, she would tell him everything, would talk to him again as she had when they counted the blue cars that passed and gave silly names to the clouds.

Chapter 12

"I'm trying to remember how they look." Shammai sat in the conference room of Lazar's office, with not much to do other than swivel the leather chair back and forth or stare at the plastic coffee cup as its circle of steam spread across the brightly polished tabletop.

Lazar had been staring at something for fifteen minutes, ever since he'd come in. Counting the time he'd waited in the reception room, it had been half an hour. A good thing he didn't pay by the hour, Shammai thought. He'd still rather be at his own office, even if to make paper airplanes.

"Short and tall. Fat and thin. Bald, full-head of hair." Lazar's answer sounded more like a nursery rhyme than a serious response.

Wth books piled around him, brow furrowed, scratching his ear in concentration, at the moment Lazar fit more than anything the stereotype of an absent-minded professor.

"You're ruining your image," Shammai said. "Not to mention your reputation."

"Sir, it takes considerable effort, preparation and diligence to present the appearance of a respectable barrister to the public," Lazar said immediately, affecting an oratorical tone. "Now kindly show the requisite awe or keep your amusement to yourself - else I shall sue you for defamation of character." As he spoke, one hand held his place while the other guided his eyes down the stack of books. "Furthermore - ah-ha!" He stopped, fingered the books' spines and pulled out a volume halfway through the stack, ignoring those that toppled down. Abandoning the open book, he flipped through several pages of the newly retrieved volume. He found the passage he wanted, and practically threw the book down. "Thus I have a precedent!"

"Care to tell me what it is?" Shammai asked.

"I knew there was a reason they wanted to settle." Lazar slipped back into his state of excitability. "Here, read it for yourself."

Shammai leaned over and looked at the book upside down. "Where?"

"Here," Lazar pointed, and began to read, "Civil Code, Article 1479, Revision Comments: 'Mere advice, or persuasion, or kindness and assistance, should not constitute influence that would destroy the free agency of a donor and substitute someone else's volition for his own.' That, of course, is the basis of our defense."

"That seems pretty clear cut," Shammai said dubiously, leaning back.

"It is," Lazar said. "But what they will argue is here, in Article 1483." He flipped a couple pages and read again. "'However, if, at the time the donation was made or the testament executed, a relationship of confidence existed between the donor and the wrongdoer and the wrongdoer was not then related to the donor by affinity, consanguinity or adoption, the person who challenges the donation need only prove the fraud, duress, or undue influence by a preponderance of the evidence.'"

"Which means?" Shammai said, stifling a sudden urge to laugh at the language.

"Which means, if you're not family, and the deceased trusted you, it's easier to prove undue influence." He refilled his coffee.

"We didn't have any confidential relationship. You know that."

"Ah, but the court doesn't. Anyway, a relationship of confidence isn't the same thing as a confidential relationship. You did have the former - all the special attention you and your family gave to Mr. Enstein. And vice-versa. Elie was his favorite. Why? The evidence here will only be - can only be - testimony of impressions. A word here, a look there becomes significant evidence. With some clever questioning and positioning of witnesses, innocent remarks

168

suddenly become undue influence."

"Oh." Shammai noticed the coffee no longer swirled steam, that its moisture had evaporated from the tabletop. He could drink it now. His shaking hand matched the state of his confidence. "So they're not going to claim it wasn't a gift at all?"

Lazar shook his head. "I don't think so. Proving Mr. Enstein's dying intent was not to alter the will is harder than proving he acted from an impulse generated by undue influence. Given our closed circle, it seems almost too easy to get the 'preponderance of evidence' to point that way." He shook his head again. "I should have figured it out sooner. If not for the offer of settlement, I would have missed it until too late."

"I don't understand." The coffee was too cold.

"It meant they had something," Lazar explained. "An angle to give them something besides all or nothing, but not a guarantee. You see, the issues and possible strategies become, if not obvious, at least easy to figure out pretty early. If nothing else, the depositions give an idea of the possible questions and directions. But which strategy? And how to execute it? Does precedent support it?"

"Fine," Shammai said, pushing the coffee cup from him, irritated. "But how did the settlement offer give away their strategy?"

Lazar shrugged, drained his coffee. "If there's proof there was no gift and never any intention of one, why bother settling? On the other hand, if you don't have anything, you don't offer first. What's left? Something that gives them good chances, but no guarantee. That's what I was researching when you came in." He twisted, leaned over, and flipped the coffee cup into the trash. "Since we were using donation in mortis causa, they had to use -"

"Undue influence," Shammai finished, a bitter edge in his voice. "Should we even bother going?" Shammai asked.

"Oh, definitely," Lazar smiled, taking the volume and sheaf

of papers with him. "It should be fun. Drink your coffee."

"It's too cold. Why?"

"To see what they have to offer. It never hurts to listen." Lazar paused by the coffee machine, then shook his head. "Let me get a copy of this and the rest of your file and we'll go."

Shammai followed Lazar out of the conference room and to the secretary's desk.

"Make me a copy of this," he said. "I'll be out for at least an hour, probably two and maybe all afternoon." He turned back down the hall. "Just a second while I get my jacket," he said to Shammai and sprinted off. He reappeared quickly, the jacket draped in the crook of his arm and a file folder held tightly in his hand. "OK, let's go."

The secretary handed him two copies of the page in question. "Thanks. Listen, when you get a chance, make a fresh pot of coffee. That one's cold."

Shammai was going to protest that it was only his cup that had gotten cold, but decided it wasn't worth it, as Lazar had already reached the door.

"Where are we going?" Shammai asked as he got into the passenger seat of Lazar's car, a sporty Dodge.

"Downtown. One Shell Square. Twenty-third floor."

"Sounds prestigious."

"It is. Fred Findlay's an old New Orleans lawyer, with connections to half the City Council and connections to connections of the other half." He shifted expertly in and out of the mid-day traffic.

"Are we in a hurry?"

"No, but I like to keep the excitement going. It's under thirty-five," he said, referring to the speedometer.

Shammai sat back and relaxed. It was certainly a comfortable car and it took the potholes well.

"I don't have to buy braces for kids," Lazar said, smiling. Suddenly, momentarily, his face darkened.

Rarely did Lazar display awareness of his past, failed intermarriage. At those times, Shammai always felt awkward long after Lazar returned, to all appearances, to the present.

"You know, their lawyer must be another Crescent City Connection," Shammai said, regaining Lazar's attention and diverting his own.

Lazar laughed. "Maybe we should call him that in front of his clients, just to see how he explains being compared to the Mississippi River Bridge. It could be viewed as a novel insult."

"Does he know all the judges, too?" Shammai asked.

"And the juries," Lazar said, only half in jest, coming down onto Poydras, by the Superdome. "Which is one reason we don't want a jury trial."

They'd come to a standstill in mid-day downtown traffic.

"But what about the judges?" Shammai asked, as traffic started moving again.

"Oh, the judges have their prejudices, too."

Shammai laughed nervously. "So much for justice." He sighed. "I hope this doesn't drag on for years."

"The traffic or the trial?"

"Both."

"I hope you'll say the same thing after the trial."

It took almost ten minutes to go the half-dozen or so blocks. Lazar turned left at the protected arrow, then pulled into the parking garage.

As they walked to the elevator, Lazar gave him instructions. "Let me do most of the talking and try to limit your answers to 'yes' and 'no.' And say that only if you have to. We're here to listen. I don't think they expect anything more, either."

The ride to the twenty-third floor was quiet and reasonably

quick, with only eight stops at other floors.

It took them a minute to find the office, the door looking much like that of any other large corporate law office Shammai had seen: heavy wood, lots of names. Findlay's was fourth on the list.

"We could have met someplace else," Shammai said.

"Where? The Deli?"

"Your place."

"I like the chairs here better," Lazar said, opening the door.

The spacious reception area, with its firm carpet of grey and green squares, cushioned chairs, glass-topped coffee tables and a half-dozen different slick magazines neatly in the racks, radiated a refined arrogance. They probably had a special para-legal just to arrange each title chronologically.

Lazar approached the receptionist immediately, his step crisp. "Mr. Balm and Mr. Danielson. We have an appointment with Mr. Findlay for two p.m." He deliberately looked at his watch. "We're five minutes early."

She replied, "I'll let him know you're here."

After a curt nod, Lazar motioned Shammai to sit down. Lazar checked his watch again, then joined him.

Lazar didn't say anything, so Shammai automatically reached for a magazine. Lazar shook his head. "You're too busy for that," Lazar explained. "In this game, appearances are everything. Especially first ones. Our time's as important as Findlay's. More important."

Shammai shrugged and looked around. "Someone's got money."

"Or expects to get it," Lazar said.

At one minute after two, Lazar marched to the receptionist. "Excuse me," he said. She was taking a phone message and held up her hand. "Excuse me," Lazar repeated, ignoring her signal, "the appointment was for two p.m. It's after two. If Mr. Findlay can't make it, he should have notified me." He paused long enough to give her a chance to respond, clearly ready to continue if she didn't.

"I'll buzz him again," she said, putting the caller on hold and watching Lazar.

I hope he's this good at the trial, Shammai thought.

"He'll be right out," she said.

At Lazar's signal, Shammai stood, facing the glass-paneled door to his right.

Fred Findlay opened the door, quickly but deliberately surveyed the room, and at last settled his attention between Lazar and Shammai. The studied mannerisms impressed Shammai as both artificial and effective: one could never be sure of Fred Findlay, but Fred Findlay was always confident and always prepared.

Physically, however, he sloped: a large man, his greying brown curls peaked above a cleanly, balding forehead. His cheeks, just short of enough fat to be jowls, inclined straight to the respectable stomach. Shammai noticed one incongruous feature: the small eyes darted.

"Mr. Balm and Mr. Danielson," he said, looking from one to the other as if not sure of their identities, but clearly extending his hand first to Lazar. "My clients are in our conference room. They're hopeful - but I'm confident - we can reach an accommodation, mutually satisfactory, of course. Can I get you something to drink? Coffee? Soft drink?"

He held the door open for them, indicating the hallway, letting them lead by a step.

The inside of the office was, if anything, more ornate than the outside: the plush carpet patterned in bright grey and deep maroon stripes, the oak doors with engraved names, the walls of paneled wood - all announced success.

"No, thank you," Lazar responded to the offer. "While my client is, of course, quite willing to settle, I remain skeptical."

"As well you should," Findlay said. He paused outside the second right-hand door. "Balm. I don't believe we've met professionally before. What's your first name?"

"We haven't. It's Lazar. What's yours?"

The edge of a smile appeared on Findlay's lips and perhaps around his eyes (between their size and the cheeks, it was hard to tell). After just the right pause, he said, "Frederick," and opened the door to the conference room.

"My clients, Earl and Simon Osterik," Findlay said, introducing the two nephews, "though I believe you've met."

Shammai studied their faces, searching for a resemblance to his memory of them from the cemetery, finding only an imperfect, out-of-focus match. They both had strikingly round faces. The similarities went no farther: Earl, the older, was tall, narrow, with thick, dark eyebrows and nervous hands; Simon, a few inches shorter, was plump, bespectacled and reserved.

The eyes of both looked out from an internal hardness. They seemed uncomfortable with the world.

That, thought Shammai as they all sat down without shaking hands, made it hardest to believe these could be Mr. Enstein's nephews.

Findlay, still standing, began, "Thank you for coming. I --" He stopped himself as Lazar noisily stood up, then coughed and continued speaking as he sat down, eyes fixed on Lazar's mirror-like motions. "-- fully expect this joint gesture of good will to be rewarded on both sides."

"About this offer," Lazar said, drawing the letter from his file folder, glancing at it disdainfully and dropping it on the table.

"Yes," Findlay said, "a generous one, considering the circumstances. You did note the five thousand for the synagogue?"

"It's not there," Lazar said without looking.

Findlay shook his head. "My secretary must have forgotten to put it in. A late addition, at the insistence of my clients. Earl Osterik actually took the initiative on it."

"You can do better," Lazar said, leaning back and folding his arms.

A good thing I know how this will end, Shammai thought, or I'd be nervous. He wiped his palms on his pants.

"I think it a quite generous offer, considering the circumstances," Findlay said, leaning forward, switching smoothly from unctuous to imperious.

"I don't think so," Lazar said, unmoved.

"Understand, the offer is being made for only one reason: it is cheaper for my clients than retaining my services for the length of a trial."

Lazar swiveled in the chair. "Only if they're paying by the hour instead of a contingency fee."

Findlay hesitated for only a second before politely retorting, "Mr. Enstein's nephews have no wish to bankrupt Mr. Danielson, which a judgment including court costs would do. Out of respect for their late uncle's relationship with your client, they have made this offer.""

Lazar leaned forward. "The *siddur's* worth five times the offer."

"It's worth nothing if you don't win."

A good thing they weren't here to negotiate, Shammai thought.

"If you were so confident, that letter," Lazar said, pointing at it disdainfully, "would never have been sent."

Findlay leaned back and steepled his hands. "I'll reserve the case law citations for the judge. If you'd done proper research -- well, a small firm. But you have read the depositions, haven't you? Surely you see how easily a relationship of confidence can become improper. It may have even started unconsciously, who knows." He leaned out of his chair, supporting himself on his knuckles. "But in a courtroom I can destroy your client." Findlay almost snarled. "Before I'm through, he himself will be swearing he's guilty of undue influence."

Simon tugged on Findlay's arm. Findlay looked down and Simon whispered something. "Of course. But I told you it was futile." Another whisper. "No, he won't take more." He turned, speaking directly to Shammai, haughty, but without the sneer Shammai expected. "You won't, will you? Even if Mr. Enstein's nephews offered you full value for the book, you wouldn't take it. I dare say if they offered you more than its worth, you would refuse. Most of us abandon such misplaced, impractical idealism in college. Can you truly take better care of that old book than a museum?"

It doesn't belong in a museum, Shammai thought. It needs to live. It needs to be studied and used. So why did he keep it locked behind glass doors in his house? What was the difference, he suddenly thought, between his bookcase and a museum?

He didn't say anything, though, just looked to Lazar for help.

"He's not a witness, Fred," Lazar said quietly. "And if we were in court, you'd be badgering him."

"Then I would apologize, of course," Findlay said, also in a quieter tone, ignoring Lazar's assumption of familiarity. "But I know the type. And I know the law."

"Well," Lazar said, starting to rise. "I guess that says it all, doesn't it?"

"There's another reason." Earl's words, spoken carelessly, caught everyone's attention. "Will it hurt to tell them?" he asked Findlay with such disregard that, Shammai thought, he'd probably tell them regardless.

Findlay studied the table for a moment. "Probably not. If counsel for the defense is at all competent, he'll find out quickly enough. Or do you know already, Lazar?"

Lazar smiled. "We're still willing to listen to a reasonable offer."

Findlay looked at Earl, who sighed and then explained.

"We have an agreement with a museum," Earl said, his dark eyebrows animated. "A quite profitable one. But we need our late uncle's library intact. Of course the *siddur* is the centerpiece. For reasons of our own, we would like to expedite a decision." He glanced up. "One way or another."

Lazar frowned. "Unusual. Give us a moment to consult." He leaned over to Shammai. "Do you understand?"

"Sure," Shammai said. "They want a speedy trial. So do I."

"No, you don't understand," Lazar said, shaking his head. "They need money, the museum's going to give it to them, but they've got a deadline and they need the *siddur* or the deal falls through."

"So they'll make another one."

"But not so fast, and not for what they need. My guess is without this deal, inheriting from Mr. Enstein does them no good. They need money - lots of it - fast."

"Why can't they sell the rest to the museum. Even if the *siddur's* worth more than the rest combined. . ."

"I don't think the museum's interested. Libraries take old books that still have use. Museums take things "too valuable" or too fragile to use. Only the *siddur* really fits that description. Without it, Mr. Enstein's library becomes a collection for another library."

"With it," Shammai said, "his library becomes fossils for a museum. If we stall, you think they'll drop the case?"

"They might, but Findlay wouldn't. But consider this: right now, the *siddur* is in your possession. I don't think the court's going to order you to turn it over to them in the meantime."

"But it might order it safeguarded somewhere?"

"There is that." Lazar pulled at his ear. "I can get you a lot more, if you want. Maybe even full value, depending how desperate they are and how much they need. The *siddur's* not the whole estate, just the centerpiece."

"But there's also," Shammai said, "my family. Particularly my children. They're under a lot of stress. Dinah Chaya's going to camp in a few weeks, and when she gets back, it'll be to leave for school. Should I leave this hanging over our heads? And Elie." He stopped. "I don't think he's put Mr. Enstein's death behind him yet." Shammai glanced at the expectant faces of his antagonists. What of those, anonymous except for a name and date, on the inside front cover? What had they sacrificed to own it, to pass it on to the next generation? If soldiers give their lives for victory of a worthy cause, what of the *siddur's* previous owners? Were they not soldiers in a different war? How many souls had the *siddur* saved?

And who would write Mr. Enstein's name, note his role in the victory, record how he had learned from the battle by teaching others the *siddur's* message of faith and observance ?

There could be no settlement. All or nothing. Let the court decide who had 'undue influence' over whom. "Lazar, the tension is tearing my family apart. I don't want to wait. Will it make a difference, not just buy time, but change the decision?"

Lazar smiled. "It'll give me more time to become a Fred Findlay lawyer."

"Then there's no question. Get us out of here. I want to go home and look at the *siddur*."

Lazar turned around to face them. "Make us a formal offer."

Findlay smiled, a hint of triumph on his lips. "I would like to propose a joint petition for an expedited trial, based on mutual agreement and the extenuating circumstances of my clients' need to dispose of the property in a timely and appropriate manner, and the availability of witnesses." The last was said with a pointed look at Shammai.

"Agreed, but leave out the last clause," Lazar said.

"As you prefer. We will see you in court, then."

They all stood. "It will be a pleasure," Lazar said.

Findlay waited until they were at the door before responding. "I don't think so."

Interlude 4 - 1917

"*Avigdor, it's crazy! You're crazy!*"

"*I know, Yankel, but - I can't explain it, but - I've got to go back.*"

"*You'll be shot on sight. It's not like you're unknown, one refugee out millions. You're Avigdor Schindler! If the Communists don't kill you for being a Jew, they'll kill you for being rich.*"

"*I'm not rich any more.*"

"*You won't be alive any more if you go back.*"

"*I've got to.*"

"*Why? What makes you think they haven't ransacked the place?*"

"*Yankel, I took all the movables - gold, jewelry - I could. It's the siddur.*"

"*What siddur?*"

"*The one I told you about. They won't find it. I know they won't. I hid it in the attic. There's a special hiding place, impossible to find.*"

"*Assuming your house is still there, you don't think they've torn it apart? Do you think they'd leave Avigdor Schindler's house more than an empty shell?*"

"*Yankel, four years ago I saved that siddur. The thieves' market, the Communists - they're all the same. It's not just lives we have to save, Yankel.*"

"*There are other siddurim.*"

"*Not like this one.*"

"*Avigdor, there are two dozen or so men, women and children here. I can't be expected to wait nearly a week for you to satisfy an obsession.*"

"It's not a week. We're only two days outside Petersburg. I'd be back before Shabbos. But I'm not asking you to wait. Go on. There are hundreds of refugees groups and encampments. I can always find another."

"We won't wait for you. We can't."

"I don't expect you to. If it's meant to be, I'll find you, Yankel."

Yankel had been right about one thing, I thought, fighting my way through another thicket. How did these briars - if that's what they were - manage to grow in such a dense forest? It had been over a week.

I'd made it back to Petersburg by noon the second day. But getting to my house took three days of avoiding the Communists, the looters, the Loyalists and whoever had taken over the next street corner. Fortunately, the upheavals made me less recognizable. I'd been spotted only twice, once by an elderly Jewish man, who gratefully accepted half my provisions for a silence he probably would have given freely. The second time I wasn't so fortunate. I still limped a little, stiff right above the ankle where the bullet cut through. I don't know who shot at me, or who responded, inadvertently saving me.

The house wasn't quite the empty shell Yankel had predicted, but it was pretty close. Some vagabonds were using it for shelter, burning furniture and pieces of wall for heat. If they recognized me, they were too cold and hungry to care. So long as I didn't challenge them or try to share their warmth, they ignored me.

I expected the attic to be ransacked, of course, but not the floorboards. But when I poked my head through, however, I saw beams and flooring in such disarray, I worried it might all collapse. I knew then it was gone; I knew why: I was Avigdor Schindler. Not finding much of value - my stocks and certificates would be worthless and I had taken the few bits of jewelry I kept at home - they tore the house apart looking for secret hiding places.

Carefully measuring each step, I checked, just to make sure. It had been taken, and I felt like part of me had been irrevocably lost. At least I didn't see any pages lying around, so I could hope it had survived intact.

I made my way out quickly. The sudden snowstorm, the season's first, actually helped, since fewer criminals - of whatever name - were roaming the streets. People were more interested in food and shelter.

I didn't expect to find Yankel and the group, but I had no place else to start from. Besides, I thought it a good hiding place.

I had thought wrong. As I broke through the bramble into the clearing, I saw red snow. Raising my head, almost against my will, I surveyed the scene.

Yankel, arm outstretched toward where the attack must have come from, head turned back, no doubt giving orders, lay before me, shredded by bullets.

I could not look at the others. I turned away. The snow would have to bury them.

THE TRIAL

Chapter 13

Shammai unzipped his *tefillin* bag and took out the empty boxes, adjusting his *tallis* before it fell off his shoulders. As he began unwrapping the *shel yad* from his hand, the first whiff of fresh-brewed coffee reached him. He took off the *shel rosh*, encased it and wrapped the straps around the sides. The aroma grew stronger, tempting him to stay, enjoy a bagel or some herring, and join the Sunday morning gossip for a while.

He saw Elie across the room, by the *bima*, talking to his friends as he put away his *tefillin*. This morning, Shammai had made a comittment to his family and he wasn't going to be late.

He zipped the straps off his arm and loosened the *shel yad*. Then he saw Bob Sagalman, still in *tallis*, and Kashdan, in an impeccable suit as usual, approaching. It must be serious. Bob never said or did anything until he'd put his *tallis* and *tefillin* away, and Kashdan usually finished just about last.

By the time they got within talking distance, he'd put his own *tefillin* away and taken off his *tallis*.

Kashdan coughed a couple of times.

"Shammai," Sagalman said.

"Must be serious," Shammai said, folding his *tallis* along the creases. "I'm being visited by an official delegation, Jonathan's got his nervous cough and Bob's got his professional tone."

"We got a letter from the nephews," Sagalman said awkwardly.

"We being?" Shammai asked, slipping the *tallis* inside the bag and zipping it up.

"The shul. We thought you ought to know."

"What are they offering?" Shammai asked coldly.

"It's contingent on a settlement," Kashdan said.

184

"Cough's better," Shammai remarked. "How much?"

"Ten thousand," Sagalman said.

Shammai took a deep breath. Findlay had offered the *shul* five at the conference. It had doubled during the week. He straightened up and looked at them. "They offered me ten." Did Findlay plan on doubling his offer, too?

That didn't seem to affect them.

"I didn't know that," Kashdan said.

Sagalman, with only one quick glance at Kashdan, added, "You're going to take it, of course."

"I'm thinking about it." He picked up his *tallis* and *tefillin*, ready to leave. "What's the *shul* going to do?"

This time, the two officers didn't try to disguise their uneasiness, as they shifted from foot to foot and exchanged glances.

"Well, we --" began Kashdan.

"We, that is, the shul, thinks you should accept the offer."

Shammai drew himself up stiffly. "I asked what the *shul* was going to do. That letter may be legal harassment."

"Oh, no," Kashdan said quickly, "we don't think so. After all, the offer's only valid if you accept their settlement offer."

"Really?" Shammai said, raising his voice. "Let's find out. Lazar, did you know the *shul* got a letter from the nephews?"

That got everyone's attention. Catching Elie's eye, he realized he'd have to be careful what he said.

He waited for Lazar - and just about everyone else - to join them.

"Don't make a scene," Bob hissed.

"I don't intend to," Shammai said. "But I'm not going to be badgered, either. Not here."

"What's up?" Lazar asked.

"Show him the letter," Shammai said, nodding with his head.

In turn, Sagalman nodded at Kashdan, who pulled it out of

his jacket and handed it to Lazar.

"You couldn't keep this private?" Bob asked him.

"Why hide it?" Shammai answered "The whole *shul* knows about the lawsuit, the books, the will and the dying bequest. It's no secret and it affects everyone."

Lazar finished reading the letter and handed it back. Shammai, glancing around, saw Elie scowling.

"Perfectly legal," Lazar said. "Unfortunately. Phrased just right. Of course. It makes no mention of Shammai or even the lawsuit. It simply states that, upon taking possession of their uncle's inheritance, the nephews intend to sell the collection to a museum, that arrangements have been made, that no legacy was left to the shul, which must have been an oversight of their uncle's, but regardless, knowing how much the *shul* meant to him they would give ten thousand as a donation. No harassment there. It sounds very generous. Of course, it's despicable and immoral, but it's perfectly legal." Lazar turned to Shammai. "The museum must be offering more. Findlay told us five thousand to the shul." He shrugged. "A secretary's error, of course. Maybe they'll offer you more, too."

"Thanks," Shammai said, glancing back at Sagalman and Kashdan.

"Anytime," Lazar smiled. "Anything else? If not, there's a cup of coffee, a bagel and some eggs with my name on them."

Shammai shook his head.

Lazar left and, as a silence built up around Shammai, Sagalman and Kashdan, the others also dispersed. Elie, Shammai noted, was one of the first to retreat.

"Well?" Shammai asked.

"I know you'll do what's best for the shul," Kashdan said, pocketing the letter. "And of course what Mr. Enstein wanted," he added as he walked away.

Even though the two may not be the same, Shammai thought.

Sagalman closed the distance between them, put a hand on Shammai's shoulder and smiled. "We've been friends for a long time, not as long as our sons, maybe, but for long enough. I don't talk to you like Lazar, but we know each other. Don't worry about Jonathan, he won't allow that letter to split the shul. Neither will you. The years . . . I know you. You'll do what's best, what's right." He squeezed Shammai's shoulder, winked, and went off to breakfast.

And that, Shammai thought, was his best bedside manner.

#

"Hello?" Shammai said.

"Hello?" Elie said.

Shammai shut the door behind them. "I wonder where they went."

"Hello!" Elie shouted.

"Not so loud. Maybe they're still sleeping."

"It's 9:30. The only one who sleeps that late is Dinah Chaya."

"Well, it looks like we won't get to the zoo early after all."

"We just have to watch the commotion around here when everyone wakes up."

"Elie."

"Sorry," Elie grinned. "Are you really sure you want to do this?" He flipped through the newspaper until he got to the sports section.

"Of course." He hesitated. "Don't you?"

"The zoo's kind of dumb for teenagers," Elie said indifferently, without looking up. He pulled out the sport section and half the paper tumbled to the floor.

Shammai bent down to help him. "Dinah Chaya seemed excited," he said, now doubting the wisdom of this trip.

Elie started to make a comment, then changed his mind. "It might be fun as a family thing," he said softly, then added self-consciously, "She'll be leaving soon."

They stood, each with about half the now disheveled morning paper. "Anyway, I'll have time to enjoy breakfast," Shammai replied matter-of-factly. "If I can find the editorials. And don't take all morning with the sports."

"You want me to wake them up?" Elie asked as he headed for the table.

"No, not yet."

Shammai watched as his son spread out the paper trying to reassemble it. Then he noticed a loose advertising supplement on the floor. He went to pick it up and, straightening, found himself inches from the bookcase.

The *siddur*, isolated in the glass, automatically drew his attention. Once the lawsuit was settled, he'd have to get information on how to preserve it and still use it. Maybe what's-his-name the bookseller - Heuerstein - had contacts.

And yet, what had he done so far? Hadn't he treated it like a museum piece - putting it behind a glass door, not letting anyone touch it?

He looked at the other, still empty, shelves of the new bookcase, then at the other two bookcases flanking it.

Something felt out of place.

"It looks nice," Hannah said quietly. He had felt more than seen her join him.

"I agree," he said, nodding. "But something feels out of place. Maybe I need to rearrange the books. Reorganize them."

"You don't have that many," Hannah said.

"If you start moving books, we'll never get to the zoo," Elie called from the table, as though it made no difference to him, at least. He'd spread out the sports section across half the table.

"Not so loud," Hannah said. "You'll wake your sister."

"So? She doesn't need any beauty rest." He pushed his chair back. "I'm getting something to eat. You want me to put up the water for the coffee?"

"Please," Hannah said. "And I know what's out of place," She added.

"What?"

"The *siddur*. It doesn't belong there all by itself."

"Why not?" he asked, surprised.

"The *siddur* shouldn't be sitting in an empty bookcase," she said. "It shouldn't be alone. A Jewish home should have books in the house. What was that quote in the will? 'Getting a new holy book enhances all the others one already has.' Something like that. But how many others do we have?"

"Maybe we should join a Jewish book club or something," Shammai said thoughtfully. "You're right. I just couldn't figure it out before. But if I really mean to preserve Mr. Enstein's "victory" - Heuerstein the bookseller told me what it took to get it back, I can just imagine the trouble it took to save it - I've got to do more than put the *siddur* on display, like any museum would. I've got to use it. More than that, I've got to start learning. We all do."

"Are we still going to the zoo?" Dinah Chaya interrupted from the doorway, her hair just-got-up wild.

"Absolutely." Shammai said.

She made a face, brushing her hair back. "I'm leaving for camp in two weeks, you know."

She disappeared back into her room.

"I thought she liked the idea. I just wanted -"

Hannah smiled. "Don't you know adolescents always use discretion? That means she's looking forward to it."

"Oh." Shammai took a breath. "Should I wake the boys?"

"They've been in the backyard for half an hour," Hannah

said.

"Oh." He paused. "I'm hungry."

They headed to the kitchen. "By the way, how was minyan?" Hannah asked.

"Remind me to tell you about the conversation I had."

"Not before coffee."

Which meant, he thought, not for a while.

#

"I hope we can find a place to park," Dinah Chaya said, staring intently out the window at the neat, self-made rows of cars parked on the lawn, mimicking their counterparts on the lot.

"Maybe we should have walked," Elie suggested sarcastically.

"I want to see the white tiger first," Aaron cried.

"No, the seals," Moshe protested.

"We'll have time for them all," Hannah assured them.

"Right," Elie said, amused.

"But your father will determine the order," Hannah concluded.

"Not if I can't find a place to park. I think we've been up and down three times."

"Try the other side," Elie suggested.

"Or the grass," Dina Chaya added.

"It's just a guess and *hashgocha protis*," Shammai said, crossing the entrance lane to the other lot.

"How come it's so crowded?" Dina Chaya asked.

"Look how cool it is in the middle of June," Elie said.

Still unable to find a place to park, Shammai suggested, "Maybe we should go to the Aquarium instead."

"Now?" Hannah said. "It's a long drive and won't we still

have problems parking, especially in the Quarter on a summer day like this?"

"Not there," Dinah Chaya protested. "It's boring."

"You stay here, and everyone else will go watch the sharks," Elie said.

"I want to go in," Moshe said.

"Me, too," Aaron added.

Maybe a family outing wasn't such a good idea, Shammai thought. Before he could voice it, Elie shouted.

"I see one!"

"Over there!" Dina Chaya added.

"Shammai, I see it! Hurry." That was Hannah, as excited as the others.

"Calm down," Shammai said, even as he accelerated. "You'd think we just discovered gold or something. He'll be a minute getting out."

He positioned himself behind the space, far enough back to leave the occupant room to back out and be off, but close enough to lay claim to it.

As the other car, a red Ford, started to back out, another car pulled up, almost identical, differing only in shade and year.

Shammai inched up. "Mishael drives a white one of those," he said.

"Be careful," Hannah said. "We didn't come here to have an accident."

"I just want to let him know I was here first."

The first one backed out, almost touching Shammai's bumper. He sat there far longer than it took to shift from reverse to drive.

"He's trying to let the other one in," Elie said.

"Don't let him," Dinah Chaya said, "or we'll never get a parking space."

Shammai honked his horn.

"Shammai," Hannah warned.

"Don't worry. I'm just not going to give up without a fight. Anyway -" he pointed so they could see there wasn't enough room for the second one to sneak in. "He'll have to let me tail him into the spot."

Suddenly, the first one jumped, screeched and sped off, leaving for a moment an empty space. Shammai and the second car started forward at the same time.

Shammai kept his eyes only on the parking space.

"Daddy, he's going to hit us!" Dinah Chaya said.

"Shammai!"

"Relax," Shammai said, as the other driver started honking his horn. "He's not going to hit us. You think he wants to ruin his car, better than ours, as well as get sued?"

Sure enough, seeing he wasn't going to get the space, the fuming driver drove on.

"That was fun," Moshe said as Shammai turned off the engine.

"Exciting," Aaron agreed.

"Well, enough of that kind of excitement," Shammai said, trying to avoid Hannah's visual reprimand. "Let's go see the zoo."

The children, with Elie holding Aaron's hand and Dinah Chaya, Moshe's, walked ahead to the entrance gate.

"I'm sorry about that parking business," Shammai said.

"Sometimes." Hannah shook her head. "Anyway, tell me about the conversation."

"What conversation?" People were hurrying around them, most going in the same direction.

"The one in shul. The one I was supposed to remind you to tell me about." Hannah's voice rose slightly at the end of the sentences, exaggerating them.

"Oh. Well, as I'm taking off my *tefillin*, smelling the coffee and wondering if anyone had prepared something to say, Bob Sagalman and Kasdhan come over to me. Sagalman's still got his *tallis* on."

"Go on."

"They stand there for a second. Then Kashdan says -" and here Shammai faked a couple of coughs.

Hannah laughed. "Come on."

"OK. While he was clearing his throat from clearing his throat, Sagalman says, 'The *shul* got a letter from the nephews offering a donation.'"

"You should have expected that," Hannah said.

Shammai nodded. "Uh-huh. But it was for ten thousand."

"You told me -" Hannah started to say, when Moshe and Aaron came running up.

"Elie and Dinah Chaya say to hurry up," Aaron said.

"There's an elephant show in fifteen minutes," Moshe added.

Shammai looked at Hannah.

"Later," she said.

They picked up the pace, got in line beside Elie, who'd been saving a spot for them and, within minutes - which meant Aaron had only bothered three strangers with questions and Moshe had jumped on and off the bench four times before responding to the warnings - were at the window.

"We might as well become members," Shammai said, more as a question. "It's only a few dollars more."

"Go ahead," Hannah said.

So he filled out the form and wrote the check, and they went inside the zoo.

"If we hurry, we'll make the elephant show," Elie urged.

"Go ahead," Hannah said. "Take your brothers and watch them. We'll catch up."

Dinah Chaya hung back for a moment.

"What were you two talking about?"

Shammai decided to let Hannah handle this. He looked past them to the gift shop.

"Private things," Hannah said after a few steps.

"Mom," Dinah Chaya said in her who-are-you-kidding, don't-be-immature voice. "It wasn't about me, because you would have said so or come up with one of your 'you don't need to know everything,' or 'there are still some things we don't discuss with you' dodge. So it's about Mr. Enstein's will and the *siddur*, isn't it?"

"We do have more topics of conversation than you and that," Hannah laughed.

"Not lately. Not that I hear. It's either about my going away or the lawsuit this and the case that."

They'd reached the entrance to the Asian domain. Shammai, scanning ahead for the boys as he half-listened, had a sudden insight. "There's a connection here, isn't there?" he asked.

The Sun Bears were wrestling with each other.

"You're too smart sometimes," Dinah Chaya said. "Yeah, there is. I just want you to know that this business with Mr. Enstein may ruin my life. It's bad enough I had to -" she stopped, swallowed, tried again, "-had to-" She wiped her eye and took a deep breath. "Anyway, I just want you to know that."

"How so, dear?" Hannah asked. "I know your father is occupied with it a lot, but we both have made sure to spend time with you and buy you what you need and - well, it won't be easy for us, either, when you go away."

"I know, and that's not what I'm talking about. I mean, I don't want to go to camp and have this over my head and be thinking about it when I should be planning for my first year away and what friends I'm going to make and what I'll eat and what the teachers are like and things like that. I mean, what if they want me to testify and I have to come home for weeks just when I'm getting to know people and make some friends?"

"That won't happen," Shammai said firmly. "Like your mother said, it's going to be hard enough for all of us as is. I won't let this case disrupt our family any more, and I certainly won't let it ruin your first year away." He closed his eyes and took a deep breath. "Anyway, I agreed to a speedy trial. Seems they need one."

Dinah Chaya wiped her eyes with her sleeves, mumbled thank you, sniffed and straightened up. "Want me to find the boys?" she asked.

"That would be a good idea," Hannah said.

Just then the leopard, resting on a tree in his cage, recessed from the walkway, roared.

The elephant exhibit was the next one over. The show already in progress, they went to the three-tiered bench in the back and found seats. They located the boys in the crowd that had formed around the posts which bordered the dry moat that separated the visitors from the elephants' 'play area.'

The trainer had one of the elephants balancing on one foot.

"Dinah Chaya's something," Shammai remarked.

"True. Now finish telling me about this morning before we're interrupted again."

"Where was I?"

"Kashdan and Sagalman had just told you that the nephews had offered the *shul* a ten thousand dollar donation."

Shammai thought a moment, watching the elephants run around their 'theater-in-the-round,' nose to tail. "If I accept," he said quietly. "And, though I'm promised it won't split the shul, they're sure I'll do the right thing."

She matched his silence for a moment, then stood. "Typical," she laughed, walking down to greet the children.

It was not the response he had expected. As he also stood, he realized he didn't know what response he had been expecting.

Aaron and Moshe were exuberant, while Elie and Dinah Chaya traded quips. So far, at least the trip seemed to be a success.

"Where to next?" Shammai asked.

"The monkeys!" Three of the four said. Dinah Chaya shrugged her acceptance.

They walked down the path to the old goldfish pond, now covered with algae, and its surrounding broken semi-circle of wrought-iron benches, rusted a dull green from age, wind and humidity. A variety of visitors and natives took turns resting, eating, making plans or just catching their breath: old couples in sneakers, summer outfits and floppy hats, leaning back and sipping drinks; teenagers in outlandish hairstyles and costumes, chewing gum; children in social outfits squirming and munching apples - a human spectrum of summer's exuberance.

"Sometimes the goldfish grow two feet or more," Shammai remarked.

"They'll grow as big as their bowl," Aaron said.

"What happens if you put one in the ocean?" Elie asked, grinning.

"It's hot," Dinah Chaya said. This part of the zoo was not shaded.

"Me, too," Moshe said.

The complaints had started.

"Maybe we should buy some soda?" Hannah suggested.

Shammai shrugged and pointed to the food building, with a soda machine leaning against it. He pulled out his wallet and gave three dollars to Elie and three to Dinah Chaya. "Get one for your mother and me. We'll meet you at the entrance to the monkey exhibit."

The children took off to the right while Shammai and Hannah strolled through the iron gate, entrance to the old zoo before its expansion and renovation, and up the incline to the monkeys.

"It's gotten nasty, hasn't it?" he asked.

Nodding her head, she smiled at him. He forced himself to return the smile.

For half a dozen steps, he didn't say anything. "What do you think I should do?"

"I don't know all the details, but has anything changed?"

He thought about that. "I don't know. What do you want me to do?"

"Does it make a difference? I know what you're going to do." She threw up her hands and rolled her eyes. "Oh, all right, I'll analyze it for you. On the one hand, it seems like we're almost obligated, because of Mr. Enstein's dying request. On the other hand, how much do we owe him? Still, having that *siddur* is a nice thank you - you deserve that much - but then, we could have some money - which we need for the children - without all the trouble." And then --"

"Then what?"

Her voice dropped to a speaking-to-herself whisper. "Then there's the rest of the books."

"Yeah," he agreed. "But they're not mine to worry about, are they?"

She shrugged. "I hate lawsuits."

He nodded. "Me, too. Win or lose, it's trouble, money, aggravation, anger, guilt, and always wondering if you're right."

"Well, we can alway make another last-minute decision. I'm sure their offer will be good until the trial."

Hearing their children's shouts and calls, they turned and watched them run up, sodas in hand.

"That's sure to cool you off," Shammai said.

The remark was ignored as the sodas were handed around and opened.

At the first exhibit - one could hardly call it a cage, so closely did the surroundings match the natural habitat - they watched a lemur, sleeping under some leaves.

"I don't see it," Moshe cried.

"There," said Elie, pointing.

Dinah Chaya took Moshe's head and aimed it.

"I still don't see it."

"Under the leaves," said Aaron.

"Oh." A moment later came, "is that all it's going to do?"

"Well, it is a hot day," Dinah Chaya said in its defense.

"Let's see some others," Elie suggested.

At the next exhibit, they saw seven small, golden-brown monkeys. Two hastily and suspiciously nibbled pieces of apple and banana, one sunned itself, two slept by the water; but, to Aaron and Moshe's delight, two raced through the leaves and branches, swinging, leaping, jabbering and occasionally pushing.

After a few minutes, when the racers took a break under the shade, they moved on.

The black and white colombo monkeys just sat in the trees.

"They're dull, too," Moshe said.

"And they look like skunks," added Aaron.

Just then they heard a huge howl. They all turned around to see a monkey, perched at the top of a large, multi-branched pole, a pouch under its chin expanded like a balloon. As they watched, the monkey opened its mouth and let out another howl and the air-sac deflated.

They moved in for a closer look at the island full of howler monkeys.

"Listen to them," said a familiar voice. "They howl just like a monkey. Some joke, these howler monkeys, eh?"

Shammai looked behind him. "Mr. Levinsky!"

Mr. Levinksy eased his way closer, using his size and age to make a path to Shammai. "Surprised? Why shouldn't an old man like myself enjoy a Sunday afternoon watching the animals and children? It makes me feel young." He reached into a small brown bag he was holding, pulled out a peanut and held it up for the monkeys to see. He waved his hand back and forth, drew it back as if to throw, then popped the peanut, shell and all, into his mouth. "I have to deceive myself with something," he added.

A moment later, another howl came from the monkey island below.

"Don't you think that's kind of cruel?" Shammai asked.

"All they can see is my hand moving. Besides, I give enough to this zoo I should be able to enjoy hearing a monkey make a monkey of itself now and then. I spend all week watching people do it."

Mr. Levinsky glanced over. "Got the whole family. That's nice. I thought your daughter, Dina Chava -"

"Dinah Chaya," she corrected without looking up.

"Dina Chaya," he repeated, with a wink at Shammai, "had already left."

"Two weeks," Shammai said. "Our last family outing for the summer."

Mr. Levinsky nodded. "You want some peanuts? The children? They're kosher."

Shammai shook his head at each question. Mr. Levinksy shrugged and reached into the bag again.

The monkey at the top of the pole let out a howl, answered by one on a branch halfway down.

"See? They want to watch me too."

"Where's your wife?" Hannah asked.

"She doesn't like the zoo. She says the animals smell. I tell her - well," with a glance around, "she has civic work to do on Sunday. Committees, phone calls, she's very important with my money."

"Do you resent that?" Hannah asked.

Mr. Levinsky snorted. "What do you think I have it for? They should sew together all the dollar bills I make and use that for a casket?" He pointed to a monkey swinging by one arm. "That's fun to watch, right? A trick, amusing, clever - something you couldn't do. But for the monkey, it's natural. For me, making money is natural. It's my trick, amusing. But spending it -" he shrugged. "That's someone else's trick. Let those who know how to spend it right make all the noise." He picked another peanut out of the bag, held it up between two fingers, and dropped it into his mouth. "But somebody's got to buy the peanuts first."

For a few moments, the monkeys ignored their audience. The people watched in silence as well.

"You've been to *shul* a lot lately," Elie said.

"Are you keeping score now?" Mr. Levinsky said, arching his eyebrows.

"I just noticed and thought it was nice," Elie said, propping his chin on his hands and looking straight ahead.

The feeling - old, familiar - rushed through Shammai and vanished before he recognized it: the sense of being manipulated for his own good by Mr. Enstein, a bittersweet combination of frustration and triumph he thought he'd buried.

Mr. Levinsky sighed. "I'm old and tired and sensitive about how I'm seen. Don't make us into a stereotype, OK?" He held out the bag of peanuts to Elie. "Hold this. I want to see the orangutans with your father."

That was as much of an apology as Elie was likely to get, Shammai thought, glad when his son, without looking, finally took the bag.

"Your wife's here," Mr. Levinsky said with a nod of his head. "Let her come, too. She'll like the orangutans. The children can join you there."

Shammai exchanged looks with Hannah. They nodded simultaneously, then, accepting the invitation, followed Mr. Levinsky around the curve to the orangutan exhibit.

Mr. Levinsky watched the only active one swing on a rope, then use its hands to "walk" across.

"I like these the best. Orange beards, even the young look like old men. See how it swings? Back and forth, walks a tightrope with its hands." He shook his head. "You know what the difference is? He's got no choice. We make our own tightropes, tie them as high as we want, and walk across only when we want, how we want. Or so we think.

"But we all hold onto ropes - threads, lifelines. Some are stronger than they seem, others weaker. I heard once that before Moshiach, G-d's going to take all our tightropes and shake them. Shake them a lot. Just to see who can hold on. Or who's rope will snap."

He leaned on one arm and angled his head toward Shammai. "Your children, especially the older two - whatever you've told them, they don't need to hear my thoughts. What are you going to do with Enstein's books?"

Although Shammai knew this was coming, it still seemed unexpected. "I've only got one, you know." Levinsky flicked his wrist at that statement. What else should he say, Shammai thought. "Do I have a choice?"

"Of course," Levinsky said. "You could accept the offer. Oh," he said, this time preventing Shammai's protest with a wide-sweeping, very-annoyed wave of his hand, "You think Kashdan can keep quiet about anything? Besides, I got an offer too - a request to testify."

"Are you going to?"

He shrugged. "I don't know. I could make it hard or make it

easy. And who knows which side what I say will help? Of course, you could choose for me."

"Is that your recommendation, too?" Shammai said, annoyed that he'd been dragged away from his children for this.

"No," Levinsky said, his voice dropping. He hefted himself off the rail and looked at the orangutans. "I've debated for weeks whether to say something to you. Friday I get this silly letter - silly to me because I have a business to run. My wife, she knows about wherefores and whereats and maybe this and maybe that. I thought I might just call you tonight and tell you I got one.

"It made me mad, and I don't like it when someone gets me mad. I don't play that way, I don't fight that way. That's not my business. I even thought of making an offer myself - to them to go away, to you to help pay for Lazar. Whatever discount, you need help, and selling the books -" he shook his head. "But that's not my business, either.

"But then, I saw you here, with your children, your wife, and thought, nu, *beshert*, I should say something or at least ask. So I'm asking, are you going to take the offer or try to keep the books?"

"It's just one," Shammai said emphatically.

"We were asking ourselves that," Hannah said. "You knew Mr. Enstein well. What do you think?"

Mr. Levinsky spat, reached in his pocket and pulled out another package of peanuts. Before replying, he took out two peanuts and diligently concentrated on thoroughly chewing each one.

"Nobody knew Mr. Enstein well. He didn't trust anybody and to him everyone and everything served those books. The difference between him and me? For me, business is a game. I win, I lose, but I can always play again, or maybe a different one. And if I win, I make sure as many people as possible think they win too. The same if I lose. Makes it easier. More satisfying, too. But deep down, I know it's a game.

"One day, He'll ask me about *tefillin*, kosher - the Jewish part of life. The moral part, I'm OK, as good as any but a *tzaddik*, I guess, better than most. But the Jewish part - so I'll point to this person and that building and say, there's my *tefillin* and ask that one about my kosher. If I'm lucky I'll be serving meals to the *tzaddikim* in Gan Eden in six months. Until then, this is how I survive. Every day, for seventy-odd years. Nu.

"But Enstein, he's been asked, and not about *tefillin* or kosher - that's in his books, but about people, like you two, your children, like me, like even the nephews, and you know what he's done? He's pointed to his books. That's all he's pointed to since I've known him." Levinsky grew pensive, rolling a peanut between his fingers. "When we met again after - what? five years? - both smuggled to an unnamed beach and assembled, with thirty-four other desperate, fleeing souls, onto a five passenger rowboat that somehow got us to another overcrowded boat. Even then.

"Everyone could bring one bag, personal items, money, some clothes - not much and not heavy. They almost didn't let him on."

"The books?" Shammai said.

Mr. Levinsky nodded. "Even then, the one thing he took with him. The books. And now you think he gave them to you?"

"It's just one."

"Even one. One can be all of them." He examined Shammai. "That one, that *siddur*, it's become your tightrope, your lifeline, hasn't it? Make sure that it's steady. Make sure you hold on."

Shammai closed his eyes. So many images, so many questions, so many doubts.

"So I ask again," Mr. Levinsky said. "Do you think he gave it to you?"

"Yes."

The answer came as he opened his eyes, before they focused.

But voicing it made him sure.

Mr. Levinsky took a fistful of peanuts and began eating them one by one. "Maybe Lazar's that good."

"It sounds like you don't think we should fight to keep the *siddur*."

"No," Mr. Levinsky said slowly, still rolling the peanuts around in his hand. "I think you should. It's very important. You'll lose, of course. But you should fight. Somebody has to care."

"I won't lose," Shammai said.

Levinsky looked at him, then at Hannah, then at him again. "You will," he said, nodding his head. "From what I will say, or be forced to say, I know you will. But the books, they will win. They always do. Who knows?" he shrugged. "Maybe I need one or two myself, to get --"

He held up his hand, curled it into a fist, then opened it, letting the crushed pieces of peanut fall. "I don't like this place after all. It smells like business. Time to increase the donation." He wiped his hand on his pants and walked on, just as the children ran up to them.

Chapter 14

Once inside the Court building, Shammai wiped off rivulets of perspiration, though each pass of the already damp handkerchief seemed to just open a channel for more. Ridiculous - they'd only had to cross Poydras. It had to be nerves as well as the heat. Still, you never knew with a New Orleans summer.

He wiped his brow again, beginning to feel the air conditioning, set too low, like most official buildings. He started shivering from the rapid evaporation. Caught between the extremes, he'd probably come out of this trial with nothing more than a bad summer cold.

He had better things to do on a Friday morning.

He glanced at his family. Hannah and Dinah Chaya looked wilted, with Dinah Chaya's apprehension making her seem even more bedraggled. Elie, his face red and dripping in streaks, maintained his adolescent high-energy defiance - even against nature. Aaron and Moshe, of course - and again - were with a sitter.

Lazar came down the hall to greet them, his briefcase arching up and down as his wrist flicked rhythmically back and forth. "Now, remember," Lazar said, "You know your name, rank and serial number, and that's it. And you're not too sure about your name or serial number."

He looked at Shammai, then the rest of the family, shaking his head. "Do you all need something to drink?"

"A hot cup of coffee," Shammai said. "In my own house."

"Later," Lazar said, leading them to the elevator. Looking at his watch, he added, "We've got a few minutes before we're called in. Best to be there early. Executioners don't like to be kept waiting."

Shammai refrained from responding.

The elevator opened, empty. They were the only ones getting on. It started with a whoosh.

"Are they really going to make me testify?" Dinah Chaya suddenly asked, her voice quivering.

"They took a deposition from you and served you with a subpoena," Lazar answered gently, matter-of-factly.

"But why?" She said, a desperate plea in her voice. Her eyes, wide and wild, darted from her mother to Lazar to her father; her body tensed unconsciously, ready to spring.

What she had endured in, but also confined to, her imagination - the judge, the lawyers, the exposure - and the forced reliving of Mr. Enstein's death - had suddenly and clearly become tangible.

What was he doing to her, Shammai thought. What had he done to her?

"This place is meant to intimidate," Lazar said in the same steady, gentle, matter-of-fact tone. "The big spaces, the solemnity. But all of them - from the lawyers to the judge - are just people. They don't know what you know, haven't seen what you saw. You know the truth. Remember that."

The elevator slowed.

"Will her testimony be necessary?" Hannah asked, fighting to conceal her concern.

"Probably. I could have forced delays and motions and back-and-forth," Lazar reminded them.

"But at some point she would have had to testify," Shammai said.

"Without a settlement, without a compromise, as long as there's a trial, true," Lazar shrugged. "Anyway, it's best to save the maneuvers for when they're needed." He smiled at Dinah Chaya. "You'll be fine. After all, I'll be there, too."

"Yeah, but this guy Findlay can question her and question her and really give her a hard time," Elie said. "I mean, what's to stop him from doing that?"

"The judge. It doesn't look good to have children badgered in your courtroom." Lazar made a face as the elevator stopped, "Besides, judges don't like to have their time wasted. They used to be lawyers. It's their job to waste other people's time."

What a great way to prepare for Shabbos, Shammai thought.

They stepped out into the broad hall. With its high ceiling and tiled walls, it created echoes of echoes.

"I'm glad we got a baby-sitter for the younger two," Hannah whispered to Shammai.

At first, he didn't understand what she meant. Then, hearing the click-clack of shoes and the reflections of voices bouncing back and forth across the walls, her reference became clear. He envisioned Aaron and Moshe running up and down the halls, shouting and chasing each other, and laughed.

"I've gotten most of the preliminary stuff out of the way," Lazar said, dropping his voice slightly, "but there'll be some rigamarole before it starts. Around the corner," Lazar pointed to his right.

The corridor was short, and at the end waited half the shul.

"Quite a turnout," Shammai said, to no one in particular.

Josh Green approached, uncomfortably glancing over his shoulder now and then. "I just want you to know that, um, whatever they make me say, I hope you win. Everyone else feels the same way."

"Thanks," Shammai said, shaking his hand.

Lazar put a hand on Josh's shoulder. "Do me a favor. Tell those who aren't testifying to spread out, or those who do testify, if they want to stay afterwards, not to sit bunched up together in the courtroom. It'll create a bad impression if it looks like all the witnesses are in collusion against the plaintiff."

"Um, most of us are here to testify," he said. "But I'll tell the few who aren't."

As they entered the courtroom, Shammai nodded to his friends. I just hope they're still friends when we leave, he thought.

Inside the courtroom, Shammai instantly realized what Lazar had meant about intimidation: the large spaces and high ceiling, the judge's bench - raised, long, deep, solid, of ornamental dark wood - even its high-backed, red-stained leather swivel chair, all emphasized a judicial indifference to any insignificant litigant.

The position and size of the witness stand reinforced the impression: to the left of the judge's bench, small, lower, like an appendage. The court functionaries a few feet in front of the judge's bench - the court stenographer, the judge's clerk, and the bailiff - were already busy with papers and conversation at the ground level, smaller table.

The seats for observers behind the railing - at a glance, Shammai estimated twenty-five on each side of the aisle - had few occupants: Maybe half a dozen members of the community and curiosity seekers. In the far left corner, observing Findlay and the nephews, sat two men and a woman, all immaculately dressed. The woman, attention probably drawn by his, saw Shammai and whispered to one of the men. All three examined him quickly, then turned away. From the museum, he thought.

As Shammai and Lazar walked up the aisle, a young man, hair slicked back, pencil and notepad swinging carelessly, detached himself from the group of functionaries and headed toward a seat near the jury box to the right. Where had he seen him before? Oh, yes, a reporter. Just how important was his story? He shrugged. It probably depended on the outcome.

Findlay and the Osteriks, already seated, were conferring when Findlay, noticing them, gave Lazar a short nod. Simon looked away, but Earl smirked at Shammai.

The aisle ended at a waist-high swivel door, separating the spectators from the participants.

"Just you and me beyond here," Lazar said, opening it as the clerk approached. He pointed to the seats immediately behind the railing. "You all can sit there," he added to Hannah, Dinah Chaya and Elie.

Shammai sat down on Lazar's right, closest to the jury box. Right now, that reporter felt uncomfortably close. Shammai took out a pocket *tehillim*.

"Good idea," Lazar said, putting down his briefcase and snapping it open. "Don't put it away, I may get a chance to say some myself."

Lazar pulled out some papers and a legal pad, exchanging greetings with the clerk as he did so.

"How's Judge Sifer feeling today?"

"How does he always feel before a trial?" the clerk responded.

"Irritable."

"Well, that's how he's feeling."

"Which means he's in a good mood," Lazar said. "What have you got for me?"

"He wants me to talk to you and Findlay."

"One last try at a settlement, huh?" Lazar smiled. "I'm willing. Anything to speed the wheels of justice." He turned to Shammai. "Excuse me a minute. My opponent and I are going to see if we can't simultaneously save ourselves time, still make lots of money and swindle our clients. I'll be back soon." The words, Lazar's usual bravado, jarred against his grimness of tone.

With manila folder in hand, Lazar followed the clerk toward the judge's bench. Halfway, Findlay joined them. He paused, apparently poised to offer his hand to Lazar, then, changing his mind, shifting his file to that hand as they continued to the front, then huddled together.

Shammai, after reading a few verses, looked up and watched, then went back to saying *tehillim*, repeating the process throughout the conference. He saw a lot of gesticulating - waving of hands, fists on tables, arms crossed, tossing of heads, turning of backs - all seemingly pre-choreographed, like a ritual dance. Occasionally he would hear a voice, but none of the words reached him distinctly.

He felt a tap on his shoulder and turned around. Elie pointed at Hannah.

"What's going on?" she whispered.

"They're conferring. Trying to work out a compromise."

"Lazar won't do anything without your approval, will he?"

"Not if he wants to keep his job. Or stay my friend."

"Do you think they'll work something out?" Dinah Chaya asked hopefully.

"Honestly? No." Shammai shook his head. "I'm afraid you're going to have to testify. Don't worry, I don't think they'll want you to say anything more than what happened. And Lazar said --"

"Daddy, I --"

"It's fine," he reassured her. He handed her the *tehillim* and turned around, not wanting to catch her nervousness.

Lazar came back.

"Well?"

"Their final offer: twenty-five thousand. On the way back, he whispered he could get another five for the shul. Off the record, of course. Between 'colleagues.'"

"I can't speak for the shul."

"I told him that. I also told him the *shul* can't speak for you, but that he had called the president and vice-president to testify and they're waiting outside."

"What did he say to that?"

"He huffed and he puffed."

Shammai pushed his glasses up and rubbed his eyes with a thumb and forefinger. Not good, he thought. "Why'd they up the offers?" he asked, already tired.

"Honestly?" Lazar said, leaning back. "Because they knew you wouldn't accept."

Shammai took a deep breath and sat up. "They knew right."

Lazar caught the clerk's eye and shook his head. The clerk frowned and disappeared behind the judge's door.

"By the way," Lazar said drily, opening the folder and pulling out the top sheet. "Here's a copy of the agreement between them and the museum, spelling out terms of transfer, etc. The museum's agreed to pay them, based on a preliminary assessment, a minimum of a hundred-fifty thousand and as much as a quarter of a million, provided the library is intact, including the *siddur*."

"Oh."

Into the silence - a tomb-like waiting-for-the-judge stillness - Lazar asked, "Would you like to know what I offered them on your behalf?"

"Sure."

"They give up all claim to the library - the whole library - except for visiting rights."

Shammai nearly jumped out of his chair. "What?"

Lazar closed the folder and dropped it on the table, next to his briefcase. "They had the same reaction. Then I offered them the opportunity for arbitration. They would select an arbiter, you would select an arbiter, and those two would select a third."

"A *Beis Din*?"

Lazar nodded.

Shammai almost laughed. "I should be angry at you, though," he said. "I didn't authorize that. What if they had accepted?"

"You'd be better off, of course. But they wouldn't. I knew that. Not with Findlay." He smiled tightly. "So, it looks like we go to trial."

The edge in Lazar's voice disturbed Shammai.

"Do you think we'll win?" Shammai asked, feeling it a foolish question, but also feeling compelled to ask.

"Only if we're supposed to. Judge Sifer won't be pleased, but," he shrugged, "as we weren't called into his chambers for a long harangue, he hasn't made up his mind from the depositions and pre-trial motions."

"He could have decided in our favor," Shammai said.

"If he had, he would have ruled positively on my motion to dismiss, filed last week after all the preliminaries were delivered to him."

"Does that mean he thinks they're right?"

Lazar thought a moment. "I don't think so, because he also didn't issue a summary judgment for them and, further, denied their request to have the *siddur* placed in protective custody. That may be the only point in our favor. I'll try to use it as a possession-is-nine-tenths argument. Anyway," he shrugged again, "enough of trying to guess what's going on in the judge's mind. He's as likely thinking about fishing this weekend or his dinner as he is the case."

"Yeah, a great way to prepare for Shabbos," Shammai said.

Just then, the bailiff banged on the table. "All rise."

Everyone stood up as Judge Sifer, overwhelmed by his robes, walked in and climbed to his seat. Shammai had a moment to study him. The judge was a short, wiry, balding man, with thick eyebrows, a moustache hiding his upper lip, so that his lower lip, appearing as a perpetual pout, gave him a look of constant discomfort or displeasure.

"Be seated," the bailiff said.

How is it, Shammai thought, that I'm here, fighting for someone else's heritage? Because, the answer came, I, too, have dedicated myself to the *siddur*. It's my heritage, too.

Findlay stood. "Your honor," he began.

"Counselor," Judge Sifer interrupted, leaning forward and practically putting his chin in his hands, "court has not been called in session. Your exuberance will have to wait."

"Your honor," Findlay continued, "I would like to point out an impropriety of the defense."

The eyebrows and moustache went down. "Oh?"

"One of plaintiff's witnesses is in the courtroom, seated with the defendant's family."

"That's because she's a member of the family," Lazar said laconically, without rising.

"Nevertheless," Findlay continued, "Witnesses --"

"Thank you, Mr. Findlay," Judge Sifer said, "I know witnesses are not allowed in the court before their testimony is concluded. Mr. Balm, it is bad form to have a witness that hostile."

"Your honor," Lazar said, standing, "The witness is the defendant's daughter. She was quite traumatized by --"

"I'm not interested in arguments at this time," Judge Sifer said peevishly. "I'd like to get the trial started with a semblance of normalcy. Please ask the young lady to leave the courtroom until she is called."

There would be no protest to that order.

Lazar and Shammai turned around.

"Actually, I'm kind of glad," Dinah Chaya said, with a nervous giggle. "It'll be easier. I'll be OK outside. No, mom, you stay here. Dad needs you."

Elie got up. "I'll go with her," he said. "I'll get her a coke or something and make sure she's all right. I'll keep everyone posted, inside and out, like a messenger."

Dinah Chaya made her way quickly, though a bit shakily, out the door, followed by Elie.

"Now, then," Judge Sifer said. "Bailiff, call the court to order.

And then, Mr. Findlay, you may begin with your presentation."

The bailiff called the court to order and then launched into a reading of the official version of the case.

Findlay stood, fingers pressed lightly on the tabletop. For a long moment, he didn't speak, but simply stared at his fingertips."Your honor," he said, "This case is simple. My clients, Earl and Simon Osterik are the nephews and sole heirs of Mordechai Enstein, and as such are entitled by right of law to all his possessions not excluded in his will. There were no exclusions. If necessary, we will prove that the defendant's illegal possession of the most valuable single item of Mr. Enstein's property was obtained under false pretensions and through undue influence. Specifically, we will show that he used his children, particularly his oldest son, to deceive and mislead a lonely, fearful old man. Mr. Enstein had dedicated his life to, was obsessed by, his books and would never, without undue influence, have given up what he had sacrificed so much to obtain." He paused, glanced at Lazar, then finished. "However, I petition the court for an immediate judgment in favor of my clients."

In response, Judge Sifer, who had been watching Findlay with his chin-on-hands-on-table gaze, dismissed the petition by lowering his eyebrows and moustache a notch and shifting his eyes to Lazar.

Lazar stood. "As your honor knows, the dispute is over possession of one book, a prayer book of some value. Mr. Enstein gave it to my client as a dying bequest. I will show that my client had no knowledge of Mr. Enstein's will or the value of his property, and that his motive was simply concern for an elderly neighbor, who was his children's teacher, in accord with Jewish law. We will show that Mr. Enstein had full awareness when gifting the prayer book and did so of his own free will. The *siddur* was a donation mortis causa." Lazar stepped to the side of the table. "Further the claim of undue influence can only apply if it can be shown that Mr. Enstein was induced or influenced, against his inclinations, nature or interest, to bequeath the *siddur* to my client.

"We will show, however, that Mr. Enstein's life as a teacher and an individual dedicated to Jewish learning shows the opposite, namely that his natural inclination would be to leave such a gift. For, as his will states, books have souls. It is these souls, that testify to the faith and self-sacrifice of the Jewish people, that Mr. Enstein redeemed. He freed them. Would he want to imprison them, confine them to the sterility of a museum? To Mr. Enstein, books must live and they can do so only when used, when studied, when touched and held and respected.

"Finally, I ask the court to bear in mind that the prayer book has remained, with the court's consent, in my client's possession since the time of death and that plaintiff has refused to submit to arbitration by a panel of rabbis, familiar with Jewish law - to which Mr. Enstein adhered - on this matter. My client is willing to do so, even now."

Judge Sifer leaned back, his hands disappearing from view. "Call your first witness," he directed Findlay.

"I call Nehemiah Heuerstein."

Heuerstein proceeded, slowly, with tedious steps, - a pace of arthritis or irritation - past the railing to the witness stand.

After being sworn in, Mr. Heuerstein folded his hands in his lap, his glasses dangling from their chain, as if debating who to scold.

Findlay stood up. "Mr. Heuerstein, what is your profession?"

Findlay's peak of grey and brown curls shook slightly as he questioned, waving like the plume of an exotic, aged bird. A bird of prey.

"I am a bookseller."

"Could you describe the types of books you deal with?"

"Used books."

"Are they particularly valuable?"

"Some of them."

"How valuable?" Findlay asked.

"Depending on the condition, of course, I have a few items worth twenty-five, even fifty dollars. I have had volumes worth a couple hundred at various times. But that is unusual. The used book business usually caters to the curious, the trader and occasionally to the connoisseur. Rarely to the collector."

"Thank you for those details," Findlay said, taking a few steps forward. "Have you ever owned a book worth thousands of dollars?"

"Oh, no. I might have retired, then," Heuerstein said with a short laugh.

"Or a thousand or five hundred?"

Heuerstein shook his head. "No. I've never had anything that rare or valuable in my possession."

Findlay paused, considering something, his cheeks bulging with each breath.

"Tell me," Findlay said suddenly, "do you do anything besides sell used books?"

"Well, I serve as a broker or locating service, if you will. If a customer wants a particular book or edition, for a fee I will find it and arrange purchase and delivery. I have developed some contacts and established a good reputation in that regard," Heuerstein said with some pride. Findlay raised a hand, prefatory to speaking, but Heuerstein interrupted him by adding, "and I also have been asked to serve as evaluator in several estate transfers. My assessment has always been accepted as definitive."

"But surely as a locating service or expert analyst, you've encountered books worth hundreds, even thousands."

"Oh, certainly."

"Did you know Mr. Enstein?" Findlay took a pen from his

pocket.

"Yes."

"How?"

"I located books for him."

Findlay began tapping the pen in the palm of his hand. "How long did you act as Mr. Enstein's agent?"

Shammai leaned over. "What's he driving at?"

"I don't know," Lazar whispered, "but I'm going to find out."

Lazar stood. "Objection. At issue is the deceased's donation mortis causa. Mr. Enstein's business relationship with the witness is irrelevant to whether or not my client had undue influence on him."

"Ah," Findlay said, as if pointing out a flaw in a clever student's reasoning. "But there can only be a donation mortis causa if there is no undue influence. To show that there was, I am establishing Mr. Enstein's attitude toward his books prior to the defendant's intrusions."

Judge Sifer leaned back. "Overruled. However, Mr. Findlay, the point of this excursion should become clear sooner rather than later."

"Of course, your honor." He turned his smile on Heuerstein. "Now, then, Mr. Heuerstein, how long did you act as Mr. Enstein's agent?"

"Nineteen, almost twenty years."

"But, Mr. Enstein's only lived here -" the pen tapped faster -"fifteen years."

"That sounds about right."

"I had hoped so," Findlay smiled, "and as my colleague has not objected, I know so. Now then, do you know where Mr. Enstein lived before moving here?"

Lazar fidgeted. "If I object," he explained to Shammai, "it'll be overruled on the same grounds. But I'm uncomfortable."

"Why? This doesn't seem to be going anywhere," Shammai

said.

"I know, but it has to be. That's what worries me."

Heuerstein frowned. "I'm not sure. Somewhere near New York City, I think."

"Really?" Findlay said, tapping pen-on-palm like a metronome. "Do you know how many booksellers and bookdealers there are in New York City?"

"I have no idea."

"At least hundreds, I would guess. Does that sound fair?"

"More than here, anyway."

"Yes. More than here." A pause. "And yet, Mr. Enstein sought you out. Was your reputation that good nineteen, twenty years ago?"

"I can't say it was, though I'd like to," Heuerstein admitted with a smile.

"Mr. Heuerstein," Findlay said slowly, "are you Jewish?"

"Objection!" Lazar stood instantly.

"Your honor," Findlay said with exaggerated patience, "the question is important to establish Mr. Enstein's attitude toward his possessions, to show that the defendant could have obtained the most valuable item only through undue influence."

"It seems an odd question, nevertheless," Sifer said. "Still, I will overrule."

"Mr. Heuerstein," Findlay repeated, "Are you Jewish?"

"No."

"But your name?" Findlay feigned surprise. "Your names, actually."

"My paternal grandfather was. I'm named for him."

"A product of an intermarriage, yet the very observant Mr. Enstein did business with you."

"I didn't discuss my personal history with him," Heuerstein retorted.

"But he did ask if you were Jewish?"

"Yes."

"So he knew that much of your personal history?"

"Yes."

Findlay paused long enough for the pen to begin tapping his palm again. This time the crest of hair followed the beat. "Do you read Hebrew?"

"No."

"Then how did you know what Mr. Enstein wanted?"

"I can read the Hebrew alphabet enough to match words in a title request to those on the spine of the book."

"So, Mr. Enstein chose to do business - important business with some valuable merchandise - with someone far away - he in New York, you in New Orleans; he dealt with someone almost illiterate in the language critical to identifying the book; he relied on someone who, by comparison of lifestyles and life histories, he would naturally dislike, even distrust." The pen moved quite rapidly. "Why?"

There was a long pause before Heuerstein said. "He wanted it all private."

"He chose you because he wanted confidentiality?"

"Of course."

"Are you that good?" Findlay asked. "Were you?"

"I was," Heuerstein said, with some irony, "quite obscure. I am now merely unknown."

"Then why did he move to New Orleans?"

"I don't know."

Findlay stopped tapping the pen in his palm. "Is it common to display objects of value openly?"

Heuerstein fiddled with the chain of his glasses. "I don't follow you."

"I'm trying to determine why Mr. Enstein would require

secrecy prior to the purchase of his books, but keep them out in public afterwards."

"Oh," Heuerstein smiled tightly. "What's the fun of collecting if you can't have and see and touch your collection? The special joy for a collector, any collector, be it of stamps or coins or whatever, is knowing that the collection is yours and nobody else can have it. They can't even see it without your permission. Besides, nobody here would know exactly what he had or their value."

"I see. So the fact that others knew it existed would reinforce a collector's sense of ownership?"

"Yes."

"That sense of ownership is very important?"

"Yes."

"As is the completeness of the collection?"

"Yes."

"And a collector, an obsessed aficionado, would be driven to preserve the completeness of the collection and to maintain ownership? I ask you as an expert on the habits and methods of hobbyists."

Heuerstein fingered the chain again. "I would say so. Of course, there's also the urge to let at least someone know what you have. It's nice to have the appreciation or envy of another."

"I'm sure it is," Findlay said. "Would it be easy to tell the value of Mr. Enstein's library? Could a casual, infrequent visitor appreciate what he saw?"

"I wouldn't think so," Heuerstein said with a slight frown. "One would recognize a collection of old books immediately, of course. But you'd have to be in the house quite often and be told, or be quite observant and inquisitive, to know that Mr. Enstein accumulated rare and valuable book. Or figure out how rare and valuable. I'd say it would definitely have to be more than a casual, once in a while visit."

"Something like once or twice a week for a chat, or for a tutoring lesson for one's child?" Findlay said.

"Objection!"

"Sustained."

"That's all right," Findlay said, tapping pen-in-palm. "Let us assume a regular visitor has realized that the collection - books, in this case - is in fact old, rare and valuable. Is there any way for a non-expert to tell which volumes are most rare or most valuable?"

"Oh, certainly," Heuerstein said confidently. "Of course, it would be more like an educated guess, not always right. But there are many ways. The collector could simply point out the best parts of the collection. Or by observing how he treats the collection - which ones are taken out the least or with most caution, that kind of thing - one can tell. Also, most collectors have a natural way of ordering. Discover their system and you know the hierarchy."

"So the average person, with a pre-meditated interest, ready access and what we used to call a 'neighborly reception' could arrive at an approximate catalog?"

"Quite easily, I would think."

"I would think so, too," Findlay said. "Now, can you tell me anything about the book in dispute?"

"The prayer book? It's the most valuable, of course. And one of the last ones I got for him."

"So a frequent visitor would surely notice its addition?"

"Well, he'd have to be pretty familiar with the language and the library. He'd probably still have to be a frequent visitor. But, yes."

"Why was it the last one - or one of the last ones - you procured?"

"Precisely because it is the most valuable, obtaining it was subject to the most difficulties."

"Mr. Heuerstein, in your expert opinion, if a person - a

collector - an obsessed collector - went to great length to keep his transactions secret, used the Purloined-Letter technique of hiding an object in the open, and then, after twenty years finally obtained the most valuable item in the collection, would such a person part with it? Even on his deathbed?"

"If we're talking about breaking up a collection, absolutely not."

"Generosity, then, is not one of the characteristics of a person obsessed with collecting. At least, generosity with the items in the collection, especially the prized possession."

"No, if you want to put it that way. Generally, as I said, one shows off or hoards a collection. It's not broken up. Museums and libraries rely on that."

Findlay smiled at Lazar. "One last thing. Did you ever see the prayer book after you gave it to Mr. Enstein."

"Yes. The defendant brought it in and asked me to assess its value. Of course, I knew it instantly."

"And what was your reaction?"

"I was suspicious, of course."

"But you told him what it was worth."

"I had no reason to refuse."

"Mr. Enstein having died, of course."

"No, actually, Mr. Enstein was still alive then. I accused him of wanting to sell it, but he said he wanted to keep it safe for when Mr. Enstein recovered."

"And for that he had to know its price?" Findlay asked, incredulous.

"Well," Heuerstein stammered before finishing, "I didn't really believe him at the time."

"Thank you," Findlay said. He turned his crest and jowls on Lazar. "Cross-examine?"

Lazar stood. For a moment he tapped the table. "Mr.

Heuerstein, you have given quite a description of the habits of the typical collector. What are the reasons a person takes up such acquisitive habits? As an expert witness for the plaintiff."

"Well," Heuerstein said slowly, "There can be many reasons. Need for a diversion. Desire for attention. Those kinds of things."

"You dealt with Mr. Enstein for some time. What was his reason for being a collector of books?"

Heuerstein smiled. "Something in his past, I'd say. He didn't do it for a diversion or for attention. He did it because, well, I suppose because he had to."

"Like paying a debt?"

"Not exactly, but I suppose it's a useful way of putting it."

"So, was he collecting books, building a personal library to show off, or saving items of value because of an obligation?"

"Oh, I'd say, if forced to choose, definitely the latter."

"Is such a person a hobbyist, a collector?" Lazar asked, surprised.

"No, not really."

"So the completeness of the collection wouldn't be as important as to a true collector?"

Heuerstein made a face. "Probably not."

"In fact, a proper disposition of the individual items might be more important than preserving the completeness."

"It very well might," Heuerstein admitted.

Lazar rubbed a thumb over his eyebrow. "About this business of the assessment of the prayer book. You said you didn't believe my client? What didn't you believe? That he'd come by the book honestly?"

"Oh, no. I didn't think he stole it."

"That Mr. Enstein was still alive?"

"I accepted his word for that."

"That he wanted to keep it safe for Mr. Enstein when he

recovered?"

"Well, yes, I was skeptical of that."

"Why? Do you know my client well?"

"He buys from me occasionally."

"But you don't know him well?" Lazar asked.

"No."

"Then on what was your disbelief based?"

Heuerstein shrugged. "Nothing really. It was just unusual."

"Unusual? Really? You've agreed Mr. Enstein's interest was more preservation and disposition than collection. If someone gave you a valuable gift - or an item to safeguard - wouldn't you want to know how much it was worth?"

"Well, if you put it that way, of course."

"Of course," Lazar smiled. "I guess that's all. No, wait," Lazar said as Mr. Heuerstein started to rise. "I forgot there was one more question. When did you say you obtained the *siddur* for Mr. Enstein?"

"I don't know that I had."

"Well, would you mind telling us?" Lazar said. "Approximately."

"I had been working on retrieving it for some time, of course."

"Of course," Lazar said, echoing him again. "But when were you successful?"

The chain slipped from his fingers. "It would have been about fourteen or fifteen years ago."

"Thank you, Mr. Heuerstein," Lazar said. "Your honor, I have no further questions for the witness."

Mr. Heuerstein's exit was even shakier than his entrance.

Like mine might be, Shammai thought.

224

Chapter 15

"Mr. Stan Levinsky, please take the stand," the bailiff called.

Levinsky barreled his way to the witness stand.

Shammai turned to Lazar and whispered, "Why him?"

Lazar ran a thumbnail over his left eyebrow. "He's a direct link between Enstein's past and you." He glanced toward the stand, where Levinsky was being sworn in. "He's the connection that leads to undue influence."

"What do we do?"

Lazar faced front, picked up a green-ink pen - he had three before him, different colors - and poised himself to write. "We wait. And listen. It's not our turn."

Findlay approached the witness stand with slow, measured steps, waiting until he was on top of it before speaking. "Mr. Levinsky, how long did you know Mr. Enstein?"

"Hmf," Mr. Levinsky snorted. "How long have I been alive? How long did I go to school? How long have I been in this country?"

"Just - answer the question, please. Without another question."

Levinsky scrutinized the judge, Findlay, Lazar and Shammai before answering. "Off and on, between sixty-five and seventy years. Better than that," he shrugged. "Do you need?"

"It will have to do - won't it?" Findlay said with a smile of resignation. "You said off and on. Can you be more specific?"

"How much off and how much on?"

Judge Sifer, through his smile, gave him a warning. "Mr. Levinsky, the court will tolerate only so much diversion; after that, the distraction becomes contempt."

Levinsky shrugged and looked at Findlay. "It depends on which off and which on you want. Many years, we're in the same town, but don't talk. Like here. Still, we know too much about each other's goings and comings." He shook his head. "Far too much."

"Can you give us some highlights?"

Mr. Levinsky looked at the judge. "He wants an autobiography from day one? Should I be like a novel, 'I was born?'"

Judge Sifer assumed his head-in-chin position, stared at Mr. Levinsky, then turned to Findlay.

"Although I'm sure Mr. Levinsky and the deceased, together or separately, have an interesting history, please specify which highlights - and make them relevant to the case before your colleague objects."

Lazar leaned over and whispered, "I hope Levinsky didn't just use up all of Sifer's small measure of good will."

"How do you mean?" Shammai asked.

"Sifer has a good sense of humor, but little tolerance for delays, theatrics or nonsense. And he's an expert on the difference - at least in his court."

Findlay leaned over the witness stand. "What we are interested in, Mr. Levinsky, is how Mr. Enstein could afford to purchase so many rare and valuable books. Not only their price, but his method, indicate a costly venture. We are also interested in knowing what he intended to do with them."

"Objection," Lazar said, wearily getting to his feet. "Witness is being asked to speculate and provide hearsay. Also, how the books were obtained is irrelevant to their disposition, unless counsel is claiming some illegality or improper title - in which case his clients certainly have no claim."

"Your honor," Findlay said unctuously, "I am trying to establish a context. Through my first two witnesses, Mr. Heuerstein and now Mr. Levinsky, I will show that Mr. Enstein would not have given away so valuable a book, even in mortis causa, except for undue influence."

The court grew silent enough to hear the clock tick as Judge Sifer thought. Finally, he sat up and said, "Overruled."

"I would like to establish your credentials, that is, to demonstrate in what way you are qualified to speak about Mr. Enstein's source of income."

Mr. Levinsky nodded his head. "Nu?"

"Briefly -if you can - what were your encounters with Mr. Enstein before coming to this country?"

Levinsky shifted his weight and leaned on his right elbow, taking in Sifer and Findlay in a glance. "My village - but how can I call it that? Five, sometimes six, families in hovels around a central square, because in its center the well, the water." He shrugged. "The ground was hard, even when not cold, but the grass could be grazed and we had a different warmth than a short summer sun." He sighed. "Difficult, complex, ease, simplicity - who can say? It seemed a robust -" He smiled up at the judge - "a good word, right? With my accent, who would think?" He looked to the back of the courtroom, at a point just beyond the closed door. "But of course, I enjoy the now more than I could have had I stayed in the then - if the then could have survived."

Sifer and Findlay began to fidget and Levinsky switched to a matter-of-fact recitation, his unfocused stare still toward a point outside the courtroom. Knowing Levinsky, Shammai thought some of the mannerisms had to be deliberate. How much, he wasn't sure.

"We had no teacher; but a village, a real village with stores and offices and activity and lots of people, maybe a hundred or more - such a place was close enough, only an hour or two walk. And so, three times a week we went to - not really school, lessons, you'd call them - with other children while parents did business."

He stopped, his thoughts elsewhere.

"And that teacher was Mr. Enstein?" Findlay prompted.

Levinsky nodded. "Nu." He shook himself. "He was my

teacher for only two years. Somehow I got a visa. I was forced to leave," he smiled grimly, "someone had given my name as an agitator, a public speaker. So, at fourteen, I was given a ticket from one exile to another."

"And Mr. Enstein?" came the immediate prompt.

"He wasn't connected with me."

"I meant, did you lose contact with Mr. Enstein?"

"In that world, you stayed in touch with any one you could, whenever you could. You didn't dare not to."

Obviously searching for a way to phrase his question, Findlay paced across the courtroom, his crest of hair bobbing up and down. "You said Mr. Enstein was your teacher for two years, from when you were approximately twelve to fourteen. How was he paid?"

"He was paid in eggs and cakes, which he transformed into books."

"Books?" Findlay asked, stopping.

"Money was scarce, but food - scarcer." Another shrug. "But learning was the hardest to get. We paid for everything that way - medical care, too."

"And how do you know Mr. Enstein transformed his 'eggs and cakes' into books?"

"Everyone knew. Enstein, he was thin then and always growing thinner. We'd bring him eggs and cake on a Monday and when we came back on Thursday, he'd have gained a new book and lost a few pounds."

Lazar picked up his red pen and scribbled something.

"What was Mr. Enstein like? Did he enjoy teaching? Did he pay attention to his duties?"

Lazar half-stood, but decided to let the question go.

Levinsky folded his hands over his stomach. "Mr. Enstein was a good teacher. But his real love was books. He gathered them, like Divine sparks, from places of filth and unholiness. He had a one-room apartment. That's where he'd tutor, in that room. I remember books. All over the place. On the stove, on the radiator in the summer, surrounding the bed. Once I even saw a grammar book in what passed as an ice box. Books." Levinsky looked up. "On all subjects."

Findlay nodded sympathetically, making his jowls wiggle. "Did you ever borrow one of his books?"

"For what?"

"Did you ask - did anyone ever ask?"

Levinsky stole a glance at Shammai. "We knew not to, so it wasn't done."

"Now, after you were deported - 'forced to leave,' were your words - what contacts did you have with Mr. Enstein before the two of you met again here?"

Levinsky drew a deep breath and sighed. "Our contacts? One time, a year, two, maybe even three after I left, a letter finds me. This is before the war and I am - well, never mind. How he knew where- but he did manage to hide and recover all those books - his excuse-for-everything books. I could have used his talents, then. The letter, it seemed friendly enough; but from someone who turns eggs and cake into books, I should have seen a trap."

"What was in the letter?" Findlay asked.

"Oh, chatter about this and that, here and there." Levinsky waved his hand about. "The village. News that wasn't news to me."

"You said something about a trap?"

"Yes, the last page. I think Mr. Enstein liked last pages."

"What did it say?"

Levinsky suddenly broke into uncontrollable laughter. Sifer's head went onto his chin, but he didn't say anything.

"What did it say?" Levinsky said at last, stopping another paroxysm. "An accounting! An accounting! On one side, a total of eggs and cakes, in the middle, the price of eggs and cakes. The price of eggs and cakes, as it changed from week to week! Though it didn't always, of course. And then, his fee - a steady figure down the page. At the bottom, totals. And you know what?" He laughed again, but this time not so strongly. "I owed him! I owed him!"

"How much?" Findlay spoke almost in a whisper.

"Enough to buy him another library."

Did he ever collect the debt?"

Levinsky's face darkened. "Yes. During the war, when I had my own battles, a package - some books. I am to safeguard, to hide. This without asking, without an acquaintance for years. What am I to do with this precious parcel at that time? He was my teacher, though. So I hid them."

Levinsky, sullen, stopped speaking.

"So that paid off your debt?" Findlay prompted.

Levinsky, arms crossed, delayed before answering. "No. Some years after the war, again after a silence, asking the books I should return. I had one with me. The rest, I had hidden, given to others to watch - I had my own emergencies in those days, and every hour was its own. But I sent him a list of where they were, how they could be retrieved. I expected him to demand I get them. But silence."

"And that paid your debt?"

Levinsky shook his head.

"Do you still owe --?"

"He is dead. And his debt was collected. In full." Levinsky again lapsed into stubborn silence.

"Tell us how, please."

Levinsky fought the words, angry. He would give nothing but the facts, though clearly there was more behind them. "Again, nothing for years, then a thank you, a list of those he'd retrieved." Levinky's arms were locked around his chest. "Then, only shortly before he moved here, a request for money to help get back the rest he'd entrusted to me. I sent it to him."

"Go on," Findlay urged.

"There is nothing else. I kept my own account. He was paid in full."

"Did he use the same procedure with his other students?"

"Objection!"

"Ask him. Ask them," Levinsky said, before Sifer could rule.

"Sustained," Sifer said anyway.

Findlay went to his table, his back to Levinsky. "Why did Mr. Enstein move here?"

"Objection. Witness is asked to speculate."

Findlay turned around. "Your honor -"

"Sustained."

Momentarily, Findlay looked disappointed. "Were you pleased when Mr. Enstein moved here?"

"Objection!"

"I am establishing opportunity. And motive."

"Overruled."

Shammai tugged on Lazar's sleeve. "What does he mean?"

"Levinsky had motive - and showed you the opportunity."

"Findlay's nuts," Shammai said with disgust.

Lazar shook his head. "I don't think so."

Findlay, triumphant, repeated the question. "Were you pleased when Mr. Enstein moved here?"

Levinsky glared at him. "I understand you. The truth, it is not yours to twist. I survived. Enstein survived. His books survived. And my friend Shammai, he will survive. You think you have truth by the throat. You have never touched the truth in your life!"

Findlay looked at Sifer. "Will the court please direct the witness to answer the question?"

Judge Sifer pursed his lips. "Mr. Levinsky, I understand your agitation, but please answer the question."

Levinsky folded his arms. "No."

Findlay tap-tapped pen in palm. "Did Mr. Enstein try to re-establish contact with you, a relationship when he moved here?"

"He knew better. We had different worlds. He had his books."

"So you didn't speak with each other?"

"We did. If forced by circumstances."

Findlay's tapping slowed down. "Did you want to take revenge?"

"For what?"

"For - being blackmailed."

"Objection!"

"Sustained. Mr. Findlay," Sifer said, "if you cannot find a proper way to phrase your questions, I will disallow the whole line."

Findlay bowed his head slightly. "I understand, your Honor. Mr. Levinsky, did you ever have thoughts - thoughts only - about inconveniencing or discomforting Mr. Enstein the way he inconvenienced or discomforted you?"

"No. I wanted nothing to do with him. Nothing at all."

"But you did speak. When forced by circumstances. In fact, you helped each other out on occasion, didn't you? Surreptitiously, of course." As an answer, Levinsky glared. Findlay's tapping picked up speed. "How well do you know the defendant?"

"Shammai? He fixes my computer. I have a membership in his shul. Why?" Levinsky asked, suspicious.

Findlay smiled tightly. "The defendant has lived here about fourteen years. When did you first meet him?"

On his guard, Levinsky replied, "Maybe the day he moved here, maybe not for years. These things, I don't remember."

"When did you become friendly with him?"

"We are not friends."

"When did you start doing business with him?"

Levinsky shrugged. "My first computer I got a month, maybe two - maybe six, this memory is so erratic, maybe it doesn't remember who Mr. Enstein is - that's all right, your honor," Levinsky said, looking up as Sifer leaned over, "but I answer as I'm asked. Nu. Let's say six weeks after the *bris* of his last, his Aaron. I remember because we talked about it then. I bought a computer because of the program he could put in it."

"That's about six years ago. But if you weren't friends and didn't do business with him, why did you go to the ceremony?"

"I am a member of the shul," Levinsky said proudly.

"The same synagogue - the only synagogue - that Mr. Enstein was active in," Findlay said. He paused before continuing. "Why did you do business with the defendant?"

Levinsky squirmed. "Because he was good."

"Is that the only reason?"

"He needed the work."

"How did you know that?" Findlay pressed.

"Someone told me."

"Who?"

"Someone in his shul." Levinsky looked at Shammai, uncomfortable.

"Who?" There was no answer. "Who, Mr. Levinsky?" Findlay demanded.

"Mordechai Enstein."

Shammai didn't know that. What else had Mr. Enstein done behind his back? Who had had undue influence on who?

"Thank you." Findlay smiled, taking a deep breath. "I assume that was one of those forced circumstances." The pen stopped tapping. "Six years ago, the defendant's oldest son, Elie, was about seven years old. Did you know that Mr. Enstein had started tutoring Elie then?"

"Yes."

"My, my," Findlay said. "For someone who wanted nothing to do with Mr. Enstein, you certainly communicated with him a lot - taking business advice, knowing who his pupils were, maintaing membership in his synagogue and attending its functions. Circumstances must have been quite forcing, indeed."

Lazar stood. "Your honor, I ask that this entire line of questioning be stricken from the record. Even if Mr. Levinsky wanted revenge, and even if he was somehow able to convince my client to be his instrument, it doesn't show how my client was able to exercise undue influence over an individual as determined and self-disciplined as Mr. Enstein. In fact, it seems the opposite is the case."

Judge Sifer nodded. "Your point has merit. Mr. Findlay?"

Findlay cleared his throat. "Mr. Levinsky had an intimate knowledge of Mr. Enstein's character and his obsession with books. He didn't like Mr. Enstein. He also knew the defendant, who at some point had to also become aware of Mr. Enstein's character and obsession with books. The witness knew Mr. Enstein's weaknesses, probably better than anyone else, at least in this city. He may have planted the motive in the defendant's mind. Regardless, he could certainly have shown the defendant, even with a hint, how to gain an undue influence over the deceased. Further, he more than anyone would know the value of the collection in general, and the worth of individual volumes in particular."

"Are you suggesting a conspiracy?" Sifer asked, incredulous.

"No, your honor," Findlay said. "They both could have wanted to achieve the same result for different reasons, and without open communication. I simply wish to show that the defendant at the very least had access to such information."

Sifer put his chin in his hands. "I'll overrule the objection. For now."

"Your honor," Levinsky blurted out. "This lawyer, he tries to make something where there is nothing. Between Shammai and me, there's no connection like this. I never talked to him about Mr. Enstein. I never talked to anyone about Mr. Enstein."

"But you belonged to the same synagogue," Findlay said.

"I belong to three synagogues. Sometimes I belong to four. In a community so small, you get to know a little about a lot of people."

"Did you know that the defendant was practically Mr. Enstein's guardian?"

"Walking an old man to shul, getting him *challah*, some shopping, that makes you a guardian? But everyone knew that."

"When," Findlay asked quietly, coldly, "did Shammai start doing what everyone knew about?"

"I don't know." Levinsky met Findlay's stare, then looked away. "Five years ago, maybe. Six." He shrugged. "Seven."

"In other words, about the same time his youngest son was born. About the same time you started doing business with him. About the same time Mr. Enstein started tutoring Elie."

"Objection!" Lazar shouted.

"No need to shout," Sifer said. "Sustained."

Findlay dropped the pen onto his legal pad. "You said you never discussed Mr. Enstein with the defendant. Did you ever discuss the defendant with Mr. Enstein?"

It took Levinsky a moment to understand the question. "No."

"But Mr. Enstein discussed him with you. The business recommendation," Findlay added. "Tell me, when was your last conversation with Mr. Enstein?"

Levinsky rolled his eyes, thinking. "Almost two weeks before the heart attack. I go to the zoo or aquarium Sunday afternoon, then to the office. He called me as I walked in to the office."

"What was it about?"

"About books, what else?"

"Can you be more specific?"

Levinsky hugged himself. "He said he felt he would die soon. At his age - my age, too, maybe - you can feel it, I guess. But I shouldn't worry about the books, he said - as if I ever did - because they would be all right." Then he looked at Sifer, spoke only to him. "About Enstein and books, you have to understand. There, there was Enstein and books, and here, there was Enstein and books. But Enstein and books were not separate things. They were always one."

The silence lengthened, going from aftermath to prelude.

At last Findlay spoke. "Always one?" he said, drily. "Not always. Not when he had his heart attack. So, Mr. Levinsky, I ask you, if, as you say, Mr. Enstein literally spent his life for and with his books, felt one with them, why did he destroy his precious legacy? Why did he break up his collection? What could induce him to give away the last received, hardest to obtain, most valuable volume in his whole library - when he was, by all accounts, an acquisitive, meticulous, demanding, vigilant individual?"

"Objection. Witness is asked to speculate."

"Sustained."

Findlay nodded his head, his hair bobbing. "Let us summarize. Mr. Enstein used most of his wages for books. While fighting for his life, he safeguarded his books. He kept an accounting of debts, just to be able to collect and gather his books. He never gave away or lent any of his books. And in his last conversation with you, he assured you his books would be all right. So close was he to these books that, as you say, they were like one thing. Is this an accurate summary?"

"Yes," Levinsky admitted, slowly.

"And, during that last conversation, he did not give any indication of breaking up the collection, or giving a volume as a gift?"

"No."

"Even though," Findlay pointed out, "at that time, in a clear state of mind, it would have been most appropriate to do so. Instead, at perhaps his last conscious moment, he contradicted his entire life. He gave away the crown jewel, so to speak." Findlay shook his head "I have nothing more to ask the witness."

Lazar stood, his hand arranging and rearranging his three colored pens into different patterns.

"Mr. Levinsky," he said, "I only have a few questions."

Levinsky leaned backed.

"First," Lazar began, "Did you ever see Mr. Enstein buy a book with the fee you paid him?"

"No."

"So your knowledge of what he did with his payment, with his eggs and cakes, is circumstantial and hearsay?"

"Enstein was honest," Levinsky growled.

"I know that," Lazar said. "So, I assume, are you. But you can't testify of your own knowledge how he got his books, can you?"

"I didn't see him buy anything, no," Levinsky said, his curiosity obvious.

Shammai also wondered what Lazar was doing.

"And," Lazar continued, "as you say, you had no real contact with Mr. Enstein after that, even when he moved into the same town."

"There were the letters," Levinsky pointed out.

"Yes, those. But they were hardly a financial statement or a library catalogue, were they?"

"No."

"So, in fact, you don't know if Mr. Enstein had some outside source of income, do you?"

"No." Levinsky began to catch on, as the unfolding of his hands and the furtive smile suggested.

"Mr. Enstein could have belonged to the Rare Hebrew Books Club and been getting fifty percent discounts on obscure and valuable items, for all you know."

"Objection," Findlay said.

"Your honor," Lazar explained. "Plaintiff has stated that the purpose of calling this witness is to establish Mr. Enstein's character prior to being subject to the undue influence of my client. It is plaintiff's contention that Mr. Enstein, under normal circumstances, could not, by his very nature, make such a gift as he did to my client.

"This witness is supposed to know a great deal about Mr. Enstein's habits and character. I am showing that his testimony is not reliable, that in fact he knows very little about Mr. Enstein's financial interests or his inclinations regarding disposal of his property."

"Overruled," Sifer said quickly. "But please make your questions a bit more realistic."

"Yes, your honor," Lazar said. "Now, as to Mr. Enstein's obsession with books, was it unusual for a scholar to love books?"

"Then, that's what scholars did."

Lazar smiled. "Yes? How many scholars did you know- back then."

"Personally?" Levinsky shrugged. "None."

"Would you say Mr. Enstein had more books, less books, or about the same as other scholars - back then?"

"I wouldn't know."

"Oh," Lazar said. "But somehow, as an unlearned, inexperienced barely adolescent young man, you were able to determine that Mr. Enstein was obsessed with books?"

"No, everyone knew it," Levinsky said uncomfortably.

Careful, Lazar, Shammai thought. Destroy his testimony, not him. But what would happen when they got to Kashdan, Josh and the others?

"But you yourself had no first-hand knowledge of obsessions, or scholars, or book-lovers, against whom to judge Mr. Enstein?"

"No."

Lazar pushed his pens aside and looked up. "Was Mr. Enstein's account of your debt accurate?"

"I paid it."

"Was it correct?"

Levinsky nodded. "Yes. Strictly speaking, I owed him all that."

"So rather than being an obsessed collector, Mr. Enstein might have simply been a shrewd investor?"

"I suppose," Levinsky frowned.

"If that's the case, and he was an honest man, and he kept a record of what you owed him - figuring the exchange rate between 'eggs and cake' and books, is it not possible that when he owed someone - my client - he did the same thing?"

Levinsky gave him a blank look.

"Isn't it possible that he owed my client for *challah* and support and paid him back in the currency of his investments - a book?"

"It's possible, of course it's possible."

"Let me ask you this a different way," Lazar said. "You say that Mr. Enstein, when he thought his life in danger, when he thought something might happen to his books, that then he did entrust you with them, give them to you to hold and take care of for him?"

"Yes."

"Well, then, surely he must have realized he might not survive when he gave them to you. What would have happened to them?"

"They would have been mine, I suppose," Mr. Levinsky said.

"In other words, when Mr. Enstein realized he might die and

he would lose control of his life's obsession, his books, he turned to you, a former student, someone who knew him, who had listened to him, who he trusted. And he gave some of his books to you for safekeeping, knowing full well, without any request or influence on your part, that they might, in fact become yours permanently?"

The implication - that he might have done the same with Shammai - was obvious.

"Correct," Levinsky said.

"One last question. You said that Mr. Enstein rescued books from -" Lazar looked at his notes - "'filth and unholiness.' For what repository of books would Mr. Enstein use that term?"

"Libraries and museums. He didn't trust them."

"Why?"

"He called them a cemetery, a living thought's resting place."

"Then he certainly wouldn't have wanted his collection going to one, would he?"

"Objection," Findlay said. "Counsel cannot both attempt to destroy the expertise of the witness's testimony, then rely on that same expertise."

"Sustained."

Lazar smiled. "No further questions."

The judge nodded at Levinsky. Levinsky nodded back at the judge.

"We will take an hour for lunch," Sifer said.

Shammai stretched, sneaking a glance across the aisle. Simon and Earl were arguing with each other, and Simon tried to argue with Findlay, who simply stared ahead, tapping his pen in his palm.

"I'll meet you outside," Lazar said, snapping shut his briefcase. "I've got to find out how long we'll go today." He headed toward the clerk at the front.

Shammai turned around, looking for Hannah. She stood when he did.

As he squeezed between the chairs and railing, Shammai saw that Levinsky hadn't made it out.

As he walked, Levinsky looked at no one, only focusing straight ahead.

But, approaching Shammai, he slowed. Shammai waited.

As he passed, Levinsky whispered, "Like a monkey," and hurried out.

When he recovered from his surprise, Shammai thought, true, but who's the reference?

Chapter 16

Shammai sat on a bench, the State Office building behind him, City Hall across the park to his right. It used to be one could see the traffic from here, he thought, but that was before they landscaped, turning a square block of civic green into an architectural project, with sculpted mounds raising a large, centrally placed gazebo. It looked like they'd moved Monkey Hill from the zoo and given it a face list. They should have left it all alone.

Years ago, after they'd first moved here, when he'd worked downtown, he used to go to the main library on his lunch hour; it still sat across from City Hall. He had an urge to get up and go explore, but he promised Hannah he wouldn't stray.

He took a sip from the now-warm coke he'd been nursing for fifteen minutes. It had been practically frozen when he'd got it from the machine. The tree's shade cut off the sun; without a breeze, though, the air remained heavy, numbing. He should be inside, with the rest of his family, waiting for lunch from the Deli. But he wanted to think. Hannah respected that, for which he was grateful. Besides, she knew he could handle the steam-bath humidity for only a few minutes. It seemed to open his mind, though, especially after the chilling temperature inside the courtroom.

Yet the very deadness of the afternoon anesthetized any optimism. He could not sustain his confidence, any more than summer fruit its ripeness. He had entered the trial expectant, but an overabundance of hope, like a watermelon or summer peach, rapidly decomposed from its own fertility. He felt he must lose, that somehow he deserved to lose.

He shook his head. No sense in combining sophomore

philosophy with freshman psychology and trying to make sense of reality. It didn't work then, it certainly wouldn't work now.

No, his first mistake was hiring Lazar. You should never do business with a friend. At least, certain types of business. Oh, Lazar was a competent attorney, good enough for routine things like mortgages and acting as executor and notarizing and making sure Shammai's business was properly incorporated and all that. But, despite Lazar's Perry Mason tricks, Shammai knew this was out of Lazar's league.

Shammai took another sip, grimaced at the taste of warm carbonation, wiped his brow with the back of his hand and leaned forward. A car honked, another responded, and there was a ten-second chorus before he heard the sounds of traffic moving.

The real question, he told himself, was what right did he even have to the *siddur*? He wasn't named in the will. He'd never been sure Mr. Enstein had ever liked him. How could you tell with someone like that, who almost never said thank you? He thought he had a good relationship with Mr. Enstein, but maybe Mr. Enstein had just wanted to take from him - some children to tutor, Hannah's *challah* - it wouldn't matter what, would it?

Maybe he had actually needed Shammai's help on occasion. It didn't mean Mr. Enstein had to be grateful or give him something. He certainly hadn't thought about being rewarded for the mitzvos of honoring the elderly and welcoming guests. At least, not much.

And should he continue to put his family through this? No question Findlay was good. Dinah Chaya would have to take the stand. Maybe all he wanted from her were facts. But even facts could be twisted. A clever lawyer, even one with scruples, could destroy a sixteen-year old girl - or at least make her betray her father. And Hannah - he threw the coke at a trash can and missed - how she had suffered, supporting him, trying to keep things normal.

Maybe the nephews' offer was still good.

But she wouldn't let him give up the fight. She knew, even if he doubted, the *siddur* didn't belong in a museum.

He picked up the coke can. Backing up a couple steps, he tried a jump-shot. He missed again. Making a face, he dropped it in the trash and sat down again.

Something would happen with the shul. The clique lines were showing and cracking. He'd disrupted any natural readjustment that would have taken place after Mr. Enstein's passing. Now it would have to grow or die. Maybe it had been waiting for Mr. Enstein to pass on before making its decision; maybe it had come to be only for Mr. Enstein's convenience and now had to find new reasons to live. Even if he simply walked away from the *siddur*, the shul, like everything else in his life, would be changed.

He shook his head and stretched, irked with the frivolous turn of his thoughts, and annoyed that his shirt slurped off the bench. Maybe the food had arrived. He looked at his watch. About half an hour of lunch left, officially, unless the judge was having a big one. He'd better get inside, anyway. This heat was ridiculous.

What am I going to do about Lazar, he thought, wending his way back toward the court building. Lunch hour walkers and talkers hurried through the haze of sweltering air. He'd seen a side of Lazar, a professional weakness, he shouldn't have. And Lazar - surely he'd seen some part of Shammai that should never have been revealed. Could his friendship with Lazar survive?

Really, though, what had happened, what would have changed, if he lost? He still had his business, his family. The problems he had before would be the same after the judge took the *siddur* away from him. He'd just have to use the normal solutions. In fact, life would be easier, more routine.

But something would have been taken away.

Enough. He'd worry where it was cool, the air breathable.

As he reached the door, Elie dashed to meet him, a sandwich

wrapped in white lunch paper in one hand, side-somethings in aluminum foil in the other.

"It's hot," Elie declared, not referring to the food. "Lox on pita. Mezonos, so you don't have to wash. French fries, cole slaw and a pickle. Mom and Dinah Chaya are eating."

"Let's join them later," Shammai said, taking the food, shivering at the sudden change in temperature.

"Your shirt's all wet," Elie noted as they walked down the hall.

"It's called sweat."

"I know what it is," Elie said, wiping his brow. "But you've got a lot of it."

"That happens this time of year when you're outside for more than sixty seconds."

"That happens most times of the year," Elie said. He paused "Why?"

"I wanted to think," Shammai said. He stopped, made a *brocha*, and took out a few french fries.

By mutual consent, they found a corner to eat.

"You didn't have to stand out in the heat to do that."

"I was sitting."

"Whatever. I did a lot of thinking, too, but I did it in here."

"Well, cooler heads will prevail," Shammai said, taking some more french fries. "Tell me what you thought."

"Well," Elie began slowly, "If we lose, you know, it's not like we've really lost something we had. I mean, it's like, can't we live the way we did before?"

"Before I got the *siddur* or before Mr. Enstein died?"

"Come on, dad, you know what I mean." He reached over and took a couple of french fries. "I was upset when he died, and I still get upset some times. That's natural, isn't it? We spent a lot of time with him. But he didn't owe us anything and we don't owe him

245

anything."

So Elie, too, had already reached a verdict, Shammai thought as he idly unwrapped his lox on pita. He felt quite hungry and incapable of eating, at the same time. My stomach's joined the paradox, he thought.

"I've got to see it through," Shammai said quietly.

"I know," Elie said in the same tone. "And I want you to. But how important is winning to you?"

"How important is it to you? To win, you have to give up everything else. Self-sacrifice and victory - you can't have one without the other. If the goal's worth having - and I'd say keeping Judaism alive, keeping its souls - human and textual - free - is worthwhile, then everything and everyone's secondary to it." Shammai paused. "I think he wanted you to be his pupil, to be like him. Your learning justified his self-sacrifice, gave him the victory. That's why it's important to me."

"He wasn't my grandfather," Elie insisted.

"You've said that before." Shammai sighed. "In one way, I really don't care. In another, well, let's just say I think it will justify a lot."

"Like what?"

"Like being manipulated, like letting someone else have an undue influence over my children - and myself. But most of all, I guess, because, speaking of undue influence, despite the testimony about his character and what we knew, Mr. Enstein did understand the value and significance of books. The only way this *siddur* - or the rest of the books - will have any influence, let alone the undue influence they should, is if they're used, not put on display like some long-dead artifact. There's a life - many lives - in those pages. I can't just let them go."

Elie reached over and took some more french fries.

"What happened inside?" he asked.

Shammai gave him a puzzled look. Then he remembered. "Oh, that's right, you were outside with Dinah Chaya the whole time. Didn't your mother tell you?"

Elie shook his head.

"It got pretty nasty. Heuerstein and Levinsky proved Mr. Enstein was constitutionally incapable of making a gift. Heuerstein also proved I was money-hungry."

"How'd he do that?"

"I had the *siddur* appraised, remember? Before Mr. Enstein died." He opened the container of cole slaw and closed it. He was going to be very hungry at the end of the day. "And did you know that Levinsky and I were in a conspiracy against Mr. Enstein?"

"What?" Elie laughed.

"It's true. Or I was manipulated by him for revenge. Or he was manipulated by me." He scratched his head. "I'm not sure how that fit in, at all. Did you talk to Lazar?" He handed the food to Elie.

"Not really," Elie said. "He just said things were going about as well as could be expected, since it was Findlay's turn. Then he rushed off to make some phone calls or something."

"Well, I'll have to ask him about that part, then."

Elie pointed to Lazar running down the hall.

"Sooner than I thought," Shammai said.

Lazar came up to them. "Court resumes in fifteen minutes."

"And?"

"What do you think?" Lazar asked.

"I think I lost."

"I didn't get to call any witnesses."

"Did their lawyer really say that Mr. Levinsky and my father were in a conspiracy," Elie asked.

"Your father told you about that, eh?" Lazar smiled. "He didn't say, he implied. A big difference."

"I'd like to know what it was about," Shammai said.

247

Lazar shrugged. "I'd like to say a stab in the dark, but Findlay's too smart for that. So, either he thinks he found something, or even without a conspiracy, Levinsky's double involvement points to undue influence."

"How?" Shammai insisted.

Lazar took the container of cole slaw, the spoon, stopped, made a *brocha* and took a few forkfuls. "Thought food," he explained. "Look, their case is built on undue influence. That means you had to take advantage of Mr. Enstein, exploit a weakness. But Heuerstein's testimony showed that Mr. Enstein wasn't likely to give anything to anybody. Levinsky confirmed that. So Findlay's got this picture of Mr. Enstein as a stubborn, selfish, paranoid old man. Not true, but that's how he turned the testimony. Or hopes to, in closing argument."

Lazar stopped to finish the cole slaw. He took half the pita & lox and questioned Elie and Shammai with his eyebrows. They shook their heads. After making the *brocha*, he took a bite. "Problem is," Lazar continued, chewing while he talked. "How can a naive money-grubber like you fool an old veteran like him? He's going to give you not just any book, but the prize of his collection, for sending him *challah*? Levinsky showed how clever, how astute Mr. Enstein was. He would have seen right through that."

"So they defeated themselves," Elie said.

Lazar shook his head and swallowed. "No, because your father's got the book and isn't mentioned in the will and he did all those things to ingratiate himself."

"So?"

""So, since Levinsky knew Mr. Enstein so well, it wouldn't take much for your father to learn, through hints, if Levinsky got involved intentionally or careful observation if unintentional, that an old, lonely man might have a weakness for a disciple and *challah*."

They'd turned the corner and could see Hannah and Dinah

Chaya waiting.

"That's ridiculous," Shammai said.

"Of course it is. But the judge doesn't know you, Stan Levinsky or Mr. Enstein. So the scenario plays like this: Mr. Enstein would never, under normal circumstances, give away a book to anyone. But Mr. Enstein, a teacher, wanted a student - and you gave him one: Moral coercion. Mr. Enstein, obsessed with his books, wanted to show them off - and you played the flatterer: inordinate flattery. You provided both and, by clever observation - aided by Levinsky - so ingratiated yourself to him that he became confused and, because of deteriorating health, dependent: confidential relationship. Moral coercion, inordinate flattery, confidential relationship equal undue influence, or three strikes you're out." Lazar tossed the balled-up paper and container over his shoulder and into a trash container.

"So what's next?" Elie asked.

They'd reached the elevators. Hannah and Dinah Chaya had their hands full with cups.

"Do you need something to drink?" Hannah asked.

"Desperately," Lazar said. "Thanks for ordering." He took the cup from Dinah Chaya's hand.

"I meant Shammai," she said, laughing. "But I got him a coffee."

Dinah Chaya gave her father a middle-sized styrofoam cup.

The elevator doors opened and they got on, along with a few other people.

When the doors opened and they filed out, Shammai repeated Elie's question. "So, what's next?"

"Next," Lazar said, taking a big drink, "he calls up people who know you both - the *shul* - and shows your confidential relationship with poor Mr. Enstein, and how you used moral coercion and inordinate flattery, you covetous -"

"That still doesn't prove undue influence," Elie interrupted.

"You're right. Sort of. But since Findlay has shown that Mr. Enstein would not normally have given such a gift, and if Findlay shows that your father appeared to have taken advantage of a position of trust, well, in cases like this, where Mr. Enstein apparently did in fact give away something valuable against his nature, the burden shifts and it's easier to get to an assumption of undue influence." He finished the coke. "Assuming, of course, we get through your father's testimony with case intact."

"That's still an awful lot to prove," Elie said quietly.

Dinah Chaya had already sat down on the bench outside the courtroom. Elie stood waiting until the others entered.

"Yeah," Lazar said wishfully. "But it won't take much for it to all fall together. That's where I come to the rescue, leaving a path of destruction behind."

Hannah, hand on the door, stopped. "But shouldn't Dinah Chaya's testimony refute all that?"

"She's really going to have to testify, isn't she?" Shammai asked.

"Don't forget, so are you. But, yes, to both questions." Lazar said, rubbing a thumb over his left eyebrow. "Levinsky's last conversation - I was trying to research that during lunch, by the way - should show there was no undue influence.

"And, Mr. Enstein couldn't know he was going to have a heart attack, and he couldn't know that Dinah Chaya would show up at that precise moment. So, he had to give it as an impulse. And that should refute undue influence."

"So why is Findlay going to call her as a witness?" Shammai asked.

"Maybe to contradict what you say." Lazar looked from Hannah to Shammai to Elie. "But really, I don't know," he whispered.

\#

Chairs scraped floor as Judge Sifer entered, then again as everyone sat down. Shammai's reaction to Lazar's description of Findlay's strategy had been to retreat into contempt: the well-practiced pomposity of Findlay had already begun to twist intricate, personal histories into an afternoon Mardi Gras parade. Seeing Sifer seat himself like some pampered reviewing-stand VIP, with the whole pageant for his pleasure, intensified Shammai's scorn. He had to fight the impulse to simply walk out.

I should have eaten lunch, he told himself.

Sifer nodded at Findlay.

Findlay glanced at a three-by-five card as he stood. "Lawrence Kashdan."

Kashdan, having been ushered in, stood by the door, peering around, surveying the arrangement of the courtroom, much as Shammai had seen him do at his store. Then he strutted to the front, with the same self-satisfied expression he wore after a surprise inspection of merchandise and employees. His promenade seemed to catch the right combination of pretention and diffidence for the court's unrehearsed theatrics.

On the way, Kashdan winked at Shammai.

Better be careful, Shammai told himself - cynicism, if mishandled, can be deadly.

"Overconfident, as usual," Lazar whispered to himself.

Shammai saw that Lazar had been drawing circles around names, using different colored pens, then making checks and other marks, usually with another color.

"Can we trust him?" Shammai asked, pointing to the red circle around Kashdan's name.

"He won't do anything intentionally, if that's what you

mean," Lazar said, making different colored doodles around Kashdan's name. The shapeless sketches began to wander, encompassing other names. "Anyway, we have no choice."

Findlay began his examination. "How are you employed?"

"I am general manager of a Dillard's department store."

"But not an owner?"

"No."

"Ever want to be an owner? Ever want to have your own store - Kashdan's?"

"No. And no."

"Why not?"

"I like what I'm doing." Kashdan responded.

"So do we all, but current satisfaction does not preclude ambition."

"Ambition takes many forms. Sterner stuff, for one."

"Are you a wealthy man?" Findlay asked.

"Wealthy enough to be the primary financial resource when the *shul* started, among other things."

"Are you now?"

"Am I now what?" Kashdan asked. "Wealthy or the primary financial resource?"

"Both."

Another exchange of icy smiles.

"Not really and no." As Findlay was about to speak, Kashdan added, "I am wealthy enough and I am *a* primary financial resource."

Findlay consulted his notes, then rather noisily pushed his chair into the table. "Mr. Kashdan," he said. "In deposition you stated you would not testify. Yet you are here."

"The penalty for refusing a subpoena is contempt of court."

"True," Findlay said. "Yet you knew that before. Why make an assertion you knew you would not see through?"

"Objection," Lazar said, without getting up.

"Overruled," Judge Sifer said. "I assume counsel has a reason for this line of questioning, and I would like to hear it."

Findlay bowed slightly. "Thank you, your honor. Mr. Kashdan?"

"I don't like you. I don't like what Shammai's doing. I don't like the mess Enstein left. In short, I don't like any of this and I, for one, have a business to run."

Findlay turned around and the Osteriks smiled at him. "Yes, we'll get to your business in a moment. But you don't seem to like very much of anything."

"I don't like tricks and I don't like mind games and I don't like unearned assumptions of privilege."

"That sounds to me," Findlay said, turning around again, "like you're describing the defendant's relationship with the deceased."

"I was referring to you," Kashdan said.

Shammai chuckled.

"He's not doing it for you," Lazar said, hesitating between pens. "And he'll probably end up giving Findlay what he wants."

Findlay started tapping the back of one hand into the other. "Did you like Mr. Enstein?"

"No."

"How long did you know him?"

"Sixteen years, two months, one week and a couple days."

"You don't remember the hours and minutes?" Findlay asked.

"I could probably calculate the seconds if you need to know," Kashdan replied. "But you don't."

"You're right," Findlay said, tap-tapping. "You met Mr. Enstein within days of his moving to town, but you don't like him. Did you ever like him?"

"No."

A long pause. "But you did start a synagogue together?"

"Yes."

"Was anyone else involved?"

"A lot of people were involved."

"I mean," said Findlay, hand poised, "Did anyone else help you two with all the preparations, papers - whatever - of the synagogue.?"

"No."

"Why not?"

"We wanted it set up a certain way, we had the ability, and we did it."

"Were you planning on leaving or buying him out or something?"

Kashdan laughed. "I think he fully expected me to die first. He was as obsessed with the *shul* as he was with his books. More, I'd say."

Findlay shook his head. "I'm still confused. If you didn't like him, why did you enter into what amounted to a lifetime partnership with him?"

"I had the monetary responsibility for the shul. He functioned as pseudo-rabbi; he had the knowledge. Often in history and business, partners despised each other, yet recognized how successful the partnership was, and remained. As an attorney, I suppose you've never been in such a situation. "

Judge Sifer leaned over again. "Mr. Kashdan, you are almost at my limit. I will not have witnesses badgering the attorneys. They do a satisfactory job of badgering each other on their own."

Well, the judge does indeed have a sense of humor, Shammai thought.

Findlay cleared his throat and resumed. "I take it Mr. Enstein was not an easy man to get along with."

"You may take that." Kashdan paused. "In fact, he was the hardest person to get along with I ever met. But there would have been no *shul* without him. And, without him, it would not have survived until it could stand on its own. I would do it again exactly the same, and much as I disliked him, I respected him."

Lazar had picked up the green pen, but not yet scribbled anything.

"Didn't he already get testimony about Mr. Enstein's character?" Shammai whispered.

Lazar nodded. "My vote's for breach of confidential relationship."

"Tell me," Findlay said, "how long have you known the defendant?"

"A little more than thirteen years," came the cautious reply.

"Don't you know the month and day?"

"Do you need to know that?" Kashdan said sharply.

"Only if it was before or after his oldest son - Elie - was born."

"After, but not much."

Findlay checked something on his legal pad, shook his head at the Osteriks', then resumed. "Why did the defendant join your synagogue?"

"Ask him."

"Was he recruited?"

"No," Kashdan said. "We didn't really have a recruiting committee, then."

"I see. But who had the main contact with him - you or Mr. Enstein?"

"Mr. Enstein. I told you. He was the pseudo-rabbi. He had contact with every member or potential member."

"Did Mr. Enstein and the defendant always have a close relationship?"

"You don't build a friendship overnight."

"A friendship?" Findlay said, beginning to pace. "Is that what you call it? The defendant had a friendship, but you had a hostile partnership. Did everyone in the synagogue have a friendship except you?"

"No, only Shammai."

"Oh, then everyone else disliked but respected Mr. Enstein?"

"No," Kashdan said. "Most of the members liked Mr. Enstein pretty much, although his constant criticisms and tendency to - I'd say deliberately irritate, like tweaking - was a source of friction. Many times I had to smooth over his tactlessness or misplaced sense of humor."

"But not with the defendant."

"Not that I recall, no."

"What, not once in almost fourteen years?" Findlay pressed.

"For most of the early years of the synagogue, we were all fighting for survival too much for Mr. Enstein's obstinacy to have that much effect. Besides, I think he invested so much in the shul, that his involvement made us overlook things. Later on, of course, as Mr. Enstein got older and wasn't as capable as he had been, things changed."

"Objection," Lazar said. "Mr. Enstein's medical condition over the years has not been established and the witness is not a physician."

"Sustained," Sifer said. "Strike the last sentence from the record."

"That didn't answer my question, anyway," Findlay said. "I'll ask again. Did you ever have to intervene with the defendant because of something Mr. Enstein said or did?"

"Again, not that I recall," Kashdan said. "If anything, someone would have to intervene for me because Shammai was so - deferential, I'd call it, or supportive - to Mr. Enstein."

Lazar leaned over. "I guessed wrong. Inordinate flattery first."

"Why do you think Shammai showed such deference?"

"Objection. Witness is being asked to speculate."

"Sustained."

Findlay made a note on his pad. "Can you give an example of such deference?"

"Objection," Lazar said. "The question is irrelevant and the witness not qualified to answer it."

"Your honor," Findlay said, exasperated. "Mr. Kashdan has testified that the deceased made a tremendous commitment to the synagogue, almost, if not equal, to the one he made to his books. We have already established that Mr. Enstein was obsessed with his books. If he had the same obsession with the synagogue, then given the inevitable conflicts within such an organization, a trusted supporter, one who had gained a confidential relationship, would be in a position to exercise undue influence. That relationship could be gained through inordinate flattery. As the witness has stated his dislike, but respect, for Mr. Enstein, and as he has been intimately involved in those conflicts, he is most definitely qualified to answer."

Lazar stood up. "The witness is not qualified to differentiate between deference and genuine support."

Findlay sighed. "If necessary, I can establish that qualification first."

"Then do so," Sifer said firmly. "And on that basis, overruled."

"Mr. Kashdan," Findlay said. "Is your department store successful?"

"Very."

"One of the most profitable in the chain?"

"It has been," Kashdan said with some pride, "the most

profitable for fifteen years."

"To what do you attribute that?"

"Location, partially, of course. But mainly the personnel that work for me. In any business, it's the people that make the difference."

"And how," Findlay said slowly, "do you obtain or retain such outstanding personnel?"

"Well, there's a department for hiring, of course. But I spend most of my time observing - offering suggestions, too - but mainly watching and listening. Paperwork's for non-store hours."

"I see. Surely you don't get along with all the employees. What if someone is a good worker, but has a personality clash with you?"

"I keep them, obviously. Even if they spend their breaks complaining about me."

"Thank you," Findlay said with a cold smile. He turned to Sifer. "May I continue?"

Judge Sifer nodded.

"I had asked you to give us an example of the defendant's deference," Findlay said.

Kashdan cleared his throat. "Well, for instance on the issue of hiring a rabbi, which I wanted to do, even though Shammai agreed with me privately that it would be good for the shul, publicly and in meetings, he always voted with Mr. Enstein. Out of respect, he said."

"When did this become an issue?"

"Over the last couple years." Kashdan cleared his throat again. "I should point out that their relationship wasn't always like this."

"Oh?" Findlay looked up from his notes, very interested. "Elaborate, please."

"Well, it's only been in the last six or seven years that -"

"Did you say six or seven years?" Findlay interrupted.

"About the time Mr. Enstein began tutoring the defendant's son?"

"Yes, but I'd call it more teaching at first. But before that, Shammai wasn't so active, except showing up on Shabbos. He had a business to build." Kashdan cleared his throat. "Anyway, I was referring to Mr. Enstein's failing health. That's when Shammai started walking him to shul, sending *challah*, defending him and just, well, -"

"Flattering him?" Findlay suggested.

Kashdan didn't answer.

Findlay waited until it became uncomfortably clear Kashdan wouldn't answer. "Six or seven years," he said slowly. "Six or seven years ago, Mr. Enstein began teaching the defendant's son. Six or seven years ago, the defendant suddenly becomes an overactive supporter of Mr. Enstein. Six or seven years ago, Mr. Enstein's health begins to deteriorate. No further questions."

As he sat down, he looked triumphantly at Lazar.

Lazar ran a thumb over his left eyebrow, circled Kashdan's name three times with the red pen - almost tearing through the paper - and said, "I have no questions for this witness."

Shammai tugged on Lazar's sleeve, but Lazar just shook his head.

Kashdan, as he left the witness stand, began coughing violently. He got himself under control, except for a brief spasm as he passed Shammai.

Chapter 17

Findlay raised an index card, examining it like a mounted butterfly. "Josh Green."

Shammai frowned. "Findlay practically tore Kashdan apart. What do you think he's going to do to Josh?"

"A better point is, what's Josh's testimony going to do to you?"

Josh, standing at the door and ignoring the bailiff's prompts, unable to look at any one thing for more than a few seconds, brushed his hair back twice, despite its being close cut. Finally, wiping his mouth on his sleeve, he raced through the gauntlet of benches, practically collapsing in the witness stand.

"He's not usually that nervous," Shammai said.

"He doesn't usually testify against a friend, either," Lazar pointed out, pushing the pens aside and leaning forward.

Findlay, sitting on the edge of the table, casually flipped through a stack of index cards, not looking at the witness. "Mr. Green," he said, rotating through the stack, as if searching for one in particular, ""You are a friend of the defendant, are you not?"

"Sure, I've always thought so," Josh said, relaxing after making eye contact with Shammai and Lazar.

"Would you consider yourself a confidant?"

"Well," Josh said, moving his shoulders. "I don't know that anyone besides Hannah - his wife - is Shammai's confidant. He's sort of like his namesake."

"Oh?" Findlay stopped sorting and looked up. "How's that?"

"He's not exactly the most patient guy." Josh's smile didn't last long. "But we all respect him. A lot. The *shul* needs him."

"Not as much as Mr. Enstein did, I take it."

"Oh, that," Josh said, sitting back and waving his hand. "Shammai didn't do anything the rest of us wouldn't have done. I mean, what's the big deal about walking an old man, especially a founder, to shul, or bringing him *challah*?"

"Or having him teach your children, or sending them on his errands, or shopping for him, or checking on his -" Findlay caught himself.

Lazar looked up sharply.

"Well, my kids aren't old enough," Josh said, squirming a little.

"Still," Findlay said, returning his attention to sorting the cards, "isn't it remarkable -" he held one up, put it back in the stack "- that a man noted for his lack of patience would have so much of it for an individual who, it seems, lacked certain social graces?"

"Objection. Witness is being asked for hearsay and speculation."

Findlay looked up from the index cards as if Lazar was just a little nuisance. "The witness has knowledge of the defendant's reputation in the community, which is admissible hearsay. He is being asked to provide details of that reputation."

"Overruled," Sifer said.

Josh shifted in the chair. "There are different kinds of patience," he said, his voice rising in annoyance. "I've seen Shammai concentrate for hours on a project. That's a kind of patience."

"Hmm," Findlay said, "so he has patience for things and puzzles, but not people." He held up another card.

"I didn't say that."

Findlay looked at him. "I thought that was the implication. Well, we'll come back to that. Do you like books?"

"What?" The question startled Josh.

"I didn't think it a difficult question, Mr. Green," Findlay said, holding the index cards, one by one, to the light, inspecting them. "Do you like books?"

"Sure. I don't read as much as I should. Who does? But, yes, I like books."

"As much as your friend?"

"Shammai? The only one who likes books more is Mr. Enstein. Was Mr. Enstein," Josh hastily corrected himself.

"As a friend, a close friend, I assume you've been in his house?"

"Sure. Many times."

"How many books does he have?" Findlay put the index cards. "Approximately."

Josh did some quick calculations, rolling his eyes, counting on his fingers. "I don't know. A hundred, I guess. Maybe two hundred."

"Is that a lot of books?"

Josh shrugged. "How should I know?"

Findlay rested his chin in his hand, the forefinger extending up. "How many bookcases do these hundred or two hundred books fill?"

"A couple."

"Does that seem like a large collection for a person whose love for books was second only to Mr. Enstein?"

"No, I guess not," Josh said glumly.

"Your honor," Lazar said. "I think counsel has gotten his witnesses confused. Mr. Green's business is real estate, not books. I suggest this line of questioning is irrelevant."

Judge Sifer lowered his head and stared at Findlay. "You did not indicate any need to recall Mr. Heuerstein."

"I have no intention of doing so," Findlay said smoothly. "If the court will bear with me, I will establish a deliberate pattern of inordinate flattery and misuse of a confidential relationship."

Sifer sat back. "Very well. I will bear with you - up to a point. Overruled."

Findlay nodded. "So the defendant loves books, but has a rather small collection for a bibliophile. I take it then that he doesn't collect much of anything?"

"No," Josh said. "He's got an extensive collection of classical records."

"Oh, I see. Nothing particularly valuable, though?"

"No. I don't think Shammai goes in for the rare or expensive. I don't know if he can afford it."

"Did he ever show an interest in Mr. Enstein's books?"

"Objection."

"Sustained."

Findlay granted Lazar a tight-lipped smile. "You've known the defendant how long?"

"Eight or nine years."

"You've been friends that long?"

"Not for the first year or two," Josh said, relaxing. "I mean, we hit it off right away, but it took a while before we became close."

"Yes, it takes time to develop a relationship," Findlay said drily. "Especially one of trust. So how did you first become aware of his interest in books?"

Josh scratched his head. "Well, I guess it must have been right after Mr. Enstein started teaching Elie."

Shammai groaned. Lazar patted his arm a couple times.

"Oh?" Findlay said, propping himself on the table and picking up the index cards again. "Why do you say that?"

"Well, one Friday night - no, maybe it was a *yom tov*, like Sukkos or Simchas Torah - anyway, he told me he'd just been to Mr. Enstein's house and had I seen the books."

"Objection. Hearsay," Lazar said, not bothering to get up.

"I believe," Findlay said, "that it qualifies as an admission against interest."

Sifer nodded. "So it does. Overruled."

Lazar turned to Shammai. "I knew that, but I had to try."

"Thanks. At least I've still got one friend," Shammai said.

Findlay returned to examining the cards. "How is it that you remember that particular conversation?"

"For a couple reasons," Josh said, apparently not realizing what he'd done. "For one, Shammai was really excited, and he doesn't usually get real excited - I mean, wide-eyed, pumped-up excited. Then, it was the first time my wife could go out after our first child - it must have been a *Yom Tov*, come to think of it - and we were having dinner at Shammai and Hannah's. And I'd owed him a present and I remember thinking, I didn't know he liked books, maybe I'll get him one."

"And this was seven years ago? Right after Mr. Enstein began tutoring his son?"

Josh rolled his eyes and counted. "No, it'll be seven this Rosh Hashanah. That's when my Miri turns seven."

"Congratulations," Findlay said. "Was that the only time he mentioned books to you?"

"Oh, no," Josh said. "Over the years, it was something he talked about. He really admired Mr. Enstein's library. I've seen it. It really is remarkable."

"But," Findlay said, picking up the index cards again, "surely your friend talked about his own books?"

Josh scratched behind his ear. "Come to think of it, not really. Not with me." His eyes narrowed in suspicion. "It's not like we talked about books much, at all. You're looking at, what, a dozen conversations, maybe, casual, small-talk thing, over six or seven years."

"You're right," Findlay said, smiling. "That's not very many conversations, considering they weren't his books and he was doing so much for Mr. Enstein." He ruffled the index cards a couple times. "Now, Mr. Green, I'd like to return to the question of Shammai's patience - or lack thereof. In what way does he lack patience?"

Josh shrugged. "He doesn't put up with a lot of nonsense. You know, gossip, power games, that sort of thing."

"Do you mean he doesn't listen to it?"

"That and he gets angry when he sees it happening."

"How does he react to criticism?" Findlay asked, straightening the index cards into a pile which he held in one hand.

"Depends. If it's of his work and right, he's grateful. I don't know of anybody who looks for constructive criticism more, in that area. For other things -" Josh shook his head. "Well, you better be very right, and very polite or he'll give you twice what he got."

"Did Mr. Enstein ever criticize him?"

"Mr. Enstein criticized everyone.' Josh laughed.

Findlay dropped the cards on the table and stood up. "Did Mr. Enstein berate or harass Shammai?"

"Objection," Lazar said, without much conviction.

"Overruled," Sifer responded. "You know better, counselor."

Josh looked at the judge. "He gave him a lot of grief, sure. But, like I said, he did that to everyone. No one was good enough."

"Not even Elie, I suppose," Findlay said. "But we'll return to that. Let me see if I understand. Mr. Enstein reproached everyone. Did he have favorite subjects for this pastime?"

"Well, I guess you'd have to say Shammai, Levinsky and Kashdan. Though Lazar and me weren't far behind some times."

Findlay turned, stared at Lazar and, for an instant, bared his teeth. Then he faced Josh again.

"An interesting combination," Findlay said, twice tapping his index finger in his palm. Then he put his hands in his pockets and began to stroll around the courtroom. "If someone else, yourself or Mr. Kashdan, say, spoke to Shammai the way Mr. Enstein did, how would Shammai have reacted?"

Josh laughed. "Probably exploded."

"So," Findlay said, stopping to scratch behind an ear. "Shammai accepted no criticism, except from Mr. Enstein. Not only that, he went out of his way, even involving his family, to befriend and be useful to a man who censured him - something he would not normally endure."

Josh struggled to restrain himself from finding release in a nervous gesture. "We never thought of it like that."

"I realize that," Findlay said, with a short laugh. "I assume, though, that Shammai would at least get angry at Mr. Enstein for criticizing Elie?"

"Not really," Josh said, making smoothing motions over his hair. "At least, not directly at Mr. Enstein. He'd say something to me or Lazar if Mr. Enstein got harsh - usually when Elie made a mistake. But I never heard him say anything directly to Mr. Enstein. And he wouldn't let us say anything to Mr. Enstein - or himself, either." Josh, half rising from the chair, looked at Judge Sifer. "But he put up with it because of Elie. He wanted Mr. Enstein to teach him, and he'd do anything to guarantee that."

"Including," Findlay said, drawing back Josh's attention, "admiring his library. But your friend received no compensation for helping Mr. Enstein? Free tutoring or something?"

Josh waited for the question, then realizing that was it, replied, "Not that I know. Shammai certainly paid for Elie's lessons."

"Did he ever say anything to indicate he expected compensation in the future?"

"No," Josh said emphatically, practically spitting the word.

Findlay bowed his head to the right.

"Oh, come, in all that time, and with all the abuse he and his son took, the defendant - the impatient defendant - limited himself to silence?"

"No," Josh said, even more emphatically, "I didn't say that. But, well, he always seemed to take it in stride, like, what more could you expect, and Mr. Enstein was tutoring his son - that meant a lot to Shammai, giving Elie the background to be a scholar. And he looked on it as a duty, taking care of Mr. Enstein - so how could he stay angry with him?"

"How indeed?" Findlay said. "It's amazing he continued to perform so onerous a duty on a volunteer basis."

"Shammai didn't think it was an onerous duty."

"I'm sure he didn't," Findlay said ironically. "But surely your conclusion is based on something other than impressions. For instance, did he ever say anything that indicated he found the duty pleasurable?"

"Not pleasurable, but - worth it."

"What was the nature of that conversation, please?"

Lazar stood. "Objection."

Findlay didn't bother to turn around. "The defendant's comments are, again, admission against interest."

Sifer thought for a while, his chin in his hands,. "Overruled."

Findlay picked up the cards and held them up in one hand. "Mr. Green? You're under oath."

Josh shrugged nervously. "Once, a few months ago, shortly before Mr. Enstein died, Elie read the Torah and made a few mistakes. He doesn't usually do that Shabbos *mincha* - the afternoon service," Josh added, looking up at the judge who had coughed for an explanation. "Mr. Enstein acted really grumpy, and treated Elie like a - well, he didn't compliment him on what he did well, let's just say that. So I asked Shammai why he put up with Mr. Enstein's games and bluster. I was just joking around, you know."

"What," prompted Findlay, "did Shammai respond?"

Josh opened his mouth, then paled. He gave the judge one

quick look of desperation. It must have just dawned on him, Shammai thought.

"I'm waiting," Findlay said.

"He said," Josh swallowed. "He said, 'patience has its rewards'."

Findlay dropped the cards. "No further questions."

Lazar didn't bother to get up. "What was Shammai's tone of voice, Josh?"

Josh thought a moment. "Ironic, I guess. Not like there was some conspiracy. More like 'what can I do,' or - I'm not sure," he ended weakly. "I mean, we were just joking."

Lazar looked down at the table a moment, to let Josh catch his breath. "Maybe he hinted at the rabbinic dictum that a mitzvah - such as caring for the elderly - was not supposed to have any rewards?"

"Objection," Findlay said, "Counsel is leading the witness."

"Sustained."

"How long did you say you've known Shammai?" Lazar asked gently.

"About seven years." Josh had lost his exuberance.

"This admiration he expressed for Mr. Enstein's library - did he ever express a similar admiration for anything else?"

"Sure," Josh said. "A well-played symphony. Anything really artistic, I'd say."

"Was there anything unusual, then, about his admiration for Mr. Enstein's library?"

"I never thought so."

"Did anybody think there was anything unusual about his interest in Mr. Enstein?"

"Objection," Findlay said.

Lazar smiled. "This relates to the defendant's reputation in the community."

"Overruled," Sifer said.

"Josh?" Lazar prompted.

"Anything unusual about his interest in Mr. Enstein? Kashdan didn't like it. But we all thought it was, well, nice. You know that."

Lazar dropped his pen onto the table. "No further questions."

Sifer nodded at Josh, who took off again. Shammai, sitting with his arms folded, refused to look at Josh.

"He's a friend," Lazar said, unconvincingly.

Shammai shook his head.

Findlay had stood up, but Lazar spoke first. "Your honor, I respectfully request we adjourn for the day."

Judge Sifer made a show of rolling up the long black sleeve and looking at his watch. "It's barely past two o'clock. Are we suddenly competing with bankers or do you have another trial?"

"No, your honor. My client is an observant Jew and since it's Friday, he needs some time to prepare for the Sabbath."

"Mr. Findlay?"

"One moment, your honor." Findlay quickly consulted with the Osteriks. "Your honor, this is only a delaying tactic. We can continue until five, as is normal, and still leave the defendant and his attorney plenty of time - at least two hours."

Lazar leaned on the table. "I didn't realize you were such an expert on preparing for Shabbat."

Judge Sifer banged his gavel. "Enough. Counselor, how many more witnesses do you have?"

"Three or four, at least," Findlay said. "Depending on their testimony, there may be one or two others."

"Are we likely to get through even those four today?"

Findlay hesitated. "That depends on how they answer."

Sifer leaned forward and put his chin in his hands. "Of course, defense will also have to call its witnesses. As this trial will have to resume on Monday regardless, I see no reason to cause the defendant or his family any unnecessary hardship. Therefore -" Sifer rolled up his sleeve and looked at his watch again -"Court is adjourned until nine AM, Monday." He banged the gavel once.

Chapter 18

"He's not there any more."

Shammai, distracted by his son's comment, which interrupted his visionary reconstruction of the judicial maneuvers and stratagems, looked up.

In his mind's eye, he had been in the courtroom, his overwhelming oratory generating ovations and applause from friends and functionaries, his enemies cringing at his rhetoric. Findlay had been begging him for forgiveness and disbarring himself. Earl and Simon Osterik, the silent, lurking, greedy, hypocritical manipulators had been trying to sneak out, but were unable to slither away from the boos, the ridicule, the condemnation they met wherever they turned. Lazar had been dancing clownishly. And the judge and witnesses - somehow versions of himself - sat with mouths open in amazement and admiration.

His attention emerged from the mists of wishful expectations, from the disorienting wonder of where-am-I; seeing Elie, focusing on his son a few steps ahead, brought into the light the dimness of his fanciful revisions.

He should have taken the car, he thought. Too much time to think now.

He started walking again, not seeing any relevance to Elie's remark.

Elie just pointed across the street, compelling Shammai to look there, to follow the direction of his son's outstretched arm. Shifting his focus, he stared and saw they were directly opposite Mr. Enstein's house.

He scrutinized the exterior. Could it need a coat of paint already? It hadn't needed painting the day Mr. Enstein passed away.

The second step looked uneven; maybe a crack in the concrete had spread. The grass had been cut, but the hedge needed trimming and the little flower garden - with begonias, and whatevers - needed weeding. The metal railing looked fine. That reminded him, the front door had needed to be planed for years.

He should have taken the car, he thought again. Too much time to think now.

A question had lurked behind Elie's remark, presented again by Elie's expectant look and posture, but it seemed as indecipherable as Shammai's dream-only eloquence.

"We'll be late for *mincha*," he said.

Elie's response - immediate - a step, then two - evoked, by its familiarity, its confidence, the poignancy of how long it had been since he had - and so reiterated an insistent, relentless yearning to - to - to simply walk with his son.

The next dozen steps, in tandem, seemed a revelation - and a resolution - in and of themselves.

"It's not going well, is it?" Elie asked quietly.

Shammai, recollecting the impression of those few steps - as ephemeral as his fantasy of justice - with photographic intensity, again felt distracted by Elie's voice.

That's right, he told himself. Elie had not been in the courtroom. Where had he been? Outside, keeping Dinah Chaya company.

"No," Shammai said, "It's not."

"I wouldn't think he had any case at all," Elie said encouragingly.

"I've learned one thing, son," Shammai said ruefully. "Given a choice between appearance and truth, bet on appearance to win."

"You don't mean that." Elie' said.

"You're right," Shammai said after a pause, "I don't. But it's hard when your friends betray you. Did you know that I used you to

272

get at Mr. Enstein?"

"Who said that?"

He had angered Elie. "No one, but Kashdan and Josh were tricked and twisted into creating that appearance. At least, I hope they were tricked," he added, more to himself, his bitterness more because he had begun to doubt his acquaintances.

"They didn't betray you deliberately." Elie's voice trembled slightly.

"I know, but I think the unintentional in some ways hurts more." During one of Elie's many nervous glances, their eyes met. "I'm fine," Shammai assured him.

But he couldn't get Josh out of his mind. The others, well, he could make an excuse for them. Heuerstein hardly knew him; he might have some loyalty to Mr. Enstein, but how would he know which way Mr. Enstein's heart turned? Mr. Levinsky - he knew what was at stake, but then, he'd described the situation, hadn't he? If anything, maybe he'd given Lazar some help, maybe he'd misled Findlay enough. Kashdan? Well, Jonathan Kashdan was very focused on a few things, and he didn't see beyond that.

Not that any of them wished him harm, Shammai knew. They just weren't aware - how could they be?

But Josh? Josh Green had been his friend. Next to Lazar - and Lazar was different - Josh was his closest friend.

It wasn't so much what Josh had said, he told himself. It's what he didn't say. Or add. Didn't Josh realize that he'd emphasized the one point that gave 'undue influence' any credence at all? Didn't he realize that his one quotation, taken out of context, had practically destroyed Shammai's case? Surely Josh knew it was coming. Surely, he could have prepared to meet it.

Shammai understood what being on the witness stand did to people. But still, it hadn't been right. Josh had betrayed him.

What bothered him most, now, was how to deal with Josh.

Close enough to the *shul* now that Shammai could see figures in the reddening light, he peered, uncomfortable conjectures preceding his discernment. But it was only Benjie and Malachi who, lounging on the steps, waiting for Elie, waved to them. Elie didn't move from his father's side.

And what will be with the others, who haven't been called yet? What will their testimony do?

"There's nothing to it, is there?" Elie asked.

"Nothing to what?" Shammai asked back.

"To what that lawyer, Findlay's, getting them to say."

His first reaction, to explode at his son, he immediately repressed. The question had not been an accusation, but a plea for reassurance. Shammai took a deep breath.

Again, for the thousandth time - but this time more searchingly, more incisively, if possible more honestly, because he had to answer to Elie - he reconstructed his thoughts over the past thirteen or so years, even the past six years, testing links from first meetings and first impressions to distanced actions and motives. But again, for the thousandth time, all his images of Mr. Enstein blurred into a constant repetition of three scenes: entering Mr. Enstein's house to see him tutoring Elie or Dinah Chaya, then looking at the collection of books while waiting; a tedious walk to shul, having to be vigilant of Mr. Enstein's balance and ego; a discussion or service or Torah reading brought to a halt by a rebuke, a question, an interjection of Mr. Enstein's - an interruption usually correct.

In all this, somewhere, were the selfish, even greedy, thoughts that had occasionally mocked him. When had his motivation changed from gratitude or friendship or even "for the sake of heaven" to acquisitiveness?

It hadn't, he told himself. An occasional wayward thought, envy of Mr. Enstein's knowledge and resources, admiration for the books - these weren't a moral coercion or an abuse of a confidential relationship. He hadn't expected to have been included in the will - and in fact, he wasn't. If not for the coincidence of Dinah Chaya delivering *challah* when Mr. Enstein had his heart attack, he would have been given nothing. But was anything ever really coincidence?

"Dad?"

"No, of course not," he answered Elie with a smile. "Findlay's got nothing. The *siddur* is ours."

They had reached the traffic signal and were waiting for it to change.

"What if you lose?" Elie asked, with a strange intensity.

Well, what would change, he thought. He shrugged. "Imagine there had been no dying gift, no lawsuit - what would have happened if Dinah Chaya had arrived a minute earlier or a minute later?"

"But it didn't happen that way," Elie said, crossing the street.

"No," Shammai sighed, following his son. "And I guess we can't go back. But we can at least go on. But I have to follow it through because, win or lose, I owe it to him. And to you. It's my fight now, and I'll see it through."

For a moment, Elie's face reflected some profound, perhaps desperate internal struggle. Shammai, unconsciously, expected, hoped to share in it. But it passed as quickly as it came, and Elie stepped ahead to his friends.

Shammai hesitated on the threshold. He had to go in. He had to face Josh. He took a deep breath, as if plunging into deep waters, and opened the door.

Inside, Shammai made a quick count. One short for *mincha*. That was another thing. Since Mr. Enstein had died, the minyan seemed more fragile. They had nine now, as a core: Kashdan, Lazar, Shammai, Josh, Mishael, Sagalman and the three boys, Benjie, Malachi and Elie. It had been ten through May but Aryeh had left for the summer. *Shacharis* had never been a problem; at least a half-dozen other men, plus a few women and children, would always show up for Shabbos morning services. So far, they'd been able to get two or three others to rotate for *maariv* Friday night. But *mincha* . . .

They never seemed to have had a problem with Mr. Enstein around. Even though the same people as before - Kashdan or Mishael, usually, sometimes Josh - made the pre-Shabbos or minyan phone calls, the results, though often the same, now seemed somehow tentative, uncertain.

Something of the confidence had slipped away.

And, he thought, it wouldn't take many missed minyans, coming up short one or two, to start more than their confidence to stumble and fall.

Might as well get on with it, he told himself as he approached Mishael, standing by the *siddurim* and urging everyone to take one. "Good Shabbos. Where's Josh?"

"He's in the kitchen or office," Mishael said. "Ranny said he would come tonight," he added by way of explanation for the delay.

"Ranny always says he'll come." Shammai smiled. Glancing at the wall clock, he added, "It's getting late. We should *daven*."

"We'll wait another minute. Will you get Josh?"

Shammai hesitated, took a step, then said, "He'll come when he hears *Ashrei*."

Mishael looked at him curiously. Even if he's heard rumors or reviews, he wasn't in the courtroom. He doesn't know how it feels. Shammai took a *siddur* from Mishael and walked steadily but self-consciously to the seat behind where Mr. Enstein had always sat. He stared down at the open page in front of him, forcing himself not to look up at any of the voices, feet-shuffling or other commotion.

The door opened and shut, and Mishael passed him on the way to the *amud*. So Ranny had come after all.

Mishael's clear, accented voice began. At the beginning of *kaddish*, Shammai stood and, despite his earlier resolve, automatically looked around to check on the minyan.

Josh stood on the opposite side, by the office door. Their eyes met - or rather, their gazes passed each other, momentarily intersecting.

Shammai immediately looked away, trying to refocus on the words in front of him. He could guess at many things in Josh's eyes, but could be sure of seeing only the reflection of his own discomfort.

During the repetition of the *Amidah*, he forced himself to follow the words as Mishael read, though the back of his neck itched intensely from the sensation of being looked at, and not knowing exactly when or for how long.

At the closing *kaddish*, his glance again found Josh, half-turned away, and by now standing at his usual place by the *bima*.

Shammai wondered, not for the first time, if he should say the mourner's *kaddish* for Mr. Enstein. The question's pathos struck him more forcefully than ever. But he wasn't going to do it just once a week and he knew he wouldn't make it across town three times a day, every day. Besides, he'd paid the yeshiva to find a substitute, and that was more than acceptable, especially for a non-relative.

Let Earl and Simon Osterik say it, if they knew how. As if they cared.

As he sat down after *Aleinu*, Shammai thought about his options. He could just sit, ignoring everyone and hoping to avoid a confrontation; he'd probably become in absentia the focus of whatever gossip passed around until *maariv*, but he didn't think that would bother him much. He could isolate Lazar or - not Elie, but maybe Elie and his friends - not Sagalman, he hadn't testified and was where Josh had been; that way, he might avoid the problem, at least for the night. Or, he could confront Josh, which would automatically expose all the fragilities he'd been hiding from.

Josh made the decision for him. He came around the *bima*, heading directly for Shammai - the only sign of Josh's tension, a little less glad-handedly than usual.

"Missed you at your usual spot," he said, doing a poor job of pretending there was no tension between them. He put one foot up on a folding chair and leaned forward. "But I guess you don't have to run interference for him any more."

The remark - a clear reference to Mr. Enstein - so startled Shammai he forgot his internal debate, all the half-formed salutations. Did Josh truly not realize - as his bantering tone indicated - the insult - especially after his testimony - of his words? Did he really not realize what he'd done? Did his social clumsiness extend so far?

"You know that program you installed?" Josh continued. "I've gotten a bunch of phone calls from others in the business. They're interested. Maybe we can work something out, in terms of licensing or leasing."

Did Josh expect only a superficial business response?

"Your testimony didn't match your deposition," Shammai said quietly.

Josh's foot came off the chair, the only outward sign of disturbance. "I guess that answers my question," Josh said, looking away.

The silence between them spread, transmitting an uncomfortable curiosity throughout the shul.

"Lazar warned me," Josh said, tapping his foot. "He said you'd be angry and hurt. But you could have waited until after Shabbos to show it."

Shammai looked up, but remained tight-lipped. "You came over to me."

"I had to. I wouldn't have if you'd taken your usual place, put up an appearance." Hands clenched, licking his lips, eyes darting, running a hand over his short hair - Josh fought to speak, finally blurting, pleading, "Why?"

Shammai looked away.

"What was I supposed to do?" Suddenly, Josh grabbed a chair, turned it backwards and sat down. "I was on the witness stand. I was under oath! You wanted me to lie?"

"You could have remembered it during deposition. We would have had a chance to prepare."

"If I'd remembered it, don't you think I would have said it? Don't you think I would have qualified it then?"

' "If we'd known, we could have prepared," Shammai said with a sigh. He turned back to face Josh. He felt tired. "You could have been more - recalcitrant. You could have tried to - oh, I don't know - show it all differently."

"It's intimidating up in that box," Josh said apologetically. "Confusing."

"Not confusing or intimidating enough, I guess."

"I've been audited twice by the IRS," Josh said vehemently. "Both combined weren't as bad as five minutes up there."

"Come on, Josh," Shammai said. "You gave a deposition. You've talked to Kashdan and Sagalman. And Lazar. It's not like you didn't know what the case was about, what Findlay wanted to prove."

"You could have talked to me beforehand. You and Lazar," Josh said defensively. "Prompted me."

"To do what? Not quote something I don't even remember saying? To make it look like I confided in you a desire for Mr. Enstein's books?"

"I didn't do that."

"Then it was a good imitation, because Findlay got just what he wanted."

"Then why didn't Lazar cross-examine me, change the impression?"

"Because -" Shammai stopped. He couldn't bring himself to

say it.

Almost everyone had gathered behind Josh. Well, what else did they have to do between services? Noticeably absent were Lazar, Elie and the other two boys.

Josh stood up, picked up the chair, turned it around and planted it with a thud on the floor. "What I want to know is," he challenged, "are we still friends?"

But that was it. The answer came, surprisingly, without thought or effort.

"As much as we ever were," Shammai said, wearied of all the struggles just to be himself.

It all began to annoy him: Josh's anxiety, Kashdan's assurance, the Osterlik's greed, Findlay's dissections - even Lazar's sarcasm. All he wanted right now was to protect his daughter, communicate with his son and make his wife smile again. And he couldn't do that, not by giving up, not by going on. He had trapped himself.

Josh hadn't moved. Apparently, satisfied with the reconciliation, he wanted to express his sympathy. "I sure don't begrudge you some reward for your patience," he said.

Shammai almost laughed. Like everything else, even the sympathy of a friend now seemed wrong. "I didn't say you did."

"And I certainly didn't think it was anything more than that. I think Mr. Enstein just acted on the spur of the moment."

"I never thought you gave any credence to their claim," Shammai said. Now he was comforting Josh!

"I just wish Lazar had asked me that. He could have, you know."

Shammai shrugged. "Why don't you ask him why he didn't?"

"I think I will." Josh stuck out his hand in his over-friendly way. Grasping it did nothing for Shammai's tension.

Josh, relieved of any further responsibility, went over to Lazar, determined to find out why he hadn't been questioned more.

"Touching," Kashdan said. "Your greed puts Green in a dilemma, and he ends up asking your forgiveness."

Before Shammai could respond, Mishael said, "That' s not fair. You know Shammai didn't ask Mr. Enstein for anything or even try to influence him. It was just a coincidence Dinah Chaya showed up at that exact moment. It's obvious to everyone."

"That may be the critical fact," Kashdan said. "But is it the critical point of law? Clearly not. While the judge decides that, Shammai's getting destroyed. The shul's getting destroyed."

"Should I just walk away from it?" Shammai asked wearily.

Kashdan waited a moment before responding. "You could take a settlement."

"What makes you think they'll still offer one?"

"You want to ask Lazar?"

"Not really."

"My point, exactly," Kashdan said.

Sagalman spoke up for the first time. "Jonathan's right about one thing. We can't afford a scandal in the community."

"Especially if we want to grow," Kashdan added.

"Grow how?" Mishael asked.

So much, Shammai thought, so much. Books and shuls are supposed to bring people together. But there has to be a center. Here, everything was flying apart now. Was this the legacy Mr. Enstein intended to leave them?

Shammai rose, escaping from the debate, of which he remained the center, just as Josh banged for the start of *Kabbalos Shabbos*.

Chapter 19

Shammai sat in the rocking chair, eyes closed, fingertips touching at his upper lip, oblivious to the music playing around him, ignoring the counterpoint sounds of his children. Back and forth, he concentrated solely, deeply on the slight effort of his feet and legs to create the back and forth, the tidal effect of the rocking chair.

The phone rang. He fought down the impulse to answer it. Let it wait. For so few conversations, he had talked too much this weekend. Its last evening would be a true quiet, not the false silence of tension. Tomorrow's destruction would come soon enough.

Amazing how fragile one's ego could be. All he had to do was open his eyes. They would focus, automatically, on the source of his future and past - the *siddur*.

He felt a presence over him.

"You're not even thinking," Hannah said, as if the accusation made him guilty of something.

He looked up at her. "So?"

"So if you're not thinking, and you're not working, and you're not resting, and you're not really doing anything but rocking yourself into depression, you could get up and help me with the kids or the dishes."

He smiled. "Well, if those are my choices, then I was thinking."

"Oh, about what?" Hannah glanced quickly behind her, trying to do so undetected.

Shammai stretched. "Difficulties."

"Past or future?"

"Present."

"Then go do the dishes," she said.

"What?"

"If you're thinking about past difficulties," Hannah said, folding her arms, "like how hard Shabbos was, or how short-tempered Lazar was, or how crazy Dinah Chaya's going, or how much Moshe and Aaron fought, or how contradictory Elie was - well, then, considering how little cooperation I got from you handling all that, I'd let you think about it, because maybe you'd apologize."

"Wait a minute," Shammai said, standing up.

"On the other hand," Hannah continued, "if you're thinking about how our daughter's going to survive a summer away from home - she's leaving at the end of the week, you know - after all this, or if you're going to be able to walk into the shul, or if you'll even have any business left - well, then, I'd let you think about all that, too, because maybe you'd find a way to keep the family going and wake up a little. But as you're not going to apologize and you're not going to get any work done - and you sure can't do anything about the *siddur* - you can do the dishes."

Shammai raised his hand and opened his mouth, but found he had nothing to say.

"What piece is that?" Hannah asked as she turned off the radio.

Shammai knew that piece almost by heart, but couldn't remember its name. "I don't remember."

"A Little Night Music. By Mozart," Hannah said in an even-I-know-that tone.

"Have I really been that bad?" Shammai asked.

Hannah relented and sat down on the couch. She seemed to suddenly relax. "I've had worse Sundays. At least you could share your sorrows. That's one reason I'm here, you know."

"I know, and I'm sorry." Shammai looked about. "Where are the kids?"

"Moshe and Aaron are supposedly doing homework. Dinah Chaya's on the phone and Elie went out to ride his bike."

"I'll go do the dishes then, I guess." He started toward the kitchen. "Do you want the paper?"

"You can bring it to me in a minute," she said.

Cleaning up after dinner - an easy job on Sundays, when they usually ate leftover chicken or *cholent* - took his mind off the lawsuit, the *shul* and all the unsolvable problems that went with them.

It didn't actually take his mind off them - the focal point of his life remained the leitmotif of his thoughts, influencing his perspective on things otherwise unrelated - what he looked for in the paper, how he responded to certain types of questions, how he interacted with service people - at the gas station, the grocery store, the drug store.

But at least the activity of scrubbing, rinsing and stacking, distracted him. He scoured the *cholent* pot vigorously, wearing himself out disproportionately to the amount of cleaning accomplished. His arm would be sore tomorrow if he kept it up.

He poured some soap and steaming hot water into the pot and let it soak. He'd reached his limit of exercise as stress relief. He dried his hands and headed into the serenity of the living room. He picked up the paper from the table as he passed.

Hannah looked up from the rocking chair. He frowned, but she didn't get up. When had she moved? She must have been looking at the *siddur*.

He sat on the couch and dropped the paper on the floor between them.

"All done?" she asked, picking up the Metro section.

"All but the *cholent* pot. It's soaking. I had my quota of

physical therapy." He searched for the sports, but couldn't find it.

"Don't mess up the ads, I need to go through them for coupons," Hannah said.

Not finding it, and not feeling energetic enough to go into the boys' area to search, he settled for the Living section, which he knew he'd finish without reading anything in it.

He settled himself on the cushions. "By the way," he said, flipping pages, "did the phone ring earlier?"

"Yes."

"Who was it?"

"Lazar," Hannah said.

Instantly, he sat up, crumpling the paper. "Why didn't you call me? I wasn't sleeping."

"I can talk, too," she said, without looking back at him. She finished the article before speaking again. "Anyway, he wanted to talk to me."

"What did he want?"

"He wanted to know if I'd be there tomorrow."

Shammai looked down at the mass of wrinkled paper in his hand. It might be good for paper mache', he thought irrelevantly. He'd better be careful where he put his hands, sure to be smeared with newsprint now.

"Why wouldn't you be there tomorrow?" Shammai asked.

"I don't know," Hannah said.

"What I mean is, why would Lazar ask if you're going to be there? Did he assume you wouldn't?"

"I don't know," Hannah repeated. "Call him up and ask him."

Shammai dropped the paper on the floor and stood up. "He didn't ask you to testify, did he?"

"No, and if I was going to be a witness for anybody, I wouldn't have been allowed in the courtroom."

"That's true." Shammai began pacing behind the rocking

chair.

Hannah folded the paper in her lap and looked over her shoulder at him. "I don't think it's all that serious. I'd guess he just wanted moral support to be there - for himself as well as you."

"Oh, it's not that," Shammai said, waving his hand. "It got me thinking about something else. About Elie."

"Elie?" By now she'd turned almost completely around. "Dinah Chaya's the one who's going to have to testify."

"No, no, not about that - I should talk to her tonight, I guess. I was just wondering if we should let Elie come tomorrow."

"I didn't think that was even a question," Hannah said, surprised.

"Well, there is school, he's not testifying and -" he stopped pacing and stared at the *siddur* in its glass case.

"And what?"

"Well, he is only thirteen. I thought it got pretty rough."

Hannah got up and started straightening the newspapers. "He's been all right so far, hasn't he? Did you have any problems in *shul* I don't know about?"

"No. Everything was fine. After I spoke with Josh." He lowered his head on his hands on top of the rocking chair, unconsciously imitating Judge Sifer. When he realized what he was doing, he shrugged. "Just some extra nervous tension."

"Don't you want him there?"

"Very much," he said emphatically.

"Well then! And besides," Hannah said, her arms full of the paper, "he's not even in the courtroom. He's outside with Dinah Chaya." She headed to the kitchen table.

"That's another thing," he said, stretching, "considering that they haven't gotten along too well since - I can't really blame them, it's a lot of tension - is it the best thing for him to be there? I mean, a lot of our case rests on her testimony."

"Ah, it comes out at last," she said, dropping the papers on the table. "You're afraid that he'll get her upset and she won't be the star witness."

"That's not it!" he protested.

"From what I understand - which is what she told me - Elie's actually helping to calm her down, telling jokes and things. I think she wants him there. But if you don't, just say so."

He turned to face her. "I do want him there. I need his support. But I don't want to lose him."

She gave him a strange look. "What makes you say that?"

"What if I lose?" He threw his arms about. "The *siddur's* a trust, not just a thank you -"

The back screen door slammed shut, interrupting him, followed by the thud of the back door itself being pushed into place. They listened to the refrigerator open and shut.

"Wash your hands," Hannah called.

Elie appeared, breathing hard, his face setting-sun red, his hair matted and dripping, a can of soda in his hand. "Hi," he said between gasps.

"Where did you go?" Shammai asked.

"Around the park," Elie replied, heaving a few times before using his forearm to wipe some droplets from his forehead. He took a drink. His breathing slowed down a little. "Where is everyone?"

"Moshe and Aaron are doing homework and Dinah Chaya's on the phone," Shammai said, glancing at his wife. "I think."

Elie nodded. "I think I'll talk to Dinah Chaya." He took three deep gulps of air, then one of the soda.

""She's not going to let you in her room like that," Hannah said, amused.

"Sure she will," he said. "She's leaving at the end of the week."

He finished the soda and tossed it into the garbage.

"You should wash and change shirts, anyway," Hannah said. "You'll get sick otherwise."

"Okay." He said and turned around,

When he'd disappeared, Shammai laughed. "So much for our fears and worries."

"Your fears and worries, you mean," Hannah said. After a pause, she added. "I think we should take a walk."

He nodded. "You think I should talk to Dinah Chaya?"

"About what? Her summer or her testimony?"

"Well, both, I guess."

Hannah shook her head. "You'll only make her nervous about tomorrow, which will make her a nervous wreck or feel guilty or both about going to camp. Leave her alone. She'll come to us if she needs to."

"Then should Elie -"

She nodded. "She'll tell him to leave her alone if she wants to."

Elie came back, fresh shirts in his hand.

"Your father and I are going for a walk," Hannah said. "Tell your sister, the two of you keep an eye on things, and keep it calm."

He waved on his way into the bathroom.

As soon as they stepped outside, the change in humidity slapped him in the face.

"You really want to go for a walk in this?" he asked, his forehead already beginning to perspire.

She nodded.

"Why?"

"You're making everyone crazy and upset. I'd say especially me, except you're even worse on yourself. The least I can do is get you out of the house for a while and give the children some peace. Who knows, maybe you'll even talk to me."

Shammai smiled. "What about all the roaches?"

Hannah took a quick, fearful glance around the yard and sidewalk. "Stop that," she said. "You know they don't come out until it gets dark."

He looked up at the twilight sky. "Are we going to be gone that long?"

Hannah hesitated. He could see her determination to get him some air warring with her distaste for possible 'visitors'. "I'll let you know."

They started walking, instinctively, towards St. Charles and the streetcar line. One rumbled past, easily heard where they were, four blocks away.

It'll be close to an hour before one passes that way again, on a Sunday evening, he thought. A good signal of time.

He looked at the sky, the westerly clouds outlined in red, streaks of orange in the deepening blue. Twilight lasted longer now. They'd have half an hour before it began to get dark, became better not to walk some of the streets - and not just because of the insects. He glanced at Hannah. That would be their heat limit, as well.

It would have been nice to hear the streetcar returning; it would have somehow foreshadowed the 'final run' he'd make tomorrow.

He could start the conversation she wanted, but this walk had been her idea, let her begin. As he grew increasingly uncomfortable despite the increasing shade and dropping temperature, he found himself relishing his petulance, this mental prank of being obstinate. Of the emotions at his disposal, it seemed the most positive, the most appropriate farewell to Mr. Enstein.

In the meantime, until Hannah decided to speak, he could pretend to ponder how hot New Orleans stayed, or how many hundreds of times he'd made this walk, with how many thousands of changes in his life. Or, he could seem to consider his state of affairs - the project he was working on, the one he hadn't pursued, the one he should follow up on. He could think of many things - but thought only of how slowly the sky darkened and how far they would get before turning back.

After two blocks, Hannah said, as if they'd been talking all along, "So, was it worth it?"

He laughed. "Well, I lose that bet."

"What do you mean?" she demanded.

"I bet myself that you wouldn't speak until we got to the Avenue, and that you'd start with something light. I lost both parts."

"We're almost there," she pointed out. "And it depends on how you answer."

"Oh, no," he said, still trying to be amused. "There's no way to get around this one. I have to either express my deepest emotions, leading to a cathartic bonding, or listen to a lecture that will irrevocably alter my perspective on life."

Hannah laughed. "You've been here before, I see." She fell pensive until they reached St. Charles, with its honor-guard line of antique, low-hanging oaks. "Some day," she said, nodding at the residence that, with its manicured lawn and fenced-in pool, occupied a quarter of the block, "I'm going to go through that iron gate, up those stairs, ring the bell and ask who lives there."

"I'm sure you'll both be pleasantly surprised," Shammai said. "It'll probably be someone you know." They had often fantasized about that house, or one of the dozens like it along the Avenue.

"Are we going somewhere particular?" Shammai asked, as they turned toward the university.

"You're setting the pace."

"And you the direction," he said, automatically slowing down.

"Let's see how much light's left when we reach the park," she offered.

Another quiet block's walk. Maybe he'd get out of this

without a deep talk or lecture, after all.

"So?" Hannah asked.

"What?" He'd drifted off into a distanced observation of the sporadic activity around them.

"Was it worth it?"

The tension returned. "I'll take the lecture," he said between his teeth.

"Oh, no," she said mimicking him, but responding with the same edge. "You decide this one. I'll simply present the possibilities."

They crossed the street and she started.

"You've jeopardized whatever relation you had with Josh Green; you've put Lazar in a no-win situation; you've increased what I thought improbable, the disdain of Kashdan; you've alienated your daughter - who, I'll remind you again, is leaving home in less than a week; you've turned superficial communication into an art with Elie; you've -"

"I think that's enough," he said. "And for your information, Josh seems anxious to be on better terms, to remove the appearance he made in the courtroom. And I can't be accountable for Lazar's ego or competence, but whatever mistakes he's made, I'm responsible for letting him proceed. Kashdan has his own agenda, as does Levinsky - who you left out. As for Dinah Chaya, how much of it is my preoccupation - I'll admit to that - and how much is her anxiety and how much is your adjustment?"

They walked half a block without speaking.

"And Elie?" she asked quietly.

"That problem existed before. And you know it." He looked behind him.

"Did you know he's been looking at - and through - the *siddur* constantly?" she asked. "All weekend. He just flips the pages. And he doesn't want you to know."

"Really? I wonder what he's looking for."

"His father, maybe?"

"Are we through?"

"No," she said, continuing on.

"It's getting dark."

"In more ways than one," she said. "But I didn't finish. On the other side, you have the *siddur*."

"For the moment."

"So why are you holding on to it? Why are you still fighting? For the children? For Mr. Enstein?"

He closed his eyes for three steps. "You know the answer."

"Maybe. But you don't. Or, at least, it doesn't satisfy you."

"Sagalman's going to testify tomorrow." He stopped and looked at her. "Why did Mr. Enstein wait? What if Dinah Chaya hadn't come by? What if - a thousand possible misses."

She nodded, started walking again. "If it was a dying bequest of gratitude, you owe it to him to somehow preserve what he'd dedicated his life to. And you have to fight for possession to show you hadn't schemed for something like this all along. I understand." They'd reached the park. "But why did he wait, why take the risk, why gamble on a thousand possible misses?" Her words, echoing against his, brought the comfort of a mirrored experience.

"That's the unanswered, unanswerable question," he said, hoping they'd turn back.

She stood a moment, pondering. The night noises began to close in on them. "If Findlay does to Dinah Chaya what he did to the others ..." she didn't finish the thought.

"He'll try," Shammai said. "But she's my best, maybe my only, defense."

She looked up at him. "Is it worth it?"

He met her gaze. "You tell me. If you don't think so, I'll call Lazar right now. I'll accept any compromise. I'll bring it to them tonight."

She shook her head. "Answer this: If she's our only defense, why is the other side calling her to testify?"

He didn't miss her emphatic shift from the singular to plural. "I don't know. I don't think it's just to verify facts."

"OK," she said, "answer this: why did the judge let you keep it at home?"

An image of the *siddur* in the bookcase immediately came to mind. "I don't know that, either. If he favored our side that much, he'd have dismissed the case."

"One more, dear husband: do you have any doubts?"

He looked up through the trees, searching for the moon. Some passing clouds obscured it.

"It's hard watching someone twist the facts of my life - our life - making it into something it's not, trying to turn the internal battle everyone - except a *tzaddik* - fights every day, expose it and make it something dirty -" he swallowed and blinked "- it's hard not to have doubts, not to doubt yourself." He looked at her, pleading.

"Then I'll tell you what you haven't been able to say because you've been too busy being miserable. What we sacrifice for the children, he sacrificed for his books. And it's the same sacrifice: to make sure the tradition lives. The *siddur's* the testimony of one generation to the next. Putting it in a museum, makes our sacrifices an exhibition, something to be remembered but not lived. Now, is it worth it?"

Slowly, he nodded. He felt immensely relieved.

"Good." She smiled at him. "I need a husband with a clear conscience. Win or lose, that's important to me. And the children." She looked around, shivered despite the heat. "Let's go home."

As they crossed the street, free of foliage, he looked up. "It's a full moon."

Chapter 20

"Well," Lazar said as they approached the elevator. "One or two more, and then it's our turn."

"Of course, that one or two more includes me and Dinah Chaya."

"If you want to put it that way, yes."

Passing by a double glass door, Shammai glanced out at the Monday morning traffic jam. Not, he thought, the way to start a week. Not the way to start anything.

Nervous, they were all so nervous, even Lazar. It showed in different ways: Hannah's tightened lips, Dinah Chaya's trembling hand, Elie's frivolity, his own indifference, Lazar's bravado. But each gesture, each involuntary twitch reflected - just as the appearance of warped fluctuations in the air outside indirectly revealed the strength of the summer sun - the intensity of their inner nervousness. He glance outside again. He preferred to suffer the physical heat.

But, really, why should they be nervous? For Lazar, entering court was routine. He and Hannah had resolved it all last night; he would lose. Only Dinah Chaya, because she might - would - have to testify, because she was leaving before Shabbos, because she had not yet had a threshold experience, had a right to be nervous.

"Do we actually have a chance?" Elie asked. "From what I heard over Shabbos, it seems pretty bad."

"Ah, only to the inexperienced ear," Lazar replied. "The fun part of being a lawyer is allowing the opponent to build a seemingly impregnable position and then, with a few deft questions - and perhaps a surprise witness - blow him away."

"And that's what you're going to do?" Elie asked. "You're

going to blow away everything Mr. Levinksy and Josh and Kashdan said?"

Lazar smiled at Shammai and Hannah. "Elie, you haven't passed the bar yet, so I'll ask the questions - at least the embarrassing kind." He grew serious. "No, I only have to show that the evidence - mostly circumstantial - is insufficient to prove undue influence. Besides . . ."

"How are you going to do that?" Elie persisted.

"Well," Lazar said slowly, "since the evidence, such as it is, isn't in dispute, I'll just have to construct a different plot."

"Can you do that?" Elie asked.

"I don't know." Lazar paused. "Reading circumstances from the outside only distorts the true inside story." He pointed to the glass doors. "It's like looking at the atmospheric distortions from air-conditioned safety. You can see the effect of the heat, but since you don't feel it, it's not real. You have to live in it to know it."

"Which side of the glass is the museum?" Hannah said.

"What?" Lazar said, making a face.

"I don't want a compromise," Shammai said quietly.

The elevator opened before them. "Oh, I've guaranteed that," Lazar said, holding the door as they entered.

"How?"

Lazar held a finger to his lips.

Dinah Chaya's agitation prevented him from pursuing the matter for, as the doors closed, she suddenly asked "Do you think there'll be a crowd today?"

The elevator whooshed up.

Lazar shrugged. "Probably not. We'll see."

Shammai wished someone could give his daughter more comfort than that. But comfort of any kind seemed hard to find right now.

The elevator slowed to a stop.

"Lazar," Hannah said abruptly.

"What?"

"We expect you as usual Friday night, win or lose." She spoke with great deliberation.

"You might just want to wait a few hours before making that definitive," he said.

"No, I don't," she said firmly.

After a long pause, Lazar managed a "Thanks."

As the door opened, Shammai sensed the others silently accepting what he and Hannah had realized last night: it was only a question of how he was going to lose. Something mechanical had settled over them all; they had to go through the motions and had surrendered to the routine of doing so.

He had no right to the *siddur*. The cousins were right about that much - only through 'undue influence' could he justify the gift. But it had been given.

The practically deserted corridor to the courtroom, the absence of visitors and spectators, signalled that others had also lost interest or realized the case was all but over.

"At least it's a private execution," Shammai said.

"I prefer -" Lazar began to banter back, then stopped, glancing over his shoulder at the sound of approaching footsteps.

The nephews. Earl and Simon Osterik.

They had a curious look about them. Did they think racing Shammai to the courtroom would help their case?

Earl's wait-I-want-to-talk expression stopped him.

"Let's go, no fraternizing with the enemy," Lazar said.

"Shammai?" Hannah added.

"You all go on ahead," Shammai said, without looking up. "I'll join you."

Lazar started to protest, but Hannah intervened. "Leave him alone," she said. "He knows what's at stake."

Shammai glanced behind him, to make sure they'd gone ahead. Then he faced the approaching brothers, waiting. They seemed fatter, more smug now. Of course, that could just be their proximity.

"So," Earl, leading, said as they closed within talking distance.

"So," Shammai replied. "You wanted to talk?"

"Why do you say that?" Simon asked.

"Don't be silly," Earl chided. "We do want to talk, he detected it, and that's enough."

"We didn't agree, Earl." Simon said, breathing heavily.

"There's nothing to agree on," Earl said. He turned his attention to Shammai, looking him up and down like a specimen. "My brother and I have a little wager. It involves you. At any rate, it comes to this: we will double our settlement offer."

Shammai shook his head.

"We will triple it. That is more than the prayer book is worth."

"Earl."

"Be quiet. He won't accept it. You won't, will you?"

Shammai stared at them, from one to the other. "No."

"I told you," Earl said triumphantly.

"And I told you not to do it this way," Simon said. "We could have worked something out."

"After that countersuit?" Earl said, practically spitting.

"What countersuit?" Shammai asked.

Earl gave him a disdainful look.

"But today's the deadline," Simon continued, speaking to his brother.

"The museum withdraws its offer at five this afternoon," Earl interrupted, smugly explaining to Shammai. "You wouldn't believe what it takes to sell one's prized possessions. I don't think we'll get such an offer again."

"Earl, maybe we can still -"

"He won't change and we won't lose," Earl said. "He knows that. But he needs the facade of his principles." He waved his brother to go ahead. Then he said to Shammai, "If we win tomorrow, we'll sue you for the value of the lost contract." He smiled. "We'll see you in the courtroom, I trust."

With that, Earl followed his brother.

Shammai watched them go. Could Lazar make anything of the exchange? Probably not, for at any rate his refusal to compromise could always be used against him. Had the offer been serious, anyway?

He walked slowly, wanting to avoid further confrontations with anyone.

What countersuit?

On one bench outside the courtroom, Dinah Chaya and Elie sat, talking in whispers. If nothing else, maybe all this brought them closer together.

Standing, waiting for him, were the rest of the *shul* regulars.

"I can't stay long," Kashdan said immediately.

Shammai nodded. That he'd come at all said something.

"I'll be here most of the morning," Josh said. "If you need anything -"

The show of support embarrassed him. Especially when he saw Mr. Levinsky lounging against a wall.

"You better go inside," Sagalman said. "Lazar's waiting. Mishael and I were called as witnesses, so we won't be in with you. I can't stay afterwards."

"I understand," Shammai said. He looked at each of them. "Thank you," he whispered.

They also knew. They all knew the case was lost and they themselves would prove Shammai had used undue influence over

Mr. Enstein. They would be forced to prove what they knew wasn't true.

He entered the courtroom, which hadn't changed over the weekend. The clerk, bailiff, stenographer and other personnel went about setting up, following their own routine, indifferent to the content of the case. Simon, Earl and Findlay sat at their table, relaxed, looking comfortable.

Hannah looked up from reciting psalms as he passed, and they exchanged smiles.

He squeezed in next to Lazar.

"So?" Lazar said.

"So, they offered me three times the value of the *siddur*. At least, Earl did."

"Because the museum offer expires today, right?"

Shammai looked at him, nodded. "A trick?"

Lazar shrugged. "Maybe. Maybe it was honest. I think they wanted to gloat."

Shammai settled back in his chair. "I wouldn't have put it so politely."

"Nothing I can do with it, of course, since you refused it." Lazar opened his briefcase, took out his papers, arranged them, put his hands behind his head and leaned back. "Well, at least we'll see how good my debate skills are. And all the evidence is circumstantial, so it's my reading of it against his."

Which is precisely why I'm worried, Shammai thought. If only there was some real evidence. Either way.

Just then, the clerk called for everyone to rise.

The rigamarole had lost its charm and solemnity the second time around. Even Findlay appeared less imposing and more pompous, he thought.

Judge Sifer leaned forward. "Before we begin, I must ask, has either party sought to negotiate a compromise or offered a settlement since the court adjourned?"

Lazar didn't move. "Just relax," he warned Shammai. "Findlay's got to answer first. Let him sweat his clients' arrogance."

Indeed, Findlay, for the first time, looked uncomfortable. He looked from Earl to Lazar to Simon to Lazar to Shammai to Earl again, all almost too fast to follow - except that he ended up glowering at Earl.

"Your honor, my clients have not authorized me to pursue a settlement since their last offer was rejected."

Lazar whispered, "Oh, well done, noble Findlay! But have you shown Sifer something of your clients you did not want him to see?"

Sifer pursed his lips, then covered them with his fingertips. After a significant pause, he said, "I see." Without taking his eyes off Findlay, he said to Lazar, "And I take it your client has also withheld such authorization?"

Lazar sprang to his feet. "Yes, your honor."

Sifer turned his gaze on Lazar, who did not flinch.

"I expected as much, considering the suit of intervention you filed on behalf of the synagogue this morning. You realize that's rather close to a conflict of interest?"

"I was concerned about that, your honor," Lazar said, "so I researched the situation carefully. I'm sure any court would be satisfied with the propriety of my representations."

"Well, yes, the second suit *is* contingent on the first." Sifer sighed. "Mr. Findlay, do you have any motions or response regarding Mr. Balm's surprising - and somewhat unusual - maneuver?"

"None, your honor. I don't know if counselor for the defense is ingenious or desperate, but the suit is still frivolous."

Shammai tugged on Lazar's sleeve. Lazar motioned for him to be patient.

"Nevertheless," Sifer said, "I'm inclined to consider it. Be advised that I will study both the merits of the suit and its request for a pre-emptive judgment at my earliest convenience. In short, there may be a ruling on it as early as this afternoon's session. And," he paused for dramatic effect, "my decision on that may well influence my decision in regards to this case."

Shammai pulled on Lazar's sleeve again. "What's he talking about? What's Earl talking about? What countersuit?"

Lazar sat down and hastily whispered. "I didn't have time to tell you. I filed a suit of intervention this morning. Briefly, it claims that if you win, the synagogue gets the rights to the rest of the books."

"What?"

"It has to do with how Enstein's will is read, intent at the time of mortis causa, the nephews' lack of involvement as a withdrawal of privilege and some other legalese I'll explain later."

"You better," Shammai said. "Who's idea was this, anyway?"

Lazar turned away, shushing him, as Sifer cleared his throat.

"Counsel may call his next witness," he said. "I will remind both parties that, while all due consideration will be given to the merits of each side, I have no patience for tangents or playing to the jury - especially without one."

Shammai's questions would have to remain unanswered for the moment. Who's idea was it? Would it jeopardize his case? Why hadn't Lazar suggested it before - and to him?

At the first break, Shammai resolved, he'd find out. Why didn't Lazar at least tell him last night?

Sagalman had entered while they were talking. He always walked slowly, and he didn't increase his ponderous pace for the sake of the nephews or their attorney. In turn, Findlay made a show of being preoccupied with his notes.

Lazar's refusal to discuss 'the suit of intervention' forced Shammai to observe the posturings and maneuverings between witness and attorney. Friday, he might have been amused - or encouraged. Now, it only contributed to his weariness and resignation. If such was the best they had, he thought, they had nothing much at all. Maybe Findlay was right. Maybe the 'suit of intervention' was just a trick.

Once Sagalman had been seated and sworn in, Findlay wasted no time.

"Dr. Sagalman," Findlay said without rising, "what is your specialty?"

"I am a radiologist."

"Not a general practitioner? Not an internist? Not a specialist in gerontology?"

"No to all three."

"What, then, was your professional connection with Mr. Enstein?" Findlay asked.

Sagalman cleared his throat. "I was the consulting physician for the home nursing system retained to monitor his health."

Findlay leaned back in his chair, with his hands behind his head. "I'm a little confused. You just said your speciality was radiology, not a field connected with primary care or the elderly. Why were you the consulting physician?"

"The insurance provider requires an outside physician - one not employed by the home care company - to act as reviewer."

"And the insurance company asked you?"

"No," Sagalman said, "Mr. Enstein did."

"Ah," Findlay said, sitting forward. "Mr. Enstein did. Mr. Enstein requested you as consultant, even though you are far from the best qualified."

"He knew me and trusted me," Sagalman said complacently.

So far, the questions had seemed routine. Sagalman answered them, Shammai noted, with the same detachment with which he approached most things. But by now, Shammai knew Findlay had a ploy.

"He knew you and trusted you," Findlay repeated. "How well he trusted you, we'll soon see. You had access to his medical records, then?"

"Yes." The wariness in Sagalman's voice showed he suspected what was coming.

"Did you ever share them with anyone else?"

"What do you mean?" Sagalman asked, glancing up at the judge.

Findlay looked at his nails. "I think the question is obvious enough. Did you ever share the contents of Mr. Enstein's medical records with any one not professionaly authorized to have access?"

"Certainly not," Sagalman said indignantly. "That's a breach of medical ethics."

"Yes, isn't it." Findlay stood and stared down at his yellow pad for a long time. "Well, what was Mr. Enstein's condition for the month or so before he died?"

"About three weeks before his death, Mr. Enstein was diagnosed with a heart condition. Because of his age and weakened health, a heart attack, most likely fatal, within six months, was considered almost a certainty."

"Was Mr. Enstein informed about this situation?"

"Yes."

"And what," Findlay said, holding a pencil poised over his palm, "was his reaction?"

"I'd say, -" Sagalman paused, looking up at nothing in particular as he thought, "I'd say, indifference."

"Indifference?" Findlay asked, arching his eyebrows.

"Yes. He didn't seem to care."

"Let me get this straight," Findlay said, beginning to pace. "Mr. Enstein was essentially told he had no more than six months to live and he reacted as if that information was useless or irrelevant?"

Sagalman shifted his weight. "You could put it that way."

"So he made no arrangements, no review of his affairs?"

Lazar, without looking up, said, "Objection. Counsel hasn't established how witness would have access to or knowledge of the deceased's legal activities."

"Sustained."

Findlay chuckled. "Well, then, Dr. Sagalman, did Mr. Enstein say anything to you at all once he learned of his condition?"

"Nothing." Sagalman, his hands folded, stared at Findlay, who had sat down again.

Findlay fished in his briefcase and pulled out a deposition. He flipped through it. "I know it's in here," Findlay said, continuing to look. "Something about the news not changing anything."

Sagalman looked genuinely puzzled. "You mean what I said at the deposition? That Mr. Enstein said, 'So? It changes nothing.' I mean, that's not really saying anything, is it?"

Findlay closed the deposition. He had a predator's smile. "That depends. But please, try to have a more reliable memory in the future." Findlay stood up, but didn't move from the desk. "To continue. Did anyone else know of Mr. Enstein's medical condition?"

"You mean Shammai?"

"Ah-ah," Findlay said, holding up a finger and waving his crest of hair back and forth. "I didn't mention any names. Did anyone besides the authorized staff of the home care and yourself know about Mr. Enstein's heart condition?"

"I'm sure Shammai knew. And Kashdan and Josh, as well." Sagalman added, though his voice had an edge of doubt to it.

"But how did they find out?" Findlay asked in an overly-reasonable tone. "You testified a few minutes ago, under oath, that you didn't share information about Mr. Enstein's health with anyone other than professionals with a relevant interest."

"I don't know," Sagalman shrugged. "But I was asked about Mr. Enstein's health, and Shammai, at least, knew about the heart condition."

"Maybe I'll get a chance to ask him about that," Findlay said. He began tapping the pencil in his hand. "But how did you know Shammai found out?"

"Well, he asked me lots of times - once or twice a week - how Mr. Enstein was doing. Mr. Enstein's heart was mentioned in some of our conversations."

Shammai leaned over to Lazar. "I didn't know anything about his heart. I asked about several organs. It's natural to worry about the heart of an old man."

"The one we have to convince is Sifer," Lazar whispered back.

Findlay's tapping had become more rapid. "And how did you respond to the inquiries?"

"Since Shammai obvioulsy knew something, I told him whatever I felt was ethically permissible."

"Which was certainly some sort of working update on Mr. Enstein's condition," Findlay commented.

Sagalman shrugged, which almost seemed like a mountain moving itself. "Don't forget, Shammai had undertaken to provide Mr. Enstein with a sort of surrogate family. The attention - emotional and physical - was good for Mr. Enstein. It was natural for Shammai to learn how much exertion or stress Mr. Enstein could take."

"Of course, of course," Findlay said, holding up a hand. "And I'm sure the satisfaction of a job well done was sufficient compensation." he added sarcastically. "Did any other member of the synagogue make inquiries about Mr. Enstein's health?"

"Oh, sure. Everyone did, at various points."

"But none as often or with as much interest as Shammai?"

"Well, no," Sagalman said, shifting uncomfortably. "But like

I said, -"

"Yes, we have a record of that." Findlay took a walk across the length of the courtroom. "So, Mr. Enstein knew he was dying and Shammai knew Mr. Enstein was dying. Yet Mr. Enstein said nothing and made no change in his will. Interesting."

"Isn't he destroying his case for undue influence?" Shammai asked.

Lazar shook his head. "The *siddur* now becomes a bribe, blackmail payment to get him to the hospital. Coercion. All unspoken, of course. The *siddur's* now become a silent witness against you."

"Tell me," Findlay continued, "was Shammai always this interested in Mr. Enstein's health?"

Sagalman looked puzzled. "Of course not. Mr. Enstein's health used to be quite good. There'd be no reason to have any special interest in it."

Findlay dropped his pencil on the table. "Yes, I suppose you're right. One more question along this line. How long did Shammai supply Mr. Enstein with a surrogate family?"

"I don't know," Sagalman shrugged. "It just sort of developed over the years. It intensified in the last year, since Elie's bar mitzvah."

"I see." Findlay leaned over to ask the Osteriks something, but suddenly turned around. "Oh, I forgot - how long had Mr. Enstein been suffering poor health before he passed away?"

"At his age, with the hardships, it's hard to tell."

"Let me rephrase that. Approximately when did the deterioration begin? When did he begin to need home care, your involvement, that sort of thing?"

Sagalman thought a minute.

"I have the first dated record of your signature on the home care report, if that will help," Findlay said.

"About ten months, I guess," Sagalman said. The threatened "help" hadn't disturbed him. "Does that fit with the date?"

"Close enough. Would that be before or after the bar mitzvah?"

"After."

Findlay opened a manila folder, glanced at it. "After it is."

Sagalman started to get up.

"I'm sorry," Findlay said in a mock-apologetic tone, "I have a few more questions."

Sagalman eased backed into the chair.

"As part of this 'surrogate family' relationship, the defendant sent his daughter every Friday with bread to Mr. Enstein, correct?"

"I suppose," Sagalman said, becoming surly. "I didn't see her go every week."

"But you saw her frequently and heard him mention it often enough, correct?"

"If that constitutes evidence, yes."

Lazar clapped his hands quietly and winked at Shammai.

"And that began - when?"

"Informally, a few years ago. When Mr. Enstein became Elie's tutor, Hannah would send over some extra *challah* as a thank you."

"Was that common practice?" Findlay asked. "You have a son about the same age. Did you ever have your wife send over bread?"

"No."

"What about cake and eggs?"

"Objection!" Lazar said.

"Never mind," Findlay said. "Was the bread simply a thank you? Or was it also payment?"

"Well," Sagalman hesitated, "Shammai's business wasn't too old and he wasn't in the best shape financially. Mr. Enstein never asked for payment, of course."

"Of course. From cake and eggs to *challah*. But," Findlay continued, "you said it was informally. That means not on a regular basis?"

"Not at first."

"When did it become formal?"

Sagalman frowned. "When Mr. Enstein wasn't able to get around as well. I'd say in the last few years. I can't be more precise than that."

"And did you prescribe that activity?" Findlay asked.

"No."

"Was it medically necessary?"

"It probably was good psychologically," Sagalman answered.

"I have no doubt, but the question would be for whom. Did Shammai discuss any of his activities in regard to Mr. Enstein with you?"

"No."

"No," Findlay said. "In other words, he just assumed certain responsibilities without consulting an authorized or competent medical practitioner."

Sagalman looked over at Lazar for help. Lazar just shrugged. "There's the home care -" Sagalman said weakly.

"Which has no record of any such request," Findlay answered.

Sifer interrupted. "How much longer do you intend to pursue this line of questioning?"

Findlay looked surprised. "I had just finished. I do have a few more questions for this witness regarding events after the heart attack, however."

Sifer looked at his watch, pursed his lips, then looked at Findlay. "The purpose being?"

"To show that the defendant's interest in the deceased was

purely monetary and his involvement based on manipulation, not compassion."

Sifer nodded. "Proceed."

Findlay slightly bowed his wave of hair. "Thank you, your honor."

Shammai leaned over. "What did that mean?"

"Either that Sifer's getting ready to make up his mind, or he'd heard enough on that subject."

"Enough for what?"

"To fit it into whatever puzzle he's putting together. Shh," he added, pointing to Findlay, who'd started to approach the witness stand.

"Dr. Sagalman, can you tell us briefly what happened after Mr. Enstein's heart attack and before his death? Specifically, your encounters with the defendant."

Sagalman took a deep breath. "Naturally, Shammai was worried. We were in touch from right after Shabbat until -"

"Excuse me," Findlay interrupted. "Shabbat is Saturday, correct? So that would be Saturday night?"

"Right," Sagalman said. "I called-"

"One moment," Findlay said, closing his eyes and raising a hand. "I'm confused. Didn't the heart attack occur on Friday afternoon?"

"So?"

"So?" Findlay practically exploded. "So are you saying more than twenty-four hours elapsed before any contact or inquiries were made?"

Sagalman went from embarrassed to angry. "As observant Jews, neither Shammai nor I nor any member of the congregation use the phone on Shabbat. Medically, we could have done nothing for Mr. Enstein. And had we violated the Shabbat, Mr. Enstein would have been furious. And rightfully so."

Findlay smiled sweetly, his tone completely changed. "Just asking."

Shammai looked over at Lazar for an explanation. But Lazar gave him a 'not now' shake of the head.

"So inquiries were made beginning Saturday night," Findlay said. "Go on."

"He was in intensive care, of course," Sagalman continued, " in a coma. I got permission for Shammai to visit on Monday."

"Very good," Findlay encouraged. "What happened Monday?"

"When we got there, it took a phone call to clear things at ICU. Mr. Enstein had come out of the coma Sunday night, as I recall. At least, he showed a moment of consciousness."

"Yes, but at the hospital, with Shammai, what happened?"

"Nothing. He sent Elie in, but Mr. Enstein was sleeping - actually back in the coma as it turned out, so we left."

Findlay had produced a pen and began rapidly tapping it on his palm. "This is the first I've heard of Elie - the defendant's son, correct? - being a part of the visit."

"Shammai brought him along."

"And sent him in to see the comatose Mr. Enstein, instead of visiting himself?"

"Not instead of," Sagalman said forcefully. "We ran out of time. You can't exactly have a picnic at ICU."

"But one could make sure to at least pay what might be last respects, instead of sending a surrogate, if one really cared."

"Shammai cared, and Elie was no surrogate," Sagalman shouted, banging his fist.

Sifer used his gavel, once. "Doctor, please refrain from such outbursts in my courtroom."

"In other words, Dr. Sagalman, as Mr. Enstein's psychological dependence on the defendant's children intensified, so did the defendant's interest in Mr. Enstein's medical condition. But when Mr. Enstein was in critical condition, the defendant did not even see him personally!" Findlay considered a moment, then waved his hand. "No further questions." He turned his back on Sagalman.

Lazar rose slowly. "No questions at this time, your honor. I intend to call Dr. Sagalman as a witness for the defense, however."

Sifer nodded. "Dr. Sagalman, you will make yourself available for the defense."

"Gladly," Sagalman snarled, his face red. As he stormed out - amazing, Shammai thought, how much energy Bob could muster when he wanted - he made sure Findlay was aware of his passing. Enough so that it took a moment for Findlay to recover his composure.

"Mr. Findlay," Judge Sifer said, "I asked if you had any more witnesses?"

"Oh, yes. Mishael Amran."

"Now what?" Shammai whispered.

Lazar thought a moment, then wrote on his pad, "*Gabbai - kaddish?*"

Mishael came quickly into the room, practically running to the witness stand.

"Your eagerness," Findlay said after Mishael had been sworn in, "especially after the last witness's recalcitrance, is refreshing. I shall be brief. What is your position at the synagogue?"

"I am the *gabbai*," Mishael said, his accent seeming thicker in the courtroom.

"Describe your duties, please."

"I make sure the *shul* is clean. I make sure visitors are welcome. I make sure services run right. I give out the - honors, I guess is the word."

Findlay smiled. "Can you describe the honors?"

Mishael wrinkled his nose. He held up a hand to count with.

"Calling up to the Torah, leading services, and-"

"A moment," Findlay said. "How do you determine who leads services?"

Mishael smiled. "We take turns. Unless someone has to say *kaddish*. Then he has the right to lead."

Findlay scratched his head. "*Kaddish*? That's the special prayer for the dead?"

"Not exactly, but someone in mourning says it, yes."

"Who should say it?"

"A relative, like I said. Parent, child, husband, brother."

"What if there's no relative available? Or you don't know about relatives, like nephews or cousins?"

Mishael shrugged. "Someone else could say, if they have had a relative pass away already. Or you could hire an orphan at a yeshiva to say *kaddish*. That's done a lot. It makes sure *kaddish* gets said three times a day."

"But that doesn't preclude saying it at your services? Especially if a congregant really cared for the deceased?"

Mishael's expression showed clearly he had just understood the purpose of the questions. He stared at Findlay.

"Please answer the question," Findlay said, undisturbed.

Mishael still did not respond.

Judge Sifer leaned over."If you do not answer the question, I will have to hold you in contempt of court."

Lazar started to rise, which caught Mishael's attention. Lazar nodded, and Mishael relaxed.

"Yes, Shammai could say *kaddish* for Mr. Enstein if he wanted. But he paid to make sure it was said, which is more than the nephews ever thought about."

Findlay smiled. "Did Shammai pay for it all by himself?"

"The rest of us insisted on helping. He paid for half."

Findlay sat down and spread his feet. "Did Shammai ever say

kaddish for Mr. Enstein?"

"Yes," Mishael said fiercely. "At the funeral."

"What book did he use?"

"The *siddur*. Mr. Enstein's gift to him. He had a right to use it."

"Perhaps," Findlay said, putting his hands behind his head, "but obviously, once he thought he had it, he felt no obligation to use it again, at least not to honor Mr. Enstein's memory. No further questions."

Mishael gripped the rail of the witness stand, breathing fast.

Lazar stood quickly. "No questions at this time, your honor, though, as with the previous witness, I intend to call him for the defense."

Judge Sifer nodded.

Mishael got down, never taking his eyes off Findlay until he reached the benches for the spectators.

Judge Sifer looked at his watch. "I would like to break for lunch soon. Do you have any more witnesses, counselor?"

Slowly, Findlay stood. "Just two. The defendant's daughter. And the defendant."

Chapter 21

"Well, it looks like it's my turn," Shammai said, standing as the bailiff called his name. "But before I go up - who's responsible?"

"Who's the intervenor?" Lazar said. "Me. On behalf of the shul."

Shammai shook his head. "Whose idea was it?"

"Mine."

Shammai shook his head again. "I know you too well. Come on, Lazar, give me at least that much."

Lazar made a face, glanced at Sifer, then said quickly. "Your wife. Last night when I called, she asked if the rest of the books had to be abandoned. That got me thinking - a rarity." He shrugged. "A long shot. Won't affect your case. Now remember,"Lazar said, with a wink, "name, rank and serial number only."

Shammai glanced back at his wife, then at the empty two chairs behind her. He didn't want Dinah Chaya to testify. But if his words stopped her from taking the stand, he'd betray his wife, his friend and Mr. Enstein.

"Maybe it's time to just answer straight. I want the judge to see inside me before he decides if I used undue influence."

"Try it and I'll object. This is a courtroom, not a philosophy seminar." Lazar leaned back and smoothed the hair at his temples. "Now go. It's not nice to keep the judge waiting."

After making eye contact with Hannah, Shammai went to the witness stand, took the oath and sat down.

So this is what it feels like, he thought. The size of the courtroom and its activity - the height and distance of the judge, the scurrying of the bailiff and clerk, even the clacking of the stenographer - testified to his centrality, simultaneously magnifying his vulnerability.

Being a witness - this being immobilized by his own importance - was like having surgery; but a hospital staff wanted to do things for you, while the courts wanted to do something to you.

Findlay stopped a few feet from the witness box; he rocked on his heels and, hands clasped behind his back, nodded his head several times. Like a vulture, Shammai thought.

If everyone's attention was on Findlay's dramatics, why did Shammai feel as if all eyes were on him?

Findlay continued delaying, to increase anticipation of his first question.

"What is your name?" Findlay asked politely. Too politely.

"Shammai Danelson."

"How long have you lived here?"

"Fourteen, close to fifteen years."

"What kind of work have you done in those fourteen, close to fifteen years?" Findlay asked, still with the gentle, patient tone.

"It's all been in computers." Why didn't Lazar object?

"Can you be more specific, please?"

"For the first five years or so I worked for Texaco as an analyst."

"What did you analyze?"

Shammai shifted in his chair. "It was a joint project between NASA and Texaco, using satellite observation and seismic - do you really want all these details?" Why was Findlay asking all this? Shammai thought. His background had already been established. What was the point?

"Please." Findlay smiled pleasantly. "But not too technical. I am only a lawyer, after all."

Was that supposed to be a joke? "The project was designed to determine the least environmentally intrusive way of locating certain resources, such as oil."

"That sounds quite impressive. What was your task specifically?"

"My job," Shammai said, taking a deep breath, "was to design a least-interference model against which to check the data."

"You said this lasted about five years. It seems like interesting work. What happened?"

Findlay's false courtesy had become almost unbearable. What did his past have to do with the *siddur*?

"I'm sorry, did you not hear the question?" Findlay asked when Shammai didn't answer immediately.

"I heard it," Shammai said with more irritation than he wanted. He didn't like being examined this way. "Congress stopped funding the program."

"That must have been disappointing," Findlay said sympathetically. "What did you do after that?"

"I worked as a programmer for a doctors' clinic for three years. Then I decided I could do better on my own, so I started a consulting business."

"And have you done better on your own?"

He's making fun of me, and nobody sees it, Shammai thought. "In some ways, yes. The pay isn't always as steady, but it's better, the work's more interesting and I don't have to answer to anyone."

"Oh, you were pretty independent when working for Texaco, then?"

"I had to report to a supervisor, but most of the day I worked on my own."

"You don't like having a boss, do you?"

"Objection," Lazar said. About time, too, Shammai thought. "The question is irrelevant."

"On the contrary," Findlay said, "It's critical. Your honor, the whole case depends on the relationship between the deceased and the dependent. Given Mr. Enstein's vigilance and meticulous record-keeping, why did he not simply change his will? When he provided for everything else in his life, why take the risk if the defendant - or his son - meant so much to him? Under normal circumstances, Mr. Enstein made - and would have made - no provision for Mr. Danielson. But, through the constant pressure, the undue influence, when put in a life-threatening situation, Mr. Enstein felt compelled to offer something."

"Are you saying," Judge Sifer asked slowly, "that the defendant made the deceased to feel that if there had been no gift, his daughter would not have called an ambulance?"

"That," Findlay said drily, "would certainly show the relationship was such that Mr. Enstein was unable to act according to his best judgment."

"How is this line of questioning relevant to that?" Sifer asked, again with deliberation.

"Having established Mr. Enstein's character, clearly the defendent's character is very relevant. Was he capable of creating such a relationship? I intend to show that in fact he intended such a manipulative relationship."

Judge Sifer pursed his lips. "The objection is overruled."

"I think," Findlay said, a slight edge to his pleasantness, his smile an executioner's, "I had asked whether or not you like having a boss."

"Not really," Shammai said guardedly.

"I suppose that makes sense, doesn't it?" Findlay continued, an edge creeping into his voice. "You work well with computers. Computers can only do what they're told, they take orders - in short they are totally subject to human control. And the person controlling them is always in charge."

"Your honor," Lazar said, "Is counselor asking a question or trying to qualify as a psychologist?"

"Well taken, Mr. Balm," Judge Sifer. "Mr. Findlay, confine yourself to a line of questioning."

"Mr. Danielson, does one have to be patient to work with computers?"

"A lot of people aren't," Shammai smiled. "They expect instant answers because computers are so fast."

"That's not what I asked. To work with computers - to program them, design them - to do what you do - does one need patience?"

"A lot, actually," Shammai said. "Systems, designs, it all requires a lot of concentration and focused thought."

"Which you do well enough to earn a living. And yet -" Findlay paused, then nodded to himself. "I understand that in Jewish tradition, the name Shammai is associated with a great scholar of limited patience."

Shammai squirmed. "The limited patience part fits, a little."

"A little. Come, Mr. Danielson, we've heard members of your synagogue testify that you have very limited patience."

"I don't have tantrums or start yelling, if that's what you mean," Shammai said.

Findlay smiled. "Impatience has many forms. Walking away, a sarcastic remark - one's displeasure need not be overt to be felt. On a scale of one to ten, with ten being like Hillel, let's say, and one like Shammai, where do you rank?"

How dare he bandy about the names of *tzaddikim*, Shammai thought. He took a deep breath. "I resent the way you use the names of important scholars. Shammai's impatience had a legitimate cause."

"I did not mean to offend," Findlay said, "only to use terms familiar to you. The scale remains, I think, a valid measure."

Shammai shut his eyes. "Probably a three."

"With whom are you impatient? Your wife?"

318

"No, not that much."

"On the scale of one to ten?"

"Objection," Lazar said. "The question is irrelevant and intrusive."

"Overruled," Judge Sifer said.

"Six," Shammai answered.

"Six," Findlay repeated, beginning to pace up and down the courtroom. "Then to bring your average impatience level to three - and assuming you have at least as much tolerance for your clients as for your wife - then you must have very little tolerance for your children, your fellow congregants and, indeed, for just about everyone else. That would include Mr. Enstein." Findlay turned and pointed at Shammai. "Were you, in fact, as impatient with Mr. Enstein as with everyone else?"

"No."

"But he would have given you more reason: his physical limitations - typical of old age - would require more patience. You would have to restrain your pace to his, wait upon his ability to get dressed, make a decision, and so on. You had to put up with the acerbic tongue and suspicious nature." Findlay turned away from Shamai. "From your self-description, you would not have spent more than five minutes with such a person. Why were you so tolerant of Mr. Enstein?"

Shammai closed his eyes. "Because he taught my children. Because he gave them what I never could. Because he survived and preserved and kept alive our legacy, our heritage."

"Something, of course, no one else did or could do. There were no other teachers in the city. No other survivors - such as Mr. Levinksy. Only Mr. Enstein."

"I didn't say that. We just developed a friendship."

"I see," Findlay said. "Is that what you meant by 'patience has its rewards'?"

"I don't remember saying that."

"But your friend Josh Green does. In fact, he testified that when he asked why you subjected yourself to Mr. Enstein's witticisms, complaints and criticism - which you've said you'd tolerate from no other - you replied with those words. What did you mean?"

Findlay was on the attack now. Shammai would have to be careful with his answer. "Probably that what my children, particularly Elie, learned was worth it."

"We could say that about many things that annoy us. We could, in fact, tolerate almost anything with that reasoning. But you don't. The only thing you really have patience for is - computers. Your average tolerance level is three - even your wife is only a six. But computers, which you control completely - ah, a computer is what? A ten? And isn't it curious that the only person, the only human being for whom you had that much patience was - Mr. Enstein. To Mr. Enstein's slightest whim you responded. What about your wife's? Your children's?

"In short, Mr. Danielson, for people, you have little patience; but you tolerate computers and Mr. Enstein quite well. Are they the same in your mind? Didn't you, in fact, want him to expect you to respond immediately, to indulge him, so that he became dependent on your favors? All you would have to do is threaten to withhold your attention, your - patience - and that lonely, unappreciated old man would panic. Am I right?"

Shammai folded his arms. Findlay was trying to bait him, to get him to lose his temper in court. He wouldn't do it.

"Let's pursue something else, shall we?" Findlay said into the silence. "If you had such a warm relationship with Mr. Enstein, why did you do nothing for twenty-four hours after his heart attack?"

"It was Shabbat. I couldn't do anything."

"Oh, come," Findlay said. "If the synagogue needed lights

320

turned on, you would have asked a non-Jew to do it. Who took Mr. Enstein to the hospital?"

"A TEMS ambulance."

"The student ambulance service. That operates on campus, does it not? Would it have been a violation of the Sabbath to walk to Tulane security - not too far from the synagogue - and make inquiries?"

"I suppose," Shammai said slowly. "I don't know what good it would have done."

"For someone who likes to be in control, you let an excellent opportunity slip by," Findlay said sarcastically. "Dr. Sagalman was familiar with Mr. Enstein's medical history. Your whole synagogue was familiar with it. Don't you think the emergency room doctors, the cardiologists or the staff would have appreciated some insight into the conditions and status of such an old man?"

"They got it anyway."

"But not from you," Findlay said.

"I didn't think of it, OK? I was a bit shocked myself and my daughter -" He broke off without finishing.

"Yes, your daughter. We'll get to her next." Findlay said. He looked away from Shammai. "I'm sure the whole episode was traumatic, though. So traumatic that on Sunday morning, instead of going to the hospital, instead of any act of concern for the one person you consistently, and against your nature, went out of your way to be concerned about, you went to the best source to determine the worth of your 'gift.' You weren't able to think of anything to do for Mr. Enstein, but you knew right away what to do with the *siddur*."

"That's not fair," Shammai said, almost shouting.

"It doesn't have to be fair," Findlay said. "It's a fact."

Shammai looked desperately at Lazar, who just shrugged and shook his head.

"Mr. Danielson," Findlay continued, "I understand you

collect records."

"Yes," Shammai said cautiously. What now?

"Have you listened to all of them?"

"No."

"Why do you buy them, then?"

Shammai put a hand to his head and exhaled. "Because I like classical music."

"You buy the records just to have them, is that correct?" Findlay asked.

"Something like that." Shammai felt tired, beaten already.

"So others can see them and admire them?"

"If they want."

"So they can admire you?"

"Your honor," Lazar said. "Mr. Findlay has badgered my client, put a ridiculous spin on stress-caused responses - obviously illogical and often not in the best interest - and is now trying to make something sinister of an innocent hobby. Surely there's nothing conspiratorial about buying things one doesn't use. I'm sure Mr. Findlay doesn't read all the magazines in his office. Does he subscribe to them just to impress clients?"

"A good point. Mr. Findlay, briefly, what is the purpose of this line of questioning?"

"To show that, just as the defendant had no real interest in Mr. Enstein, so he had no real interest in Mr. Enstein's 'legacy.' His only interest was to own, to collect, an item or items of extreme value."

"Even if true," Lazar said, "and Mr. Findlay hasn't proven that, it remains irrelevant and immaterial. The question is not what Mr. Danielson's motives were, the question is whether or not he had undue influence over Mr. Enstein."

"From his motives, we can deduce the effects of his actions," Findlay said. "We know what the defendant did. We know what Mr.

Enstein did. The question is why. I think it's obvious. Mr. Enstein's perception of the defendant's motive explains the bequest in mortis causa. Did Mr. Enstein give it of his own free will? We cannot ask Mr. Enstein, but we can determine what Mr. Danielson intended to do and infer that Mr. Enstein responded to the motive as well as the act."

"And how do these questions determine my client's motive?" Lazar asked skeptically.

"His actions after the fact demonstrate, by implication, his intent before the fact," Findlay said.

There was a pause while Judge Sifer thought.

"You've made your point about the records," Judge Sifer said. "You may proceed, but keep the questioning brief and to the point. We don't need much to see the validity of a particular line."

That, Shammai thought, surely was a victory for Findlay, despite the reprimand.

"Thank you, your honor," Findlay said. He faced Shammai. "You collect records. Do you collect books?"

"Not really."

"But you just bought a new bookcase."

Shammai fidgeted. "I needed someplace to put the *siddur*."

"To show it off or to protect it?"

"To protect it."

"Oh, come, it's natural to want to show off such a - 'find,' shall we say? But never mind. Is it normal - to buy a bookcase for one book?"

"I don't understand the question," Shammai said.

"Let me rephrase it," Findlay said. "Do observant Jews usually buy a bookcase for one book?"

"I don't know."

"Do observant Jews usually buy books?" Findlay asked.

"Yes, sure."

"And they need someplace to put them, don't they?" Findlay asked.

"Yes."

"So they don't buy bookcases just to protect a single book. Or to show it off. Do they?"

"But this *siddur* is two hundred years old," Shammai protested, looking at the judge.

"What kind of bookcases did Mr. Enstein have?" Findlay asked.

Shammai looked at him. "Regular bookcases, I guess."

"Not a special one to protect or show off the *siddur*?"

"No," Shammai said, realizing where this line was going.

"Nor did he take any special precautions for the hundreds of other valuable and precious books he had, did he?"

"No," Shammai answered reluctantly.

"Yet, when you gain possession of just one, you go out of your way to do so. Why?"

Shammai bit his lip. Scanning the courtroom, no one would meet his eyes. No one except Hannah, whose own were filled with tears. "I'm not Mr. Enstein," he said quietly.

"No, you're certainly not," Findlay said. "Mr. Danielson, I only have two or three more points I want to cover. I think we can get through them quickly. When someone passes away, after the funeral, what is normally done?"

"You mean during the mourning period?"

"No, I understand that there is a week of mourning and restricted activity for a month. What kind of memorial or service is performed?"

"You mean saying *kaddish*?" Shammai asked.

"Yes, that's it," Findlay said cheerfully. "You are saying *kaddish* for Mr. Enstein, are you not?"

"No."

324

"No?" Findlay acted surprised. "Why not?"

"He's not a relative. If anyone, his nephews should be saying it."

"Well," Findlay smiled, "my clients are not so well versed in the intricacies of Jewish observance as you. They're also not on trial. But you mean to say no one is saying *kaddish* for Mr. Enstein? That is a shame."

"I made arrangements with a yeshiva for someone there to say it."

"Oh. Does Mr. Enstein have a relative we don't know about?"

"I don't think so. I didn't even know he had nephews."

"I'm sure of that," Findlay said. "But then why would a complete stranger say *kaddish* for Mr. Enstein, when you, who knew him so long and so dearly, do not?"

"It's a common practice," Shammai said, trying not to sound annoyed.

"Paying someone else to fulfill your responsibility, you mean?" Findlay said.

"That's not what I mean."

"Are you not allowed to say *kaddish*?" Findlay asked.

"I can say it," Shammai said. "But I knew I wouldn't be able to do it for a whole year three times a day."

"Because Mr. Enstein wasn't a relative?"

"Right."

"Let me understand," Findlay said, beginning to pace again. "Saying *kaddish* shows respect and a close relationship. It's said for relatives, but can be said for others."

"Under certain circumstances," Shammai interrupted.

"Conditions which you met. Rather than be inconvenienced - how difficult would it have been to say *kaddish* three times a day for a year?"

"I would have had to rearrange my schedule. The only place to do it everyday is on the other side of town."

"Most inconvenient. But you could have done it? You would have done it for a relative?"

"Yes."

"Is there anything preventing you from saying *kaddish* at your synagogue when you do have services?"

"No," Shammai said uncomfortably. "But there would have been no point. He wasn't a relative and *kaddish* was being said for him. I made sure of that."

"Yes. You made sure of a lot of things, it seems. But just to continue the clarification: you could have said *kaddish*, even on a partial basis, but have chosen not to because - why? It's inconvenient? It doesn't matter?" Findlay paused. "Whatever the reason, it hardly fits with your earlier description, that you felt so close to Mr. Enstein as to change your nature, or at least feign patience for otherwise intolerable irritations."

Shammai clenched his jaw.

"Let's see," Findlay said, going to the table and picking up his notepad. "Ah, yes. You've done some work for Mr. Levinsky. Has he ever discussed Mr. Enstein with you?"

"No."

"Not at all?"

"Not directly. Only in connection with the synagogue and superficially."

"Did you - never mind." Findlay stopped himself. He flipped some pages, nodded to himself, smoothed his hair, put the notepad down and approached Shammai. "We're almost done. I just want to ask you a couple questions about your children."

"My children?"

"Yes. Do you love them?"

"Of course."

"Did they enjoy learning with Mr. Enstein?"

"Sure." Now what, Shammai thought. He felt hot and sweaty.

"Both of them?"

"Well, Dina Chaya not as much. She stopped a few years ago."

"But she still brought Mr. Enstein *challah* every week?"

"Not every week," Shammai said. "If she had time before Shabbat, or was staying at a friend's house. Maybe half the time."

"Did she do anything else for Mr. Enstein?"

"Like what?"

"Clean his house," Findlay said. "Do shopping for him."

"No. We sent our cleaning lady over at least once a week and Dina Chaya's just learning to drive."

"Did she cook for him?"

"No."

"Never?" Findlay pressed.

"Well, occasionally she'd bake him cookies. Or if she was making dinner for the family, like macaroni and cheese, she might make some extra for him." Shammai wiped his brow. Nobody else seemed uncomfortable, so the air-conditioner must be working.

"Did she volunteer to do this."

"Sure."

"All the time? You never suggested it?"

"Objection," Lazar said. "He's leading the witness."

"Overruled," Sifer said. "The extent and the manner of his daughter's involvement is of the utmost importance, considering she was present when the *siddur* was gifted. Mr. Danielson, you will answer the question."

"I must have suggested it on occasion," Shammai said angrily. "It's only natural. There was nothing sinister about it."

"No one has suggested that yet," Findlay said. "But did you suggest that she make cookies or dinner for anyone else?"

"No one else needed it."

"Yes or no, Mr. Danielson."

"I'm sure I did."

"Who?"

"I can't remember."

"Mr. Danielson," Findlay said, "Yes or no - did you tell your daughter to prepare meals for anyone else with the frequency or urgency with which you instructed your daughter regarding Mr. Enstein?."

Shammai lowered his head. "No."

"I can ask your daughter this," Findlay said gently - the threat was clear, "but it might be better if you answered. Did she enjoy cooking for Mr. Enstein or did she resent it?"

"Sometimes she enjoyed it, sometimes she resented it. Sometimes she resents doing her chores."

"That's different," Findlay said. "Let me ask it another way - and I hope I won't have to ask her to confirm this - did she share your comittment to provide for Mr. Enstein?"

"No."

"Did she resent having to provide for him?"

Shammai ground his teeth. "Probably, but no more so than resenting anything else we asked her. She's a teenager."

"Yes or no, Mr. Danielson."

Lazar, who'd been crouching over the table, shouted, "Objection. He's harassing the witness."

"Overruled," Judge Sifer said. "The question seems quite straightforward. I think the court can make due allowance for adolescent ambivalence. However, Mr. Findlay, I think it would be best to use a less strident tone. You wouldn't want the court thinking you're threatening the defendant while he's on the stand."

"Of course not, your honor," Findlay smiled. "Mr. Danielson - Shammai - did Mr. Enstein appreciate Dinah Chaya?"

"Definitely."

"No, no," Findlay said, shaking his head and a finger. "I didn't ask if he appreciated her efforts or what she brought, I asked if he appreciated her."

"What do you mean?"

"We've had some testimony that Mr. Enstein had an extraordinary affection for your son. Did he have the same affection for your daughter?"

"No."

"Did he have any affection for your daughter?"

"I'm sure he did."

"Did he demonstrate it in any way?" Findlay asked, gathering his papers.

"No."

"Did he thank her for her efforts?"

"He didn't thank any of us."

"I'll take that as a no," Findlay said, straightening his note cards. "Isn't it true that the mistrust or aversion was mutual?"

"They didn't hate each other."

"That's not what I asked. I asked if the disdain - I'm trying to be polite - was mutual."

Shammai turned to Sifer. "Your honor, he's trying to twist things. Maybe Dina Chaya was a little jealous of Elie, or resentful of things I asked her to do, but it was just normal family tension, part of growing up, being a teenager. Mr. Enstein, well, since Dina Chaya didn't want to learn, though she could have, he was critical of her. But he was like that with others, too. He felt that if you didn't share his passions, you were rejecting him. So he pushed you away, to protect himself."

"And knowing this," Findlay said, "You continued to press, to insist that they interact. And so, the one person Mr. Enstein felt least comfortable with, least able to rely on, was the one person who happened to be there when he had a heart attack. No wonder Mr. Enstein felt compelled to do something against his nature, against his will."

This is crazy, Shammai thought.

"No more questions," Findlay said.

Shammai looked from Findlay to Sifer to Lazar. Lazar just shook his head. Behind him, Hannah sat, head in her hands, shoulders shaking from sobbing.

"I don't wish to cross-examine the defendant," Lazar said quietly. "But I am planning to call him as a defense witness, if necessary."

"You may step down," Judge Sifer said.

In a daze, Shammai went back to the table. He ignored the stares.

"Why didn't you ask me something?" he demanded in a whisper.

"Because," Lazar said, "You're in no condition to answer anything and I want to limit Findlay. If you're my witness, he can only ask you about my questions, not his. Hannah --" He stopped as Findlay started to speak.

"I have one last witness, your honor," Findlay said. "The defendant's daughter, Dinah Chaya."

Chapter 22

Findlay named her. Sifer called her. The bailiff went to get her.

Dinah Chaya.

Shammai had expected it, had anticipated it, had, he thought prepared for it. But hearing his daughter's name mentioned in the courtroom shocked him.

Hannah's gasp, quickly suppressed, startled him, magnifying his disorientation, unbalancing his slowly returning self-control. Alarmed, doubly shaken, he turned, but Hannah seemed less distressed than he'd imagined.

But her lapse had shattered *his* composure, his facade. The bailiff, opening the heavy wooden door in what seemed like slow motion, blocked his view of the outside. He knew, though, where she sat. In his mind's eye he saw her reaction, Elie's unreceived assurance, her rigid rising from the bench, her -

He grasped Lazar's arm. "Call it off."

Lazar tried to pull away. Shammai's grip increased until he sensed Lazar stop resisting.

"I can't do that."

"You're my lawyer. Call it off."

"Shammai, it's-"

"That's my daughter. It's not worth it."

"Relax," Lazar said, tentatively trying to free his arm. "She'll be fine. I coached her, remember?"

"Like you coached Josh and Sagalman? Like you coached me? You saw what Findlay did to them. Look at what he did to me! What's he going to do to her?"

The judge's gavel sounded for the third, fourth, fifth time.

"You can't back out. The suit of intervention, remember?" Lazar said. "There's no compromise now."

"There never was. End it."

"Listen," Lazar said, "I'll get us a recess and you can talk to her. Then decide."

The judge's gavel sounded for the sixth, seventh, eighth time.

"Shammai, you've got to trust me a little bit."

The judge's gavel sounded for the ninth, tenth, eleventh time.

Shammai let go of Lazar, then nodded once, briefly.

Before the judge's gavel could sound again, Lazar rose. "Your honor, I request a fifteen minute recess."

Sifer stopped himself, surprised by the request. "On what grounds, counselor?" he asked, lowering the gavel gently.

"My client has been attacked rather strongly. He would like an opportunity to get himself together before his daughter takes the stand."

"If the two parties had reached a settlement," Sifer reminded him, "his daughter wouldn't have to be called as a witness at all."

"Your honor," Findlay said, leaning over, his fists on the table, "I have no objection to a short recess. My colleague may be able to persuade his client to agree to a settlement in that time."

Lazar faced away in disgust. "Overconfident windbag," he whispered to Shammai. After a pause, he added, "But we've got the recess."

Sifer went into a chin-on-hands deep think. "Fifteen minutes," he said suddenly. "And counselor, remind your client his daughter will be under oath."

"Yes, your honor. Thank you," Lazar said, hurrying Shammai out. Hannah waited at the door, already having gotten up as soon as Lazar made his request.

"Sifer wants me to talk you into compromising," Lazar said as they exited. "I've just tried. I could get you, say, ten thousand dollars, but Findlay won't accept a deal unless I drop the suit of intervention, which I won't. So it's all or nothing. Now, then." He steered them into a corner, motioning for Dinah Chaya and Elie to join them.

"What's the problem?" Hannah asked. "I thought she was just supposed to say what happened." Shammai noticed the redness around her eyes and winced.

"Shammai's afraid Findlay'll go after her like he went after every one else, including him," Lazar explained.

"Why should he?" Hannah asked. "Didn't he do as much damage as he could to Shammai?"

"Maybe," Lazar said. "Maybe he just wants to rattle us. Despite the dramatics, I don't think he's got a better read on Sifer than I do."

"Rattle us? He's out to destroy us!" Shammai said.

"Dinah Chaya's not Josh," Lazar said quietly.

"I don't want to take the chance," Shammai said, shaking his head. "Do you?" he asked Hannah.

"Chance of what?" Dinah Chaya asked, as she and Elie arrived.

"What happened? Why are you all out here?" Elie asked. "It's not over, is it?"

"No," Lazar answered, leaning against the wall. "It's not over, though it might as well be. I could get paid for wasting my time, you know," he said to Shammai.

"Wait," Hannah said, shutting her eyes and holding up both hands. "Why did Findlay agree to this recess? Or the nephews?"

"Does it make a difference?" Shammai asked.

"It might," Hannah said.

"What's going on?" Dinah Chaya pleaded.

Lazar, still leaning against the wall with his arms folded, said, "If all of you will be quiet for just ten seconds, I can fill every one in and maybe even explain the options." He looked at each of them to make sure he had their attention. "First, Findlay agreed to the recess because the nephews still want a compromise. They want a compromise because they have a sale deadline, and even if this trial doesn't go over it, the suit of intervention effectively blocks it. Also," he said with a conspiratorial glance around, "between you and me, Findlay's a bit conceited and he's gloating, but he doesn't have a guarantee and he knows it.

"Second," he continued, holding up two fingers, "Shammai panicked when he heard Dinah Chaya being called to testify, which after the grilling he took is understandable. Third, there's some merit to his panic, because even though Dina Chaya will only be asked about what happened when Mr. Enstein had his heart attack - Findlay can't stray too far from the deposition, after all - nevertheless, he's in high gear and wasn't likely, without a break, to cease and desist his demolition derby just because the witness happens to be a teenage girl.

"That, though, might have worked in our favor, since rule number thirteen - or is it seventeen? - I forget - it doesn't matter - is never make a child or young woman cry on the stand. Unless you want them to confess something. So," he said pushing himself off the wall and standing straight, hands in his pockets, "while it gives us a chance to recover and think, it does the same for him."

"I didn't think I had a choice," Dinah Chaya said.

"You don't," Lazar said, "unless Shammai gives up."

"So I *don't* have a choice," Dinah Chaya said.

"I could just concede everything," Shammai said.

At first, no one responded.

"There is that," Lazar said.

"Shammai," Hannah said, "You're not seriously thinking of just - just dropping it? Quitting?"

Shammai nodded.

"How can you do that?"

"The how," he said, speaking with difficulty, "is easy. The why is simple. I don't want my daughter hurt."

"I can handle it," Dinah Chaya said.

If he'd had doubts before, hearing her voice tremble and seeing her hands shake removed them. He shook his head.

"You saw what he did to me," Shammai said to Hannah.

"Let me rephrase it," Hannah said firmly. "You can't do this. Not to me. Not to the children. Not to Mr. Enstein. And not to yourself."

"And not to me," Lazar added.

"Not to you? You're supposed to be my lawyer, not - not--"

"A litigant?" Lazar asked. "Once you accepted responsibility for that *siddur* - for Mr. Enstein - you made us all - the whole *shul* - litigants. You represent us, as surely as that *siddur* represents the rest of his books - in fact, the truth that there's life, sacredness in Torah.

"Why do you think I filed that suit of intervention? As a technicality? No, because when Hannah asked me about the rest of the books, I realized what this case has to be about. If you didn't exert undue influence, if Mr. Enstein gave you that *siddur* as a gift in mortis causa, then it's because *that* fulfilled his will. And the will states the collection has to remain intact."

Lazar exhaled deeply, as if winded.

"Shammai," Hannah said gently, "Don't do this to the *siddur* and those who sacrificed who-knows-what so that it would survive and be used, not hidden away like some fossil."

"Besides," Elie added, "You're going to win."

Shammai had to smile. "How do you know? You haven't heard anything."

"I've gotten reports. And Lazar hasn't had his chance. Don't you have any confidence in him?"

Lazar clapped his hands in delight. "There's a psalm about

that," he said.

"You don't even need a good lawyer," Elie continued. "But you've got to let Dinah Chaya testify."

"Why?"

"Because she's going to win the case for you."

Shammai looked puzzled.

"It's what I told you. It's our strategy," Lazar said. "And if Elie can figure it out, so can Judge Sifer. The very fact that she just happened to be there - that the gift was a result of coincidence - proves there wasn't undue influence. If there had been, the will would be different. That means he meant you to have it, a token that, as the suit of intervention claims, gives the *shul* a priority claim on the collection. It's the only way to read the will if there isn't undue influence."

"Well," Shammai said slowly, "I guess we could even interpret his dying words -- "Give it to your father. It's for --" to support that idea."

"But she has to testify," Lazar pushed. "We have to refute Findlay's implications. That means he has to make them first."

"We're not going to settle it standing here," Hannah said. "Dinah Chaya, can you handle it?"

Biting her lip, she nodded.

"She's sixteen, Shammai. Trust your daughter," Lazar said.

He looked from his friend to his wife to his daughter to his son, all waiting, each in their own way: Lazar arms folded, Hannah lips tight, Dinah Chaya eyes averted, Elie - walking back to the courtroom.

"Okay," he sighed. "Let's go save the *siddur* and honor the deceased."

They made quite a little spectacle, Shammai thought, as they marched back inside, single file, each to their assigned place. He felt the eyes of the judge, the bailiff, the court clerk, the newspaper

336

reporter - and of course Findlay and the Osteriks - judging their little procession.

No need for Elie to stay outside now. He took the aisle seat.

As Shammai sat down at the table with Lazar, he looked back at his family and was surprised to see Josh and Levinsky enter. They nodded at him and found a place in the back. Come to offer condolences, he thought. The others would have been there, he thought - and hoped - even Kashdan, if they could.

Did they know about the suit of intervention? Did they approve?

"Are we ready to proceed?" Judge Sifer asked.

"Yes, your honor," Lazar said.

"If the young lady will come forward and be sworn in," Sifer said gently.

Shammai could at least hope that would set the tone for how she was treated.

Aside from some trembling, which occurred randomly at various intervals, Dinah Chaya managed the trip from the spectators' benches to the witness stand - under everyone's scrutiny - relatively poised.

Findlay got up and began to approach her, when Judge Sifer motioned for him to stop.

"Young lady," Sifer said, "I just want to assure you that you will not be badgered or persecuted in my courtroom."

"Thank you," Dinah Chaya replied, forgetting to add his title.

"In return," Sifer continued, ignoring her breach of etiquette, "I only ask that you answer the questions honestly, even if they're difficult or painful."

"I'll try."

"I know you will," Sifer said with a smile. "It's a scary thing to be on the witness stand. Especially in these circumstances. But you are under oath, which must take precedence even over what your parents might have told you in confidence. I'm sure you'll tell the truth." He smiled again, then motioned for Findlay to proceed.

Standing in the middle of the courtroom, Findlay started to speak, then stopped. He walked up to the witness stand and leaned over, then backed up a few steps. Clearly, he didn't want to do anything to antagonize the judge.

Finally, he settled on standing by the stenographer.

"I only have a few questions," he began. "I'll just be asking you about what happened. You don't have to be nervous."

Dinah Chaya glanced at the judge. "It's just that it's taken so long to forget what happened and now I'm going to have to remember. I never saw anybody die before."

Findlay, apparently, had 'figured out' Dinah Chaya and decided on an approach, because he next spoke with his accustomed assurance. "We all understand your trauma," he said, with just the right touch of sympathy and firmness. "None of us are inured to the death of a loved one - a friend. To see it happen -" he shook his head. "Personally, I admire your courage, how you acted. I want you to know that.

"Of course, you're going to need that courage, that nerve of the young, again today. I'm afraid I am going to have to ask you to recall an unquestionably unpleasant incident. I'm going to ask you for details, and I apologize in advance if that will make you uncomfortable. You know you're under oath, of course, so I have no doubt you'll tell the truth, whatever the consequences. I just hope," he smiled, "that we can avoid making it painful for you to tell the truth."

Shammai clenched his fist in anger. He didn't mind that Dinah Chaya would be questioned - he'd reconciled himself to that - but he resented Findlay's condescending treatment, making her look so immature.

"Go on," she said, getting more tense.

"What were you doing that Friday afternoon? Why were you going to Mr. Enstein's house?"

Dinah Chaya swallowed. "I was bringing *challah* to Mr. Enstein like I do almost every week."

"Were you the only one who brought it - this *challah*?

"It depended on who had time. Usually me, but occasionally my brother."

"Did your father ever bring the *challah* himself?"

"Sometimes. It depended on whether he was driving or walking to shul, whether Mr. Enstein was going, a lot of things."

"I see," said Findlay. "Was that the only contact your family had with him?"

"No," Dinah Chaya said. "He'd call us a couple times a week and we'd call him. For groceries, ask how he's doing, things like that."

"Was he grateful for all that you did?"

"Mr. Enstein?" Dinah Chaya said, looking at her father. "Mr. Enstein wasn't grateful for anything."

"I detect some resentment in your voice," Findlay said. "Did you resent helping him?"

"Sometimes," she admitted, visibly trembling for a moment.

"Did you express this resentment to your father?"

"Sometimes," she said quietly, her body still.

"And what was his response?"

"He got angry at me. He said it was our duty, things like that."

"Did you ever think there might be another reason?"

She looked up, tears in her eyes. "Sometimes."

"What might that reason be?"

"That Mr. Enstein would give us something for being so nice."

"And what made you think that?"

"Because Daddy was always so patient with him, and with nobody else. But I know that's wrong."

Judge Sifer interrupted Findlay by asking, "How do you know that?"

"Because my father's not like that, not greedy. And when I think that he is, I know I'm just being a teenager."

"Then why the difference?" Sifer asked.

"I think because he expects so much from us, and expected so little from Mr. Enstein."

Shammai had to fight his own tears. He hadn't thought she understood him.

"You may continue, counselor," Sifer said.

Findlay nodded, obviously not pleased. "Now tell us what happened when you got to Mr. Enstein's house that day."

Her tears had stopped, but she now looked like one suddenly trapped. "Well," she said, licking her lips, "When I got there, I rang the bell, but there was no answer. I rang again. Then I tried the door and it was open." She stopped, sobbed once, wiped her eyes, sighed, and went on. "He was sitting in his chair, one hand on his heart. His eyes were wide, bugged out. At first he didn't recognize me. He just stared and stared."

"What did you do?"

"I called his name, softly, because I was afraid and I thought - I don't know, but like I shouldn't shout and surprise him. But I couldn't help myself. When he didn't move, I screamed his name."

"And then?" Findlay prompted.

"It was like he just woke up or something. I think he started to get up. I mean, I think he tried to, but he just ended up sliding halfway off his chair."

"Not all the way? Not onto the floor?"

"No. I remember that, because it was strange and surprising to see him there, with his eyes-" she made a gesture around her own

- "and breathing hard, and his hand on his chest and his face in such awful pain, and he still didn't just, you know, fall down." She started shivering again; she took a deep breath, which only made her agitation more visible.

"Go on," Findlay said carefully.

She tightened herself. "I, um, I panicked. I screamed. More than once, I think. It's hard to remember, not that I want to, and I can't always tell what's a real memory and what's a leftover from my nightmares."

"I understand," Findlay said, but not as soothingly. "After you panicked and screamed, what happened next?".

Findlay blocked Shammai from seeing her clearly. She stretched and contorted to look around Findlay, but didn't quite succeed.

"I don't know," she said, sinking back. "At least not for sure. But I do know he pulled himself back up a little, sort of trying to stand." She shuddered. "Then he looked at me and I couldn't tell if it was really me he was looking at or what, but it was a hard look. And he fell."

She buried her face in her hands, but now Findlay didn't give her much time to recover, prompting her almost immediately. "That was it? How did you get the *siddur*? Surely, you didn't just take it. So what did you do?"

Shammai, angered by Findlay's sudden change of tone, started to get up. Lazar yanked on his sleeve.

"He's going to get the information," Lazar said. "If we interfere now, it'll make it harder for Dinah Chaya and worse for you. Trust me. I'll object if it gets bad."

Findlay's tone had angered Dinah Chaya as well, who now glared at him before answering. "Well, I called 911. And my parents. Then I just stood there and sort of babbled at him and asked if he wanted water or whatever. I didn't know what else to do. I think he fainted or blanked out, even though his eyes were still open, real wide, too."

"You didn't do anything to try to revive him?" Findlay asked, pretending to be surprised.

"I don't know CPR," Dinah Chaya replied. "And I told you. I was scared. Maybe you've seen a lot of people die, but I haven't."

"Please, I understand how frightful it must have been. I'm really not trying to upset you," Findlay said soothingly.

Shammai clenched his fists and kept his thoughts to himself.

"However," Findlay continued, "I'm trying to ascertain - to understand - two facts about the case. One, how did you get the prayer book and two, what did you do while waiting for the ambulance?"

"Which do you want answered first?" she asked, rather defiantly.

"Either one," Findlay said with a smile.

"Well, the first one's easy. Mr. Enstein gave me the *siddur*."

"Just like that?" Findlay exclaimed. "He's lying on the floor, dying from a heart attack, and he just hands you the book?"

"Not exactly," she said uncomfortably.

"Not exactly," Findlay repeated. "But that's just the point. We need to know exactly." He took a deep breath, as if exasperated. "Let's try to do this together, all right? Where was the prayer book when you walked in?"

"On his little table, I guess."

"You guess?"

"Well, it had to be there," she said, looking up at the judge. "But I didn't see it right away, because he had a lot of books on the table. He always had a lot of books on the table."

"So it was on the table and he was on the floor. Did he jump up and give it to you?"

"Mr. Findlay," Judge Sifer interrupted, "I said the witness

would not be badgered. Save your sarcasm for one who deserves it. Or can appreciate it."

Findlay nodded. "Let me rephrase it," he said more gently. "Something's missing. If you're standing by the door, Mr. Enstein's lying on the floor and the book is on the table - how did you get it?"

"He had it with him when he fell."

"Oh! This is news!"

"Well," Dinah Chaya said defensively, "You didn't give me a chance to give all the details."

Findlay paced back and forth for a moment.

"I'll give you time now. Describe the table please," he said, coming to rest where he started.

"Mr. Enstein had this little table in his living room, like a card table, but a little bigger and sturdier and he studied at it and tutored Elie at it and it always had books all over it."

"When you came in, then, he had the prayerbook in his hands?"

"A trap," Lazar whispered to Shammai.

She shrugged. "I don't know. I mean, one hand was on his heart. So his other hand, his free one, when I came in, was on - or holding - I'm not sure, he could have been marking a place with his hand, but he had one of the books."

"Good," Findlay said. "So far, then, you come in and see Mr. Enstein with one hand on his heart, the other on an unknown book. You call his name, he doesn't respond, you scream. He starts to stand. Do I have it correct so far?"

She nodded.

"Good. Instead of standing, Mr. Enstein slips in his chair. You scream again. He stands, stares at you, then falls. Right?"

"Yes, I think that's the way it happened."

"And he had a book in his hand the whole time?" Findlay asked.

"No," she said tentatively.

"So he had a book in his hand, or under his hand, when you came in, and a book in his hand when he was on the floor, but not anytime in between?"

"I don't know," she said, getting upset. "When he fell, he pulled it down with him."

"You're sure?"

"Yes!"

"No need to shout," Findlay said. He paused, noticing, as did Shammai, Judge Sifer's frown.

Lazar wrote on his pad and shoved it at Shammai. "Dangerous ground," it said.

"Were they the same book?" Findlay said.

"I don't understand," Dinah Chaya answered, shaking her head.

"The book he had his hand on when you came in and the book he grabbed as he fell - were they the same?"

She furrowed her brow. "I don't know."

"So," Findlay said reasonably, "They could have been two different books?"

"I guess."

"She's getting confused," Shammai whispered, concerned.

Lazar chewed on his lower lip. "It doesn't matter. We may be in trouble."

"Now we're in trouble?"

Lazar nodded. "If the books weren't the same, but he thought they were - listen!"

Findlay moved away from Dinah Chaya, symbolically giving her breathing room. "Did he look at the table or the books? Did he make the switch deliberately?"

"Objection," Lazar said immediately. "The witness testified she didn't know if the books were the same. That doesn't mean they weren't, which counselor is implying."

"Sustained."

Findlay flashed him a just-checking grin and turned back to Dinah Chaya. "Did he look at the table or the books or otherwise indicate he deliberately chose the book he gave you?"

"He didn't look, not before he fell. Afterwards, he couldn't really - I mean, he was in a lot of pain, was he supposed to check the title and say, I meant to give you another one? But he knew what he was doing. When he finally fell, he made sure he had a book and he struggled hard to make me take it."

"But it could have been any book. What was important was that you take a book, not that particular one, correct?"

"Objection, counsel is leading the witness and asking her to speculate."

"Sustained."

Findlay sat on the edge of the table, tapping away. "So as he fell, he pulled a book with him, maybe deliberately, maybe not, maybe intending the *siddur*, maybe not. Once on the floor, he still didn't examine the book he made sure you took, did he?

"Right."

Shammai leaned over. "What's he trying to prove?"

Lazar grimaced. "That the book he gave you - Dinah Chaya - may not have been the one he intended. Among other things."

"Let me ask you something else. You're being very cooperative and very accurate in difficult circumstances, by the way. What I want to ask," Findlay said, "is what did you mean that he struggled hard to make you take it?"

"Well," she said, swallowing hard. "He made gurgling sounds, and he tried to motion to me, and he kept on looking at me, and he tried to get up, like on his elbow and - I don't remember what else, but it was clear he wanted me to take it."

"I see. By the way, what did you do with the *challah*?"

She stared at him.

"Didn't you understand the question?" Findlay asked.

She nodded. "I - I held it the whole time. I forgot I had it."

"Even when you screamed?"

She nodded again.

"Even when you took the prayer book?"

She went pale and looked like she was about to faint. "No. When I - when I bent down to take the book, I - I gave him the *challah*."

Judge Sifer banged his gavel several times before the courtroom quieted down. The implication was clear.

"Please explain," Findlay said, his voice hissing.

"I took the *siddur* with both hands and dropped the *challah*."

"Was this before or after you called 911?"

Dinah Chaya didn't answer. Tears flowed, unattended.

"Was this before or after you called 911?" Findlay repeated, more harshly.

Dinah Chaya still didn't respond.

Judge Sifer leaned over. "You must answer the question," he said gently.

She looked at him. "Before. I was in shock. When I touched the *siddur* and dropped the *challah*, I realized - I didn't -"

"No, you didn't," Findlay said calmly. "No one thinks there was any intent or malice on your part. But Mr. Enstein - given the pattern, the relationship your father established - well, we won't know what he might have thought." Findlay drummed his fingers on the table. "I want to thank you for your cooperation. I know testifying has been difficult. I just have one more question. Did Mr. Enstein say anything to you?"

Dinah Chaya glanced at her father. "He said, 'Give it to your father. It's for -'"

"That's all?" Findlay said, standing. "'It's for'? It's for

346

what?"

She shrugged.

"'It's for.'" Findlay let the words hang for a moment. "And those were the last words he spoke," Findlay said triumphantly, waving her down.

"Well, not exactly," Dinah Chaya said, remaining in her seat. She seemed suddenly strong, self-assured. Everyone's suddenly returning interest even made her smile. "He talked to my brother Elie."

Chapter 23

"What?" Findlay and the Osteriks and Judge Sifer and Lazar cried simultaneously.

Shammai twisted around, looking for his son. Where? There, sitting in the back by his mother, with the silliest why-is-everyone-looking-at-me grin. What had Elie been hiding from him?

Dinah Chaya's disclosure he never doubted: she had no reason to lie, was too nervous to consider it - and Elie's self-consciousness revealed it had been planned.

But when had he talked to Mr. Enstein? Had Elie lied? Or convinced his sister of a fantasy to save their father from embarrassment?

Instinctively, he looked to Hannah, sure that a moment's eye contact would suffice to restore, not just the hope, but the certainty of truth.

But she, focused on Elie, had momentarily withdrawn awareness from all but her son - isolated, too far to touch - shrinking from him as the deceiver of her husband. Then she stretched out a hand, spoke his name; she looked to Shammai to reach Elie, to acknowledge and appreciate the greater burden he had carried.

He felt, through her, Elie's words must be true.

But where and when had Elie spoken to Mr. Enstein after the heart attack?

The answer made Shammai light-hearted, faint.

In the -

"Hospital!" Lazar cried, grabbing him.

Like a juggler suddenly aware of the pieces, the motions, the audience, Shammai suddenly saw all the details, the mistakes, what Mr. Enstein had meant, what Elie had accepted and what he himself had misunderstood; but, like the same juggler forced to think, to count, to reconsider, rather than simply do, he could no longer hold all the pieces together, make a coherent puzzle from the insight.

The courtroom had, of course, erupted. That fact - with the contrapuntal, building tempo of Judge Sifer's gavel - slowly penetrated, reorienting Shammai. The effect of his daughter's announcement would have to be dealt with.

Dinah Chaya herself sat, at last calm, smiling at Elie, reassuringly glancing at her parents. She had done her part, had succeeded enough to relax.

Earl and Simon were shouting at each other, almost pushing. Findlay attempted to intervene, and they both turned on him.

The audience - Levinsky, Josh - hardly moved, shocked, not comprehending. Or maybe comprehending too well.

Lazar, the most excited, scribbled notes, agitatedly waiting for Sifer to restore order. "We've got it," he said, catching Shammai's attention by pulling on his sleeve and shoulder. "I had only hoped we'd be okay with Dinah Chaya. I had doubts. Really, I thought we'd lose, even if I could - but it doesn't matter. When Findlay started on her and turned everything crooked, I'd given up. Now, with Elie's testimony, we've got it! We've got it and Findlay knows it!" Lazar exulted.

Judge Sifer increased the tempo of the gavel's beat, his loss of patience accelerating with each stroke. He had allowed the consternation sufficient time, given the participants enough room to recollect themselves.

And Shammai had.

They didn't know what Elie would say. They just assumed that it would give him the *siddur*. But it couldn't - because otherwise Elie wouldn't have waited.

The noise began to diminish as the gavel got louder. Earl and Simon sat down, surly; Findlay straightened his coat and began tapping pencil to palm, ready to proceed as if Dinah Chaya had said nothing.

Judge Sifer, order restored, waited.

Lazar was out of his chair, ready to pounce, knowing he needed only one, maybe two questions during cross-examination.

"Lazar -" Shammai started.

"No," Lazar almost snarled. "We've been through that with Dinah Chaya. He testifies or we're through. Don't be selfish. This isn't for you or about you any more - if it ever was. Don't you realize what your son's willing to sacrifice - what your daughter and wife have sacrificed - what we've all sacrificed? And you're going to throw it away? Why? Because of your pride? Because Mr. Enstein didn't talk to you?"

"That's just it," Shammai said. "I don't want and never wanted anyone else to go through my torment."

"Findlay got this much right, Shammai," Lazar said harshly. "Mr. Enstein never talked to you. He talked through you. To Elie. And that's how you're going to get the *siddur*."

Judge Sifer interrupted. "Counselor, if you need a recess to discuss things with your client, ask for one. Otherwise, if you continue to prevent the plaintiff from proceeding, I will find you in contempt."

"Sorry, your honor," Lazar said. To Shammai, he whispered, "Ask your wife."

Shammai looked behind him. Hannah nodded her head.

Shammai sat down. "Your witness," he whispered to Lazar.

When he had everyone's attention, Findlay dropped his pencil on the table. "I have no further questions for this witness. However, I request that her last remark be stricken from the record."

Sifer leaned back in his chair. "Overruled. Really, counselor, I'm surprised. You invited the response by your own comment. And even if your request was granted, the defense attorney could surely get the same information." He sat up. "As you have no further questions, I'll ask defense to proceed."

"Thank you, your honor," Lazar said. "I'll be brief. Dinah Chaya, how do you know your brother spoke with Mr. Enstein?"

Dinah Chaya smiled. "He told me. After Shabbos."

"Did he tell you anything else?"

"Yes," Dinah Chaya answered. "He said that if it looked like my testimony was being used against Daddy, or if he - Elie - gave me a signal, I should mention that he'd talked with Mr. Enstein after the heart attack."

Lazar nodded. "Thank you. No further questions."

Dinah Chaya quickly walked to the back of the room, sharing a hug with her mother.

The silence grew protracted, until Judge Sifer at last asked, "Counselor, do you have any more witnesses?"

Findlay looked up, his face clouded. "No, your honor."

"Then I will ask the defense to proceed."

Lazar stood. "I call the defendant's son, Elie."

"Your honor," Findlay said, a small smile appearing and disappearing, "he is not on the witness list."

"Your honor," Lazar responded, "the fact that Mr. Enstein spoke with Elie - that whatever he said were Mr. Enstein's last words - has just come to light. Obviously, any communication from the deceased is critical."

Sifer nodded. "Proceed."

The clerk called Elie. Eyes downcast, Elie stopped, for an instant, without looking up, by his father.

After Elie had been sworn in, Lazar stood for a moment, thinking. "Well," he said, "You've given us all some unexpected excitement. Why? Why didn't you tell us before?"

"Why did I wait so long?" Elie blinked rapidly, his eyes misting over, his voice stumbling once in a while. "Why didn't I say something before? It meant so much to my father, this *siddur*. He loves books, he appreciates them. He never bought very many. He had to spend his money on food and a house and his family. And he's not a scholar."

"But he wanted you to be one?"

"Yeah. He wanted me to be a scholar and Dinah Chaya to be, well, I'm not sure what, but something he couldn't be."

"He was ambitious for you?" Lazar asked.

Even I know that's leading the witness, Shammai thought, a bit detached. Findlay must really be in shock.

"Yeah, he was ambitious for use." Elie stopped and sniffled. "Do you know what it's like to watch your father turn his life over to you?"

"No," Lazar said softly. "I don't even know what it's like to be the father in that situation." He shook himself back to the business at hand. "And so," Lazar said, his own voice still subdued, "you wanted him to win the *siddur* on his own, without any help or interference from you, is that right?"

Elie nodded and wiped his eyes. "For all those years, to see my father watching, giving Mr. Enstein such undue influence over him, because Mr. Enstein could teach me what was in the books - and that's the key to them, isn't it, owning what's inside them? - well, it hurt. It still hurts."

"You were like a silent witness to your father's pain and hopes, weren't you?" Lazar asked.

Elie shrugged. "I just know he should have, he could have. I know he could have been a scholar. But he had to work to support us."

"What does this have to do with the *siddur* - and your revelation?"

Elie shrugged again. "My father wanted to earn at least the *siddur* on his own, to believe that Mr. Enstein saw wisdom in him, could trust him as he had trusted Mr. Enstein.

"And I thought it could happen. No one had to know. How could I take it away from him? I wanted to be - what did you call it? - a silent witness. But my father deserves the truth. Even if -"

He covered his face with his hands.

Lazar waited, but when Elie didn't move, he called. "Elie." He waited a count of ten. "Elie, I need to ask you some more questions."

Elie nodded and, with effort looked up. "I know. You only really need two."

"One, I think," Lazar said. "What did Mr. Enstein say to you in the hospital?"

Elie smiled, briefly. "When I walked in to that room, I was scared. He was hooked up to all these machines and he looked so old. I thought he was already -" he gulped. "Except that he was breathing so deeply. I went up close and whispered his name.

"I didn't expect him to answer. My heart's pounding just remembering it. But he called me. He said 'Elie', like he was hopeful and not-believing at the same time. I said I was there. Then he asked me, 'Did you get it?' I knew right away what he meant. I said my father had it for me." He looked straight at Shammai. "That wasn't a lie, Dad."

"Go on," Lazar urged.

Elie shrugged. "It's funny, because this whole trial's about my father having an undue influence on Mr. Enstein, when it was the other way around. And it hurt, hurt so much to see it and not be able to speak."

"Elie," Lazar said, "What did Mr. Enstein say?"

Elie had faded into his own world, his eyes unfocused. "It's mine. But I don't have the words, not yet. And I don't know if I'll ever have the wisdom, not like my father. Sons inherit from fathers, but today, maybe a father will inherit from his son."

"Elie," Lazar said again, "What did Mr. Enstein say?"

Elie stared at Lazar, but saw something past him. "I didn't believe him," Elie said. "I didn't want to. Without a note, or a letter, or something, I wouldn't have to take it. It could just be my father's. I didn't worry about it or think about it until the trial started. I figured I could wait until I was an adult to tell him. And then they came, his nephews who he never spoke about, who no one knew about, they came demanding it, so I had to believe him."

He sighed. "I thought maybe there might be a way without me. But then, when things starting going bad, I had to find proof or we'd both lose it. I didn't want to, but I looked in the *siddur*." He looked at Shammai. "You know I didn't want to, because all those months I never did. Now you know why. It made me uncomfortable. How could I take it away from you?

"But it's there, Dad. In the back. Mr. Enstein wrote it, dated it. Just like all those in the front, remember? The names and dates of the owners. But there wasn't room in the front cover. So Mr. Enstein wrote a name in the back cover. I know his handwriting. He wrote my name, Dad. It's mine. I would have told you earlier, but I didn't know. I didn't want to deal with the *siddur*."

"What made you look?" Lazar asked.

Elie said, looking around the courtroom, explaining to everyone, "I knew Mr. Enstein hadn't acted without thinking. I just knew it. He had it planned. But there was nothing in the will. Until now I didn't care. And then, Friday night, it hit me. The answer had to be in the *siddur*. I looked at almost every page. I had to do it secretly, so no one would see. I was so stupid. It wasn't until Sunday night that I found it.

"I must have gone through the *siddur* three or four times looking for something. Finally I noticed that there wasn't any room on the inside front cover - it was filled with names - and I turned to the back. It wasn't there, I guess because it was too hard to write on the cover, because the *siddur* was so old. I turned back one page and there it was. My name, Eliyahu ben Shammai. And the date of my Bar Mitzvah.

"The funny thing is, I couldn't find Mr. Enstein's name."

He was crying freely, not trying to stop his tears or weeping.

"Elie," Lazar said again, "What did Mr. Enstein say?"

Elie looked once at Lazar, then again centered his attention on his father. "He only said five words. He just said -" Elie let forth a loud sob, "He said, 'The *siddur*. All for you.' And those were his last words."

Chapter 24

Shammai tested Dinah Chaya's suitcase, lifting it a few inches off the ground once or twice. Considering they'd already checked in the duffle bag and large trunk, which he'd needed Elie's help to carry, he hadn't thought she'd bring the rest of the house in her suitcase. He should have let Elie, who'd gallantly put it into the car, carry it down to the gate as well. Fortunately, it had wheels, so if he could keep it balanced, he could roll it through the terminal.

He'd told the others to go ahead and check in while he struggled with her luggage.

Strange how things work out, he thought, as he wrestled the suitcase into the elevator. Five days ago at this time, they were on their way to court, expecting to lose the *siddur* with who knew what reactions. Now, Friday morning, they were putting Dinah Chaya on the plane to camp. And they'd hardly mentioned the trial or the *siddur* all week.

The elevator opened and he dragged the suitcase out behind him, having to hit the doors once so they didn't close on it. They should be through with the ticket counter by now, so he might as well head for terminal B. He weaved in and out among the other travelers and their families and friends, avoiding the hawkers and outstretched hands while fighting to keep both himself and the suitcase balanced.

She probably had an empty purse.

After Elie's testimony, of course, the trial had been over for all practical purposes. Findlay had tried a few tactics, but Elie's words ended all discussion. In fact, the Osteriks had wanted to leave during the cross-examination, but were constrained to wait. They didn't need to wait long, for Judge Sifer came to a decision immediately. He hadn't even bothered to have the *siddur* brought, to verify Elie's claim.

Findlay had perfunctorily congratulated Lazar, and then, outside, had come the real celebration, with Josh treating everyone to dinner.

Truthfully, though, Shammai hadn't felt much like celebrating. He just felt relieved.

The security line wasn't too long. There was so much stuff in this suitcase, though, that the x-rays or whatever they screen with probably wouldn't get halfway through. The thought of lifting it up onto the belt made him wonder about hernias.

That night, they had all been too tired and drained to talk about it, and for the next few days, had been too busy getting Dinah Chaya ready to leave and Aaron and Moshe ready for camp to have a real discussion.

There'd been some legal technicalities to clear up, such as the assigning of Shammai as trustee until Elie came of age. But Lazar had taken care of it all, only needing Shammai for an hour of autographing official documents.

He took a deep breath and heaved the suitcase up and, surprisingly, onto the belt on the first try. No pulled muscles, either. He went through without setting off the alarm, took down the suitcase - letting it drop a little - and hurried down to the gate. The slight incline of the terminal helped.

He heard a lot of children noise, but couldn't distinguish Aaron or Moshe's unique sounds among them. He should have asked Elie to help him.

"Leaving town with the stolen goods, eh? Only, they're not stolen, not all of them, are they?"

He turned around to see Mr. Levinsky, a small travel bag in one hand and a garment bag in the other, catching up with him.

"That suitcase and my weight, a good match," Levinsky said pleasantly. "We'll walk together to the gate, and even at the same speed." So saying, he matched steps with Shammai, though he could have gone a bit faster. "Sorry I didn't go the victory party, but one more you didn't need."

"Actually, I don't know that I needed the party at all, but Josh insisted."

Levinsky nodded. "False guilt will do that. Makes one generous, often in the wrong way. I should know. You're going where?"

Shammai looked down at the suitcase. "To Gate 10 to get rid of this thing. Also, to send Dinah Chaya to camp for the summer. She and the rest of the family are already there."

"That's my gate, too. So the flight won't be so lonely."

"Oh?" Shammai said, hesitating. Should he ask? It seemed Levinsky wanted him to. "Why are you going to New York? Businesss?"

Levinsky frowned. "Business, yes. But not mine. Or, it wasn't until Monday, but maybe it should have been, much earlier." He smiled strangely. "What Elie said - Mr. Enstein's last words - even as an old man I have to give him the honor of a 'mister' - 'All for you.' And that suit of intervention. Your friend's more clever than he realizes. How do you preserve a library? I know a few lawyers and a few of my business associates know some booksellers." He shrugged. "Maybe he meant to give them all to Elie." He smiled. "After Shabbos. On Sunday. Who knows. And of course, maybe the nephews have other ideas. If so, maybe these ideas have a reasonable asking price."

Shammai stared at him, hardly conscious that he was moving. "Why are you doing this?"

Levinsky answered immediately, as if prepared for the question. "Because I like you. Because he liked Elie." He paused. "Because, maybe I still owe him something - or the other way around. Anyway, I want to be finished. So, I'll see. And I'll let you know if anything's possible." He pointed. "There's your family. Go ahead. I'm heavier than that suitcase, it seems."

Shammai, dazed by Levinsky's declaration, nevertheless moved ahead. They'd be boarding soon and, turning his attention to his family, Aaron and Moshe would not behave much longer.

Aaron ran up to him and Dinah Chaya waved.

"For a suitcase small enough to fit in an overhead compartment, this is rather heavy. You sure it won't tip over the plane?"

"You're not mad at me, are you, Daddy?" she asked.

It was the voice of his little girl. Even at sixteen, she was five.

"No," he said. "Not about anything. Just have a safe summer and be a good counselor."

"I will."

He gave her the suitcase, which she rolled without trouble.

"They'll be boarding soon," Hannah said to her. "I want to tell you a few things. Shammai, watch the boys."

He nodded and guided Aaron and Moshe to the window where they could watch the planes land and take off. He checked his watch. The clerk announced the boarding of families with children or those needing special care. He'd have time for one more goodbye.

Elie had followed him, and now stood next to him, looking out the window. As a jet roared down the runway, he said quietly. "What about me? Are you mad at me?"

Shammai smiled and shook his head. "No, Elie. Actually, I'm very, very proud of you."

Elie took that in. "But we haven't talked about the trial or Mr. Enstein or the *siddur* all week."

"I know. We've been busy." Shammai focused on an empty spot on the runway. Nearby, Aaron and Moshe were animatedly discussing all the activity going on around the belly of the plane: the loading of luggage, the men in orange shirts with thick orange pointers, the trucks and drivers. "We haven't had time to just talk."

"We have time now," Elie invited. "Don't you want to ask me some questions?"

"Not," Shammai said, "apparently as much as you want to answer them. Okay, when did you take Dinah Chaya into your confidence?"

"Monday morning. Early," Elie said, relieved to be talking. "I heard all Shabbos how bad things were going. Everyone was discussing their testimony and you were so angry. I thought about what to do all Shabbos and then, Saturday night, I decided. But I had to do it in secret. I didn't know what Mr. Enstein had written, or even if he had written anything, and I didn't want to say anything without proof. If I had to, I'd volunteer what he told me, but I knew that would hurt you and I didn't think it would do any good. I mean, they could have said he wasn't in his right mind then, either."

Elie looked up at him.

"A theoretical problem for Lazar," Shammai said.

"I just didn't want you to lose the *siddur*."

"It's not mine," Shammai interrupted.

"It is as much as anything I own or do will be," Elie insisted.

359

He waited for Shammai to respond, but Shammai didn't say anything, letting Elie decide where the conversation should go. He did, however, put a restraining hand on Aaron, who had gotten up to wander off.

"Anyway," Elie said, "I decided that if it looked like Dinah Chaya's testimony wouldn't be enough - and I hoped like Lazar it could be - but if it wasn't - or it was made to look - anyway, then I'd tell - what happened." He watched a plane take off before resuming. "So I told her, right before you all came out, that if it looked bad, or if she got a signal from me, to mention that I'd talked to Mr. Enstein after she had. I said, just work it into an answer. I figured that would be enough to get me on the witness stand. If I'd known how bad it was, I would have said something right away. I just didn't know Findlay would do that to you.""

"Did you tell her everything?" Shammai asked.

Elie looked at him, shuffling a foot. "Kind of. I just told her that Mr. Enstein had told me something that could let you keep the *siddur*, but it was supposed to be a secret. So I didn't want to tell anybody, but I would if I had to."

Shammai nodded. "And she didn't press you for the secret?"

"No."

Amazing, Shammai thought. "I'm pleased you two trusted each other so much."

"Well, she was nervous, after all. But you do understand why I couldn't tell you?"

Shammai realized that Elie had taken his remark as a reprimand. "Yes." He certainly hadn't intended it as such. "I really meant that Elie. Without any qualifications." Now it was Moshe's turn to be restrained. "I don't know if I would have accepted the truth from you earlier."

"You're really not mad at me, are you? Or upset or anything?" Elie asked.

As he thought about his answer, the conversation with Levinsky came to mind. "No. I'm upset with myself for confusing myself, for - I don't know what. And I should have seen it. You did see Mr. Enstein. You asked me if I had. I should have been more concerned, more aware. All the times over the weekend I saw you sneaking a look at the *siddur*." He smiled. "I was so proud of myself for not saying anything, for restraining my impulse to tell you not to touch, or be careful. Had I only known." He looked at Elie, surprised at how mature and yet how much still a little boy he was. "We both had a similar motive, I guess, honoring someone we respected." Elie smiled at that. "Are there any more answers I should ask questions about?"

"I guess not."

Shammai stared out the window, obliquely noting that Moshe and Aaron had run off to Hannah. "We should rejoin your mother and sister," he said, but neither of them moved.

A plane took off. Elie still stood by his side.

"What are you thinking?" Elie asked.

He thought about change and sacrifice and generations and tradition and books. A lot about books. But how to answer?

Silently, he hugged his son.

Interlude 5 - 1990

So old. I am so old. Where is that girl, anyway? Erev Shabbos, getting too late for the girl to bring my challos. My challos should have been here. That girl is always late. So much potential, she had. It would be wasted, though, unless they got her to the right school. I'd tried to work with her, but I was just too old. No patience any more.

The boy, Elie, is different. Since he was seven, since his youngest brother was born, it had been obvious. The father, so anxious, had been easy to convince. Almost too easy. It was - it is - a feeling - this wanting, this longing - I understood, still understand. I'd feel sorry for the father, but he got something, too.

Besides, what can he know of sacrifice? Let him spend years, like me, years of gathering, of searching, of keeping records of cake and eggs. It is my legacy, my duty, to collect them and preserve the books. Would the father have taken the beatings, suffered the hunger, given up a family for the books?

I learned early to take precautions: use an unknown bookseller. Create layers of documents. In learning to gather, to discern, to create a network to buy, I learned how to hide, to conceal and deceive. That's what saved them when the darkness came. What saved me - well, I had to bring them home again. No one else could.

It took so much longer to regather, to find them. But I had planned well. Any other way and they would have been lost. Thank G-d, I lived long enough.

And to think that, at long last, I have found someone. Elie wants to learn. The father wants the boy to learn. The father envies the books, but no matter.

I should stop pacing. A bad habit. It comes from teaching too *much.*

Everything must be passed on, must be preserved. That is the duty, that is the task. The minds and the books. Together, they will survive.

Survival is not something I had planned. It has happened. But now it is over.

And if I had not survived?

It would have. The siddur would have surfaced again. When the leaf falls, it covers the struggling ant, giving it shelter.

Do not step on the leaf.

I still remember how I found it. Warsaw, 1938. I was passing through, going home from a meeting in Vienna. Filthy city, Vienna had been. But I had a suitcase of manuscripts. I couldn't resist a walk, and a walk always seemed to lead to old stalls and second-hand bookshops. And there it was, beneath a pile of old Polish cookbooks. I almost missed it. But I saw its value immediately.

A pain. No, a twinge only. Sore muscles. What time is it? If one of them - the boy or the father - doesn't get here soon, I won't be able to go to shul.

The shul. I even built a shul here, just for the books.

Years of hiding, of plotting, of teaching - all for a roomful of books.

Where was that girl with the challah? Maybe the father was bringing it this week.

Another twinge, in my shoulder.

Thinking about it, maybe I do feel sorry for the father. Smart, hard-working - impatient like his namesake, but a good man, ready to do a mitzvah. But for all that, too late to learn. It was never too late, but the father made it so.

What time is it? Almost Shabbos.

Let me check one more time.

So, here's the siddur. I tried to find the family - or families.

With all those inscriptions, one of them should have left a trace. Strange how the names changed. Yaakov Strasbourger. Mattis Katz. Chaim Ephraim Tzivies. Avigdor Schindler.

Should I write my name, now, above his?

No. Six months ago, on his bar mitzvah, though he knows it not, it became his. Let it be that way.

Here, on the inside back cover. The date and the boy's name. Like all the others before. The boy's name - it will have to satisfy the father.

Where were they? Someone was always here by now - the father, the sister - the boy.

The bell. Open the door yourself. The bell again. Open the door.

My chest hurts.

It is her - the girl. I must give it to her, then. No, underage - legal problems. Let the father know. He must make sure. Give it to your father. It's for -

GLOSSARY

Aleinu: concluding prayer

Amidah: also known as *Shemoneh Esrei*, the standing, silent prayer, central to the service.

amud: cantor's lectern

Bar Mitzvah: when a boy turns 13, he becomes an adult according to Jewish law

brocha: blessing

beis din: rabbinical court

bima: the pulpit or lectern from prayers are led

Birkat HaMazon: Grace after meals, said when a meal commences with *HaMotzi*, the blessing over bread

bris: ritual circumcision, takes place on the eighth day, if the boy is healthy

challah: braided loaves of bread, used at Sabbath and holiday meals

Chevra Kadisha: burial society

cholent: special Shabbos stew

daven: pray

gabbai: synagogue caretaker

halacha: Jewish law

hashgocha protis: Divine Providence

Havdalah: a short ceremony marking the end of Shabbos

hesped: eulogy

Kabbalas Shabbos: prayer service welcoming the Sabbath

Kaddish: mourner's prayer

Kiddush: sanctification of Shabbos or festivals, includes a blessing said over a cup of wine

kohen: member of the priestly family, a descendent of Aaron

Lag B'Omer: thirty-third of the forty-nine day period between Passover and Shavuos. During this period, some festivities are restricted, except on Lag B'Omer.

Maariv: prayer

mazel tov: congratulations

mezuzzah: a scroll affixed to the doorpost. See Deuteronomy chapters 6 and 11

Mincha: afternoon service

minyan: quorum of ten men needed for certain prayers, such as the Kaddish

mitzvah: a commandment

niggun: a wordless, spiritually moving tune

parsha: weekly portion of the Torah

Pesach: Passover

Purim: literally, Festival of Lots - see the Book of Esther

rasha: a wicked person

sefer Torah: a Torah scroll

Shacharis: morning service

sheva brochas: the seven blessings said at a wedding

shiva: the seven days of mourning immediately following the burial

shul: synagogue

Shulchan Aruch: Code of Jewish Law

siddur: prayer book

Simchas Torah: Holiday of Rejoicing with the Torah - last of the autumn season holidays

Sukkos: Tabernacles - follows Rosh Hashanah and Yom Kippur

tallis: prayer shawl

tefillin: phylacteries

Tehillim: Book of Psalms

tzaddik: a righteous individual (pl. - *tzaddikim*)

tzedekah: charity

yahrtzeit: the anniversary of a person's death

Yom Tov: festival or holiday

www.ingramcontent.com/pod-product-compliance
Lightning Source LLC
Chambersburg PA
CBHW051446260626
47162CB00001B/275